A WORLD RAGE ™

CW01502026

By Bruce Baugh, Chris Campbell, Jackie Cassada,
Nicky Rea and Adam Tinworth

Credits

Authors: Bruce Baugh, Chris Campbell, Jackie Cassada, Nicky Rea, Adam Tinworth

Developer & Additional Material: Ethan Skemp

Editor: Aileen E. Miles

Art Director: Aileen E. Miles

Art: Jeremy Jarvis, Jeff Rebner, Alex Sheikman, Ron Spencer, Melissa Uran

Cover Art: William O'Connor

Back Cover Art: Jeff Rebner

Layout, Typesetting & Cover Design: Aileen E. Miles

735 Park North Blvd.
Suite 128
Clarkston, GA 30021
USA

WHITE WOLF
GAME STUDIO

For a free White Wolf catalog call 1-800-454-WOLF.

Check out White Wolf online at

http://www.white-wolf.com; alt.games.whitewolf and rec.games.frp.storyteller

PRINTED IN THE USA.

Special Thanks

Phillipe "Ministry of French-Canadian Culture" **Boulle**, for spot-checking a thing or three. Mercy bow-coop.

Ken "Filial Duty" **Cliffe**, for taking time off with the folks, thereby letting E&D do whatever the hell they wanted for a week.

Fred "Commish Lousy Fredo" **Yelk**, for resurrecting Wolf Blight and filling the conference room with groans of despair once more.

Mike "Weeping All the Way Home" **Tinney**, for superior sportsmanship.

James "A-Town Broken-Down Machine" **Stewart**, for learning the hard way there's more to the game than just punching whatever's at hand.

Justin "Powers-that-Be" **Achilli**, for demanding to go forward with the booking. It's *his* fault!

Brian "Airplane Spin" **Glass**, for scoring the first victory — on the test circuit, that is.

Aileen "Ten Miles of Bad Road" **Miles**, for quitting while she was on top of the game.

Authors' Special Thanks

• Thanks to Lorna Ebersole for her Germanic knowledge and constant inspiration, Thérèse Gaughan for championing all things Irish and Catherine Stoneman for advice from the heart of the Eurohub.

• More thanks to Phillipe Boulle for furnishing the Canadian perspective, and to John Malcolm Buckmaster for further suggestions from the Great White North.

• Thanks also to Astrid Mosler, Oliver Hoffmann and the gang at Feder & Scwert for the extra German spot-checking.

A Quick Note

Although we've done our best to represent the various nations of the world fairly, we're first to admit that we haven't done so *precisely* accurately. In specific, we've taken a few liberties with the mood. If countries seem a bit grimmer or bleaker, if the standards of living are portrayed as a notch or two below what one would expect, just remember — it's the World of Darkness. It's our job to make the world look less hospitable than our own. So don't hold any alterations that are apparently made with mood in mind against us.

On the other hand, if we've screwed up geography, it's okay to rail at us. We probably deserve it.

A WORLD OF RAGE™

Contents

Chapter One: The Americas

A World on Fire

As territorial as werewolves might be, even they have to concede that the world's a big place. There's an almost uncountable number of irons in the fire around the planet, from the battle for South America's rainforest to the recent tyrannical reign of Black Tooth, the genocidal Simba king. However, these areas of concern have been scattered throughout dozens of supplements, in some cases left without an update for years.

Until now.

A World of Rage is your guidebook to the World of Darkness, specifically focusing on the areas and subjects that are most important to the Garou and other shapeshifters. Within these pages you'll find out the latest word on the ongoing struggles such as the cover wars for Russia and the Amazon, as well as hints at strange new troubles erupting in unlikely places like Australia. There are literally hundreds of possible story ideas within this book — all it takes to use them is a little willingness to take your chronicle outside the usual sept boundaries.

It's a great, big, hostile world out there. Have fun touring it.

Canada

The Canada of the World of Darkness is a wide, vast, beautiful land — one that isn't particularly forgiving of human residents. The long winter nights make young souls old quickly, and the suicide rate inches up a little bit every year. Every so often, tourists pilot their snowmobiles down the wrong stretch of pine valley, and never come home again. French and English Canadians resent each other just that little bit more, and violence between various ethnic groups flares up more frequently (and viciously). When winter descends on Canada, hope seems to die out a little. When a chemical truck spills its payload across the highway and the surrounding ground, an effective cleanup is all the slower in coming — if it comes at all.

It's a harsh land, particularly away from the cities — and one that suits the Garou.

The Basics

Canada is frankly immense — Russia is the only larger country in all the world. It stretches more than 5,500 kilometers (over 3,400 miles to Americans) east to west, encompassing six full time zones. Its north-south axis is no less impressive; Canada's northern-most point is almost 2,000 km north of the Arctic Circle. And for all this land, Canada's population is roughly a tenth of that of the United States, and most of its people live within 160 km of the Canada/US border — nearly 90% of the country is unsettled.

At least, by humans.

Geographically, Canada is almost a basin — wide prairies and lakes at the center, bounded by mountains on the west, east and northwest. To the north, there's an expanse of permanent snow and ice; to the south, the Interior Plains, a continuation of the United States' Great Plains. The Rocky Mountains and Appalachians both stretch up into Canada, and the land boasts a few mountain ranges solely its own (such as the Mackenzie and Richardson Mountains). The earth itself ranges from tundra and permafrost in the furthest north, to highly fertile soil that feeds Canada's breadbasket.

There are three major types of forest in the land — the eastern forests along the Appalachians, the tall-timber forest along the Pacific Coast, and the coniferous taiga that constitutes the majority of Canada's woods. The natural grasslands to the south have been mostly plowed under and turned into a region of heavy agriculture.

And of course, it's cold. Those living along the Pacific coast receive the best of it; their summers are fairly cool and their winters mild. Everywhere else receives fairly long winters and short summers; everywhere east of the Rockies gets plenty of snow for three to six months every year. The farther north you go, the less hospitable it gets. The tundra regions experience winters where the average temperature never crawls above freezing, and the summer temperature never really climbs above 10° Celsius (50° Fahrenheit).

Canada makes a lot of its money from its natural resources; the land is rich in petroleum, coal and other minerals, and the lumber, paper and agricultural industries are particularly robust. Most of the country's power comes from hydroelectric dams, which have become remarkably widespread. Regional governments seem perfectly happy to place dams wherever they can, turning the rivers into sources of "clean" power — even if some of the land along the banks suffers in the process.

Canada is also without a doubt werewolf territory. The country's plains and forests support a wolf population that's almost certainly the most stable in the New World (for whatever that's worth), making it prime breeding grounds for the Garou. The human population is ethnically diverse in the cities, but scattered and almost meager across the land itself. Canada's population of vampires is comparatively low, and the Leeches that do call Canada home are either immigrants or decidedly young (as vam-

pires measure their years). There are, of course, a few of the ancient undead who have settled into the country, but for the most part, it's not the vampires that the local Garou have to worry about.

But the country is far from perfect — like everywhere else in the World of Darkness, the wild places are under attack. Human companies log and dam and strip-mine the land, leaving little but repositories of dangerous chemicals and industrial waste in their wake. Monsters out of darkest Native American myth skulk in the isolated corners of the land, feasting on whomever they can catch. Spirits of murder and vengeance haunt the sites of old battlefields and massacres. The werewolves of this country, particularly towards the cold north, must be strong to resist their rivals and enemies.

The Garou

Most of Canada's Garou are Fianna, Get of Fenris, Silver Fangs and Wendigo. The first three arrived alongside the earliest European settlers, and found something of their old lands' appeal in the northern woods. Of course, the Wendigo had already claimed Canada as nothing less than their tribal protectorate, and the result was all too predictable. The fires of hatred have dimmed down a little since — but werewolves are creatures of rage, and the anger still smolders.

The Wendigo are stronger in Canada than they are anywhere else, save perhaps Alaska — not only is the land the heart of their original protectorate, but they find the harsh winters virtually fortifying. They still hold a number of caerns here, calling on their Gifts and spirit allies to drive away or kill intruders with lethal cold. Unfortunately, the more remote caerns are on their own when it comes to defenses as well. At least two caerns in the last two years came under air attack from military-style helicopters — only the power of mighty storm-spirit allies was able to deflect the missiles and bring the helicopters to the ground. The Wendigo know they were lucky, and don't look forward to the next attempt; it doesn't help that they're not sure just which of their enemies funded the assault.

Most of Canada's population is of French or British descent, and the Silver Fangs have Kin representatives in both. A few Fangs claim that their ancestors set foot on the land when Samuel de Champlain first founded Acadia, but others of their tribe are more dubious. The Canadian Fangs' pedigrees do go back a few centuries, though, and the house of the Unbreakable Hearth is firmly rooted in southern Canada. King Cyrus-the-Bald commonly travels north from America in the summers to discuss politics with the local elders, and King Albrecht of the nearby protectorate in New York has offered his support to the Unbreakable Hearth — even if it wasn't in the courtliest language.

Canada's Fianna are similarly mixed, although the ratio of British to French descent is much steeper. The Canadian Fianna have a slightly better reputation for dealing with the native Garou, although there are still plenty of blemishes on their record. The tribe is generally a little more given to urban caerns in Canada, partly because their Kin blend seamlessly into the local population, and partly because they don't care so much for the stoic ideal of surviving a harsh winter in the

Métis vs. Metis

Just in case you didn't know, there's a significant difference between the metis (MET-iss) and the Métis (may-TEE). The former is, of course, the Garou breed; the latter is an ethnic group of mixed American Indian and European blood.

Also on the subject of terminology, the term "Eskimo" isn't something that the Inuit find complimentary — it means "eaters of raw meat," and was given to them by other tribes. They prefer to call themselves "the only people."

northernmost areas. (One waggish theory put forth by the Bone Gnawers also holds that the Fianna were mildly traumatized the first time they tried to call a stag-spirit and got a moose-spirit instead.)

The Get in the area mostly arrived in the last 300 years or so, although the tribe claims that some of their number were here since the 10th century. Some of the local Fenrir can trace their ancestry back to the late 1700s, when the German-founded town of Lunenburg was becoming prominent in local maritime affairs; others claim descent from British Get who arrived elsewhere. The Fenrir have been more successful than most European tribes at adapting to the colder climes; they apparently find it an excellent test of their endurance.

The other tribes are also present to varying degrees, of course. The Red Talons have a strong presence in Canada, where they take full advantage of the comparatively healthy wolf population. There's a slight tendency among these Talons to be more forgiving of humans in general (since they have more territory to themselves) and more vengeful to specific humans (not being used to the damage humans can do to the land and its life). Likewise, the Uktena are scattered here and there, mostly sharing space at Wendigo caerns where they're welcome as advisors. The tribe also shares a particular sympathy for the Métis, whose mixed blood gives them something in common with the Uktena.

The Black Furies, Children of Gaia and Shadow Lords have very few caerns of their own in Canada; in fact, each tribe probably has no more than one tribal caern to their name in the country. They tend to focus their attention on the human population, which means that they spend most of their time around the more populated south of the country. The Shadow Lords are generally the most outgoing of the three; the tribe's Crows have made some connections among the Red Talons, Fenrir and Wendigo of the northern areas, offering the tribe's help should it be needed.

In the cities, the Glass Walkers are probably about even with the Bone Gnawers as numbers go. Although the Gnawers are highly sympathetic to the blue-collar population of most Canadian towns and cities, relatively few felt comfortable tagging along with the Get, Fianna and Silver Fangs to what was clearly a hostile tribe's territory. Most of Canada's Bone Gnawers are scattered throughout the towns and cities along the corridor from Quebec City to Windsor — which is also where the majority of Canadian Glass Walkers dwell. Both tribes are at their thickest in Toronto, where the Glass Walkers maintain at least two caerns.

The Silent Striders and the Stargazers are the two most distinct minorities among the country's tribes; neither tribe is known to hold any caerns in the area, or even gather in numbers of more than two at a time.

The Maritime Provinces

The Maritime Provinces account for very little of Canada's overall land area, but they are rich in petroleum, natural gas and other resources. This makes them a prime target for many of Pentex's activities. As a result, industrialization has been rapidly working its way into the easternmost provinces, bringing some jobs along with it — but imperiling other jobs, and more besides, as it goes.

New Brunswick

New Brunswick perches on the east coast of North America, just north of Maine. The province is heavily forested, with most of the human population concentrated along the coast and the Saint John River valley. Of course, the woods are considered quite the useful resource, and the logging industry (particularly for pulp and paper) is important to the local economy. This doesn't please the local werewolf population much; a pack of Fenrir is currently entertaining plans to severely monkeywrench Edmundston, one of the major centers of the industry.

About one third of New Brunswick's population is French-Canadian, largely descended from the settlement of Acadia, established in 1604. Most of the province's larger towns and cities are on the coast, whether that of the Bay of Fundy or the Gulf of St. Lawrence. The coast also has a scattering of Acadian villages, often marked by flags resembling the French tricolor with a yellow star in the upper part of the blue stripe. Rumors persist among the neighboring septs that a few of these villages are homes to a cult that worships some sort of Wyrm-beast under the waters, but the local packs haven't yet had the leisure to investigate these rumors in depth.

The Fundy Islands are a popular spot among outdoor types such as birdwatchers, whale-watchers, fishermen and the like. The world's second-largest whirlpool churns off the coast of Deer Island, and the place is a nexus for spirit energy. The place would make an excellent caern — if werewolves could breathe water, of course. A rumor making its way around Garou circles (and some human circles as well) says that huge sharks have been seen in the whirlpool's area, hinting that the Rokea are aware of the site's significance.

New Brunswick doesn't have a large werewolf population, and most of the local Garou are Get of Fenris of mainly Saxon descent. Of them, the most notable is Jarl John Golden-Boar, who's famous for single-handedly overturning six logging trucks in a single run, without so much as breaking stride.

Newfoundland

This island province is an extension of the Appalachians, and is as rugged as that would imply. On average, the island is home to less than four people per square mile. It has quite the local history — the first European settlers after a failed Viking settlement were sailors who jumped ship, preferring to eke out a living on "the Rock" rather than spend another day at sea. A number of bogs and heaths squat in the more poorly drained areas of the island, and at least one boasts a Fianna caern. The Fianna are rather content on the island; the locals' personality works well with their own. Storytelling is a long-standing tradition among "Newfies," and their speech is an unusual blend of West Country English and the dialect of southwest Ireland.

As mentioned previously, the island was the site of a 10th century Viking settlement, one that apparently included a few Fenrir in its number. The Wendigo and Get tell conflicting stories of the settlement: the Wendigo claim that the Fenrir were poor guests, and immediately fell to attacking the native people, while the Get maintain that the so-called "Pure Ones" offered violence to the newcomers, and that the Fenrir merely retaliated. Whatever the actual story of the settlement, it didn't last more than a few decades. However, there are persistent stories that a few of the Get remained behind and began to run with Wendigo and Uktena, becoming Fenrir by totem alone. If these rumors are true, there's no proof to be found on Newfoundland — although descendants of "Ymir's Sweat" might live on elsewhere.

Despite the influence of the local Fianna, Newfoundland is the site of heavy iron mining, at least some of which is overseen by Harold and Harold. The natives aren't particularly happy about the province's reliance on natural resources — what happens when the wells and mines run dry? — but as long as mining and drilling provide jobs, it's hard to turn away from them.

The most significant change on the wind — at least to Garou perspective — involves the Hibernia oil fields, a multi-billion dollar project taking place just off St. John's east coast. This project has the potential to be very profitable, if the oil reserves prove to be as rich as the investors hope. And unfortunately, one of those investors is Endron International. Endron currently has two Menantol platforms under construction off the Newfoundland coast, and are planning others should the payoffs — in crude oil, natural gas and…other resources — be there.

Nova Scotia

"New Scotland" is a relatively small province; it'd be an island if not for the Isthmus of Chignecto, which attaches it to the mainland. Its rivers are short and its woodlands plentiful, and despite its natural resources, the province isn't very urbanized. Most Nova Scotians are of British descent, although there's a sizable minority of French Acadians. The province's prosperity hasn't been anything to brag about for some time; Nova Scotia has a history of receiving a large share of financial aid from the federal government, and unemployment is a chronic problem. As a result, the local government is becoming increasingly receptive to corporations like Endron who are quite interested in offshore drilling for petroleum and natural gas. Forestry, fishing and tourism are all well and good, but they're not the same kind of moneymakers.

Nova Scotia was originally home to the Micmac, and a few members of this nation still live in the province. Most of the area's tourism focuses on Cape Breton Island, a place where the economy is nonetheless at its worst. Bad things have been known to happen to tourists every once in a while here, as a few fomori are spontaneously born every year and start causing trouble.

Unsurprisingly, the most populous tribe in the area is the Fianna, who have been drifting here since the late 18th century. The tribe has been devoting most of their effort to bettering their human Kin's lot in life; the province's economic hardships are much more important to the Fianna than they would be to most other tribes. The local werewolves have been known to travel into the coalmines when they need to bind spirits of a particularly grim or forbidding aspect into their fetishes. At least one abandoned coal mine, though, had to be abandoned because it was too close to awakening something horrible that slept below the earth. The Fianna don't enjoy the time they spend in the mineshafts, but as they put it, better that they go down there from time to time than leave the shafts open so that the Black Spiral Dancers can move in.

Prince Edward Island

Prince Edward Island (a.k.a. PEI) is by far the smallest of the Canadian provinces. In many ways, it's also the least imposing; the terrain is a gently rolling plain and most of the original forests are gone, cleared long ago to make room for settlements. The island's human population is dense, but not urbanized. The towns that dot the island aren't particularly large, but they leave little room for wilderness caerns.

There are no full-fledged septs on PEI; a few families of Fenrir, Silver Fang and Fianna Kinfolk make their homes here, but any children who undergo the First Change are sent to septs elsewhere. These Kin are also likely to call in their werewolf relatives if trouble seems to be brewing, but if their Garou cousins are busy with other concerns, help can sometimes be a long time coming.

The Central Region

The provinces at the heart of Canada are also the most densely populated; proximity to the United States border, ample natural resources and a relatively forgiving climate make Quebec and Ontario the place to be in the eyes of many. This section of Canada is also where the greatest mix of Garou tribes can be found; almost all of the tribes are adequately represented in these two provinces.

Quebec

The largest eastern province, Quebec is also the heart of French-Canadian culture. The residents are fiercely proud of their language and culture, to an often obsessive level. Quebec is famous for its separatist outlook, and to some extent that's not surprising. The province is surrounded on all sides by English speakers, making some Quebecois feel as if they're stranded on an island — and others to feel besieged. Many residents are downright angry at the intrusions of English-language culture (particularly American television), and resent being lumped in with the rest of Canada when the rest of Canada's culture is so clearly different from their own. Quebec has regularly striven to gain independence from the rest of Canada, becoming a nation in its own right. So far, it hasn't happened, but one never knows.

Although most Quebecois are bilingual, there's no doubt that they favor French; it's rare to spot an outdoor sign with English information anywhere in the province. Most of the province's human population is centered in the southwest, along the St. Lawrence and the border with the US. The province extends up into polar bear territory in the north, and there's also an ample wolf population away from the more urbanized areas. Of course, the north woods support a heavy forestry industry, one that infuriates the Red Talons that call northern Quebec home. The province also has a thriving manufacturing industry, although this is more concentrated in the southwest.

Although Quebec's capital is the distinctive Quebec City, most people who think of Quebec think of Montreal. Montreal is the second-largest French-speaking city in the world, right behind Paris. And as a result, it's prone to the troubles that plague most urban centers in the World of Darkness. This does mean Weaver-energies, of course; the webs are strong around the city, particularly around the Parc Olympique (the remarkably expensive sports complex that wasn't fully completed until 11 years after the Olympic Games it was built to serve). It also means vampires, and the undead that cluster in Montreal seem to be a particularly cunning and vicious lot. Black Dog Game Studio prints their tainted products at a plant nearby, quietly eluding Garou notice because there's just so much else that needs doing in the area.

According to Garou oral history, somewhere in Montreal's vicinity is the site where one of the more powerful and malevolent Banes of the New World was bound long ago. This tale has passed along from Garou to Kin and beyond, with the unfortunate result that the story is now familiar to some occult circles. The local Garou, a sept of largely Silver Fang extraction entrenched in the Laurentians, worry that the more scholarly Leeches of Montreal might chance across this legend and decide to make trouble. The locals also suspect a small coven of Black Spiral Dancers has also slipped into the city in search of clues telling how to free the evil spirit, but the number of vampires in the city makes any search parties a risky prospect.

Ontario

Canada's most populous province, Ontario is both highly modern and unusually wild in pieces. The south portion of the province is filled with towns and cities; the north portion with lakes, bogs, moose and mosquitoes. The Great Lakes run along Ontario's south border, and Hudson Bay defines its northern limit.

As befits its sizable population, Ontario is home to plenty of industry, including the ever-present mining and forestry, but also a fair bit of manufacturing and agriculture. Virtually everywhere there *could* be a hydroelectric dam in the province, there is one — and even then, Ontario requires nuclear and fossil fuel power plants to meet its energy needs. With the exception of Hallahan (and even they are somewhat active in Hudson Bay), every Pentex subsidiary with an interest in Canada is quite likely present in Ontario somewhere.

The province is also home to Canada's largest city. Toronto is a remarkably busy city, with a bustling downtown; it serves as the headquarters for the country's radio and television broadcasting. Toronto boasts a pair of urban caerns, one largely populated by Glass Walkers and one mostly run by Bone Gnawers, which are both notably

multitribal. Most visiting Garou with business in Canada tend to drop by one of these septs to be caught up to speed; this is particularly true of tribes other than the well-entrenched Get, Wendigo, Silver Fangs or Fianna.

Algonquin Provincial Park is an important issue among the local werewolf population. For one, there are several packs of wolves hanging on in the park — ironically, they're part of what draws tourists in droves. In August, park naturalists are known to take campers out in groups to howl into the night, hoping to raise a response from the wolves in the park. For another, the park is being heavily scarred by industrial pollution and logging companies. Because the park is so prominent in the locals' eyes, the werewolves in the area know that violent reprisals will have to be carefully orchestrated so as not to rend the Veil — but as more trees are plowed under and more streams polluted, the urge to claim payment in blood gets harder to resist.

Ontario is notable among the provinces for the sheer number of ethnic groups that make up its population; it's not surprising that its werewolf population is similarly mixed. As mentioned before, Glass Walkers and Bone Gnawers concentrate in Toronto; the Uktena also have a scattered presence throughout the province. In fact, although they might not hold caerns of their own, virtually every tribe has permanent residents somewhere in Toronto — the only ones that can't be proven to live there are the Silent Striders and Stargazers, and even then it's possible they just haven't been noticed.

The West
British Columbia

British Columbia stretches from Alaska down to the state of Washington, straddling the Pacific Ocean. It's a notably mountainous place; the Rockies, Columbia Mountains and Cassiar-Omineca Mountains all run through the province. British Columbia is Canada's third most populous province, and about half of the locals are immigrants from other provinces, territories or countries. Half of the province's population lives in Vancouver, and fully 75% is concentrated along the southwest coast. The north portion of the province is virtually empty of human life, but there are several wolf packs, as well as both black and grizzly bears, roaming the area. Generally speaking, the climate's rather mild in B.C., at least in the more settled areas.

Although the province does draw a fair amount of money from tourism, B.C. also has a healthy forestry industry (particularly in the north) and plenty of mining (mostly in the southeast). A few Children of Gaia been strive to use their resources to encourage tourism, hoping that the more people who see the land's natural

beauty, the more people will object to the blatant abuses common to the forestry and mining industries. The Red Talons of the province are something of a thorn in the side of this plan, of course. It also doesn't help that the resident Silver Fangs would rather see as few visitors as possible, so that they can execute their missions with little fear of rending the Veil.

The province's capital, Vancouver, is particularly notable as the site of a "noble experiment" — an experimental treaty between the

city's vampires and Garou, which required both sides to set aside their eternal grudge in the name of peace. This compact was struck in 1972 — and it lasted over 26 years before disintegrating.

Nobody's sure who fired the first shot, but when the esteemed Glass Walker Roger Daly was killed defending his urban caern — a caern that was lost — the Garou knew that something stank in Vancouver. Recent intelligence reports confirm that someone has built a shiny new casino atop a toxic dump, a dump previously proven to be a full-blown Wyrm-caern. The only thing preventing it from being a Hive proper is the absence of Black Spiral Dancers — but the casino is apparently under the vampires' protection. One particularly ugly bit of rumor has it that Daly's skin, somehow preserved in Lupus form, hangs in the lobby.

The truce is off, and the werewolves of British Columbia are asking themselves some hard questions about trust. Although they don't have the numbers to wage an open war against Vancouver's Leeches (and whatever allies the undead might have), a covert war is about to erupt into being.

Alberta

The westernmost of Canada's prairie provinces, Alberta is somewhat harsher than its neighbors. Excepting the southeastern portion (where grasslands are the prevalent terrain), Alberta is subject to the short, cool summers and long, cold winters that outsiders associate with Canada. The Canadian Rockies stretch through the province, meeting forests and even tundra and glaciers as the province stretches north. The people here tend to be the equivalent of Canada's cowboys; Alberta's notorious for macho pursuits like rodeos, hockey and Gold Rush revivals.

There are plenty of Garou concerns in Alberta. Historically, Alberta was once the stomping grounds of a number of Plains Indian tribes, including the Blackfoot Confederacy; the failing fortunes of these tribes sparked a number of werewolf attacks on local settlers around the end of the 19th century. The petroleum business is profitable and heavily entrenched here, with Endron — as usual — among the worst offenders of the industry. Alberta's also home to the largest surviving herd of wild bison that has apparently fallen under the protection of a multitribal sept dedicated to the totem of Bison.

A Get of Fenris caern based out of the Kananaskis Provincial Park, not far from Calgary, is particularly notable for offering intensive battle training to members of other tribes. The students undergo a brutal training regimen and even more brutal sparring sessions, but those that "graduate" are among the fiercest and most technically proficient warriors of the Garou Nation. The werewolf who quietly mentions his training at the Stone Heart Sept receives a healthy amount of respect from those in the know.

Also of particular note is the West Edmonton Mall, the infamous "largest in North America." This monument to shopping, with over 800 stores and the largest indoor amusement park in the world, has boldly pushed its way into caern status. The spirits of Cockroach's brood, particularly spirits of commerce, breed here in great numbers; its hardly surprising that a local sept of Glass Walkers has claimed the mall as their territory, and hold moots there after hours.

Saskatchewan

The province of Saskatchewan is pure prairie country; mountains are few and far between in this portion of Canada. The province's name means "fast river" in a native dialect, and true to form, the hydroelectric power industry is quite busy along the various rivers of the land.

Saskatchewan makes a good deal of its money from agriculture, but its family farms have traditionally been troubled. The Depression of the 1930s hit brutally hard, and today the vagaries of weather aren't being particularly forgiving. The family farm is becoming an endangered species, as an increasing shift toward corporate farming moves across the province. And as with so many other places in the World of Darkness, the "big business" treatment of agriculture leaves much to be desired. Chemical treatments bathe the crops, sometimes even leaking out of their containers to seep into the land. Over-farming is causing a severe erosion

problem. And the people who know how to take care of the land become increasingly unable to do so, as the poor harvests continue to hurt them. The province also suffers from an ever-increasing number of forest fires; locals are beginning to suspect that an arsonist or arsonists are responsible. The werewolves of the province, of course, have their own opinions.

Saskatchewan's most prominent sept of Garou is a mixed sept of Wendigo, Uktena and Red Talons who guard a caern of Honor in Prince Albert National Park. However, as the park's fortunes fade (the money hasn't been coming in the way it's needed), park officials strive harder to increase tourism. The sept leaders are worried that if the park is successful, a confrontation between tourists and well-meaning caern guardians is inevitable — and if it isn't, then the park might lease out its mineral rights. As of yet, no solution has presented itself, and the clock is ticking.

Manitoba

Manitoba is fairly representative of Canada's terrain; the south is seasonally temperate prairie, while the northern two-thirds of the province are heavily forested and sparsely populated. The province's capital is Winnipeg, a multicultural city that often unknowingly sponsors multitribal moots in Kildonan Park (a park that, like New York City's Central Park, was designed by Bone Gnawer Kin Frederick Law Olmstead). The city is something of a neutral ground among the various Garou, although the Wendigo, Get and Fianna are notable for voicing old grudges at the Kildonan moots.

A large portion of the province is covered by lakes, one of which takes up a good portion of the province on its own. Lake Winnipeg is a remarkably large body of water, second only to the Great Lakes. However, overdevelopment is a very real problem along its shores, one that has incensed a local sept of Fenrir. These Get are fairly prone to covert attacks on local fishing boats and development companies, particularly those that seem to take an… unusually professional interest in converting the land for their purposes.

In fact, Manitoba's economic activity is a matter of concern to most of the local Garou. The province is home to almost all the problematically abused industries settled in Canada — fishing, mining, forestry, commercial agriculture and even heavy tourism. The most recent near-disaster took place near the northern town of Flin Flon, where blasting at a copper mine stirred up a bed of Thunderwyrm-like beasts that spread throughout the area. It took weeks for the Wendigo and Fenrir septs in the area to hunt all the beasts down, and even now they're not sure that they caught every last one.

The Northern Territories

Canada's territories are distinctly werewolf country, particularly Wendigo and Red Talons. The lands are very sparsely populated, boast modest numbers of wolves, and proportionately more native Kin are present. Of course, the climate makes the territories less than desirable to many people, but the Wendigo seem to thrive on the bitter cold.

Unfortunately, the Wendigo's Kin don't seem to have the same fortitude. Although the Inuit and other natives are able to make a living in the harsh terrain, their existence isn't anything to be envied. The suicide rate among the native peoples is horrifying — alcohol and drug addiction is a sadly ever-present problem. The Wendigo and other native shapeshifters do what they can to fight against this miserable situation, but the depression settled over the Inuit and other native nations has little to do with Banes. There's nobody to "kill and make it better" — and although the Wendigo are surely capable of things other than outright violence, they haven't been able to do more than preserve the sanity of a few Kin families. The situation is horrible, and no easy solution is in sight.

Northwest Territories

The Northwest Territories (or sometimes NWT) are very sparsely settled, with most settlements topping out at a few hundred people. Considering the size of the territory, the human population seems all the more rare. Rivers and lakes cover more than half of the land, and much of the area is tundra proper. The summers are fairly hospitable, with sunlight for up to 20 hours a day, but when winter comes the NWT become a harsh and unforgiving stretch of land.

The NWT support a surprising amount of animal life, particularly given the conditions of permafrost that cover the north. Timber wolves inhabit the southern forests, while the tundra is arctic wolf territory, and that means Wendigo and Red Talons. The ecosystem is dangerously fragile, though; one poor season can ravage the plant life, decimating the rest of the food chain. Although the animal species have always recovered over time, the encroachment of southern development and increasing Wyrm-influenced intruders threaten to throw the balance off for good. Most of the Garou's battles in this area take place far from human civilization, where there's nobody to interfere — on either side.

Nunavut

Canada's newest territory is still just a fledgling — but one with an unusual twist. In 1999, the Canadian government formally set aside a portion of the NWT as the territory of Nunavut, a territory placed directly in the hands of the native people. This step hasn't been the solution to all of the local natives' woes, to be sure, but most Canadians see it as a well-intentioned, progressive step. The fact that Nunavut isn't exactly the most hospitable of terrain probably doesn't hurt their generosity.

This almost unprecedented move has some people looking for werewolf influence; it would certainly seem like the sort of agenda that the Wendigo, Uktena or even the Children of Gaia would pursue. However, no Garou has come forward to claim the responsibility, and the renown that would surely follow. Some Garou are hesitant to believe that the humans could have come up with this idea on their own; to others, it's not such a hard idea to swallow.

Ultimately, the responsible parties don't really matter — what matters are the new opportunities. Now the Wendigo are doing what they can to place their Kinfolk in the local governments, and Parliament if possible. Legislation isn't a tool they're used to using, but they refuse to let a chance like this slip away.

Nunavut is no more immune than any other province to the depression and addictions that plague the native nations. Of course, there are plenty of people who manage to overcome these demons, particularly in light of the new opportunities opening up — but, as always, there are people who aren't as lucky or strong. If there's one bright spot, it's that the increased Wendigo influence and sparse population makes it easier for werewolves to detect, isolate and destroy the Banes that come to feed on the human population's misery. Unfortunately, those Banes are a symptom, not a cause of the disease of the spirit; as long as the humans are subject to pain and oblivion, the Wyrm-spirits will keep coming.

The most prominent sept in Nunavut is, naturally, a Wendigo sept, one located along the Chesterfield Inlet. Nungak Shifting Ice, a powerful Philodox skilled in battle, diplomacy and spirit mastery, leads the sept. The Sept of the Cold Sun has sponsored many packs who have distinguished themselves well in battle and vision quest; some prophets predict that the sept will produce the Wendigo's champion in the Final Battle.

Whether Nunavut will earn a reputation as a failure with noble intentions or a genuine betterment for the lot of Canada's native people remains to be seen. The Wendigo are certainly going to fight for the latter prospect — should the onrushing Apocalypse allow them any time to do so, of course.

Yukon

The Yukon Territory is famous for being mountainous, forested and cold — the 1896 gold strike in Klondike fixed the territory firmly in the world's perception. And for a short time, gold flowed freely out of the mountains. A very short time. By 1902, there just wasn't as much gold to be had. Within a decade, the boom had gone bust. The locals turned to mining zinc, silver and other minerals, but this was a poor substitute. The territory is currently in a depression as the world mineral markets are in a slump. The Yukon has turned to tourism, particularly with the gimmick of Klondike nostalgia, as a possible way to make ends meet — but this has its drawbacks as well.

Nearly 20% of the local population are either full-blooded or mixed-blood Native American; the Inuit population is negligible. Among them, the most prominent group is the Dene, who have lived here for perhaps 60,000 years. The remainder of the population is generally European, of fairly mixed pedigree.

The Garou are fairly strong in the Yukon; the mountainous, forested territory suits them. The Wendigo and Red Talons are a notable presence, as is an enclave of Shadow Lords who have come north to make their name fighting the more abusive mining corporations. There are said to be a few Gurahl in the territory as well; certainly the salmon runs along the Yukon River attract their ursine Kin. The Pentex Board of Directors is well aware that the Yukon is a prime example of "territory likely to be guarded by shapeshifters," and is prone to dispatching First Teams and other heavy security to guard their mining — and other "prospecting" — interests in the region. More than a few bloody firefights along the slopes have been the result.

The Changing Breeds

If Canada belongs to anyone other than the Wendigo, then it's surely Corax territory. The Corax have lived in the northern woods since before the humans were telling stories of how Raven stole the sun to keep the world warm. Canada's raven population is moderately healthy, and since the Corax don't particularly require Kin bloodlines to pass on their gifts, the wide selection of human partners is plenty beneficial.

Canada is also the tribal home of the Qualmi, the werelynxes who hoard mystical knowledge, both new and ancient. The riddling lynx-shifters tend to avoid contact with the European settlers' descendants, although a few have cautiously padded into the cities proper in order to pry out whatever information catches their tufted ears. The Qualmi have very little by way of central organization, instead relying on a gossip network of sorts to exchange important news. The Corax occasionally act as messengers for the werelynxes, but this isn't common; an old feud, centuries or even millennia past, has left the two sides moderately wary of each other. The Corax claim that the chill relations stem from a Qualmi fondness for

pulling tail-feathers, but considering the wereravens' usually easy-going nature, this is probably a euphemism. A few Pumonca also make their homes in Canada, largely in the mountains of the western provinces, but they are significantly fewer — the werelynxes have precedence here, and the cougar-shifters know it.

There are plenty of coyotes in Canada; the adaptable little canines have done quite nicely at settling into the majority of the country. With them come the Nuwisha, of course, who enjoy both the increasing coyote population and the diverse selection of humans who might make enjoyable partners. As a result, a moderate portion of the world's Nuwisha has been born in Canada, although like the rest of their kind, they find it difficult to put down roots. They aren't particularly influential — but they're there.

The vast spaces also afford a few Gurahl ample places to hide; the bears across Canada are numerous and varied enough to serve as Kin for all four tribes, including the Ice Stalkers of the north. There are precious few Gurahl active, but Canada seems to have more of them than does any other country save Russia — it helps somewhat that the local Wendigo don't mind the werebears' presence, and the Europeans aren't inclined to believe that any survive. Still, one werebear has made open contact with the Garou — an Ice Stalker named Kucirak the Splitter. Kucirak is on fairly decent terms with a Fenrir sept on the Alaskan border, and he has joined their war parties on several occasions, most notably making two Endron EEPS and the First Team guarding them disappear from the face of the earth. His Fenrir friends have so far been very loyal, but Kucirak hasn't dropped his guard around them; he knows full well that should he display any hint of dubious moral character or weakness, the werewolves' estimation of him will plummet.

Finally, the Ratkin aren't as populous in Canada as they are in the United States, but they find the prairies fairly appealing and the cities moderately interesting. Common gossip among the wererats talks of a few Rat Race militias that have been setting up ranches far from civilization, or of Gamine deserters who are trying to either form their own plague or claim cities in the name of Madame DeFarge.

Most of the remaining Changing Breeds have a few representatives in Canada, but only incidentally. At least one Pumonca is said to roam the Rockies north of the border, presumably guarding the site of a long-buried Bane. The few Ananasi that inhabit Canada tend to focus on the cities; they seem to find nothing of interest in the wilder places. And although an occasional Mokolé comes north to see the midnight sun for himself, the sun-aspected Dragon Breed has a natural dislike for the climate. There are no perma-

A World of Rage

nent Mokolé residents in Canada, and it's unlikely that any visitors of the Breed will stay long.

The Enemy
Black Spiral Dancers

The Wyrm's own tribe is everywhere, and Canada is no exception. However, despite ample wilderness to hide themselves in, the Dancers aren't as prolific here as one might guess. The greatest deterrent holding them back is the presence of the Garou Nation's strongest warrior tribes — the Get of Fenris and Wendigo both flourish in the frozen north, and there's a fair number of Fianna, Uktena, Silver Fangs and Red Talons to back them up. As a result, the Dancers have generally restrained themselves to worming their way into Canada's metropolitan centers, where the wilder tribes don't tend to go. It's certainly safer for them.

Pentex

The various corporations under Pentex's banner are, of course, highly profit-driven — and Canada is a place with ample profits to be made. In particular, Endron has been making constant (if slow) progress toward bleeding as much petroleum and natural gas out of the land as they can get. And because they promise the ever-seductive bait of jobs, they have plenty of allies in Parliament. Good House International is a major buyer for the Canadian forestry industry, and the company is probably strongest in Canada. Good House has made a number of investors quite rich, at the expense of the nation's forests. Harold and Harold Mining, Incorporated is also firmly entrenched in Canada, where they vigorously tear as much of the local mineral reserves out of the earth as possible.

While these three are the most prolific Pentex subsidiaries in Canada, many of the others aren't too far behind. Ardus Enterprises has several profitable branch offices up north, where there's lots of land to bury waste and few people to complain. Hallahan Fishing Corporation is heavily involved off both coasts, the Atlantic in particular; their current practices are making it hard for local fishermen to turn a profit, while still ensuring high profit margins for the company.

The subsidiaries that produce everyday products and entertainment are also doing quite well for themselves. As a general rule, the influence of American culture in Canada is a tremendous asset. Canadians grab meals at O'Tolley's, watch OmniTV shows, leaf through Vesuvius publications on the bus, and play Tellus and Black Dog games. The most notable exception is King Breweries and Distilleries, which has the unfortunate distinction of producing recognizably American (which, to the Canadian palate, means "weak") beer. That

hasn't stopped the King family from doing their best to buy out local breweries and start pushing Canadian beer under a different label — with the appropriate King "touch," of course. So far, they haven't made that purchase, but it might not be long.

United States: Pure Lands No Longer

There can be little doubt that humans have essentially reconfigured the American landscape. Today, more than 85 percent of the virgin forests of the United States have been logged, 90 percent of the tallgrass prairies have been plowed or paved, and 98 percent of the rivers and streams have been dammed, diverted, or developed. In the process, hundreds of species have vanished completely, many others have declined to the point of endangerment, and still others are drastically reduced in number.

— David S. Wilcove, *The Condor's Shadow*

Sprawling from the Atlantic coast to the Pacific shore, the United States presents modern Garou with a host of challenges. Land of opportunities lost and found, the vast nation that has, for the better part of the last century, assumed the leadership of the world serves as a crucible in which the three-way struggle of Wyld, Wyrm and Weaver manifests in a multitude of forms. Though greater battles against the Wyrm take place in the Amazon on a daily basis, the United States harbors many smaller battles on a multi-sided front. Many Garou believe that the final battles against the Wyrm will take place on American soil. They may be wrong, but no one can dispute the fact that America offers the Garou a splendid practice field on which to hone their skills for the inevitable conflict.

History

Of the three Garou tribes that originally settled in the Pure Lands, which consist of the continents of the Western Hemisphere, only the Uktena and the Wendigo remain. The stories they tell of the history of their homeland speak of great wars against Wyrm creatures followed by a time of peace and prosperity before the invasion of the European Wyrmcomers. The other Garou tribes, who arrived in the "New World" with their Kinfolk from Europe, tell a different tale — of a land in need of strong guardians able to defend it in ways the local Garou could not fathom. Together, these tales make up an epic story of struggle and conquest, of lessons learned and knowledge lost.

The Pure Lands

During the time of ice and cold, three Garou tribes, along with other Changing Breeds, crossed the great land bridge from Asia with their Kinfolk. The land they found stretched before them in unspoiled glory — vast forests, expanses of tundra and taiga, towering mountains and fertile prairies. Spirits of all kinds, including many hostile creatures of the Wyrm, filled the Umbra and walked about in the physical world as well. The newcomers also found humans and members of other Changing Breeds already living in the Pure Lands. The new arrivals joined with the indigenous dwellers to hunt down and either destroy the Wyrm-spawn or bind them in spirit prisons or deep within the earth itself.

After the time of binding, the Garou and their charges spread out to make their homes in the land given to them by Gaia. The Wendigo and their Kinfolk remained, for the most part, in the northern forests and icy lands of North America. The Uktena and Croatan traveled further south, to warmer, more temperate climes.

In the southwestern United States, the Uktena shared the land with the Pumonca and the secretive Ananasi. The Croatan wandered toward the Great River and, beyond, to the eastern ocean. They, too, encountered a few Pumonca and, in the swamplands of the most southern regions of North America, the strange and uncommunicative Mokolé. The Nuwisha, at that time, were everywhere.

The War of Rage had not left behind as many scars in the Pure Lands as elsewhere in the world; the Changing Breeds managed to coexist in relative harmony with one another, respecting each others' territories and acknowledging that there was room enough for all of Gaia's children.

Over the centuries, the people of the Pure Lands prospered. In the fertile valley of the great Mississippi River, the civilization of the mound builders grew and flourished. They traded with other cultures, including the empires far to the south. In the northern forests and the deserts of the southwest, other cultures rose and fell. The Garou watched over the societies of their Kinfolk, acting as messengers from the spirit world to their chosen humans but otherwise leaving them to their own devices.

The humans of the Pure Lands did as humans everywhere — they harvested the riches of the earth, hunted the creatures given to them by the spirits they honored, traded among each other and made war for many reasons. The Garou tended their caerns and bred with their Kinfolk. Occasionally they met with other Changing Breeds — not always on friendly terms, but never with the ferocity that characterized the Garou tribes in other lands, where the War of Rage still bred enmity.

Some stories say that the Garou of the Pure Lands grew complacent; others, that they grew proud. Most legends speak of the Wyrm-spirits of jealousy and greed that took shape across the ocean and impelled the humans of Europe to sail across the ocean in search of new sources of wealth and power. In any case, the centuries of relative peace known by the creatures of the Pure Lands came to an abrupt end with the sight of sails upon the eastern horizon and the approach of strangers from across the sea.

Dreams provided the first warnings of impending change. Garou Theurges saw visions of strange creatures, their skins pale with death or blotched from sickness, arriving from the east. Omens spoke of dark clouds blotting out the light of the moon and covering the land with their blighted shadows.

When the ships led by Columbus made landfall on the islands of the Caribbean, most Garou of the Pure Lands did not realize that their world would change forever. Only gradually did they sense the oncoming peril. But by then, it was too late. The Wyrm had arrived once more in the Pure Lands.

Forever Changed

The Spaniards arrived in the 1500s, as De Soto led his troops of soldiers and priests from Florida through the southeastern portion of North America. His travels brought him into contact with many of the native peoples, who suffered from De Soto's ruthless tactics of conquest and subjugation. Werewolves, along with the other Changing Breeds of the Southeast — the Pumonca and the Mokolé — harried the Spaniards, many of whom disappeared in the forests and swamps. But the foreign infestation had begun in earnest and left its mark in burned and looted villages and disease-ridden people, who died by the thousands from unfamiliar illnesses. Although De Soto finally succumbed to malaria and most of the Spanish withdrew to Florida, other Europeans followed swiftly in their wake. The French created settlements along the Gulf Coast and carried out a brisk trade in furs in the northern forests. More Spaniards invaded North America, coming up from Mexico and creating a string of missions in the southwest and up the California coast. In the northwest, Russian fur traders carried on a lucrative business with the people of the Pacific coast. Finally, the English came to the shores of North America — establishing their first colony on Roanoke Island, near the coast of what would one day be called North Carolina.

With the Europeans came the werewolves of the Old World. Fianna, Get of Fenris, Silver Fang, Bone Gnawers, Warders, Black Furies and Children of Gaia came with their Kinfolk, eager to flee the overcrowded cities of Europe and the increasingly oppressive presence of Wyrm and Weaver. A few Red Talons made the journey as well, searching for new sources of Kinfolk among the wolves of the New World.

Along with the newcomers, however, came the Wyrm-tainted. Some of those who settled in the new

colonies were not humans, but fomori, whose Bane riders drove them to latch onto the uncorrupted lands and claim them for their master. Leeches came, as well, gathering in the new cities and establishing their own territories to prey upon the blood of their victims.

Many of the Pure Lands Garou, like the humans of the New World, greeted the newcomers cordially, at first, hoping that their dreams and omens were wrong. But the European Garou carried themselves with the same arrogance as the human settlers. Believing that they possessed greater knowledge of the world than the primitive seeming "natives," the new werewolves laid their own claims on the Pure Lands, heedless of the territorial rights of the tribes that had protected the land for centuries.

Sacrifice and Loss

Accompanying the colonists who founded the settlement at Roanoke, the powerful Wyrm-spirit known as Eater-of-Souls quickly made its presence known in the Pure Lands. The entire Croatan tribe, along with their Kinfolk, perished in the now-legendary act of sacrifice in order to banish the monstrous creature from the world. Though the Croatan's heroic action succeeded, the repercussions proved costly. The Wendigo blamed the Uktena for not coming to the aid of the Croatan, while the Uktena maintained that they knew nothing of the Croatan's intentions. The rift that opened up between the two remaining Pure Lands tribes made the encroachment of the European Garou a relatively easy task.

As the European colonists embarked on a campaign of expansion, claiming native territories for their mother countries, the werewolves from Europe seized the lands once protected by the Uktena and the Wendigo. Hampered by the loss of many of their Kinfolk to disease or forced removal, many Pure Lands Garou abandoned their caerns and relocated to lands as yet untouched by the Europeans. The American Revolution opened the door to massive westward expansion — and for more waves of immigrants. As the territory claimed by the United States grew larger, the Uktena and the Wendigo saw their own lands and Kinfolk diminish.

The Other Side of the Coin

Many European Garou, of course, tell a different story. Upon their arrival on the shores of the New World, they encountered the native Garou and expressed their desire to share the land. They soon realized, however, that the Uktena and Wendigo had little knowledge of European ways and that they would become easy prey to the weapons and ploys of the newcomers. Placing the need to protect Gaia before all else, the Garou from Europe assumed the role of caretakers of the new lands. The European werewolves speak of how their Pure Lands cousins met their offers of friendship and cooperation with hostility and enmity, forcing them to go to war to secure the land against the Wyrm-taint that had arrived with the colonists.

For the Garou of Europe, the Pure Lands offered hope and opportunity, both qualities missing from the Old World, where Leeches and other Wyrm-creatures had gained the upper hand. They did not understand the reluctance of the native Garou to accept the help and leadership they offered. Unfortunately, the seeds of the Wyrm had already taken root and grew into a legacy of rivalry and bitterness among the European Garou.

The Pure Lands Despoiled

The outbreak of the Civil War saw the European Garou divided among themselves. As Kinfolk entered into the conflict on both sides, the Garou found their loyalties likewise divided. After the war, many Garou joined the movement westward as the philosophy of Manifest Destiny drove the United States to establish its boundaries "from sea to shining sea." The Uktena and Wendigo once again found themselves driven out of their territories, leaving their caerns either sealed and abandoned or else in the hands of usurpers. In the Umbra, the abandonment of caerns once belonging to the Pure Lands Garou weakened many of the controls placed upon Wyrm-spirits. In 1830, the powerful spirit known as the Storm Eater burst loose from its bindings and rampaged through the Umbral lands of the western United States. It wasn't until 1889 that the Garou, through the sacrifice of one of the greatest heroes of each tribe, managed to seal away the massive Bane/Weaver-spirit hybrid once more.

The latter half of the 19th century saw a consolidation of effort by the United States to solidify its borders. Railroads crisscrossed the land, telegraph wires stretched across the continent and great cities formed a gigantic

Weaver's web from the Atlantic to the Pacific. By the end of the century, most of the wolf population had been brought to near-extinction in the continental United States. This paucity of lupus Kinfolk brought home to the Garou the precariousness of their position and made them aware of just how close they were to losing the vital essence of wolf-blood. Finally, even the European werewolves realized that their new home lay in grave danger from both Weaver and Wyrm. Efforts at conciliation with their Pure Lands cousins began, but too many years of bitterness made it difficult for the Uktena and Wendigo to put aside their enmity for the Garou who had stolen their lands.

A Century of Rage

The 20th century began with a worldwide war that resulted in plunging the heretofore isolationist United States into the midst of world affairs. The Second World War brought home to the werewolves the true strength of the Wyrm and the Weaver as the nuclear age placed terrible weapons of destruction in the hands of mortals. In the United States, European and Pure Lands Garou finally realized the need to find some common ground. As a sense of global community spread throughout the world during the second half of the 1900s, werewolves in the United States gradually attempted to heal some of the wounds caused by 300 years of infighting — years during which only the Wyrm truly profited.

Although intertribal differences still surface — particularly those involving the Wendigo and any other Garou — the werewolves of the United States now strive to unify themselves in order to present a strong enough force to bring the battle to the Wyrm. The fate, not only of the "Pure Lands" but also of the world, hinges on their success.

Geography: Where the Garou Are

Although Garou tend to be territorial, the migration patterns of their Kinfolk in the United States have resulted in a wider distribution of tribes than in most other parts of the world. Nevertheless, some tribes predominate in certain regions — largely due to the presence of significant Kinfolk populations.

Northeast

The sprawling megalopolis that encompasses much of New England and the Mid-Atlantic and includes the cities of Boston, New York, Philadelphia, Baltimore and Washington, DC has fallen under the firm control of the Weaver. The Glass Walkers and Bone Gnawers, with their predilection for the urban wilderness and their acceptance of technology, have a strong presence here. Other Garou tribes make their homes in the less populous areas, such as rural New Hampshire, Vermont, Maine and upstate New York. The Fianna, Get of Fenris and Silver Fangs predominate among Garou of European descent. A few Uktena live here along with a handful of Wendigo who remain near the remnants of their Kinfolk.

Southeast

The coastal lands of Virginia and the Carolinas, along with the southern Appalachian states of Kentucky, West Virginia, Tennessee and Western North Carolina serve as home to Garou from many tribes. Although the Fianna and Get of Fenris predominate, due to the high incidence of Scot-Irish and German settlers, Silver Fangs and Children of Gaia also make their homes in this region. While none of the cities of the Southeast approach the size or congestion of the Northeast or Midwest, urban centers such as Richmond, Raleigh, Greenville, Columbia, Knoxville and Nashville contain enough stimulation to attract a significant number of Glass Walkers. Bone Gnawers exist not only in the urban centers of the Southeast, but also among the rural and mountain populations of Appalachia. A few Red Talons roam the isolated forests of the Great Smokies, the Blue Ridge and the Cumberland mountains, while Uktena reside among their Cherokee Kinfolk in the mountains of North Carolina and Tennessee.

Midwest

The large number of German and Irish settlers who populated the Midwestern United States has ensured a predominance of Get of Fenris and Fianna Garou and Kinfolk. The cities of Chicago, Milwaukee, Kansas City, Indianapolis and other urban centers of middle America have their share of urban Garou tribes as well as a good representation from tribes such as the Black Furies, Children of Gaia, Silver Fangs and Shadow Lords.

Deep South and Florida

The region encompassing Georgia, Alabama, Mississippi, Arkansas, Louisiana and Florida has fewer large cities than most of the rest of the United States. Nevertheless, Atlanta, New Orleans and Miami provide large population centers and serve as gathering places for Glass Walkers and Bone Gnawers, along with a few representatives of other Garou tribes. In the rural South, the Uktena have made a resurgence due to their decision to seek Kinfolk from the large African-American population in the area. The Everglades region of Florida hosts a sizeable Uktena population as well.

Southwest

The southwestern United States consists of the vast deserts of New Mexico and Arizona, the varied landscape of Texas and the salt flats of Utah. As expected, Glass Walkers congregate in the cities of Phoenix, Houston, Dallas, and other urban centers. In the wilderness regions, the Uktena have a stronghold due to the presence of many Native American Kinfolk. A few Wendigo dwell here as well, although the warm climate does not suit their cold natures; the Sept of the Painted Sands in Arizona is one of their most prominent caerns. The rest of the tribes are represented in smaller numbers.

The Rockies

The states of Colorado, Montana, Idaho and Wyoming boast some of the nation's most dramatic and wild scenery as the Rocky Mountains dominate large portions of the region. Denver hosts the largest number of Glass Walkers in this portion of the United States. Other tribes have scattered throughout the sparsely populated areas. Both Uktena and Wendigo live near the reservations belonging to their Kinfolk. The return of the wolves to Yellowstone National Park has attracted a fair number of Red Talons in the last decade.

Pacific Northwest

Washington and Oregon boast large tracts of forestlands that attract many Garou concerned with their preservation. Except for Alaska and Canada, the Wendigo have their largest concentration in this part of the country. Silver Fangs of Russian descent along with Get of Fenris and a few Fianna also make up a significant portion of the Garou population, while the Red Talons have a small but important voice in the community of werewolves. Relatively few Uktena live in this region; those who do have chosen to live among their Kinfolk relocated in the last century to reservations in the Northwest, or the increasing numbers of Asian-Americans. The cities of Seattle and Portland hold the greatest concentration of Glass Walkers and Bone Gnawers in the area.

California and Nevada

The West Coast, along with Nevada, contains a varied mix of Garou. The cities of San Francisco, Los Angeles and Las Vegas are meccas for the urban werewolves, while the redwood forests of northern California provide a haven for the Children of Gaia and other European Garou. Stargazers also have a distinct presence in California, where many of their Kinfolk live among the state's large Asian-American population.

Alaska

The relatively unspoiled lands of Alaska provide a hospitable environment for the Wendigo, who exist here in greater numbers than in many other regions of the United States. The wolf population in Alaska serves as a prime lupus breeding stock for the Red Talons, as well, who have migrated to Alaska to seek out lands where fewer humans dwell. Other Garou tribes exist here in small numbers — many of whom have come to address the environmental concerns in America's largest state and, to date, its most unspoiled.

Hawaii

Garou are not native to Hawaii, but some werewolves do inhabit the tropical island state. Stargazers live among their Polynesian and Japanese Kinfolk, while Glass Walkers have come to Honolulu to enjoy the benefits of urban living in the midst of "paradise." Other Garou visit the region and occasionally remain to get involved in preservation efforts.

Other Changing Breeds

While more Garou exist in the United States than any of the other Changing Breeds, nearly all of the shapeshifters have a presence in America. Pumonca inhabit den realms in the southwest and in parts of the southeast, where "painters" (panthers or mountain lions) once roamed freely. A few Qualmi live in the Rockies while most reside in Canada alongside their feline Kin. The few American Gurahl inhabit the forests of the southeast, the Rockies, the Alaskan riverways and the Pacific Northwest. In the Everglades of Florida and the bayous of Louisiana, a few Mokolé make their homes. Corax have spread throughout the United States, while the Ratkin inhabit most of the nation's cities. Along the coastlines and in Hawaii, the Rokea make themselves known upon occasion.

The Present

The Garou in the United States face an uphill struggle against the forces of both the Weaver and the Wyrm. Vanishing wilderness, urban pollution, toxic waste and other environmental disasters-in-the-making pose a constant threat to the land. Many caerns once protected by the Uktena and Wendigo remain lost to modern Garou. The ancient bindings that held powerful Wyrm spirits at bay are weakening at an alarming rate, and there aren't enough Uktena Banetenders to guard them all. Most Garou attribute the increasing violence among the human population to the effect of Wyrm-spirits on the population. And, of course, the specter of Pentex dominates much of corporate America, infusing modern society with its unique brands of Wyrm-taint. The signs of the Apocalypse grow more and more evident as the true millennium approaches and many Garou feel that their efforts have come too late to make a difference. Still, they try — and some of their efforts succeed.

The Reign of Albrecht and the Demise of the Seventh Generation

The recent ascension of Lord Jonas Albrecht, grandson of Jacob Morningkill, to the throne of the Silver Fangs has brought new life to the tribe. By custom and tradition, the Silver Fangs have claimed leadership of all Garou. While few tribes accept this claim as valid and binding, many Garou acknowledge the position as symbolic of the unity of all Garou in their fight against the Wyrm. Certainly, Albrecht's recovery of the legendary Silver Crown has gone a long way toward convincing his tribemates of his fitness to rule.

One of Albrecht's first actions as king was the destruction of the organization known as the Seventh Generation, a Defiler Wyrm cult dedicated to the corruption of children through systematic abuse. Under the rule of Jacob Morningkill, the Silver Fangs refused to accept the existence of the Seventh Generation, exiling Loba Carcassone, the Silver Fang Theurge who urged her tribe to take action. However, Albrecht's experiences during his own exile made him more receptive to the ideas of those outside the tribe. His recall of Loba from exile and his decision to wage war on the Seventh Generation met with resistance at first from more traditional tribe members. The resultant successful war, however, not only proved the wisdom of his decision but also served as a great morale boost for the Silver Fangs.

Since then, Albrecht has gone on to take the fight to the Wyrm in other places, advocating an aggressive stance that many Garou feel is long overdue.

Albrecht has his critics, of course, primarily among the older members of the tribe who oppose the new king's sometimes-unilateral decisiveness and would prefer to spend years planning and discussing actions before actually putting them to practice.

Signs of the End Times

Apart from the concerns of the modern world, many Garou also believe that the final days prophesied in the Silver Record have arrived. The appearance of a mysterious red star in the Umbra, coupled with the miraculous birth of a perfect cub to two metis, has brought together Theurges, Galliards and Philodox from all the tribes to determine what, if any, course of action the Garou should take. For the most part, these seekers spend their time in discourse and research, trying to piece together fragments of lore — both written and oral — and prophecy in order to discover the meaning of these two very potent signs of the Apocalypse. A few, however, have undertaken quests into the Umbra in search of more information from the spirits. While many Garou dismiss these actions as peripheral to the "real fight," others wonder if, just perhaps, the visionaries might have a clearer view of the years to come than most Garou.

A Dying World

Environmental concerns in the United States remain a prominent focus for most American Garou. The predations of Pentex aside, the prevalence of disastrous practices such as the clear-cutting of forests, exploratory drilling and mining operations, nuclear waste disposal and unmonitored dumping of toxic chemicals keep many Garou busy taking action to stop the destruction of the ecosystem. While awareness increases among the human population, the Garou feel that not enough is happening to make the changes necessary to halt the onslaught of environmental disaster. Various movements among the Garou have arisen to handle the crisis on multiple fronts. Some Garou, particularly the Children of Gaia, have chosen to concentrate their efforts on educating the masses and lobbying for legal change. More volatile Garou, such as the Fianna and Get of

Fenris, have joined forces with various environmental activist groups. The Glass Walkers have taken the struggle to the World Wide Web, rallying support through online newsgroups and maintaining a series of web pages to disseminate information. In addition, some Glass Walkers have sought to encourage the growth of eco-friendly businesses, hoping that cooperation with the Weaver can lead to the defeat of the Wyrm.

Movers and Changers
Albrecht, King of the Silver Fangs

Background: Born to Silver Fang Kin, Jonas Albrecht's intensity and his inclination to speak his mind alienated many of his tribe and incurred his exile by his grandfather, the former Silver Fang king, Jacob Morningkill. Traveling to New York City, Albrecht befriended the local Garou and gathered a small pack together. His contacts with Garou of other tribes gave him a broader picture of the overall struggle against the Wyrm and prepared him for his destiny.

The untimely death of Jacob Morningkill brought Albrecht, in a roundabout fashion, to the throne of the Silver

21

Fangs. His ability to inspire confidence in others and his unclouded vision concerning the true purpose of the Garou have led many to believe that he is, indeed, the leader needed to unite the Garou for the final battles against the Wyrm.

Image: Tall and well built, with angular features and fine silver-blond hair worn past his shoulders, Albrecht displays the aristocratic carriage of his noble ancestry. His preference for worn jeans and casual clothes, however, indicates his true opinion of outer seemings and unearned status. In Crinos form, Albrecht becomes a huge, white-furred engine of death. His lupus form displays white pelt of his Pure Breed.

Roleplaying Notes: You didn't ask to be king, but since Falcon chose you, you might as well make the best of it.

Micah Farwatcher, "Prophet of the End Times"

Background: Raised by his Kinfolk father, a noted astronomer, Micah came by his love for the stars honestly. Claimed by his Stargazer mother soon after his First Change, Micah accepted his Garou heritage but also insisted that he pursue his education, gaining a Ph.D. in astronomy from Stanford University. He has used his scientific knowledge to interpret many of the prophecies concerning the red star and other cosmic portents and has gained a reputation as a prodigy among his tribe. Although he spends much of his time studying the legends of the end times, the Galliard has also traveled extensively in the Umbra searching for answers and studying the impact of the red star on the spirit world. So far, he has uncovered more questions than answers, however. His next self-imposed quest consists of finding the truth about the metis cub and attempting to judge for himself the importance of this occurrence.

Image: Of mixed Asian-American heritage, Micah stands just under 5'7" in homid form. He has dark hair and eyes, with a definite Asian caste to his features. In Crinos form, Micah is 8' tall, with silver-streaked black fur. He dresses like a professor unless he is geared for battle or preparing to embark on an arduous journey.

Roleplaying Notes: Your knowledge of the stars comes from science and legend and you see no disparity between the two. You have dedicated your life to solving the mysteries of Garou prophecy, and it seems that you are engaged in a race against time to do just that. You have little time for anything else other than your life's work, since you believe that the Apocalypse is literally just around the corner.

Fainche Battlesinger, "Avenger of the Land"

Background: Fainche grew up in an activist family. Her Garou father coached her carefully from childhood to hold the Earth as sacred and to hate any who would destroy Her through accident or design. When her First Change came, the young Ahroun joined the local sept and quickly formed a pack of like-minded Garou. Accepted as pack leader for her outspoken opinions and confident attitude, Fainche quickly plunged into the world of eco-terrorism. She and her pack delight in galvanizing normally peaceful environmentalist groups into actions of sabotage, believing that only those who put their beliefs on the line will ever accomplish anything. To date, she has been arrested four times for her actions, but has managed to escape imprisonment through the efforts of one of her pack members, a Glass Walker attorney.

Image: Fainche is a stocky young woman in her early 20s, with dark auburn hair cut short and hazel eyes. She prefers clothing that allows her plenty of freedom to move — drawstring pants and loose shirts — unless she is engaged in clandestine activities that require dark clothing. Her Crinos form stands nearly 9' tall.

Roleplaying Notes: Gaia is dying, and you have to do something about it. It's all so very simple once you put things into perspective. You can afford to give up most of the comforts of modern existence in order to concentrate your efforts on an endless string of rallies, protests and more direct (and less legal) activities. So what if you spend a little time behind bars for your beliefs. The world needs risk-takers, and you are nothing if not that.

Mexico

I heard the music of Palenque
I heard your mother's cry
Faded footprints
On a blood-stained soil
And the sacrificial lullabies
　　— Annie Lalley, "Mexico"

The land of Mexico comprises a portion of the Ring of Fire, a Pacific region characterized by seismic and volcanic activity due to the interaction of three tectonic plates. Natural disasters such as the eruption of the Chinchon volcano in the early 1980s frequently alter the environment and create havoc among the people and creatures of the country. Some Garou and other Changing Breeds claim that this disturbance of the land stems not from natural causes, but from Gaia's displeasure at what has happened to Her once beautiful land.

History

The earliest stories of Mexico told by the Garou and other Changing Breeds relate the travels of the Pure Ones and their shapechanging companions from their ancient homes to a new land. Some of the tales told by the Kinfolk of Mexico describe several ages of the world, each of which ended in a great disaster and a new beginning for living things. Other stories recount a long journey from beneath the earth to the surface of the world. So many stories exist that no one knows which tales are true but most believe that each tale contains the seeds of the real story.

The first werewolves to arrive in Mexico came with their human Kin who would eventually form the Aztec Empire. Traveling from their ancient home of Aztlan, in what would one day be called Colorado, a few Uktena accompanied their human charges into the fertile mesas of central Mexico, where they found other people dwelling. These earlier civilizations, descendants of the Olmecs, the Toltecs, the Mixtecs and the ancient people of Teotihuacan, already lived in large cities and drew their sustenance from the fruits of their fields. The Balam knew these people as their Kinfolk and jealously attempted to protect them from those who would try to conquer them.

Some stories tell of how the Garou and the Balam fought a long a vicious battle over territorial rights to this part of the Pure Lands. During this time, when both Changing Breeds were distracted from their true duties, ancient and powerful creatures of the Wyrm moved in and worked a subtle influence over the Aztecs, encouraging them to make terrible and devastating war on the older civilizations. These old ones, probably vampires, controlled the priesthood and demanded the blood of their captives as sacrifices. Many Kinfolk of the Garou died upon the altars of the gods. Other stories whisper of even darker forces working beneath the land, demonic creatures and Wyrm-spawn who encouraged the bloody impulses of the Aztecs.

When the Garou and the Balam realized that their struggles had cost them the people they had been trying to protect, they called a truce and attempted to rectify the damage, but they were too late. By this time, the Aztecs had developed a taste for blood, war and empire. They turned their desires to the rich land of the Yucatan peninsula, where the civilization of the Maya flourished.

Like the Aztecs, the Mayan culture fell under the influence of bloodthirsty supernaturals despite the attempts of the native shapechangers to protect them. The Mayan empire disappeared under the weight of invaders from first the Toltecs and, later, the Aztecs. Their culture faded into obscurity after their abandonment by their "gods."

In 1519, Hernan Cortes landed with his conquistadors on the coast of Mexico. The Aztecs believed that Cortes, because of his pale skin, was the reincarnation of Quetzalcoatl, one of their greatest and most beloved of gods. This misconception opened the door to the rapid conquest of the Aztecs — and later, the rest of Mexico — by the Spanish. Within a few years, the mighty cities of Mexico lay in ruins beneath the heels of the conquistadors, who plundered them of their riches and made slaves of their people, using them to work in the gold and silver mines and on the farms and plantations. Along with the Spanish armies came missionaries, who worked to convert the native population. Used to obeying their own priests, the people recognized the new authority that now ruled their lives. One more factor contributed to the utter conquest of Mexico — the arrival of diseases for which the natives had no immunity.

With the Spaniards who came to live in Mexico came a few Garou who fell into the same conflict with the native shapeshifters that marked the colonization of both North and South America. The native Garou and the Balam found themselves and their Kinfolk outnumbered and retreated — the Balam to their Den-Realms and the Garou to places deep within the jungles away from the population centers.

Other supernatural creatures followed, including vampires who encouraged the growth of large cities to feed their hunger for blood. To augment the native labor force, the Spanish brought in slaves from Africa.

In 1824, Mexico gained its freedom from Spain. Twelve years later, Texas rebelled against Mexican rule, only to be annexed by the United States in 1845. Under the leadership of Benito Juarez, a member of the Zapotec tribe and Uktena Kinfolk, the new government of Mexico attempted a number of reforms intended to redress the injustices suffered under Spanish rule. Economic disaster resulted and European forces invaded Mexico to secure their financial investments. Juarez and his followers began a campaign of guerilla warfare. Native shapechangers likewise fought their European counterparts in bloody battles for the right to protect the land.

The Garou, still few in number, played little direct part in the evolution of Mexico during the latter half of the 19th and the 20th centuries. In the less populated parts of the country, however, both Garou and Balam tried to protect what they could from further despoilment by minions of the Weaver and the Wyrm.

Geographic Regions
Mexican Plateau

The most heavily populated region of Mexico consists of a large plateau that extends from the US border to the Isthmus of Tehuantepec, rising from 4,000 feet above sea level in the north to 8,000 feet in the south.

The northern region of the Mexican Plateau — La Mesa del Norte — contains an arid region bordered by the Sierra Madre Occidental to the west and the Sierra Madre Oriental to the east. Over the ages, the erosive action of streams and rivers has carved deep canyons through the mountains, including the Barranca del Cobre, which rivals the Grand Canyon in size and spectacle. Some mountains of the Sierra Madre Oriental reach a height of 13,000 feet, while the peaks of the Sierra Madre Occidental attain elevations of up to 9,000 feet.

La Mesa Central extends southward from La Mesa del Norte to Mexico City and beyond. Flatter and wetter than the northern plateau region, La Mesa Central contains many rich valleys of volcanic soil surrounded by mountainous areas. This region holds Mexico's breadbasket as well as some of its highest volcanic peaks including Mounts Popocatepetl and Ixtaccihuatl, both over 17,000 feet.

Gulf Coastal Plain

Stretching from the border with Texas to the Yucatan peninsula, the Gulf Coastal Plain contains a series of swampy lowlands and lakes near the shore and gentle hills and plains that proceed inland toward the high mountains of the Sierra Madre Oriental. Much of this land serves as pasture for cattle.

Pacific Lowlands

The narrow strip of land west of the Sierra Madre Occidental consists of a varied mix of geological formations — mesas, valleys and strips of coastal plains surrounding numerous river basins. Stretching for 900 miles from the Mexicali Valley southward to Tuxpan, this predominantly arid region has undergone extensive irrigation in the 20th century and now serves as an agricultural area for Mexico.

Baja California Peninsula

The Gulf of California separates this narrow strip of land from the rest of Mexico. Baja California extends southward from California for 800 miles and consists of a pair of mountain ranges — the San Pedro Martir and the Sierra de Juarez — with peaks that exceed 9,000 feet. The eastern mountains drop off dramatically to the Gulf of California, limiting access from that direction. The gentler slope of the western mountains allows for more habitable conditions. In general, rainfall is sparse throughout Baja California, although the southern portion of the peninsula experiences moderate rainfall during the summer.

Balsas Depression

The Balsas Depression gets its name from the Rio Balsas, the region's major river system. Small basins alternate with hills to form a varied and impressive landscape just south of the Mexican Plateau.

Southern Highlands

Mountain ranges and plateaus make up the Southern Highlands of Mexico. The mountains of the Sierra Madre del Sur, along the western border of the Highlands, extend to the sea. The beaches along the coast attract many tourists to their clear, warm waters and the presence of cities such as Manzanillo and Acapulco have garnered the area a reputation as the "Mexican Riviera." Inland, mountain basins and valleys provide a harsh if habitable basis for local farming. The Mesa del Sur, a region of secluded valleys and low-lying ridges, lies to the east of the mountains. Here, in the valley of Oaxaca, the Zapotec Indians preserve their culture amid an atmosphere of harsh living and subsistence farming.

Isthmus of Tehuantepec

A narrow strip of land between the Southern Highlands and the Chiapas Highlands forms the Isthmus of Tehuantepec. Made up of a central ridge of low hills flanked by narrow coastal plains, this area contains heavy jungles along the interior. The coastal cities of Salina Cruz and Coatzacoalcos form the terminals of a trans-isthmus highway and oil pipeline.

Chiapas Highlands

Extending upward from the mountains of Central America, the Chiapas Highlands consist of a series of faulted mountain ranges which encompass an elevated rift valley. The Sierra Madre de Chiapas hugs the Pacific coast, leading to the interior valley of the Rio Grijalva. More mountains extend from the valley to the Gulf Coastal Plain.

Current Events

The last decade of the 20th century has seen almost unabated turmoil in Mexico. Attempts to spur the country's economy through means such as NAFTA have not had the desired effect and political assassinations and guerrilla warfare have fostered a climate of uncertainty and unrest. While a few people hold the purse strings of the country, poverty has become a way of life for most of the people of Mexico. The border between the United States and Mexico remains a hot spot for illegal immigration and illicit drug traffic.

A World of Rage

For the Changing Breeds, Mexico presents a land of challenges against almost insurmountable odds. Although only a few Garou remain within the borders of Mexico, the Balam still prowl the Yucatan region and other untamed places.

Mexican Standoff

Mexico City has a population of over 20,000,000 people and represents one of most troublesome cities in North America for the Garou. Despite the reform efforts of President Ernesto Zedillo Ponce de Leon, who has held power since 1994, violence and corruption still hold sway. Leeches and Weaver-mages are heavily entrenched in the city's political maneuverings and, in the last few years, evidence of Malfean forces has also surfaced. Some suspect that the earthquakes that all too often devastate the city are to blame; local shapechanger superstition has it that things from deep beneath the earth are awoken with each quake, and quickly find their way up to the nourishing stew of humanity above. Most Garou avoid the city, turning their efforts to areas where they have some chance of reclaiming the land for Gaia. Only a few Glass Walkers, Bone Gnawers and Children of Gaia linger within the city's confines, acting as protectors of Kinfolk and, where possible, liaisons and information sources for Garou on the outside.

Secrets of the Yucatan

The Yucatan peninsula, though it attracts a fair number of tourists and visitors, still contains much unspoiled jungle. Here lie the ruins of the ancient civilization of the Mayas and, rumors say, the tombs of powerful creatures best left asleep. The Balam patrol the Yucatan, determined not to let Wyrm-tainted individuals into — or out of — the region.

Paper Chase

The decision by the government of Mexico to allow international paper companies to insert eucalyptus plantations in the Chiapas Highlands and parts of southeastern Mexico has sounded an alert to local Changing Breeds. One of the greediest of plants in terms of its demands for soil and moisture, eucalyptus plantations can cause rapid depletion of the land and drastic changes in the environment.

While the hand of the Wyrm has not yet revealed itself overtly in this scheme, packs of Garou and even a few Balam have begun to investigate the possibility of Pentex interference in the environmental balance of southern Mexico.

The Changing Breeds in Mexico

Though their numbers are few, most Garou tribes can be found in Mexico. While the native Uktena keep mostly to the mountains where their Kinfolk still keep the old traditions, Glass Walkers and Bone Gnawers brave the cities and bring the war for Gaia to the urban jungle. Garou from other tribes occasionally visit Mexico, many of them on their way to the Amazon. In addition to the Garou, the Balam have a significant presence in Mexico, where both the Aztec and Mayan civilizations venerated the jaguar as a sacred animal. The Ratkin are also present in significant numbers in densely populated urban areas such as Mexico City.

The Garou
Manuel Soledad, El Mano de la Tierra (Hand of the Earth)

Background: Born to a family of Kinfolk in Mexico City, Manuel experienced his First Change during one of the outbreaks of violence that erupted in the city. Brought to the attention of local Garou, Manuel soon acclimatized himself to his new role as one of Gaia's warriors — although as a Glass Walker Theurge he seeks more subtle ways of fighting the Wyrm than frontal assault. His pack, Los Compañeros, patrols the streets of Mexico City looking for a chance to reduce the number of Leeches that infest their home. Manuel has managed to insinuate himself into middle management in an international banking firm and uses his contacts to monitor evidence of Pentex investments in local companies and to track the movements of *vampiros*, Weaver-mages and other supernaturals within the city.

Image: In Homid form, Manuel presents the flashy image of a successful Latin businessman, with short black hair, dark eyes and a trim mustache. He's distinctively tall and well built, although not so muscular that his tailored European suits seem out of place. His cultivated demeanor drops away when he takes his dark-furred, nearly 10' tall Crinos form.

Roleplaying Notes: There are times when you wonder why you remain in a city that reeks so much of evil and corruption. Then you and your pack have a night when it all comes together and you corner one of the ubiquitous Leeches and send him back to his Wyrm-father. Other times, you have the satisfaction of knowing that you have managed to forestall the movements of Pentex by moving a few funds around and putting a few choice words in your bosses' ears. At times like those, you know that you are doing the work you were meant to do.

Floricita, "The Little Flower"

Background: Despite her noticeable limp, Floricita manages to carry on her battle against the Wyrm in Mexico's Chiapas region. An Uktena metis born under the Galliard's moon, Floricita spends most of her time with her pack, who accepts her despite the shame of her birth. Currently, she haunts the lands coveted by the paper industry for development, seeking for signs of Wyrm-taint in the Umbra nearby. Her impassioned speeches among the local Mayan population have helped them organize protests against intrusions of big business into a land that cannot tolerate outside environmental stress. Her equally ferocious actions with her pack discourage those who do not respond to more peaceful means.

Image: Floricita is a pretty young woman in homid form, with dark skin and long black hair. Her features display the Mayan ancestry found in both her Garou parents. She occasionally wears traditional clothes, particularly when she is acting as an organizer among the people of the region. In her birth form, she stands just over 8 feet tall.

Roleplaying Notes: Your weak leg makes you less effective as a fighter, but your ability to inspire your packmates makes up for your lack of combat skills. You prefer working as an organizer to arouse the emotions of the humans who live near your caern and to galvanize them into action against those who would destroy their environment and bring the Wyrm — or even the Weaver — to yet another part of your country.

The Balam

Night-Eyes, Watcher of the Ancient Ones

Background: Archaeological teams exploring the Mayan ruins that dot the Yucatan countryside claim to hear the eerie cries of some ghostly animal haunting their campsites in the wee hours of the night. Occasionally one of the members of a dig goes missing. While the jungles of the Yucatan hold their dangers and anyone spending time there accepts certain risks, the disappearances common to certain places have led to the cessation of work in these areas. When an archaeological survey team picks up camp and moves to a safer location, the young feline Balam known as Night Eyes knows that she has done her bit to prevent dangerous discoveries from coming to light. The stories told by the Balam of the Yucatan recount how in the first times, ancient creatures from the realms of the Unmaker came to the land and made their lairs deep within the earth. Later, the Mayans built great temples above these lairs. Now it falls to the Balam to prevent curious humans from unearthing more than artifacts from the ruins of these cities. Night-Eyes prides herself on her ability to drive away the weak-hearted with her unearthly songs. Those who are too foolish to leave, however, meet more than her music — and disappear forever into the depths of the jungle.

Image: In her human form, Night-Eyes appears as a young woman of Mayan stock, with long brown hair and a trim, muscular body. She seems simple-minded to the diggers and scientists she encounters in her capacity as menial laborer for various archaeological teams, for she shares more in common with the jaguars who birthed her than with any human society. In her Crinos form, Night-Eyes has luminous eyes that mesmerize her victims before she dispatches them.

Roleplaying Notes: There are some secrets that should never be known — at least not by humans. It is your task to make certain that the lairs of the Unmaker's children remain undiscovered and the ancient wards that bind them remain unbroken. You have a hard time mixing with humans and they often seem to treat you like a mere kitten, but you do it anyway so that you can learn which ones need to be driven away or destroyed. The more time you spend in the company of humans, however, the more fascinating you find them. You divide your time between their company and your den-realm, where you try hard to purge yourself of the strange customs the humans have taught you.

Central America and the Caribbean

But our own America, which has had poets
since the ancient times of Nezahualcóyotl;
which preserved the footprints of great Bacchus,
and learned the Panic alphabet once,
and consulted the stars; which also knew Atlantis…
and has lived, since the earliest moments of its life,
in light, in fire, in fragrance, and in love…
our America lives. And dreams. And loves.
   — Rubén Dario (Nicaragua), "To Roosevelt"

Central America

The isthmus that connects North and South America contains the countries of Belize, Costa Rica, Guatemala, El Salvador, Honduras, Nicaragua and Panama. From Guatemala and Belize, on the southern border of Mexico, Central America stretches for 1,200 miles to the border between Panama and Colombia.

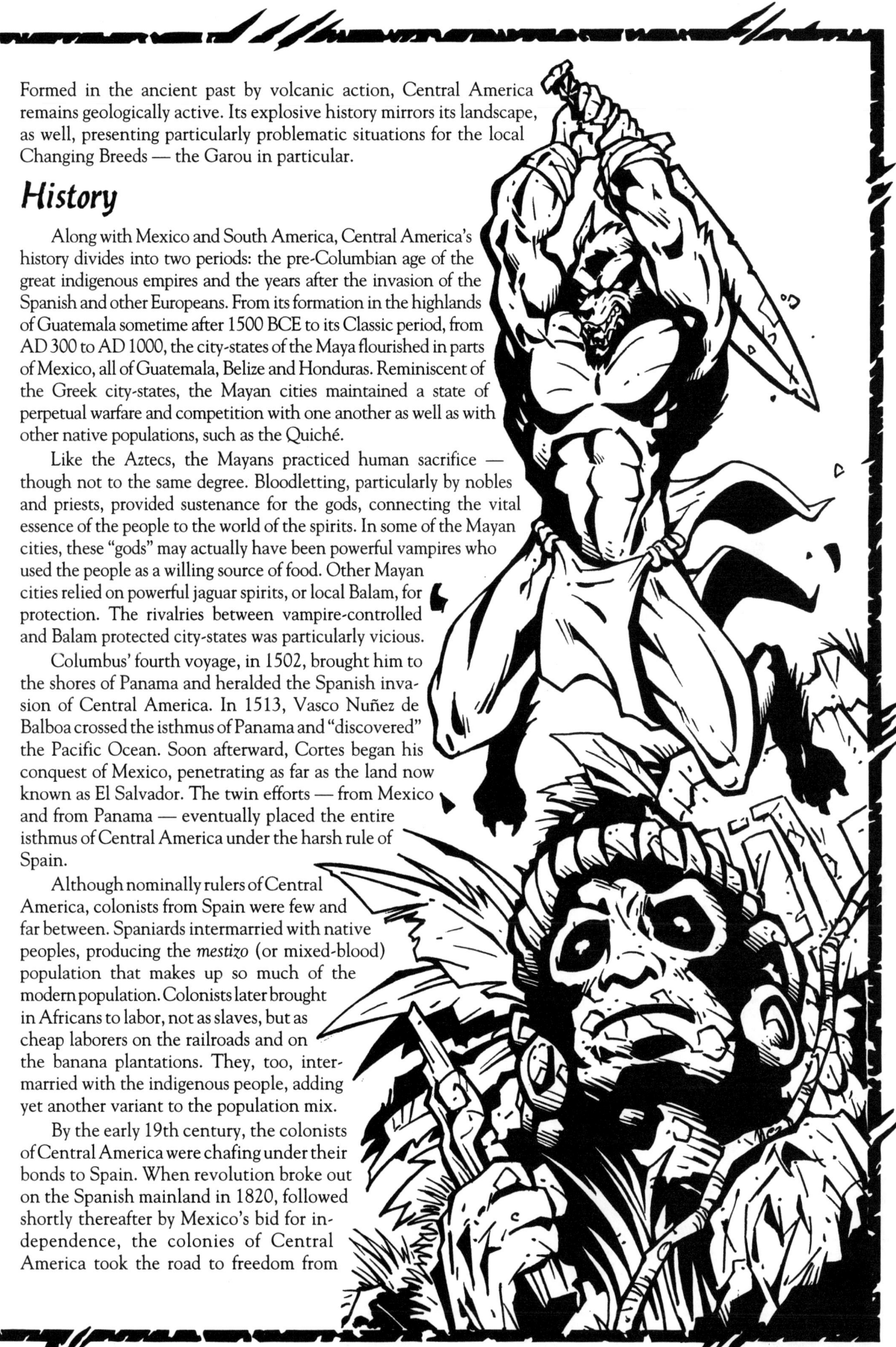

Formed in the ancient past by volcanic action, Central America remains geologically active. Its explosive history mirrors its landscape, as well, presenting particularly problematic situations for the local Changing Breeds — the Garou in particular.

History

Along with Mexico and South America, Central America's history divides into two periods: the pre-Columbian age of the great indigenous empires and the years after the invasion of the Spanish and other Europeans. From its formation in the highlands of Guatemala sometime after 1500 BCE to its Classic period, from AD 300 to AD 1000, the city-states of the Maya flourished in parts of Mexico, all of Guatemala, Belize and Honduras. Reminiscent of the Greek city-states, the Mayan cities maintained a state of perpetual warfare and competition with one another as well as with other native populations, such as the Quiché.

Like the Aztecs, the Mayans practiced human sacrifice — though not to the same degree. Bloodletting, particularly by nobles and priests, provided sustenance for the gods, connecting the vital essence of the people to the world of the spirits. In some of the Mayan cities, these "gods" may actually have been powerful vampires who used the people as a willing source of food. Other Mayan cities relied on powerful jaguar spirits, or local Balam, for protection. The rivalries between vampire-controlled and Balam protected city-states was particularly vicious.

Columbus' fourth voyage, in 1502, brought him to the shores of Panama and heralded the Spanish invasion of Central America. In 1513, Vasco Nuñez de Balboa crossed the isthmus of Panama and "discovered" the Pacific Ocean. Soon afterward, Cortes began his conquest of Mexico, penetrating as far as the land now known as El Salvador. The twin efforts — from Mexico and from Panama — eventually placed the entire isthmus of Central America under the harsh rule of Spain.

Although nominally rulers of Central America, colonists from Spain were few and far between. Spaniards intermarried with native peoples, producing the *mestizo* (or mixed-blood) population that makes up so much of the modern population. Colonists later brought in Africans to labor, not as slaves, but as cheap laborers on the railroads and on the banana plantations. They, too, intermarried with the indigenous people, adding yet another variant to the population mix.

By the early 19th century, the colonists of Central America were chafing under their bonds to Spain. When revolution broke out on the Spanish mainland in 1820, followed shortly thereafter by Mexico's bid for independence, the colonies of Central America took the road to freedom from

Spain. In 1823, a congress of the Central American colonies established the Provincias Unidas del Centro de America. This Federation struggled to maintain its integrity, but suffered from internal friction and shattered in 1842. Ideological, economic and political differences have caused a constant state of unrest since the beginning of Central American autonomy. Political assassination has accounted for more turnovers in government leadership in the region of the "banana republics" than elections or retirement.

After a particularly bloody period of civil unrest, guerilla warfare, insurgency and counterinsurgency during the latter half of the 20th century, the nations of Central America once more seek peaceful resolutions to their problems. Overwhelming poverty and economic stress have led to plans for an economic union of the countries that comprise the link between the Pure Lands of the North and South.

The Land

Though predominantly tropical in climate due to its latitude and general humidity, the mountainous landscape that comprises about one third of the isthmus possesses a temperate climate marked by cool weather and mixed vegetation. The Caribbean side of the isthmus experiences rainfall throughout the year, while the Pacific coast and the interior receive rain only during their summer season.

Highlands

The Pacific coast of Central America consists of a rugged range of volcanic mountains that stretch from the southern region of Guatemala all the way to Panama. Much of the rest of Central America contains high plateaus that resulted from ancient movements of the earth's crust in response to seismic and volcanic activity. Along the Caribbean coast, a series of ridges and valleys form the major features of the land. Though less populous than the mountainous regions, the eastern lands of Central America contain a wealth of minerals.

Lowlands

Low-lying lands make up a large part of northern Guatemala. In addition, lowlands occur along the coastlines of the Pacific and the Caribbean as well as near Lake Managua and Lake Nicaragua.

The Countries of Central America

Most of Central America has suffered the throes of revolution and political upheaval for much of the 20th century. The Garou place a portion of the blame for this on elements of the Weaver and the Wyrm, citing the influence of Leeches and Pentex dollars as the twin culprits. Though only a few members of the Changing Breeds dwell in Central America, they serve an important role in preserving the native culture and the remaining wild places of the region.

Belize

Physically isolated by the Maya Mountains from the rest of Central America, Belize, located west of Guatemala on the Yucatan peninsula, suffers less from political unrest than most of its neighbors. Belize's population of around 250,000 people are a mix of nationalities and ethnic backgrounds, including Creole, *mestizo*, Garifuna, Mayan and German Mennonite. English is the official language of Belize, which remains a member of the Commonwealth of Nations despite being a self-governing country. Prime Minister Said Musa has led the country's government since 1998.

The European influence in Belize has led to the presence of a few Garou from European tribes. These Garou remain mostly near Belize City, on the Caribbean coast.

Off the coast of Belize is the 175-mile-long barrier reef known as the Cayes. Only Australia's Great Barrier Reef is longer than this string of tiny islands, many of them relatively uninhabited. Other islands provide popular destinations for tourists. At least one Rokea makes his home near the Cayes. Western Belize contains a large expanse of tropical jungle as well as some of the most impressive Mayan ruins and a large system of limestone caves. Balam and Ananasi make their homes near their Kinfolk in this region. Oddly, the presence of a Mennonite community serves as a Kinfolk population for a few Get of Fenris who make Belize their home. Pharmaceutical corporations have recently turned their attention to the gathering and harvesting of local medicinal plants in western Belize, as they have in the Amazon. The government of Belize encourages the interest of the medical industry, seeing economic prosperity in their future. Southern Belize contains old-growth rainforest as well as villages of traditional Mayans. In addition, this portion of the country is home to many Garifuna, or Black Caribs, descended from African slaves and native Caribs. Northern Belize contains the Community Baboon Sanctuary, for the endangered black howler monkeys, the Crooked Tree Wildlife Sanctuary, which shelters many species of migratory and resident birds, and the Rio Bravo Conservation and Management Area, a privately managed rainforest preserve.

Costa Rica

Located between Nicaragua and Panama, with coasts on both the Pacific and the Caribbean, Costa Rica ("rich coast") has fallen prey to commercial interests and the tourist trade. The country, however, also contains some of the most distinct scenery in Central America and the oddest collection of wildlife in the region.

Inhabited by various Carib tribes for thousands of years before the advent of the Spanish, the land and its indigenous populations fell to the Spanish greed for gold — a misplaced desire, since the precious metal did not exist in any quantity in the area. Given over to agriculture instead, most of the great forests disappeared under the axe and fires to make way for pasture and fields. The native people vanished as well, claimed by disease and war. The descendants of these pre-Columbian nations now comprise only 1% of the Costa Rican population.

Costa Rica gained its independence from Spain in 1821. In 1917, a brief dictatorship soon gave way to democratic and constitutional forces. A civil war in 1948 led to the abolition of the nation's army. Afterwards, the nation evolved as a democratic republic without a standing army, though a force of guardsmen (*guardia*) provides armed protection for the country. Both banana and coffee plantations make up much of the Costa Rican economy, but tourism also ranks as one of the country's leading economic boosters. The relative peacefulness of the political environment makes this an attractive place for visitors to Central America.

Costa Rica has a population of over 3 million people, over 95% of whom are *mestizo* with the rest claiming African, Amerindian or Asian descent. President Miguel Angel Rodriguez has held office since 1998, representing the Social Christian Unity Party.

The capital of San José lies in the Meseta Central, a rich and fertile valley known for its wildlife and mountain scenery. Though the city itself suffers from typical urban problems, the surrounding lands provide a sharp contrast to overcrowding and pollution. Parque Nacional Volcán Poás contains a geologically active volcano that erupts intermittently — a phenomenon that has continued since 1989. The Parque Nacional Braulio Carrillo contains over 113,000 acres of rainforest and serves as a home for many species of rare wildlife. The country's primary archaeological site, Monumento Nacional Guayabo, lies within the rainforests along the slopes of Volcán Turrialba and contains artifacts from many of the ancient indigenous tribes, including petroglyphs, aqueducts and evidence of a sophisticated road system. The dry Costa Rican lowlands in the western part of the country contain the country's primary cattle-grazing lands, remnants of the region's original dry forests and a number of active volcanoes. The Caribbean coastal region of Costa Rica contains jungles, mangrove swamps and a variety of wildlife. A few Balam inhabit the Parque Nacional Tortuguero, keeping an eye on their jaguar Kin. Other werejaguars have den-realms near the Reserva Biósfera La Amistad, a site that contains not only a small jaguar population but also many pre-Columbian archaeological sites. Only a few Garou find Costa Rica worth their while as a place for honing their skills against the Wyrm.

El Salvador

One of the most violent countries of Central America, El Salvador lies between Honduras and Guatemala. The Pacific Ocean forms its southern border. The land dubbed "The Savior" by the Spanish is both the smallest of the Central American states and the only one which does not have a Caribbean coastline. Known as the Land of Volcanoes, the violence of the land echoes the tumultuous history of its people. Originally settled by distant kin of the Mayan and Toltec people, El Salvador fell to Spanish rule in the 16th century. After attaining independence in 1821, the new country devolved into a 20-year-long civil war. Even though Spain no longer governed El Salvador, Spanish and other outside interests swarmed the small country to make their fortune through the cultivation of the coffee bean. Society in El Salvador quickly stratified into two distinct classes: the wealthy white owners of the *haciendas* (or coffee plantations) and the *campesinos*, or indigenous laborers. Not only the people but also the land suffered from this focus on intensive agriculture. As the coffee industry grew, the wholesale deforestation of the land to make room for more plantations increased — as well as the poverty of the majority of the residents of El Salvador.

The Depression of the 1930s paved the way for unrest and violent actions among the *campesinos*. Many working class people saw a solution to their poverty in the philosophy of communism. At the height of the Cold War, in the 1960s, the American government sought to lend aid to the economically deprived countries of Central America — but their aid came with anticommunist strings attached. Conflicts between El Salvador's military regime and popular leaders led to the rise of the infamous death squads and the systematic murder of thousands of dissidents in the name of law and order — and capitalism. The Catholic Church became caught up in the conflict, with some activist priests and nuns siding with the revolutionaries — and falling to the guns of the military.

In 1992, a series of peace accords attempted to bring about a resolution to the conflict. President Armando Calderon of the National Republican Alliance has held office since 1994.

The few Garou who make their home in El Salvador spend most of their time protecting their Kinfolk, a full-time occupation for them in this troubled and Weaver-touched land. The mountains of western El Salvador remain the domain of the Balam, who jealously guard the wild beauty of the volcanic land. Rumors that Wyrm creatures have made a home for themselves near Volcán Izalco, a relatively young volcano born the late 18th century, have caused great disturbance among the werejaguars in recent years. There are also old ghosts in the lands; rumors of vicious Banes or restless dead lingering in the wake of the death squads' trails persist among the country's shapeshifters.

Guatemala

Bordered on the north and west by Mexico's Yucatan region, with Belize on the northeast and Honduras and El Salvador on the southeast, Guatemala contains over 100 different ethnic groups using 20 languages. Since achieving independence from Spanish rule in the early 19th century, Guatemala has suffered almost continual political unrest stemming from the rise and fall of numerous dictators, many of whom received their support from the United States (so long as they eschewed any ties with the Soviet Bloc). Native populations, including Mayans, Garifuna and Quiché, endured — and still endure — oppression from the Ladino ruling class. The horrors of the death squads and the phenomenon of *los Desaparacidos* ("the disappeared") have not yet faded from a land striving for political stability despite the odds against it. Political parties in Guatemala include the National Centrist Union, the Christian Democratic Party, the National Advancement Party, the National Liberation Movement, the Social Democratic Party, the Revolutionary Party, the Guatemalan Republican Front, the Democratic Union, the New Guatemalan Democratic Front and the Guatemalan National Revolutionary Union. Since 1996, Alvaro Enrique Arzu Irigoyen, of the National Advancement Party, has served as president.

The western highlands north of Guatemala City contain the preserved ruins of Mixco Viejo, where pristine temples and ball courts pay tribute to the glory of Mayan civilization. A popular tourist attraction, Mixco Viejo boasts a pair of watchful Balam guardians who make sure that visitors do not stray into places best left alone. This area also contains one of the largest indigenous populations of the country, many of whom are Kinfolk of both the few native Uktena as well as the more numerous Balam. The city of Chicicastenango has the distinction of being one of the few places in Guatemala where the ancient religious practices of the Maya take place alongside the traditional practices of Catholicism, apparently with Church approval. The mountainous region of Ixil gained notoriety as the site of some of the worst depredations during the years of violent conflict between the Guatemalan Army and indigenous revolutionaries.

The lowlands of the Pacific coast hold most of Guatemala's agricultural lands. Here, great *fincas*, or plantations, produce the nation's crop of coffee, sugar and bananas. Most of the Changing Breeds avoid this region. The Peten region of northern Guatemala contains the largest forest reserve in Central America as well as the great Mayan city of Tikal, now one of the most popular stops for tourists on the Mayan pilgrimage route. The lands of central and eastern Guatemala have a history of bloody warfare dating from the vicious battles between the Rabinal Maya and their Quiché foes to the massacres perpetrated by the Guatemalan army on the indigenous population during the 1970s. Garou and Balam in this region often find themselves coming into frequent conflict, as if the land itself harbors spirits of war and violence. This region is also the land of the quetzal, the sacred creature of the Mayan Empire and modern Guatemala's national bird. Despite efforts to preserve the quetzal, such as the Biotopo del Quetzal, deforestation has disrupted much of the native habitat of this rare and beautiful bird.

Honduras

Resting on the shores of the Caribbean, between Guatemala to the west and Nicaragua to the East, Honduras bears the dubious status of the original "banana republic." Primarily an agrarian country, a tiny percentage of the population actually owns the land, while the majority of the people either work as farm and industrial laborers or in the service industry. Over half the population is below the poverty level.

In pre-Columbian times, the Maya settled in the western portion of the region. As their empire declined in the 16th century, the Lenca civilization arose. Columbus' landing near Trujillo — on the northern coast of Honduras — marked his "discovery" of mainland America. Although the Lencas put up a strong resistance to Spanish conquest, the Spaniards overcame the native people through deceit and assassination, murdering the Lenca chief Lempira during a "peace conference."

Spanish rule in Honduras followed the pattern prevalent throughout the Hispanic-claimed lands of the New World — gross exploitation and decimation of the native population. Other nations of Europe soon made their presence known in Honduras. The British formed colonies along the eastern coast of Honduras and supported privateers who based their operations from the nearby Bay Islands just off the coast.

A World of Rage

Honduras gained its independence from Spain in 1821, though the British remained until 1859. United States' interest in Honduras grew to significant proportions with the end of Spanish rule. US dollars supported economic expansion and subsidized the plantations and mining interests while the American government backed up friendly politicians. When Nicaragua erupted in the late 1970s, the US used neighboring Honduras as a staging area for troops, while Nicaraguan *contras* received their training on Honduran soil. Honduras became one of the many Central American locations for political and social terror and human rights violations.

Since 1998, President Carlos Roberto Flores Facusse of the Liberal Party has held power in Honduras. Despite efforts to improve conditions in the country, an entrenched military and judicial system still present obstacles to reform. The recent devastation caused by Hurricane Mitch, which ravaged Honduras in 1998, has only added to the nation's problems.

Not far from the capital city of Tegucigalpa, Parque Nacional La Tigra preserves one of the country's remaining cloud forests. Home to a number of indigenous animals, including pumas, La Tigra also serves as the physical connection for a Pumonca den-realm. In western Honduras, home of the Maya and the Lenca, Balam watch the ruins of the great Mayan city of Copan. The eastern highlands have garnered a reputation for internecine violence — mountain families carry on feuds that have lasted for generations. The British influence on the Mosquito coast originally brought a few Fianna Kinfolk to Honduras, leading to a small number of Fianna of Honduran birth.

Nicaragua

Sandwiched between Honduras and Costa Rica, with long coastlines on both the Pacific and the Caribbean, Nicaragua has seen a long period of bloody revolution and counterterrorist activity. Originally settled by nomadic and farming tribes nearly 10,000 years ago, Nicaragua fell to the Spanish in 1502, who established the two major settlements of Granada and Leon. The presence of gold drew the Spaniards, and soon the indigenous people found themselves forced to labor in the gold mines for their conquerors. Rival cities of Granada and Leon continued their fierce ideological and economic competition even after Nicaragua gained its freedom from Spain in 1821. Conservative Granadans preferred a more traditional form of government, while the more liberal element in Leon attempted to introduce reforms patterned after the French and American revolutionary model.

War broke out between Conservatives and Liberals, lasting until the US intervention of marines in 1912. In 1927, Augusto César Sandino raised an army to protest US power in Nicaragua, using guerilla tactics to harry US Marines for more than six years. His assassination at the hands of Nicaraguan National Guard leader Anastasio Somoza paved the way for one of the most repressive and ruthless military governments in Central America — the Somoza regime. Though Somoza was assassinated in 1956, his sons Luis and Anastasio succeeded him.

Founded by student leader Carols Fences Amasser, the Sandinista National Liberation Front waged a serious guerrilla war against the Somoza government. The United States had an interest in maintaining Somoza's rule, particularly since the Sandinistas demonstrated a markedly leftist leaning. As the conflict grew more and more bloody, media attention displayed the violence to the world — highlighted by the televised murder of ABC news journalist Bill Stewart by the Nicaraguan National Guard in 1979.

This led to the eventual victory of the Sandinistas — and the outright hostility of the United States, who feared a communist foothold in Central America similar to Cuba's presence in the Caribbean. Counterinsurgents (*contras*) trained in Honduras to combat the Sandinistas, supported by the Reagan administration.

The elections of 1990 placed a conservative regime in power, undoing many of the accomplishments of the Sandinistas, who nevertheless acceded to the orderly transfer of power. President Arnoldo Aleman Lacayo, elected in 1997, represents the Liberal Alliance, a coalition of several parties with ambitions to restore Nicaragua's damaged economy and institute needed reforms.

The Garou in Nicaragua tend to stay clear of the cities, where Weaver and Wyrm have seemingly joined forces with human elements of destruction and despoliation to create sinkholes of poverty and despair. Southwestern Nicaragua, on the Pacific coast, contains the greatest population density in the country. This region also contains two areas of note — Masaya National Park, home of Volcán Masaya, and Coyotepe Fortress, site of a notorious prison for Sandinistas and the scene of numerous atrocities perpetrated by the National Guard during the Somoza years. Both these sites evidence strong Wyrm-taint. The volcano's history includes many instances of human sacrifice by the ancient tribes and casual murder by Spaniards who lowered laborers into the crater (and to their deaths) in attempts to retrieve the volcano's "liquid gold." Coyotepe Fortress resonates with the stench of death and cruelty. Rumors of a Hive of Black Spirals have

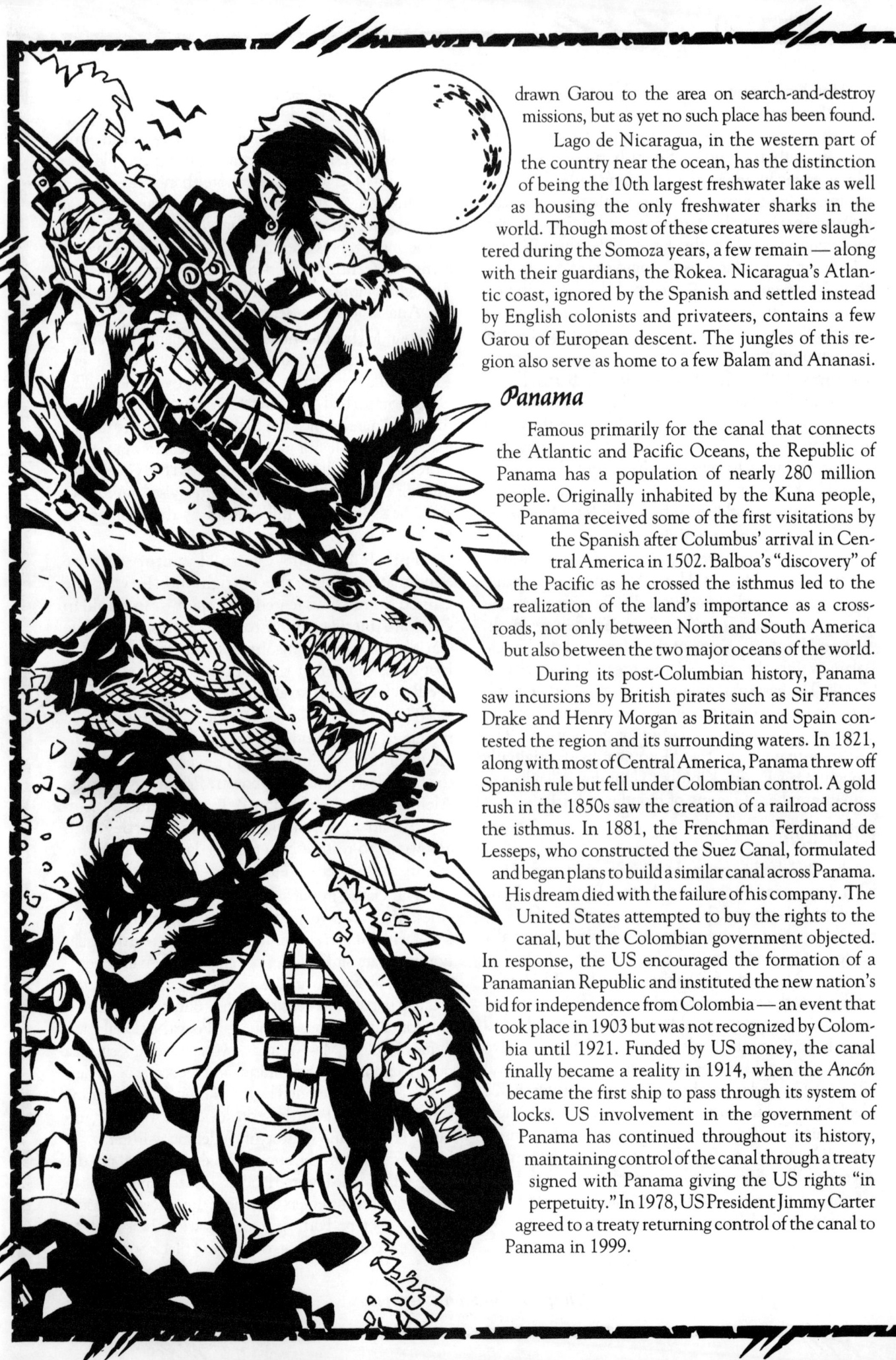

drawn Garou to the area on search-and-destroy missions, but as yet no such place has been found.

Lago de Nicaragua, in the western part of the country near the ocean, has the distinction of being the 10th largest freshwater lake as well as housing the only freshwater sharks in the world. Though most of these creatures were slaughtered during the Somoza years, a few remain — along with their guardians, the Rokea. Nicaragua's Atlantic coast, ignored by the Spanish and settled instead by English colonists and privateers, contains a few Garou of European descent. The jungles of this region also serve as home to a few Balam and Ananasi.

Panama

Famous primarily for the canal that connects the Atlantic and Pacific Oceans, the Republic of Panama has a population of nearly 280 million people. Originally inhabited by the Kuna people, Panama received some of the first visitations by the Spanish after Columbus' arrival in Central America in 1502. Balboa's "discovery" of the Pacific as he crossed the isthmus led to the realization of the land's importance as a crossroads, not only between North and South America but also between the two major oceans of the world.

During its post-Columbian history, Panama saw incursions by British pirates such as Sir Frances Drake and Henry Morgan as Britain and Spain contested the region and its surrounding waters. In 1821, along with most of Central America, Panama threw off Spanish rule but fell under Colombian control. A gold rush in the 1850s saw the creation of a railroad across the isthmus. In 1881, the Frenchman Ferdinand de Lesseps, who constructed the Suez Canal, formulated and began plans to build a similar canal across Panama. His dream died with the failure of his company. The United States attempted to buy the rights to the canal, but the Colombian government objected. In response, the US encouraged the formation of a Panamanian Republic and instituted the new nation's bid for independence from Colombia — an event that took place in 1903 but was not recognized by Colombia until 1921. Funded by US money, the canal finally became a reality in 1914, when the *Ancón* became the first ship to pass through its system of locks. US involvement in the government of Panama has continued throughout its history, maintaining control of the canal through a treaty signed with Panama giving the US rights "in perpetuity." In 1978, US President Jimmy Carter agreed to a treaty returning control of the canal to Panama in 1999.

The latest direct intervention in Panamanian politics came about in 1989, when the US used force to overthrow the corrupt government of General Manuel Antonio Noriega Moreno, withdrawing their former support for Noriega's regime. President Ernesto Perez Balladares of the Democratic Revolutionary Party came to office in 1994 and instituted a strong economic reform program to take advantage of the privatization of the canal.

The strong American interests in Panama have brought a few Garou to the region out of curiosity, though not many remain there for long.

Panama City attracts a few Glass Walkers and Bone Gnawers, who have established a network of contacts to keep Garou in Central and South America informed about movements of Pentex and other actions by hostile supernaturals — including Leeches and Weaver-mages. In the less populous region of Kuna Yala (San Blas), the indigenous Kuna people serve as Kinfolk to a small population of Balam, as do the Embera and Waunan people of the Darién jungle region.

Islands of the Caribbean

Originally settled by the Arawak people, the islands of the Caribbean have seen centuries of war and bloodshed. The Caribs, in the 14th century, invaded the once peaceful islands and destroyed the civilization of the Arawaks. In turn, the Spanish arrived and conquered the fierce Caribs. Other islands of the Caribbean saw conquest by English, Dutch and French explorers.

Although these picturesque islands eventually gained their independence or quasi-independence from European control, the dominion of the dollar soon replaced outright political rule. Foreign interests in commodities such as coffee, bananas and sugar cane vied with tourism as a means of economic control.

Few of the Changing Breeds reside in the Caribbean, although Garou and Bastet often visit the islands in search of relaxation or out of sheer curiosity. Some of the larger islands, such as Haiti and Puerto Rico are home to a few Ratkin, drawn — as most ratfolk are — to the teeming urban environment of San Juan, Port au Prince and Santo Domingo. A few Russian-born Silver Fangs have taken

advantage of the fall of the Shadow Curtain to visit Cuba, seeking to combat the vestiges of vampiric involvement in that country's affairs.

The most dominant Changing Breed in the Caribbean is the Rokea, who ply the waters off the coasts of the islands and act as protectors for the marine wildlife threatened by over-fishing and tourism.

Hot Spots

Like Mexico and South America, Central America suffers from general environmental stress as the forces of the Wyrm, the Weaver, human greed and economic self-interest wage a one-sided war of attrition on the once-Pure Lands. Deforestation, pollution, overpopulation, offshore drilling and other ecological nightmares afflict the region despite efforts to curb these activities. The Garou, along with other Changing Breeds, have their hands full just holding the line — but they cannot be content with just maintaining the status quo.

Los Desaparacidos

In recent years, both Garou and Balam have noticed that their Kinfolk are vanishing, not only in countries such as Nicaragua and El Salvador, where political turmoil has led to the disappearances (and likely deaths) of dissidents and activists, but in less troubled countries like Belize and Costa Rica. Some Garou fear that agents of the Wyrm have undertaken a concerted effort to destroy the breeding population of the Changing Breeds. Others blame the machinations of other supernaturals who might covet either the potent blood or latent power of the Kinfolk for their own dark purposes. Several groups of Garou as well as a few Balam have launched their own investigations into the problem, but so far they have not succeeded in turning up any concrete information. No bodies have turned up, leading to the hope that the vanished Kinfolk are alive — and salvageable.

The Good Fight

The constant struggle to preserve the remaining wild places continues in Central America. As foreign nations seek offshore drilling rights, buy land for paper mills and mining concerns and invest heavily in tourism, the jungles, rainforests, swamps and rivers of Central America steadily diminish. The Garou, Balam and other shapeshifters of the region — though too few to mount a full-scale effort — consider the protection of the environment one of their top priorities in Central America. A few Garou — particularly Glass Walkers, Bone Gnawers and Children of Gaia — advocate the path of compromise. They seek to find eco-friendly businesses that can lend their financial clout to the preservation effort through environmentally constructive practices such as harvesting renewable rainforest resources and creating wildlife preserves with limited access to tourists. The opposition to this effort comes not only from obvious allies of the Wyrm, such as Pentex, but also from short-sighted local governments who see immediate economic gains from foreign corporations as the only way out of an economically depressed environment. Many Garou choose to sabotage these intruders whenever possible.

Hide and Seek

Central America contains many active volcanoes and labyrinthine cave systems. Persistent rumors have reached the ears of many changers concerning secret Pentex laboratories and Black Spiral Hives tucked away in the depths of the earth. Occasionally a pack of Garou follows one of these rumors. While the Balam claim to know part of the truth behind these enigmatic hints of Wyrm-lairs, they are reluctant to share their information with Gaia's "dogs."

The Changing Breeds in Central America and the Caribbean

Garou and Balam are the most numerous of the Changing Breeds in Central America and the islands of the Caribbean, though even their numbers are few. The jungles of the region serve as home to a few Ananasi, while the ocean waters harbor a handful of Rokea.

The Garou
Johann Meister, Landspeaker

Background: Born into a small community of Get of Fenris Kinfolk who dwell inconspicuously among the Mennonites of Belize, Johann underwent his First Change in the company of his uncle, an older member of the tribe.

Together with a few other local Garou of other tribes, Johann and his mentor form a pack dedicated to the watchful care of the island. Primary among Johann's concern is the influx of foreign interest involving the medicinal plants of the country's rainforests. As a Philodox, Johann considers carefully the implications of "harvesting" the rainforest, seeing it as an unfortunate but necessary compromise in the light of the alternatives — deforestation and outright exploitation. Brought up as a Mennonite, Johann has a distinct aversion to Glass Walkers and avoids technology and machines whenever possible. This extends to his combat tactics, as well — restricting him to knives, machetes or his own natural weaponry.

Image: Standing well over six and a half feet in Homid form, Johann has collar-length dark blond hair and blue eyes. Although he is not extremely muscular, his body is athletic and strong. He dresses in simple, functional clothing, though he affects traditional Mennonite attire when visiting his family. His Crinos form exceeds 10 feet in height. He is quick to smile, though he most often appears thoughtful and somber.

Roleplaying Notes: The values of your Kinfolk differ from yours in many ways, but both your Mennonite ancestry and your Garou heritage emphasize respect for the natural environment and avoidance of unnecessary complications to living. Despite the urge you sometimes feel to leave Belize and confront Gaia's enemies in a more spectacular fashion, you know that even here, your work is important and you refuse to abandon your duty for mere glory — although other Get may consider your attitude a strange one.

Padre Atilano (Father Attila), "Gaia's Urban Missionary"

Background: Though often mistaken for a priest because of his gentle ways and good deeds, the Bone Gnawer Theurge Atilano Mendez considers himself a true missionary of Gaia to the lost and homeless of El Salvador. Basing his operations in the squalid city of San Salvador, Padre Atilano spends his time ministering to the unfortunates that make up the bulk of the city's population. While he uses his Gifts (more or less discreetly) and his paramedical knowledge to bring healing and comfort to his charges, he also checks those he "doctors" for Wyrm-taint. Whenever he finds such an individual, he makes certain that, despite his "best" efforts, the tainted one does not survive. Such is life in Central America.

Image: At 5'7", Padre Atilano does not present an imposing figure. Scrawny to the point of appearing frail, he nevertheless possesses a hardiness that enables him to forego many comforts in pursuit of his mission. He dresses in clothing that neither confirms nor denies his calling as a "priest," a ruse he finds useful in many circumstances. In Crinos form, he grows to nearly 8 feet tall but still remains relatively unimpressive; hence, he tries to avoid that shape whenever possible.

Roleplaying Notes: Other Garou can fight the Wyrm in the Amazon or attack secret Pentex holdings and pit their skills against fomori and Black Spiral Dancers. You prefer to do what you do best. Your medical skills are passable, but Gaia has blessed you with healing Gifts and you enjoy doing your part to comfort Her human children in this godforsaken land. Of course, when you can rid the world of one of the Wyrm's spawn, you don't hesitate for a minute just because the creature inhabits a poor or starving body.

The Balam
Sarito Quickstride, Guardian of the Ruins

Background: The Mayan ruins of Mixco Viejo, north of Guatemala City, attract many tourists each year to its many pyramid groupings and dramatic scenery. Posing as one of the local guides, Sarito insinuates himself into tour groups to make certain that no one strays off the beaten path. The ancient ruins contain secret passages beneath some of the pyramids that have only recently yielded some of their finds to Sarito and his companion, Ema Hides-the-Moon. The two werejaguars have uncovered strange markings that seem far older than any of the human-made constructions of Mixco Viejo, glyphs that — while indecipherable — suggest the presence of some bound creature or spirit. Sarito also makes it his business to follow any suspicious individuals that come to the ruins — particularly if they come alone and at night. To date, he has strongly "discouraged" over a dozen such interlopers — including one who carried about him a strong Wyrm-taint. Attempts to follow certain tunnels under the ruins have led Sarito to dead ends, but he persists in exploring Mixco Viejo's underbelly in hopes of finding a passage that leads to his goal — whatever it may be. What he plans to do if he finds it, he has not yet decided. But both he and Ema are determined that no one else will discover it first.

Image: Sarito appears as a *mestizo* male in his mid-20s, with dark hair and eyes and dusky skin. His body shows evidence of strenuous exercise. He dresses in modern clothes when doing "pyramid duty." In Crinos form, Sarito stands nearly 8 feet tall and his long legs are even more apparent than in his human form.

Roleplaying Notes: You have all the social graces down and can mingle with almost any group of people, although you feel as if you are playing a role when you do so. You are most at home wandering through dark passageways and nosing about strange places, even if some of them make your fur stand on end.

South America: Jungles of the Heart

The fourth-largest continent, South America accounts for approximately one eighth of the Earth's landmass and occupies an area of 6,878,000 square miles. Bordered by the Atlantic Ocean on the east, the Pacific Ocean on the west and the Caribbean Sea to the north, South America extends from the Isthmus of Panama all the way to the island of Tierra del Fuego at its tip near the Strait of Magellan.

The continent has four distinct climates: tropical, temperate, arid and cold. The Amazon and Orinoco Basins, along with the Guiana Highlands and many of the foothills of the Andes experience the consistently humid temperatures and heavy rain that characterize tropical climates. Most places within this equatorial region receive over 100 inches of rain every year and the temperature ranges from 65° to 80°F. Southern Brazil, Paraguay, Uruguay and northeastern Argentina enjoy a more temperate climate with cool winters and hot summers. The regions near the ocean experience more moderate effects due to the tempering currents. Chile's interior climate resembles that of the Mediterranean, while southern Chile has cooler year-round temperatures and year-round rainfall.

The deserts of the continent's west coast and the Argentine interior, along with parts of northeastern Brazil and coastal Venezuela have a dry climate due to the patterns of wind and the cold coastal waters. The Peruvian coast and northern Chile enjoy a cool but relatively humid climate despite the having little rainfall. The southern portions of Argentina and Chile as well as the highest parts of the Andes experience generally cold average temperatures. High winds characteristically sweep through the southernmost portions of the continent, including the island of Tierra del Fuego.

History

In ancient times, according to the legends of the Garou, groups of humans, animals, werewolves and other shapeshifters migrated across the land bridge from Asia into the vast twin continents of North and South America. The migrants spread out to settle their new home. While the Garou remained mostly in North America, a few continued on with their human Kin into the lands of Mexico and, even further south, into South America.

In the wild jungles and mountains of South America, the werewolves encountered other humans, whose tales of origin told how they arose from the land itself or came by sea in even more distant times. The Garou also encountered the jaguar-people of the Amazon jungles, the Balam, whose temperament and nature seemed more suited to life in the southern Pure Lands. Eventually, the Garou largely left South America, but some of their Kinfolk remained behind in the Amazon jungles, the Andes highlands and the southern plains and deserts.

In what would later be known as Peru, the Inca civilization developed great cities and a highly sophisticated culture. The Inca religion acknowledged many gods, including Inti, the sun god, Mamaquilla, the goddess of the moon, Illappa, the god of thunder and Pachamama, the earth mother. While Gaia's influence was strong among the Incas, the Weaver, too, worked her designs in the hearts of the Inca people. Grand settlements such as the fortress of Sacsahuaman, near Cuzco, and the city of Machu Picchu once stood as testimonials to the Weaver's skill.

In other parts of South America, particularly in the jungles of the Amazon, cities did not proliferate. Instead, tribes of humans dwelled in harmony with their natural surroundings, watched over by their spirit-kin, the Balam and the Mokolé.

Columbus' arrival in the Americas in 1492 brought great upheaval to the people and Changing Breeds of South America. The Treaty of Tordesillas, in 1494, divided the "newly discovered" continent of South America between the kingdoms of Spain and Portugal, even before the advent of the age of explorers. In 1500, Pedro Alvares Cabral, a Portuguese explorer, landed on the coast of Brazil and claimed the entire continent for Portugal. Not long afterward, in 1532, the Spaniard Francisco Pizarro reached the coast of Peru with his conquistadors and began the subjugation of the Incan empire in the name of Spain. With the capture of Atahuallpa, the Incan king, the fall of Incan civilization was assured and in less than three years, a rich and glorious civilization disappeared into the annals of history.

Along with the armies of Spain and Portugal came agents of both the Weaver and the Wyrm. European sorcerers, eager to explore the strange new world and describe its limits, sought to codify the places of power and reduce them to lines on maps and words in books that supposedly chronicled the true history of the region. As some explorers delved deep into the interior of the jungles in search of ancient cities such as the legendary El Dorado, other discoverers sought to eradicate all signs of the supernatural in the name of "a progressive world."

European werewolves came to the new southern continent as well. Black Furies who were willing to attune themselves to the ways of the Amazon and accept the customs of its people found a cause and a home in South America. Other Garou tribes, however, made the same mistakes as their counterparts in the Pure Lands of North America. Believing themselves better caretakers of the land than the native Changing Breeds, they antagonized many of the Balam, driving them from their den-realms and setting up caerns in places that had once belonged to the werejaguars.

Eventually, the rest of Europe eyed the riches of South America and began staking their own claims to the southern continent of the New World. As both Spain and Portugal declined in power, the English, Dutch and the French took advantage of the opportunity to gain their own territories. These newly emerging world powers developed settlements along the northeastern coast of South America in the lands that would become the Guianas as well as in Venezuela and parts of northern Brazil. Along with these new settlers came more Garou from Europe — Silver Fangs, Get of Fenris, Fianna, in particular. Bone Gnawers and Warders arrived as well, making their homes in the large port cities such as Rio de Janeiro and Buenos Aires. A few Children of Gaia made their way to South America, seeking to act as liaisons with the native Changing Breeds — with only minimal success.

The European pattern of subjugation of the natives and exploitation of the natural resources led to the enslavement of the native human population of South America. In addition, the Europeans imported slaves from Africa to work their great plantations and labor in the fields. A few Silent Striders made their way to South America at this time to lend their support to their enslaved Kinfolk. In addition, a few Swara and Bagheera managed to overcome their reluctance to travel and made the long journey from their native Africa to South America to be with their human Kin.

By the 19th century, popular revolutions against the oppressive European governments aroused the imagination of the people of South America — and their Changing Breed kin. Led by Simon Bolivar and Jose de San Margin, successful campaigns against Spanish rule resulted in the eventual severing of ties between South America and Spain. The end of European rule, however, did not mean a rebirth of independence for the native populations of South America. The new governments, most of them patterned on the surface after the republican model of the United States, continued to make distinctions between the European and native or African people. Wealthy landowners continued to exercise excessive amounts of control and most governments in South America eventually came under the control of military despots or political dictators (*caudillos*) who concerned themselves with their own wealth and power. In the major cities of South America, vampires and Weaver mages exercised their sinister influence, making circumstances difficult for the few Garou who chose to remain in the continent's large population centers.

Yet another force worked behind the scenes in South America to destroy the beauty and richness of the once-Pure Lands. As the economic importance of South America — and particularly the fertile Amazon Basin — grew in the eyes of the world community, many international corporations sought to establish their claims to the resources of the southern continent. One of these companies, the Pentex multiconglomerate, made its move in the Amazon, targeting the rainforest's wealth and natural power with its tentacles of destruction.

Beginning in 1986, Pentex established a foothold in the Amazon Basin and initiated its program of burning and clear-cutting of the rainforest. Eventually, the Garou discovered the existence of Pentex's secret base of operations — and the war for the Amazon began.

Land Features

More than 150 million years ago, the South American continent broke off from the land mass of Gondwanaland, migrating westward to its current position in the southern half of the Western Hemisphere. Tectonic activity and volcanic eruptions during this time of migration resulted in the formation of the Andes Mountains along the western spine of the continent. Other land formations developed later as the continent settled into its new position in the world.

Guiana Highlands

The Guiana Highlands lie to the north of the Amazon River. These ancient mountains, akin to those found in the Brazilian Highlands, lie beneath a thick cover of vegetation. The highest peak in this region, Mount Roraima, reaches a height of 9,094 feet. The Guiana Highlands stretch from the coast of Brazil all the way to Venezuela and Colombia.

Andes

The Andes Mountains, the longest mountain chain in the world, make up the western coast of South America. Extending all the way from Venezuela, on the continent's northern coast to Chile, 5,000 miles to the south, the towering peaks of the Andes form a portion of the Ring of Fire, volcanic mountains that gird the Pacific Basin. Still geologically active, the Andes had their birth during earth's Tertiary period, more than 65 million years ago.

Consisting of a series of mountain ranges, or *cordilleras*, interspersed with knots of mountains, or *nudos*, and high plains, or *altiplanos*, the Andes form a spine-like ridge that acts as a wall against the Pacific Ocean. The northernmost Andean Mountain group,

the Nudo de Pasto, consists of three ranges that extend from the border between Ecuador and Colombia in a northwest direction into the western tip of Venezuela. Bogota, the capital of Colombia, sits atop one of the broad plateaus that lie within this portion of the Andes. Many of the mountains in this region exceed 15,000 feet although the lower mountains seldom exceed 12,000 feet in height. The Ecuadorian Andes consist of a pair of parallel volcanic ridges, along with their mountain basins. Mt. Chimborazo, the highest mountain in Ecuador, towers more than 20,000 feet. The basins of the Ecuadorian highlands range from below 6,000 to more than 9,000 feet and contain volcanic soil that once served to sustain the majority of Ecuador's population.

The Peruvian Andes consist of several separate ranges that demarcate high plateaus. While the mountains of northern Peru stem from non-volcanic origins, volcanic activity is responsible for the high peaks in southwestern Peru. In general, the Peruvian Andes extend over a wider range than their northern counterparts and attract world-class mountain-climbers to their snow-capped peaks. At 22, 204 feet, Mount Huascaran is the highest mountain in the Peruvian Andes.

The *altiplano* (or high plain) occupies an area that includes southern Peru, the northern regions of Chile and Argentina, and the western portion of Bolivia. From north to south, the altiplano descends from around 15,000 feet to 12,500 feet. The largest lake in South America, Lake Titicaca, has its home in the elevations of the altiplano, making it the world's largest navigable inland lake. South of the altiplano, the Andes Mountains pass through Chile and Argentina. Though generally not as high as in the north, these mountains contain the highest peak in all of the Andes — Mt. Aconcagua, which rises to a height of 22,831 feet as it straddles the border between Chile and Argentina. Volcanic activity marks many of the mountains in the Chilean Andes.

The geological activity of the Andes makes habitation problematic. While the volcanic material provides fertile soil for farming as well as a wealth of mineral resources, the frequency of earthquakes and eruptions, along with the rugged and often impassible terrain, act as a deterrent to large populations.

Amazon Basin

From its source in the Peruvian Andes to its eventual outflow into the Atlantic Ocean close to the equator, the Amazon River and its tributaries form the second longest river in the world. Nearly 4,000 miles long, the Amazon feeds life into two-fifths of the South

American continent and supports one of Gaia's richest and most diverse ecosystems. Parts of Brazil, Columbia, Venezuela, Ecuador and Peru depend on the waters of the "Mar Dulce" — the sweet sea.

The Amazon River basin contains a wealth of animal and plant life: hundreds of thousands of species of plants and trees, over 500 types of moths, 2000 species of fish, as well as numerous species of birds, reptiles, insects and mammals.

Brazilian Highlands

Ranging from the mouth of the Amazon River all the way to the interior of Uruguay, the Brazilian Highlands also encompass the eastern portions of Paraguay and Bolivia. The Highlands drop dramatically to the ocean along the Atlantic coast, while inland regions consist of hills and plateaus. Pico da Bandeira, the highest mountain in the area, reaches 9,482 feet. The rock formations that make up the Highlands contain some of the oldest geological samples in South America, dating from the Precambrian era. Volcanic sheets blanket some parts of the Highlands while other areas of the region benefit from rich soil near the Parana River. Erosion and overuse have marred the northern regions, near the Amazon River, leaving a land where only scrub growth survives. Mineral deposits in the Highlands provide much of Brazil with a source of wealth.

Gran Chaco Plain

South of the Amazon Basin, in Paraguay, lies the alluvial Gran Chaco Plains. Formed from an ancient seabed, these humid plains contain sluggish rivers and soils with high clay content. Hardwood forests alternate with cacti and palm trees along the Chaco. Rainfall during the summer creates impenetrable marshes, while during the winter, much of the land suffers from a lack of rain, becoming dry and cracked. Near the Paraguay River, the land provides a suitable environment for raising cattle.

Pampas

Extending southward from the Chaco, the vast treeless expanse known as the Pampas covers much of Argentina. From east to west, the Pampas rises toward the Andes, becoming drier as its elevation increases. The rich pastures of the Pampas serves as grazing land for the cattle that form much of Argentina's economy.

Patagonia

Southern Argentina contains a region of extensive plateaus and river valleys known as Patagonia. A few gentle mountains, including volcanic cones, break up the generally flat landscape. Lava sheets extend over a good portion of the arid, treeless region. Only a few cities exist in Patagonia and the sheep industry provides the primary economic basis for the region. Near the Andes, the northern region contains great forests dotted with clear lakes, while the island of Tierra del Fuego, or "Land of Fire," emerges from the southernmost tip of the continent.

Orinoco Basin

The Orinoco River flows through Venezuela between the Andes and the Guiana Highlands. Its basin extends for more than 220,000 square miles and forms the Orinoco Basin, also known as the Llanos. This low-lying region consists of winding rivers that overflow their banks during the rainy season and grass-covered plains. Palms and other trees line the riverbanks of the Llanos.

Parana Basin

The Parana Basin lies between the Andes and the Brazilian Highlands in southern Brazil, parts of Uruguay and Paraguay and eastern Argentina. The Parana, Paraguay and Uruguay Rivers all provide water to this rich basin. These rivers drain into the Rio de la Plata, a gulf between the coasts of Uruguay and Argentina. Massive waterfalls and cascades characterize the rivers of the Parana Basin. Hydroelectric dams harness the rivers to provide power for the region.

The Politics of South America

Although the Garou and most of the Changing Breeds concern themselves less with cities and human politics than with the natural environment, political and economic institutions bleed over into environmental problems that demand a response from Gaia's warriors.

Venezuela

The Republic of Venezuela, located on South America's northern tip, covers an area of 912, 050 square kilometers and holds a population of 22 million people. The capital city of Caracas, situated on the coast, boasts a population of 3.5 million. Since November 1999, Hugo Chavez Frias has ruled as president. A prosperous country, Venezuela gains much of its wealth from oil. Currently in the process of drafting a new constitution, the government of Venezuela is also concerned with its position in the world market.

Guyana

The Cooperative Republic of Guyana, located between Venezuela and Suriname on the northeastern coast of South America, occupies a territory of 83,000 square miles and contains a population of just over

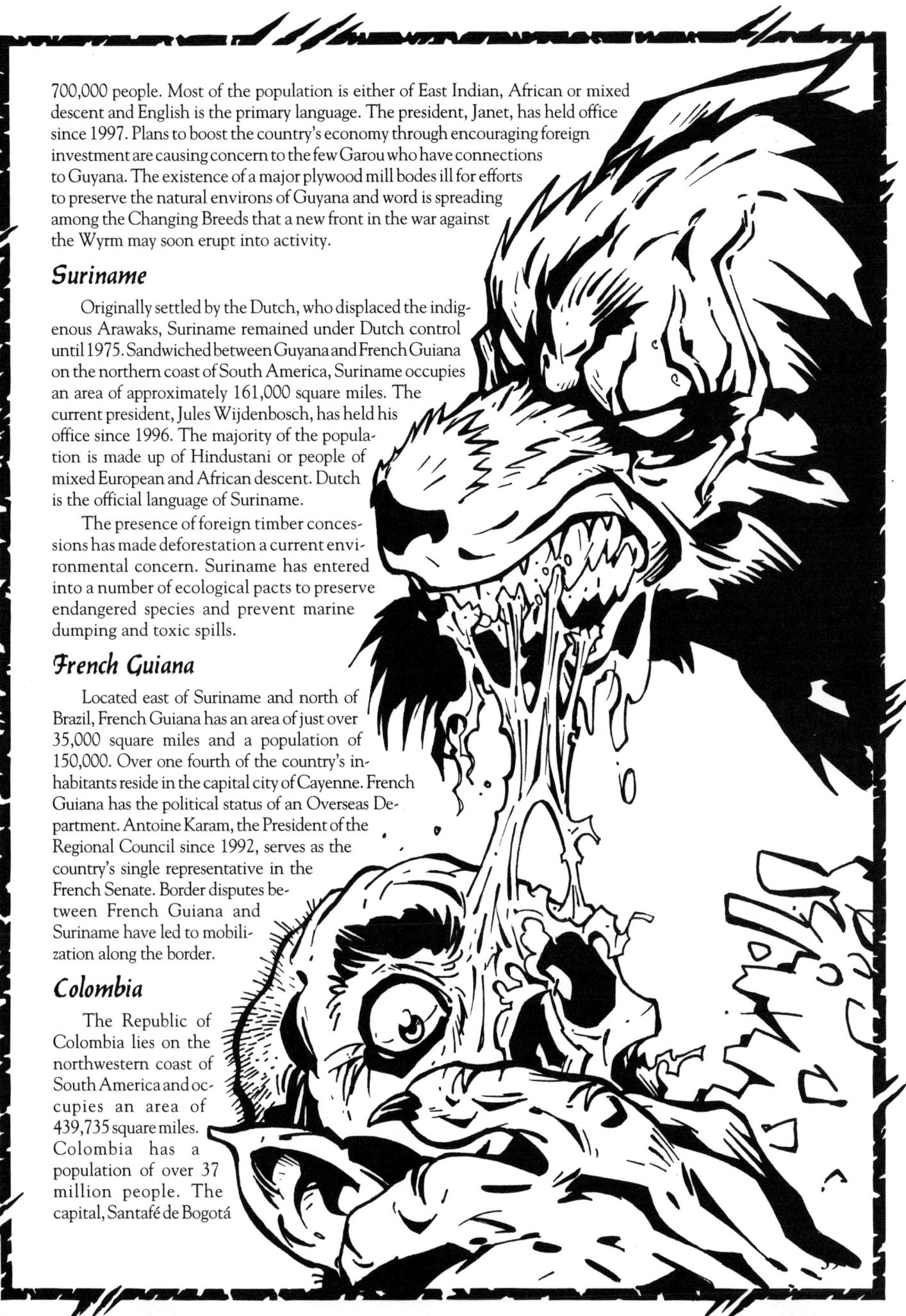

700,000 people. Most of the population is either of East Indian, African or mixed descent and English is the primary language. The president, Janet, has held office since 1997. Plans to boost the country's economy through encouraging foreign investment are causing concern to the few Garou who have connections to Guyana. The existence of a major plywood mill bodes ill for efforts to preserve the natural environs of Guyana and word is spreading among the Changing Breeds that a new front in the war against the Wyrm may soon erupt into activity.

Suriname

Originally settled by the Dutch, who displaced the indigenous Arawaks, Suriname remained under Dutch control until 1975. Sandwiched between Guyana and French Guiana on the northern coast of South America, Suriname occupies an area of approximately 161,000 square miles. The current president, Jules Wijdenbosch, has held his office since 1996. The majority of the population is made up of Hindustani or people of mixed European and African descent. Dutch is the official language of Suriname.

The presence of foreign timber concessions has made deforestation a current environmental concern. Suriname has entered into a number of ecological pacts to preserve endangered species and prevent marine dumping and toxic spills.

French Guiana

Located east of Suriname and north of Brazil, French Guiana has an area of just over 35,000 square miles and a population of 150,000. Over one fourth of the country's inhabitants reside in the capital city of Cayenne. French Guiana has the political status of an Overseas Department. Antoine Karam, the President of the Regional Council since 1992, serves as the country's single representative in the French Senate. Border disputes between French Guiana and Suriname have led to mobilization along the border.

Colombia

The Republic of Colombia lies on the northwestern coast of South America and occupies an area of 439,735 square miles. Colombia has a population of over 37 million people. The capital, Santafé de Bogotá contains nearly five and a half million people. Andres Pastrana has been president since 1998 and has battled severe economic problems, including recession and unemployment. A legitimate exporter of coffee, petroleum and gold, Colombia also has the dubious reputation as a major exporter of illegal drugs, including cocaine, cannabis and opium poppies. Although this is a serious form of corruption, many shapeshifters feel no compulsion to interfere with this trade; as some of their animal-born members might put it, "if the humans want to kill themselves, let them."

Ecuador

Recent actions by the president of Ecuador, Jamil Mahuad, to block drilling for oil within two national park preserves have dealt a blow to the efforts of Endron to harm that land's endangered species. In addition, the homelands of the Tagaeri and Taromenare peoples lie within the protected region. In 1997, under pressure from environmental organizations as well as from local Changing Breeds and their Kinfolk, British-based mining industries announced their intentions to withdraw from their operations in the Intaq region, home to the fragile cloud forests of Junin as well as to several endangered species including the jaguar, spectacled bear and howler monkey. This pullout occurred too late to prevent the contamination of the Junin River, however, by exploratory copper mining efforts.

Brazil

The Federative Republic of Brazil occupies about two-thirds of the area of South America and is the largest single country on the continent. President Fernando Henrique Cardoso has ruled Brazil since 1995. Brazil has a population of over 170 million, about four-fifths of whom live in urban areas. Portuguese is the official language of Brazil, but English, Spanish and French are also spoken. Although Brazil is famous for its rainforest, it's a mistake to assume that most of the country is jungle — the vast surface area of Brazil includes pastureland, highlands and plenty of other terrain types besides forest.

The indigenous people of the Amazon include a number of tribes that have survived the centuries of occupation and exploitation since the arrival of the Europeans and the discovery of the vast resources of the rainforest. The Arawete, who still have only limited contact with the outside world, retain many of their traditional customs, although the trappings of the modern world hold a great interest for them when they are exposed to such things as CDs and digital cameras. The Assurini live along the Xingu River in the heart of the Amazon. Visitors to the Assurini, if they win the trust of these people, are warned to stay close to the villages at night because of the jaguars that roam nearby. Those who anger the Assurini or otherwise offend them do not receive this warning — and many of the offenders disappear if they stray too far from the safety of the villages. The Kayapó live near the farthest reaches of the Indian Reserve within the Amazon. Early contact with European settlers, loggers and miners has resulted in the loss of many of their traditional customs, although a few members of the tribe still retain the old ways. Satellite dishes and other symbols of the technological world are not unknown among the Kayapó.

Bolivia

Southwest of Brazil, the Republic of Bolivia occupies an area of 1,098,580 square kilometers and has a population of nearly 8 million people. Nearly one third of Bolivia's population are Quechuan speakers and Quechua, along with Spanish and Aymira are the three official languages of the country. The city of La Paz serves as the seat of government for Bolivia, while the city of Sucre is the legal capital and the home of the country's judiciary branch. Hugo Banzer Suarez has served as president of Bolivia since 1997. The President's campaign to improve Bolivia's failing economy consists of an anticorruption campaign and a plan to encourage more investment in the country. Bolivia has recently completed a natural gas pipeline to Brazil with which it hopes to energize its economic recovery.

Peru

Located on South America's west coast, bordered by Ecuador to the north and Chile to the South, Peru occupies an area of 1,285,220 square kilometers. Peru's population stands at about 26 and a half million people. Alberto Kenyo Fujimori has ruled as Peru's president since 1990. The presence of mining interests in Peru concern a few Garou who have traveled to that area after leaving the Amazon Basin. Other concerns include deforestation and overgrazing, the erosion of soil from desertification and the pollution of rivers from the mining industries.

Paraguay

The Republic of Paraguay lies just northeast of Argentina in the central region of South America. Occupying an area of 406,750 square kilometers, Paraguay has a population of over five million with an overwhelming majority of mixed Spanish and Amerindian people. President Luis Gonzalez Macchi has held office since 1999 following the resignation of Raul Cubas Grau earlier in the year. Deforestation has affected Paraguay to a great degree as well as water pollution and inadequate waste disposal.

Uruguay

Located along the coast of southern South America between Argentina and Brazil, the Oriental Republic of Uruguay has a population of 3,308,523 people, most of whom are descended from Spanish and Portuguese colonists. Julio Maria Sanguinetti has held the post of president since 1995. Uruguay's economy is linked closely to that of its neighbors, Argentina and Brazil. The country's major environmental concern deals with the prevention of pollution from Brazil's nearby power plant.

Argentina

The Republic of Argentina, located in the southern portion of the South American continent, has a population of 36 million people. Buenos Aires, Argentina's capital, lies on the eastern coast along the Rio de la Plata and houses a population of over 12 million people. The current president, Carlos Saul Menem, presides over a country that occupies more than a million square miles and boasts one of the most prosperous economies of all of South America. A Peronist in his political beliefs, Menem has opened Argentina to foreign investors and cut the nation's inflation rate dramatically. Food processing and agribusiness, in the form of sheep and cattle along the fertile pampas, are the country's major industries. Although Spanish remains the official language, English and other European languages are also spoken. In addition, descendants of indigenous natives speak their tribal language such as Quechua, Guarani or Mapuche.

Over 20 national parks preserve much of the indigenous wildlife of Argentina, including puma, guanaco (or native llama), the ostrich-like rhea and the Magellan penguin. The island of Tierra del Fuego, which Argentina shares with Chile, contains not only wildlife preserves but also oil drilling operations — a concern targeted by the few Garou who have diverted themselves from the Amazon War to investigate other problems in South America.

Chile

The Republic of Chile occupies a narrow strip of land along the western coast of South America and encompasses and area of 756, 950 square kilometers. Chile's capital is Santiago. President Eduardo Frei Ruiz-Tagle has held office since 1994. Chile has a prosperous, free-market economy with exports in copper, fish and lumber. The resulting deforestation has lead to a loss in biodiversity and has threatened the natural resources of the country. The Andean wolf, a species native to the Chilean Andes, has become the special project for a group of Red Talons who have settled in the region in order to act as protectors for their wolf Kin.

The Amazon War

By far the most significant ongoing crisis for the Garou and the other Changing Breeds in South America consists of the battle to prevent the defoliation and destruction of the great Amazon rainforest. Since the times of the first explorations into the Brazilian jungle, many factions including agents of both the Wyrm and the Weaver have sought to control, tame or annihilate the wild regions of the Amazon Basin. The arrival of Pentex in 1986, however, initiated a concerted effort to break the power of the Wyld once and for all.

Since 1986, Garou from many parts of the world — but particularly from North America — have flocked to the Amazon to aid in the great fight. Under the leadership of Golgol Fangs-First, a remarkable Get of Fenris Ahroun gifted with both tactical expertise and the ability to unite others under his command, the Garou have battled the forces of Pentex and its Black Spiral Dancer allies. Unfortunately, old grudges between the Garou and the native Balam and Mokolé have consistently weakened the forces of Gaia and made a true joining of forces difficult, if not impossible.

In 1990, due to guerrilla-style activity from the controversial Swiftclaw Pack, Pentex's "research organizations" came under fire from government and environmental agencies that exposed their fraudulent practices and threatened them with legal as well as military action. The forces of the Wyrm found themselves on the wrong side of the Amazon War's offensive. **Rage Across the Amazon** chronicles this tale as well as the early years of the War for the Amazon.

Today, though the war continues unabated, new tactics have changed the face of the war effort. These changes fill some Garou with hope while arousing the suspicion of others who see yet another subtle maneuver by the Wyrm or else fear that the Weaver, too, has joined in the fray to further her own agenda.

Pharmaceutical companies have awakened to the demand for "natural" remedies and have discovered that many of these wonder drugs exist in the rainforests of the Amazon. To this end, several environmentally friendly companies have attempted to establish operations in the Amazon with the intent of encouraging the harvesting of renewable herbs and the discovery of heretofore-unknown medicinal plants. Some Garou view this development as a positive sign that the outside world has finally realized the importance of preserving the Amazon's endangered plant species; others see this as just another ploy by the Weaver's chosen to extend their control over the Wyld. Opponents of the pharmaceutical operations also suspect the hand of Magadon though they have not yet been able to discover any real evidence of their involvement.

The Plight of the U'wa

Since 1996, the U'wa people of northeastern Colombia have battled to save their land from the depredations of the oil industry. Plans to drill for oil on lands long inhabited by this 5,000 member tribe threaten not only the U'wa's way of life but their very existence. Tied inextricably to their land, the U'wa have vowed to do anything — even allow themselves to be annihilated — rather than give up their homes.

In September 1999, the government of Colombia granted permission to a major oil company to initiate exploratory drilling of the U'wa lands. In November, several hundred members of the tribe gathered at the intended drill site and established a settlement on the spot, hoping by their presence to prevent the drilling and to call attention to their plight.

Acts of violence on U'wa leaders and activists have not had the intended effect of intimidating these proud and determined people. The crisis of the U'wa has brought together both Garou and Balam in an unprecedented putting aside of differences, for the tribe contains Kinfolk of both Changing Breeds.

Clearcutting the Rainforests

Actions by several rain forest action committees supported by the Garou and other Changing Breeds have resulted in some progress in the prevention of clear-cutting by companies that supply wood for construction. A few major lumber distributors have agreed to forego using ancient forests as sources for lumber intended for construction. In addition, the government of the Brazilian state of Amazonas has recently begun discouraging investors in logging companies in a belated effort to save the rainforest from destruction.

The Changing Breeds in South America

With a few exceptions, South America contains no native Garou. Due to the pressing conditions in the Amazon, however, nearly all the Garou tribes have a presence in the southern continent of the Pure Lands.

The Garou
Golgol Fangs-First, War Lord of the Amazon

Background: This sixth-Rank Get of Fenris Ahroun has led the Garou in the War for the Amazon since the early 1990s. His military expertise and charismatic leadership have elevated him to the status of a near-god for most of the Garou under his command. Born on a battlefield during World War II, Golgol honed his fighting skills in Vietnam and put them to use in the Amazon. He is a natural leader who commands respect from his underlings but who also knows how to give praise and encouragement where it is most needed. Although he recognizes that the Amazon War has taken a more subtle turn, he is determined not to allow the Garou to let down their guard.

Image: Though he is nearly 60 years old, Golgol Fangs-First has not appeared to age since his arrival in the Amazon. He stands over 7 feet tall in homid form and his Crinos appearance is even more formidable. Although his hair shows signs of gray, his body displays the marks of a warrior in his prime — muscular and fit with quick, decisive movements. Golgol's face has hardened into a soldier's mask and he bears the scars of his many battles against the agents of the Wyrm. He wears a specially made battle harness and has decorated himself with glyphs that celebrate his many victories.

Roleplaying Notes: You display an inordinate calm in the midst of battle, which gives courage to those who fight alongside you. Unlike many of your tribe, you come across as an even-tempered, rational warrior who uses his head fully as much as his prowess to win not only the battle but also the war. Your experiences have taught you much about the nature of warfare and you constantly look for ways to put your knowledge to use. You know that other Garou look up to you and you try to present them with a worthy model.

Electra Shieldmaiden, Chronicler of the War

Background: Born to a close-knit Greek Orthodox family in Spartanburg, South Carolina, Electra grew up in an atmosphere of increasing social consciousness. She underwent her First Change during a bloody and violent demonstration for women's rights in the 1970s. Although she has only recently arrived in the Amazon, she has taken it upon herself to put together a cohesive history of the Garou's battle against the armies of Pentex in the rainforest. She grudgingly accepts the leadership of Golgol Fangs-First but maintains her own autonomous pack of

Black Furies that acts as a long-range scouting patrol throughout the Amazon region. She is an Athro Galliard who has risen to the position of pack leader through her skill in war and through her ability to interact with the local population — whoever they may be.

Image: Electra is an imposing woman in her 50's. Her dark hair, which she has cropped close to her skull for her stay in the Amazon, shows only a few silver hairs and her body is lean and hardened from fighting and exercise. In Crinos form she presents an impressive and ferocious appearance. She wears battle fatigues when necessary and otherwise dresses in clothing suitable for trekking through the jungle.

Roleplaying Notes: The Black Furies were among the first of the Garou to join in the Battle for the Amazon and you carry with you the burden of living up to your tribe's formidable reputation. You accept the leadership of Golgol Fangs-First because you have no choice, but you keep close watch on him for any signs that he is beginning to fail in his duties as a war-leader. Your primary concern, however, is preserving the tale of the battle to save the rainforest from the Wyrm so that its heroes, living and dead, will long be remembered in moots throughout the world.

Manuel Swift-Paws, Gaia's Enforcer

Background: A Bone Gnawer Theurge from Brooklyn, Manuel grew up in a low-income neighborhood and learned his fighting skills in the schoolyard and the streets. His First Change took him completely by surprise, but he soon adapted to his new life as one of the Garou. He traveled to the Amazon after hearing about the war from a wounded returnee. Once there, however, he realized that life in the jungle was just not for him and he asked for reassignment somewhere his talents and street savvy could better serve Gaia. Manuel ended up in Bogotá, where he serves to keep an eye on the progress of the drug trade, sabotaging it wherever he can and monitoring the Colombian underworld for signs of direct involvement by the Wyrm. He has made the acquaintance of a few Glass Walkers in Bogota and has even touched base with a few of the Leeches who claim to control the city. More than a few shipments of drugs have gone missing — along with their carriers — through the efforts of Manuel and his allies.

Image: A scrawny Latino man in his late 20s, Manuel has an infectious charm and a lighthearted manner that belies his deep dedication to the eradication of the drug trade. He dresses in worn street clothes and maintains the image of a Colombian petty criminal. His shoulder-length black hair is neat but not deliberately styled and his body is graceful if a bit undernourished in appearance. In Crinos form, Manuel stands around 9 feet tall but still looks a little underweight.

Roleplaying Notes: You have learned to blend in with the other street scum who make up the low-level forces of the drug trade. You keep an eye on the movement of drugs through Bogotá and cause "accidents" whenever you can. Jungle warfare didn't suit you, but learning how to hurt the Wyrm in its pocketbook is right up your alley. Sometimes you hate yourself for the person you appear to be, but a Garou's gotta do what a Garou's gotta do — and you're so good at doing it!

A'ala Mother's Heart, Protector of the Homeland

Background: The youngest daughter of a family of U'wa Kinfolk, A'ala underwent her First Change as part of a vision quest. Brought into the society of other native Uktena, A'ala learned the art of peacemaking and mediating, skills that appealed strongly to her as a Philodox. When a large oil concern announced its intention to establish a drill site on the homeland of her Kinfolk and to relocate the U'wa to make room for their equipment, A'ala decided that she could not ignore the call to defend her human Kin. Upon her arrival back at her village, she was stopped and challenged by a young Balam who, like her, had decided to take action against the oil company. What began as a fight evolved into a wary state of mutual cooperation. Now both A'ala and I'mo work together to harass the drilling operation and to prevent more acts of violence upon the U'wa.

Image: Small-boned and agile, with dark hair, skin and eyes, A'ala has a gamin-like face that displays a quick, shy smile toward her friends and a look of fierce determination toward her enemies. She wears tribal attire whenever possible and does not call attention to herself unless she is forced to. In Crinos form, A'ala stands around 8 feet tall and all hint of the waif is gone from her appearance.

Roleplaying Notes: The Earth Mother's children are in trouble and you must defend them at all costs. You have learned the art of talking as well as the art of fighting, however, and this ability has made it possible for you to win over one of the mistrustful jaguar people. Now you and I'mo are allies; tomorrow, if you succeed in your battle against the Wyrm's servants — and survive, you may both go your separate ways again. But

somehow you think you may have begun something — a kind of trust that might help heal old wounds between the Garou and the cat-folk.

The Balam

The werejaguars are native to the Amazon and to other parts of South America. The Amazon War strikes close to home for most of the Balam, since their Kinfolk belong to the many Indigenous Peoples of the Amazon region. Solitary by nature, the Balam keep largely to their den-realms in the Amazonian Umbra unless forced to emerge to destroy some Wyrm-creature or some errant Garou. The Amazon War, however, has led some Balam to consider distant cooperation with the Garou who are, after all, fighting to protect lands sacred to the werejaguars. Many Balam, however, consider merely allowing a werewolf to live a "cooperative" effort.

I'mo Silent Heart, Stalker of the Land

Background: Raised as a child with his U'wa family, I'mo Silent Heart left his Kinfolk shortly after his First Change. Securing a comfortable den-realm in the jungle surrounding his U'wa village, I'mo kept a distant watch on his human family when he was not busy stalking the jungle and ferreting out secrets in the Umbra. Then the oil companies came with their machines and their plans to dig holes in the ground where I'mo's people had lived for centuries. I'mo decided that someone must come to the aid of his human Kin — and that he would have to be that someone. Only a few nights after he began making his regular rounds of the U'wa territory, he encountered a female who stank of "dog." Challenging her to a fight, he soon discovered that she was not only stronger than he but she also seemed reluctant to prolong a battle with someone she insisted was not her enemy. Eventually, I'mo overcame his dislike of A'ala Mother's Heart and the two of them decided to join forces to cause twice as much trouble for the oil conglomerate.

Image: I'mo is a lithe U'wa male in his Homid form, with dusky skin and dark hair and eyes. As a jaguar, he is a gold and black image of grace and speed. I'mo dresses in native U'wa attire when interacting with his Kinfolk. He prefers to attack his enemies in either his jaguar or his Crinos form.

Roleplaying Notes: You hold yourself alert for betrayal at all times, since you can never be sure if your closest ally in the struggle to save your Kinfolk may turn on you due to her dog-like nature. Still, you are fascinated by this opportunity to study one of the notorious Garou and so you take the opportunity to ask the questions you have always wanted to ask — such as "how does it feel to be inferior to the Balam?" Despite everything, you find your attitudes changing and you might even wish to continue your association with A'ala after you have gotten rid of the threat to your people.

Other Bastet

Although the Balam are the only Bastet who are native to South American, a very few Swara (werecheetah) and Bagheera (werepanthers) have made their homes in parts of the Guianas and Suriname. Descended from African Kinfolk brought over by the colonials as slaves, the few outsider Bastet have learned to love their adopted home and have joined in the struggle against the Wyrm whenever it reaches too close to home. For the most part, however, Swara and Bagheera keep a very low profile since they respect the prior claim of the Balam to the lands of South America and they wish to stay as far away from the Garou infestation as possible.

Ananasi

The Amazon rainforest is home to many varieties of spiders, and also provides a perfect environment for the Ananasi — the spider folk. Secretive by nature, the werespiders are distrusted by the other Changing Breeds due to their affinity for drinking blood. Consequently, the Ananasi in South America either migrate to the large cities, where they can lose themselves in the crowd and revel in the decadent nightlife of Rio de Janeiro, Bogotá, Caracas or Buenos Aires or else secret themselves in the jungles of the Amazon.

Mokolé

The werecrocodiles exist in small numbers along the mighty rivers of the Amazon, Orinoco and Parana Basins. Solitary by nature, the Mokolé reserve their strongest affections for their Kinfolk, caring little, if at all for anyone else. Touched closely by the contamination of many of the rainforest's rivers by pollution from mining and refuse from deforestation and burning, the Mokolé have their own methods for avenging the wrongs done to their lands and Kinfolk. While they recognize the Garou's efforts to fight the Wyrm in the Amazon, the Mokolé prefer to work on their own — discouraging all trespassers, whether they are creatures of the Wyrm or well-meaning Garou.

Alejo Eyes of the River

Background: His emergence as one of the Mokolé caused Alejo to leave his village on the shores of the Rio Negro and take to the lowlands near the river mouth. Although he spends much of his time in crocodile form lazing along the shallows of the river, Alejo occasionally rouses himself to action against those who would despoil (and have already despoiled) his homeland. Disguising himself as a native guide, Alejo takes parties of tourists, developers and potential investors in the industrial destruction of the rainforest on an unforgettable ride down the river — a ride from which few of them return.

Image: In Homid form, Alejo is a tall, stocky man of mixed Indian origin. His short curly hair and heavy-lidded eyes mask a fierce temper and a determined nature. For his expeditions as a boatman, Alejo wears simple European dress and affects a deferential attitude. In his Crinos form, Alejo is the stuff of nightmares.

Roleplaying Notes: You keep to yourself most of the time, but occasionally you feel the need to make a strike against anyone who threatens your home. Fortunately, those times coincide with the arrival of strangers and fools — who soon become drowned strangers and fools. You say little to these people except, perhaps, "goodbye!"

Chapter Two:
Eurasia

Europe

The young Glass Walker glanced nervously around her. She wasn't comfortable in the wild at the best of times and the atmosphere in the Sept of the Night Sky was like nothing she had ever encountered.

The craggy outlines of the Carpathians lumbered above the huge, blazing bonfire. Elizabeth thought of the tales of the vampires in these mountains she had heard as a pup and shivered slightly.

Garou in the full range of forms from Homid to Lupus laughed, drank, told tales and fought all across the central area of the caern. From the accents she could make out, it appeared that several different tribes were represented here — something of a rarity in this part of the world.

A burly black wolf paced toward her, finally shifting into the form of a scarred woman in her late 40s. "Come with me," the older Garou said simply and strode off away from the fire.

Elizabeth's guide led her to a clearing off to the side of the caern's center. As her eyes adjusted to the gloom away from the firelight, she could make out a lean figure, cloaked in dark fur, sitting on a rock. A heavy, well-maintained sword lay across his lap.

Litany be damned, he was attractive. Tall and muscular, with not a spare pound on him anywhere. He held himself with utter confidence, his gray hair and beard neatly trimmed. There were several other Garou in the clearing too, but she was so entranced by the figure on the rock, she barely noticed them.

"Welcome, Elizabeth Genereader," said the figure, his deep voice sending a shudder down her spine. "I am Margrave Yuri Konietzko of the Shadow Lords. A trusted advisor of mine tells me that you have much to share with us about the deeds of your own tribe. I have neither the time…" he paused, inclining his head a fraction, "…nor the inclination to visit the Scabs overmuch. Perhaps you can tell us how Gaia's warriors fare there?"

Konietzko sat back and motioned for her to start talking. Elizabeth gulped, feeling her mouth go dry. She offered a quiet prayer to Cockroach that she was doing the right thing, for if she was mistaken she could be dooming many of her tribemates to death and the tribes to civil war across the continent.

Feeling the weight of many eyes upon her, she began to speak.

Introduction

The sheer diversity of people and culture contained within the relatively small land area of Europe is mind-boggling. Over two dozen nations make up this continent, which covers a mere 8% of the world's surface. An impressive 730 million souls live in a land area of only 4 million square miles — that's over 140 people for every square mile. The need to house all these people has eaten up the countryside to a degree that American Garou would find horrifying.

The Garou of Europe have responded to the space constraints by becoming fiercely territorial. Some countries have long been contested ground—Great Britain has seen the Fenrir, Fianna and Silver Fangs struggling for dominance for centuries, while the Black Furies only recently consolidated their hold on Italy as their rivals, the Glass Walkers, lost interest. Conversely, others have long been regarded as the protectorate of individual tribes.

As the wild places of Europe rapidly disappear under the ever-expanding cities the territorial boundaries have actually become more defined. As the Apocalypse approaches, even Europe's proud, stubborn Garou are beginning to see the need for cooperation in the face of overwhelming threats.

In recent years, an upsurge in activity from the forces of the Wyrm, particularly in Scotland and the Balkans, has focused the minds of the tribes admirably. They have little other option.

Europeans

The diversity and territoriality of Europe's Garou is a mere shadow of that found in the continent's human population. Each of the countries of Europe has at least one language of its own; some countries have several languages.

For instance, within the United Kingdom the primary language is English, but there are significant numbers of Scots Gaelic speakers in Scotland and Irish Gaelic (a different, but related tongue) speakers in Northern Ireland and the Gaeltacht of the Irish Republic. In Wales, Welsh is taught in schools and most signposts are written in both Welsh and English. Towns are known by both their English and Welsh names: Swansea and Abertawe, for example.

Some countries, like Switzerland, have no primary language. In different regions of Switzerland people speak French, Swiss German, Italian or Rætoromanic.

The most widely spoken languages across the continent are English, French and German; most people speak at least one other language, although plenty of Europeans still speak nothing but their own country's native tongue.

These days, upsurges in nationalist beliefs are unsettlingly common, reminding many of the rise of the nationalists in Italy, Spain and Germany that helped to trigger World War II. Stereotypes and ancient enmity between nations persist, despite the European Union's move towards European integration.

Geography

Europe can be divided into four main areas. There's the northern upland and mountainous area, running across northern Britain and Scandinavia. Then there's the great central plain that stretches right across France, Germany and across Eastern Europe into Russia.

A second mountainous zone spreads from the Pyrenees Mountains of Portugal and Spain, along the Alps, which run through southeast France, along the top of Italy into Eastern Europe. The Carpathians complete this region, forming an arc through Eastern Europe. Finally, there's coastal area along the Mediterranean.

Climate

The climate across Europe varies wildly. The far north, particularly Scandinavia and Iceland, experiences Arctic conditions. The southern edge of Europe, along the Mediterranean Sea, is blessed with warm days and cool nights.

Much of the rest of the central plain has a temperate climate. The summers are warm and fairly dry, while the winters are cold. In the mountains and the northern stretches of central Europe summer is short and winter long, dark and bitterly cold.

This southern part of Europe is still tectonically active, with occasional earthquakes and volcanic eruptions, particularly at the eastern end. Sicily's Mount Etna erupts regularly, most recently in early 2000. Iceland, an island to the far north of Europe, is also volcanically active.

Rivers

Several great rivers make their way through mainland Europe. The Danube rises in Germany, runs through Austria, before turning southeast through Slovakia, Hungary and Yugoslavia and Bulgaria. It then runs northeast through Romania and the Ukraine before entering the Black Sea

The Loire rises in the Alps in southern France, travelling north then east through the country, before draining into the Bay of Biscay. The Loire Valley is particularly famous for the numerous beautiful castles (chateaux) along its length.

The Seine runs from northeastern France into the English Channel, while the Rhine rises in the Alps, flows through France and Germany and then into the Netherlands and the North Sea.

The Oder runs from the Czech Republic north to the Baltic Sea; for at least part of its length, it forms a natural boundary between Germany and Poland.

Kin Animals

Europeans have had something of a love/hate relationship with wolves. The peoples of northern Europe equated the animal with evil, while the people of southern Europe associated it with fertility. This disparity can been seen when you compare the Norse legends of the fearsome Fenris wolf with those from Italy of the she-wolf who nurtured and raised the legendary founders of Rome, Romulus and Remus.

The result of these differing attitudes can be seen even today in existing wolf populations. In the north of Europe, they were ruthlessly hunted to extinction. They were gone from England by the 13th century. Tradition holds that the last wolf in Scotland died in 1848, by which point they had been virtually eliminated from the rest of Northern Europe as well.

However, populations still survive in Italy, Spain, Portugal, Sardinia and the Balkans, as well through much of Eastern Europe. Some packs have recently begun migrating to Germany from Poland. They remain under threat, though, and not just from man. One of the biggest dangers to the remaining wolf packs is that of hybridization through interbreeding with their distant relatives, dogs. Once the wolf line becomes a dog line, the wolves stop being Kinfolk.

Big cats are all but extinct in Europe. A few lynx survive in Scandinavia, the Balkans, Greece, the Pyrenees and areas of Eastern Europe; more are being introduced into German and Austrian forests. The pardel or Iberian lynx is on the verge of extinction, with only a handful surviving in Spain and Portugal. European wildcats can be found in the highlands of Scotland, central Germany and much of southern Europe; these are really the only evidence other shapeshifters have of the once-strong Ceilican.

Brown bears can be found throughout Scandinavia, as well as in isolated parts of northern Spain and Portugal, central Italy and southeastern Europe.

Ravens are commonplace and can be found across most of the continent. They are particularly numerous in northwestern Europe, Britain, Germany, Scandinavia and Iceland.

History

When you look at the history of Europe, there is one theme that runs clearly through it: war. From the skirmishes between the early Indo-European tribes in the days of prehistory to the NATO military intervention in Kosovo that saw out the 20th century, there has never really been a time when the continent has truly been at peace.

Here rose the Greek city-states and the Roman Empire, which was eventually laid low by the Germanic tribes. The Celts were born somewhere in the shadow of the Alps and spread across most of Europe. The Norse went a'viking and spread their culture across the Atlantic.

The feudal system arose in central Europe in the Dark Ages and came to dominate the continent, until the Renaissance started in southern Europe in the 17th century and slowly brought sweeping reforms to Europe.

The 18th and 19th Centuries were times of conquest. Many of the European nations carved out empires for themselves across the world, by colonization and invasion. Notably, the United Kingdom carved out the British Empire, which was so large at its peak that, famously, "the sun never set on the empire" — there was always some part of the world claimed by Britain in daylight. The 19th century also saw the Industrial revolution and the sudden, rapid growth of Europe's cities.

Then came the 20th century, the first half of which was dominated by war. The assassination in Sarajevo of the Austrian archduke Franz Ferdinand and his wife was the spark that caused Europe to burn in the flames of war. Pent up rivalries between European nations, which had built up over the centuries, were unleashed in a tide of destruction — the Great War — that swamped Europe for five years.

Sadly, the conflict that many called "the war to end all wars" didn't live up to its name. The rise of the fascist political groups in Italy and Germany triggered the Second World War scant decades later. Once more Europe became one large battlefield. Many cities were bombed into rubble, destroying a legacy of centuries. The heavy shelling destroyed whole areas of wilderness, and the march of thousands of soldiers, tanks and other military vehicles reduced vast areas of the countryside to mud. Entire populations, but particularly Jews and Rroma, were systematically slaughtered in Germany's "Final Solution" — better known as the Holocaust.

In the aftermath of the war, the Iron Curtain fell into place, bisecting Germany and keeping much of Eastern Europe isolated from its Western neighbors. The fascist government in Spain lingered well after World War II ended. As Eastern Europe experimented with communism, Western Europe gave itself over to the free market. The nations of Europe concentrated on rebuilding their economies in the decades that followed. Trade treaties fostered closer links between nations that were once at each other's throats.

By the 1980s, parts of Europe were slowly moving towards political integration. The European Union now unites 15 nations in a loose political, social and economic federation. The collapse of communism and the fall of the Iron Curtain reunited Germany and allowed free congress between all the nations of Europe once more.

However, in other parts of Europe, the movement is the other way. In the last decade, Czechoslovakia split into two nations, the Czech and Slovak Republics, while the Yugoslavia that existed in 1990 has slowly torn itself apart in a series of civil wars. The country which now claims Yugoslavia's name occupies only a small fraction of the land its predecessor once covered. Even in Italy, the Lega Nord campaigns to split the northern half of the country away from the poorer southern half.

Europe Today

While the memories of the two World Wars still linger across the continent — for each country that would like to forget, there's another who won't let them — Europe has new challenges to face, not least of which is the growing population. In certain areas of Europe, particularly the UK, pressure to give up green field land for new housing development is becoming overwhelming. With more people marrying later and the divorce rate ever on the up, the number of one-person households grows every year.

Current predictions suggest that the UK will need over one million new homes by 2016, most of them in the area of southeast England that surrounds the capital, London. Builders want to put the new homes on green field sites in the countryside. Residents of the countryside want them to go on old, often heavily contaminated industrial sites in city centers. Neither option is exactly attractive.

A similar picture can be found right across Europe. Over 730 million people cram themselves onto this tiny continent and the Wyld is squeezed out of the land by the Weaver's webs a little more every year.

By contrast, the Wyrm has a strong hold on the continent and its influence is growing. If the damage wrought by the two World Wars wasn't enough, intensive farming methods introduced in the post-war period to up productivity on short-handed farms have done serious long-term damage to the environment. The use of chemical fertilizers and pesticides and the destruction of the natural habitats of hedgerows to make larger fields for more efficient farming have pushed many species onto the endangered list. The environmental consequences of decades of landfill trash dumping are only just being realized, too. Many of these sites are leaking pollutants into the ground around them at an alarming rate, creating new Hellholes and Blights across the continent.

The more developed countries are just waking up to the problems caused by the car. In many countries congestion is reaching critical levels, despite a strong public transport system. While some measures have been made to curb the worst environmental impacts of petrol by a general move to unleaded fuel, most Europeans are a long way from ending their love affair with the car.

The European Union

The EU evolved out of the European Economic Community, which was established by the treaty of Rome in 1957. Successive treaties and agreements have moved the member nations towards greater economic, political and legal unity, most recently with the Maastricht Treaty in 1991.

The EU has launched a common currency — the Euro — but only a limited number of member nations have adopted it so far. Many nations are openly skeptical about the idea of ceding further sovereign right to the growing European superstate and are worried about losing their own cultural identities to a United States of Europe.

Members

Founding members: Belgium, France, Germany, Italy, Luxembourg and the Netherlands

1973: Denmark, Ireland and the United Kingdom

1981: Greece

1986: Portugal and Spain

1995: Austria, Finland and Sweden

Current applicants for membership:

Bulgaria, Cyprus, the Czech Republic, Estonia, Hungary, Latvia, Lithuania, Malta, Poland, Romania, the Slovak Republic, Slovenia and Turkey

However, if Europe belongs to any of the Triat, it is the Weaver. While Europe can't claim the world's biggest cities, it can claim one of the highest concentrations of them to be found anywhere.

The Eurohub

The sweep of land from London in England, round via Paris in France, taking in Belgium, Northern Germany and the Netherlands is the most urbanized region on the face of the planet. This so-called "Eurohub" is so tightly bound in the coils of the Weaver that few non-Glass Walkers dare step sideways for fear of calcification into the Pattern Web.

The Weaver's influence is increasingly being felt in the political move towards unity in Europe. The EU claims greater and greater power over its individual members with each passing year. Legislation continues to do its best to reduce social, economic and political obstacles to uniformity. The culture of each nation is eroded a little more as the native currencies are replaced progressively by the Euro.

At the center of the Eurohub lies Belgium. 98% of the country's 10 million people live in an urban environment. The largest city, Brussels is the very core of the Weaver's power over the region, and home to many of the core European Union institutions:

• the European Commission, the EU's "civil service," which can propose legislation but cannot make decisions on it

• the Council of Ministers, made-up of EU national ministers who come to discuss matters pertaining to their portfolio (e.g. agriculture)

• the European Parliament (which is actually based in Strasbourg in the Alsace region of France but has a building here too)

Any sense of the city's own personality has been swept away in the last few decades as it has become the administrative center of the continent. Nearly a third of the million people living in the city are now non-Belgians. Not surprisingly, the few Bone Gnawer packs that have tried to make contact with the City Father report that the spirit has clearly become a servant of the Weaver and no other.

The Penumbra

American Garou stepping sideways almost anywhere in Europe are horrified by the degree to which the continent is wrapped in the webs of the Weaver. Even the Blights and Hellholes of the continent have a Weaverish element to them. Twisted webs reminiscent of barbed wire often surround the areas of corruption. Slimy, oozing knots in the Web indicate spots where Banes have only partially been calcified into the strands.

After all, the Weaver has only had a matter of centuries to really wrap up the former Pure Lands in her webs. She's been cocooning Europe for millennia.

The effect is even more pronounced as one approaches the Eurohub. Despite the best efforts of the Ratkin, Paris is truly under the spell of the Weaver. The spiritual reflection of the Eiffel Tower stabs even higher into the Umbral sky than does its physical counterpart. From its sides stretch vast webs that blanket most of the city center.

Approaching Brussels in the Penumbra is even more difficult (and some would even say nigh impossible). Whatever route a pack takes, the closer they come to the city itself the more their progress is impeded by thicker and thicker webs. Guardian-Spiders are common and easily disturbed if the Garou try and force their way through.

By the time they enter the reflection of the city's suburbs it is almost impossible to move without attracting the attention of Weaver-spirits, particularly Pattern Spiders. Attack Geomids prowl the streets, searching for anything that would disrupt the Pattern Web.

In the distance, the buildings of central Brussels can only be vaguely seen as shadowy forms through the webs that enshroud them all. Vast sheets of webbing hang between them, making progress along streets virtually impossible. Electricity elementals flash backwards and forwards between the buildings. The occasional Strand-spider can be seen moving over the cityscape and along the road and rail links, building ever-stronger connections with other cities in the Eurohub.

There are a few places largely free of spiritual webbing, but they're few and far between. The depths of the Scottish highlands, the high mountainous regions and some of the more remote areas of Scandinavia are small areas of refuge. Small islands like Corsica, Malta and Elba have yet to be overrun, as do small portions of Ireland and small portions of the very rural sections of East Germany and Poland. Although much of the Black Forest is in very real danger, the Weaver has been violently pruned out of a few remote valleys and mountaintops within; Freiburg, the largest city in the Black Forest, has managed to remain comparatively free of the Web, thanks to an emphatically "green"-minded population.

Too much of Europe feels the coils of the Wyrm round it as well. Germany, France and Austria have yet to truly recover from the spiritual damage inflicted

during the World Wars. Umbral reflections of the battlefields of both wars are dangerous to travel; the battlefields on the Marne in France are so ravaged that healthy plants refuse to grow there. The Penumbra of the former Yugoslavia is a great network of Hellholes, with new Banes being birthed almost daily.

The poverty and misery endemic to the Eastern European countries during the later years of communist rule have gifted their cities with more than their fair share of Blights and plenty of Banes to people them.

The Shoah

There is one area of Europe's Penumbra to which few Garou ever travel. The areas of the Penumbra corresponding to the sites of the Shoah, the camps where the Nazis imprisoned and murdered thousands of Jews, Rroma, homosexuals, communists, socialists and others during the Second World War, are strange, dark places quite unlike anything else found in the Umbra. Even traveling near these sites can bring a Garou to the very edge of Harano.

Only Silent Striders dare venture into those areas and then only in times of dire need. They return even more grim and tight-lipped than usual. None ever speak of their experiences there.

The Garou of Europe

Just as war has plagued the humans of Europe, so too has it preoccupied the Garou. The continent is home ground to at least four tribes: the Black Furies, Fianna, Get of Fenris and Shadow Lords. The result has been a tense interplay between these tribes down the centuries, often to the point of all-out war.

In recent decades, though, the boundaries of each tribe's territory have been more firmly set. As the cities grow and true wild places become rarer, each tribe has had to consolidate to its main caerns to protect them from the unstoppable growth of the humans' Scabs.

The Black Furies dominate Southern Europe. The Fianna are heavily entrenched throughout Great Britain, with the exception of England (where they still contest territory with the local Get). They also have a strong presence in France. The Get of Fenris hold Scandinavia, Northern Europe and Germany. The Shadow Lords now regard Eastern Europe as their sovereign territory, as centuries of warfare with the Silver Fangs have finally ended in the Lords' favor. They finally cemented their ownership of the territory when they reclaimed the powerful caern that is home to the Sept of the Night Sky in Wallachia from the Silver Fangs. These boundaries are likely to hold for the foreseeable future, for the werewolves of Europe

Death of a River

On January 30, 2000 a dam in a Romanian mining works burst. Over 100,000 cubic meters of contaminated water swept into the Somes River. From there it continued into Hungary and the Tisza, a tributary of the Danube.

The water was contaminated with cyanide. The Tisza died.

Clean-up workers removed 12,100 tons of dead fish from the river. The toxins killed everything right down to the level of bacteria.

As predators ate the dead fish, the cyanide began to work its way up the food chain. Foxes and otters were among the first to start dying. One of five remaining pairs of ospreys in the region died after eating poisoned prey.

The poison carried on into Yugoslavia, where 80% of the river's life died — in an area already under severe ecological strain following the NATO air strikes on oil refineries in 1999. Thankfully, by the time the polluted water reached the Danube, the cyanide was diluted enough to no longer pose a threat.

It will take 10 to 20 years for the river to return to anything like normal. Several species have been completely destroyed.

Of course, the humans living along the Tisza suffered as well. 2.5 million people found their drinking water supplies threatened. 15,000 people in the fishing industry saw their livelihoods destroyed.

The operator of the mine claims that excessive melt-water from heavy snowfalls caused the dam to burst. The local Garou suspect that the contamination was planned. Whatever caused the disaster, the Wyrm's legions have been feeding on the resultant misery and ruin ever since. Banes were drawn to the devastation in vast numbers. By the time the poison entered Hungary, the river's Penumbral reflection was a seething mass of Wyrm-corrupted spirits. As the front edge of the contamination was carried down the Tisza, the whole length of the river became little more than one long Hellhole.

When this wave-front hit the Hellhole caused by the oil spills the year before, two things happened. The combined taint of the two incidents was enough to create a massive Wyrmhole surrounding the lower reaches of the Tisza. The second was to fuse many of the pollution spirits already present with the poison and corrupted nature spirits and create something new from them all. This monstrous new spirit wallows in the polluted Umbral river, its oily toxic bulk bathed in the foulness the Tisza has become. Every now and again it swallows another twisted fish or otter-spirit and grows a little bigger.

For now it seems content to bide its time and enjoy the misery that caused its birth; the Garou packs that have tried to put it down have so far been unable to meet the challenge, and have yet to penetrate its lines of defense. Eventually, however, the nascent spirit will grow bored and seek to spread its own brand of corruption elsewhere.

---

can ill-afford to be fighting amongst themselves as the Apocalypse draws ever closer. However, these boundaries are by no means absolute; many septs tolerate packs of other tribes in their territories, at times even welcoming the help. Just so long as the guests know their place, of course....

Europe birthed the Black Spirals, too, and the fallen tribe still has a strong presence here. The numerous wars that have raged across the continent, along with the areas of heavy pollution that are a legacy of the Industrial Revolution, have left many areas Blighted. While the Garou do their best to cleanse the Blights as they find them, they are few and the Blights rampant.

If they are to stand any chance of surviving the Apocalypse, the Garou of Europe desperately need to put their differences behind them and start to deal with the multitude of threats facing them.

Black Furies

"Surely we are on the very verge of the Apocalypse. For thousands of years we have protected this land, sought to teach man his place and honor Mother Gaia. Yet now, on the edge of the lands we call home, the Wyrm has built itself a stronghold the like of which we could never have imagined.

Prepare yourselves, sisters. The time for petty squabbling with the other tribes is over. We must fight beside them to rid the land of the Wyrm once and for all. If we fail, the work our ancestors have done for generations is as nothing."

— Kelonoke Wildhair

Imagine the horror that the Furies felt when, after centuries of fighting for the rights of women across the world, they found atrocities being committed against them right on the tribe's very doorstep.

Rape and mutilation of women has become all too common throughout the Balkan regions caught up in the struggles of the past decade. The dehumanizing horror of "ethnic cleansing" has led to some racial groups treating others as less than human — objects to be used, abused and destroyed as they see fit. Unsurprisingly, women and children often suffer the worst. Reports of gang rapes and mutilations continue to trickle out of the region even after the theoretical cessation of hostilities following the NATO intervention in Kosovo.

However, what has made the situation worse, from the point of view of the Furies, is that there is precious little they can do about it.

The attitudes that spawn the Balkan atrocities spring from the humans themselves, not from servitors of the Wyrm. Human prejudices and grudges are much harder to fight than a multi-legged horror spawned from a Blight. Also, the decade of atrocity has turned the Balkans into a breeding ground for Banes and fomori. The Furies seem to spend too much of their time putting down these monsters.

The European Furies' numbers have been steadily declining for many years, as attrition, the tribe's custom of giving away male infants and the general decline in Garou numbers take their toll. At their current numbers, it is all the tribe can do to keep the Wyrm's forces at bay, let alone try and deal with the human problems. With great reluctance, the Furies have decided to concentrate on defeating the Wyrm and have left the human consequences for later.

Uneasy Alliance

The Furies rarely ask for help from anyone. However, their situation looked so bleak and their numbers were stretched so thin that when an offer of aid came from the Shadow Lords, they actually listened. Kelonoke Wildhair from the Sept of Bygone Visions (see **Caerns: Places of Power**, reprinted in **Rage Across the World Volume 1**) traveled by moon bridge to the Sept of the Night Sky and met with Margrave Konietzko, the sept's leader. She found much to admire in the seasoned warrior and an outlook on life not unlike her own. She spent a week as his guest, joining him in hunting down a nest of vampires and in talking to Swift-as-the-River, a representative of the Red Talons.

When Kelonoke returned to the Miria Caern, she recommended to the Outer Calyx, one of the ruling circles of the tribe, that they enter into a temporary alliance with the Shadow Lords. After much heated debate, they agreed but not without severe misgivings on the part of many of the tribal elders.

So far, Kelonoke's judgement has been vindicated. The Shadow Lords, Red Talons and Black Furies form an effective fighting group; they are beginning to root out the Blights and Hellholes that are spawning the fomori in Kosovo and are making plans to push north towards Serbia.

The fact that all three tribes' patience with humans has reached the breaking point is helping to keep them bonded together. Amongst the slaughter the humans are inflicting on each other, a few extra fatalities at the hands of the war packs are hardly noticeable.

Or so the theory went. Early this year, a small pack managed to wipe out a band of fomori that had taken control of a Balkan village. When an equally small group of humans entered the village not long afterwards, the werewolves reacted far more brutally than was necessary. To their surprise, these humans turned out to be immune to the Delirium and imbued with some form of supernatural abilities. Four of the humans were killed and the other two driven off; two werewolves also perished.

While some of the survivors theorized that these were a strange new breed of fomor bred by the region's violence, the pack's Theurge remains adamant that they were not Wyrm-tainted.

The Fianna

"The last advice I offer you is this: have your Galliards sing songs of our ancestors and their battles against the fallen White Howlers. Learn the lessons of the past and prepare to face the future as one tribe. For, if you do not, the return of the Árd Cruimh Beithíoch will mark the fall of the Fianna."

— Brendan O'Rourke, during his final address as Ard Righ

There's a long-standing misconception among American Garou that Fianna means Irish werewolf. The slow evolution of their New World Kinfolk into the "Plastic Paddies" so despised by the Irish back home certainly hasn't helped.

In truth, the Fianna and their Celtic Kinfolk once had much of central Europe to themselves, before eventually being pushed back to the western fringes of the continent by the invading Germanic and Nordic peoples. The interbreeding of these peoples through the centuries means that the Fianna have a strong presence throughout the UK, areas of France and, to a lesser extent, Spain.

Britain has long been contested ground between the Fianna, the Get and the Silver Fangs. However, the actions of House Winter Snow centuries ago saw

The Balkans

The countries that make up the "powder-keg of Europe" have seen the start of more wars than any other region of Europe, a tradition they are maintaining even today.

In the early 20th century the area erupted into warfare, seeking to free itself from the rule of the Ottoman Turkey, with partial success enshrined in 1913's Treaty of London. Fighting broke out for three months that summer as the newly liberated nations fought to establish new boundaries.

Tensions between Bosnia-Herzegovina, part of the Austro-Hungarian Empire and Serbia grew in the aftermath. These tensions culminated in the assassination in June 1914 of Archduke Franz Ferdinand, heir to the Austro-Hungarian emperor, by a Bosnian student working for the Serbian nationalist movement called the Black Hand (no relation to the vampiric sect of the same name). The empire sought to punish Serbia, and Germany committed its support. Russia allied itself with the Serbians, and World War I was born.

Events in the aftermath of World War I saw the Balkan nations united into what became the Federal Republic of Yugoslavia. In 1991, it all fell apart. Two countries, Croatia and Slovenia, declared themselves independent. Serbia objected and used federal troops to impose its will. Serbia quickly struck a deal with Slovenia allowing its independence after a 10-day war. The war with Croatia, on the other hand, raged until the end of the year, when the United Nations brokered a cease-fire between Croatia and the remainder of Yugoslavia. By this time, several of Yugoslavia's other constituent countries had declared their own independence.

Croatia, Slovenia, Bosnia-Herzegovina (often known simply as Bosnia) and Macedonia all became independent nations, while Serbia and Montenegro remained as Yugoslavia.

The problems were only just starting. Bosnia erupted in civil war as the ethnic Serbs attempted to establish their own state, independent of the rest of Bosnia. By the end of 1992, they held 70% of Bosnia's territory. The Muslim and Croatian residents were systematically driven out in a process that was called, euphemistically, ethnic cleansing. Tens of thousands died and nearly two million people were forced out of their homes.

The United Nations slammed economic sanctions on Yugoslavia, as the perceived instigator of the civil war. By the end of 1993 these, and the threat of air strikes from NATO, pushed the Yugoslavian government to pressure the Bosnian Serbs into accepting a UN peace plan.

In 1997, Serbia found it had its own problems. Kosovo, a formerly independent area within its borders populated mainly by ethnic Albanians, started to protest against the Serbian government. The Kosovo Liberation Army was formed, and declared its intention to integrate Kosovo with Albania. The Serbian forces reacted in predictable fashion: they instituted a program of ethnic cleansing, which was eventually ended by a prolonged air assault from NATO troops.

The decades of violence have, inevitably, attracted the attention of the Wyrm. The Black Furies, whose homelands border the area, sent several packs into the area to try and deal with the rape camps that had sprung up. None were heard from again. The Shadow Lords in the lands to the north of the Balkans were also suffering losses to the growing Wyrm forces concentrated in Bosnia and Serbia. The two tribes entered into an uneasy alliance to root out the problem.

The more cautious packs that first started to penetrate the area came back to report groups of fomori preying on the refugees. Margrave Yuri Konietzko, a Shadow Lord Theurge of formidable reputation, started to take a personal interest, coordinating strikes against the fomori which have allowed the Furies, pushing north into Kosovo, and the Lords, striking south into Bosnia, to score significant successes against the Wyrm's minions there.

However, neither tribe has yet found any central spiritual source to the corruption. Both are beginning to suspect that the real source of the corruption lies deep within Serbia itself.

the effective end of Fang rule in Britain. The Get, while they haven't relinquished any of their caerns in the UK, have been forced to spend more of their time and resources in protecting their homelands in Germany, northern Europe and Scandinavia.

As a result, the Fianna have a stronger grip on the UK than they have had in a long time. The tribe is also more united than it has been in its recent history. The tentative success of the peace process in resolving the situation in Northern Ireland took the wind out of the

Mixing It Up

Multitribal septs are rare indeed in Europe. The European tribes have long shared the fierce territoriality of their wolf Kin and many caerns that lie on the borders between two tribes' territory have changed hands repeatedly over the years.

Throughout history there have been exceptions to the rule: the Fenrir and the Fianna frequently shared caerns during their long campaign to reclaim Scotland from the White Howlers, for example. Today, each tribe's territory has been won through centuries of warfare with tribal rivals and so they are reluctant to give another tribe so much as a foothold in their caerns. Still, the value of cooperation is not lost on the European Garou and multitribal packs are often formed for particular missions in cooperation between several septs, in some cases scattered across the continent.

The major exception to the rule of "one caern, one tribe" is the Sept of Sun's Glory, in the Alps between Switzerland and France. The sept has been in existence since the Dark Ages, when it was led by Guillaume Sun's Glory, an elder Silver Fang with an abiding hatred of vampires.

When Sun's Glory finally fell in battle, the sept was renamed in his honor and adopted his mission as his own. Werewolves from all over the continent, and even further afield, regularly gather in the alpine valley that houses the quiet, frozen lake that is the heart of the caern. There they discuss the Leeches and exchange tactics for dealing with them. Young packs of Garou often travel to the sept to learn from the more experienced Leech-hunters that make their home there.

The sept has also maintained its reputation for strict neutrality in tribal politics that Sun's Glory enforced in his heyday. A disproportionate number of Philodox make their home here and, in recent decades, several territorial disputes that would normally have led to major skirmishes between two tribes have actually been settled through mediation.

The infiltration of human politics is not the only threat from within the tribe. The blood of the Picts, the Black Spiral Dancer Kinfolk, has long been mixed with that of their own Kinfolk. As each year passes, a few more Fianna dance the Black Spiral or are forced to undertake a quest through the Umbra for Stag's blessing to stave off the corruption from within. The fall of the Silver Fang's House Austere Howl to the same legacy has proved an object lesson to the Fianna, and one they have taken to heart.

North Wales, areas of rural Ireland and the north of Scotland represent the last vestiges of the Wyld under the tribe's protection that have not fallen to the webs of the Weaver or the corruption of the Wyrm. The Fianna know they must remain strong and united as a tribe if they are to preserve them. Regrettably, a few of their Theurges fear this realization might have come too late.

Homecoming

Scotland has been the Fianna's land for over a millennium. When the Scots traveled from Ireland into what is now know as Scotland, they steadily drove out the Picts, the Kinfolk of the fallen White Howlers.

Over the centuries, working with the Get of Fenris and the Silver Fangs, the Fianna drove back the Black Spiral Dancers to the one Wyrmhole they were never quite able to cleanse, the Caern of the Mile-Deep Loch. This island off the west coast had been the home of the leaders of the White Howlers. It was the last Howler caern to fall to the Wyrm, and it fell the furthest. The loch itself, at the center of the island, is reputed to lead into Malfeas and the Black Labyrinth itself.

The Fianna contented themselves with making sure than nothing went to or from the island, and called Scotland cleansed. It never truly was, though. The Spirals had riddled the Highlands with tunnels, which the Fianna, remembering the fate of the Howlers, were loath to enter. In the centuries that followed new incursions of Spirals would crop up every few decades or so, before being put down.

That carefully maintained balance has now been disrupted. A series of acquisitions, mergers and reverse buyouts so obscure that they barely made the pages of the *Financial Times* in early 1999 led to several of the refineries in the town of Grangemouth on the Firth (a Scots word for an estuary) of Forth in east Scotland becoming subsidiaries of Endron Oil. Within months safety standards had dropped and a series of "accidents" contaminated the Firth of Forth several times.

Around the same time, packs living in the Highlands reported the first major skirmishes with Spirals

sails of the Eire Fundamentalists and the Brotherhood of Herne to the point where both groups are now more fringe gatherings than true camps of the tribe. The growing problems in Scotland have focused the minds of the Fianna away from human politics and onto the imminent Apocalypse so much that when the peace process tottered on the brink of collapse, the tribe's attention did not return to human politics.

A World of Rage

in over a century. In early November, a pack of Fianna found a group of wildcat and human corpses near Caithness. The bodies were defiled with marks of the Wyrm. Two months ago, a caern in the Ochils near Dollar fell to the Dancers, in the first of a series of assaults that have made the Fianna's hold on Scotland tenuous indeed.

It appears the Spirals have come home, and the Garou Nation would dearly love to know why. A few Fianna suspect that they know. The watchers assigned to the coast near the Sept of the Mile-Deep Loch have reported seeing something rising from the waters there. One or two Galliards of the tribe have noted similarities between the sightings and tales of the Árd Cruimh Beithíoch, a mighty Wyrmspawn that fought alongside the Black Spiral Dancers to defend the Mile-Deep Loch. While the old songs tell of the beast's destruction at the hands of several packs of Garou, the fear is that those tales have grown too far in the telling and that the beast lives still.

Tribal Politics

Bron MacFionn, former leader of the Sept of the Tri-Spiral at Brugh Na Boinne in County Meath, Eire (again see **Caerns: Places of Power**), recently ascended to the position of Ard Righ of the Fianna and has taken up residence in Silver Tara. His mentor Brendan O'Rourke, the former Ard Righ, stepped down to undertake an Umbral quest after the attempted invasion of Silver Tara by Black Spiral Dancers. He and his trusted packmates would give no details of where they were going or why, save that he had received a vision from Stag that made it clear that the tribe's future is at stake.

Bron has taken the opportunity his new role offers him to pursue his dream of a world where werewolves, fae and humans live together in harmony. Feeling that the Fianna need allies in their battle with the growing strength of the Wyrm in England and Scotland, he has turned to the old alliances with the sidhe, leaving others to build bridges to the other tribes. He spends more and more time caught in the endless dance of changeling politics, trying to win their support, and less and less attending to the needs of the tribe.

The decline of the Brotherhood of Herne has seen the Dyn a drowyd yn flaidd — the Welsh Fianna — take a more active role in Fianna politics. These fierce Garou who have been so successful in keeping their lands free of both the Wyrm and Weaver are bringing a much-needed hard edge to the tribe's policies.

Meanwhile, younger members of the tribe, particularly the Grandchildren of Fionn, are finding more common ground with members of other tribes. Son-of-Moonlight, Bron's successor as Righ of the Sept of the Tri-Spiral has started negotiations with Margrave Konietzko of the Shadow Lords behind the Ard Righ's back. The lupus Theurge feels that other werewolves are likely to prove more reliable allies than the notoriously capricious fae.

Get of Fenris

"The Fenrir have kept this land free of the Wyrm for centuries, for we are strong. Today is no different from yesterday. The howl of Fenris echoes from the mountains and the creatures of the Wyrm cower."

— Mikki Rethgar, Fenrir Ahroun

The Fenrir occupy a broad swathe of land from the north of Italy through Germany, Austria and Denmark into Norway, Sweden and Finland. The sparsely populated Scandinavian countries are the tribe's homelands and they protect them ruthlessly. The harsh, unforgiving climate suits the tribe perfectly. The weak do not survive in the semi-arctic wilderness where many of the Get's septs dwell. They wouldn't have it any other way. The weak are not fit to fight for Gaia as true warriors of the Fenrir.

The tribe still manages to maintain entire villages of Kinfolk in certain areas. While once common practice for all the European tribes, the greater mobility of humans in the 19th and 20th centuries has made this impractical elsewhere. These Kin have been successful in actively campaigning against the construction of further nuclear reactors in the area. The wolf packs that roam Finland provide the tribe with a healthy proportion of lupus members, too.

The werewolves of northern Europe compete against each other to hunt down wandering feral vampires, and packs of Scandinavian Fenrir are always the first to respond when a cry for assistance comes from a sept anywhere in the world. Many travel to the Amazon to spend time fighting alongside the almost legendary Golgol Fangs-First.

Still, the Wyrm continues to provide plenty here to keep the tribe busy. They have been warring against Wyrm-beasts that tunnel beneath the land since the Dark Ages, with no signs that they are decreasing in number. Indeed, in recent years packs of Fenrir venturing into these tunnels have found that the tunnels may be more extensive than they ever realized. New passageways and caverns have opened up in areas that the Fenrir thought cleared and thoroughly explored centuries ago. A series of carefully planned expeditions have discovered, at the cost of many lives, that the tunnels now seem to reach far beneath the North Sea, and may in fact reach as far as Scotland.

A few members of the tribe are finally starting to defy tradition and suggest that they should follow the second tenet of the Litany a little more literally and "Combat the Wyrm Wherever It Dwells and Wherever It Breeds." That means packs traveling into the deepest Wyrm tunnels and finding where these monsters are coming from. Ah, what a battle that will be.

Germany

Germany has become something of a blemish on the Get's honor. Not only do they live with the knowledge that members of the tribe chose to side with the Nazis during World War II, but they have been unable to defeat the forces besieging its strongest caern in the area.

Indeed, although the tribe would have others believe otherwise, their hold on the German countryside has never been terribly secure. Memories of the Inquisition are strong among German and Austrian members of the tribe. As recently as the 17th century, werewolves were occasionally hunted down by the humans. The most famous incident took place in Eschenbach at the end of the century.

Rumor has it that some of the Get of Fenris who sided with the Nazis during World War II were a little too free in dropping hints about their true nature. This has made the Fenrir fanatical about upholding the Veil. Any human in Germany who sees a Garou change, dies. Any werewolf allowing a human to see him in any form other than Homid or Lupus had better have a watertight excuse, or they are severely punished. The Get's definition of severe means that precious few offenders survive long enough to be sent on a quest to redeem themselves.

The sudden rise of a new breed of human hunter with certain supernatural talents has brought back too many bad memories of the Burning Times for the Fenrir to ignore. Packs of Get strive to wipe these new threats from the face of Europe whenever they can.

The increasing number of fomori, or *Zerrütteten* as the German Fenrir know them, in central European cities is also a point of serious concern to the tribe. Occasional and begrudging co-operation with septs of Glass Walkers has allowed some success in keeping their numbers down.

Finally, the unrest among the human population is feeding all the wrong kinds of spirits. The reunification of Germany was far from flawless; the differences in economical prosperity are still pronounced, inspiring no small amount of envy in the former East Germany. This problem is often linked to an even more severe one — the growing numbers of racists, particularly neo-Nazi skins, in the country. As Bertolt Brecht put it, "the womb that they grew from is still fertile."

The Battle for the Schwarzwald

The tribe's best-known sept in the region, the Sept of the Blood Fist (see **Caerns: Places of Power**) deep in the heart of the Schwarzwald — the Black Forest — has been under siege for over half a decade. An alliance of Black Spiral Dancers, Banes and Leeches has launched repeated attacks on the caern. While each and every one has been successfully repelled, the mounting cost in Garou lives has been staggering.

Of the sept members alive when the siege started, only Else Kirchenwald, known as Wyrm-Guard, the Gatekeeper survives. Jarl Torgus Firemane, the sept leader, was killed three years ago in a battle with a Black Spiral wielding a fetish sword called Wyrmblade. The Jarl's sacrifice allowed the Get to capture and destroy the blade but his absence is keenly felt. Since then the leadership of the sept has passed from one young werewolf to another, none of whom has the experience or tactical knowledge to stand long against the forces that surround the caern.

Septs from all over Europe have been providing reinforcements for the caern. While this has seriously depleted their numbers elsewhere, the UK in particular, the tribe refuses to let a caern touched by the talons of great Fenris himself fall to the Wyrm. Neither will they ask for help from the weaker tribes. This is a battle they must win on their own, whatever the cost.

Italy

Tensions between the Black Furies and the Get run high in Italy, as they have for centuries. The Get first arrived in the land alongside their Kinfolk as the Germanic tribes sacked Rome. Centuries later the Get are still there, skirmishing with the powerful Leeches in many of the Italian cities and warring in the Umbra against the Banes that are drawn to the corruption that seems endemic to Italian politics. As one Fenrir Ragabash once observed, the only thing that changes more often than Italy's government — 56 governments since 1945 and counting — is the Jarl of a Fenrir sept.

The Get have a quiet respect for the Black Furies in the south of the country, as fierce warriors who are fighting pretty much the same fights and who are nearly, but not quite, as strong as the Get. This, of course, goes utterly unappreciated by the Furies, who see in the Get everything that is worst in the often-misogynistic Italian society.

In recent times, the skirmishes between the two have dropped to a minimum. Neither tribe can afford to lose many more members to intertribal warfare with everything else they have on their plates. Still, if two packs meet while pursuing Banes through the Umbra, it only takes a single thoughtless word and the two tribes are at each other's throats again.

Glass Walkers

"I understand the value of using the Weaver's tools against the Wyrm. But what if we suspect that the Weaver is a potentially bigger threat to Gaia than the Wyrm? If only more of our tribe asked themselves that question."

–Elizabeth Genereader

Wherever there are cities, there are Glass Walkers. As a result, they are the most widespread and possibly the most numerous tribe in Europe.

During the Renaissance, the tribe's focus was on the cities of Italy that ignited the cultural advances that swept the continent. In the last century, though, the focus of corporate activity in Europe has largely moved to two cities: London, England and Frankfurt, Germany. Naturally, the Glass Walkers followed.

The growing financial integration of the European Union countries has been a boon for the Corporate Wolves. Multiple septs of Glass Walkers all across the continent, and even further afield if need be, can mobilize against a Wyrm-tainted company without any of them ever having to leave their offices. The single European currency, the Euro, and its benefits and dangers is a point of debate among the CEOs of the various Glass Walker-funded and run companies.

Frau Zalewsky, chairman of the Frankfurt-based Wirken & Weben GmbH & Co. KG, has long been a proponent of the Euro. She argues that it facilitates co-operation between members of the tribe in different countries, making it harder for Pentex to trace its attackers through the financial markets.

Her most vocal opponent is Charles Meadwell, a Philodox and CEO of Fenestre Holdings, a company with offices in London, Manchester and Oslo. He argues that currency speculation and exchange rates are a valuable tool, especially in hostile takeovers and that the Euro removes those weapons from the financial armory.

New Markets

The Glass Walkers are finally getting the foothold in Eastern Europe they have long sought. The strength of the Shadow Lords in the region in the last century or so coupled with the problems posed in getting a foothold in communist-run economies had made it difficult for the Glass Walkers to have any great influence, until now.

With most of the former communist countries throwing their doors wide open to foreign investors in a bid to kick-start their economies, the tribe has walked right into many of the major cities of the region. The Shadow Lords have enough on their plates in the Carpathians and the Balkans that they have done nothing about it, as yet.

The greater threat has been Pentex subsidiaries trying to do just the same. It's a battle many Corporate Wolves and City Farmers enjoy fighting.

Life on the Street

Of course, it's not all boardroom battles. With Bone Gnawers relatively scarce in Europe (thanks to past emigrations to the Americas), it's up to the Glass Walkers to deal with the Wyrm's growing influence on many cities with only minimal aid.

A pack loosely attached to Charles Meadwell's Fenestre Holdings was successful in cleansing the site of the Millennium Dome on the Greenwich Peninsula in London early last year. The site, a former gasworks earmarked for the UK's largest millennium project, was the most heavily contaminated piece of land in Europe. Despite heavy opposition from Wakshaani and H'rugglings, the pack was able to hold the site long enough for the Fenestre Sept's Master of the Rite to perform a rite that cleansed the land.

As pressure grows across Europe for greater development of similarly abandoned industrial sites, young Glass Walkers have to become more proactive in driving out the Wyrm-taint before the builders move in. Otherwise, their problems just grow as the Banes start corrupting the construction workers and eventually the new development's occupants, providing a steady supply of fomori to further the Wyrm's aims.

Still, the number of fomori on the streets of Europe's cities is growing at a frightening rate, and increasingly the hard-pressed Garou are merely dealing with the symptoms and not the cause of the corruption.

The Flip Side

There are two other losses showing on the tribe's European balance sheet.

Italy, once the tribe's stronghold, is rapidly becoming a problem. The Glass Walkers' influence within the Mafia is not what it once was. The Kinfolk that they had strategically placed in the most powerful families have slowly been weeded out and "retired."

The tribe is actively seeking a way of reestablishing its power base, with little success as yet.

Two major European cities — Vienna and Venice — remain almost completely inaccessible to the tribe. Venice is off-limits due to an "understanding" reached with the vampires there. The dealings between the Glass Walkers and these insular vampires are fragile at best, but they often lead to quiet secret swapping about the corporations under Pentex's banner. This agreement remains a dirty little secret, one that the Glass Walkers sincerely hope the other tribes never find out about.

In Vienna, Garou rarely survive long. The resident Leeches seem to be able to detect and hunt-down werewolves with disturbing ease. Rather than lose any more packs, the tribe has chosen to handle its business there in a different manner: their corporate operations in both cities are generally handled by Kinfolk.

The Weaver's Call

The biggest single worry comes from within the tribe, though. The Glass Walkers of Belgium, the Netherlands and areas of France and Germany are becoming altogether too close to the Weaver for their tribemates' comfort. The Cyber Dogs camp of the tribe almost completely dominate the region and they embrace technology to an unhealthy degree. Glass Walkers from other European septs have noticed a marked tendency for them to call upon Weaver-spirits rather than Gaian spirits during their rites.

The more traditional members of the tribe are torn as to the best course of action. Using the Weaver's tools against the Wyrm is one thing. Embracing the Weaver herself is quite another. Still, acting against members of one's own tribe rather goes against the grain and they don't seem to be doing that much harm yet, argue the elders.

In the meantime, more and more of the younger members of the tribe accept the enhancements the Cyber Dogs offer. By the time the tribal elders decide to act against the Cyber Dogs, they may well find themselves in the minority.

A small group of younger werewolves, an uneasy mix of members of the Urban Primitives and Random Interrupts camps, aren't prepared to let this happen. Frustrated with their elders' indecision, they are starting to make overtures to the other tribes hoping to nip the problem in the bud.

Elizabeth Genereader, a young Dutch Philodox, sounded out an acquaintance among the Shadow Lords and discussed the problem with her. One thing led to another, as it so often does when one deals with the Shadow Lords, and several months later she found herself deep in the Carpathians talking to a grizzled old Theurge. Out of her depth and out of her element, she has begun to suspect that she may have made a mistake that will cost the tribe dearly.

Shadow Lords

"The Garou of America are weak, merciful and laughable. Let us show them how the warriors of Gaia really fight. First we shall win the war on our own soil. Then, perhaps, we will deign to rescue our cousins."

— Margrave Yuri Konietzko

The Shadow Lords have known nothing but war for centuries. From their holdings in Eastern Europe, they war continually with the twisted vampires that haunt the Carpathian Mountains.

From the Sept of the Night Sky near the Danube in northern Hungary, Margrave Yuri Konietzko conducts endless campaigns against the Leeches with a ruthlessness that chills even his fellow Lords. His frustration at being unable to destroy a fortress of vampire wizards that has stood for centuries burns fiercely and he takes revenge on every group of vampires that can be found. Only one thing matters to the Margrave: winning. The war was going well for him, too, until the latter half of the last decade.

As the atrocities in the Balkans grew worse, slowly the Margrave found himself fighting a war on two fronts: the vampires in the Carpathians and the fomori and Banes swarming out of the former Yugoslavia to the southwest.

On top of that, the tribe is also trying to deal with the growing number of Wyrm-tainted foreign companies that are investing in the Eastern European territories that the Shadow Lords claim as their own. Rooting out such insidious threats is far more time-consuming and challenging than simply tearing apart a band of vampires.

The prospect of fighting on multiple fronts intimidates even the Margrave. No Shadow Lord wins as much respect from the tribe as Konietzko without seeing ways of turning any situation to his advantage. All the native tribes of Europe face major threats. If he can be the werewolf that unites them against their enemies, what renown could be his?

His careful overtures to the Black Furies and Red Talons have met with success. The three tribes have been cooperating successfully and are just beginning to turn the tide in the Balkans. The next step is to try and bring the Fianna on board. While their new Ard Righ has proved difficult to deal with, younger members of the tribe seem more accommodating.

Konietzko Ascendant

Konietzko has called a moot to address the threats facing all the local tribes as well as the issues raised by the sudden collapse of the Shadow Curtain. Representatives of all the European tribes have agreed to attend, even the normally insular Get of Fenris. Of course, Konietzko, always the astute politician, has already thrashed out the details of his deals with the majority of the other tribes well in advance. The moot is merely for show.

The one exception has been the Glass Walkers, who refuse to communicate with the other tribes in anything more than a perfunctory manner. Since 1999, however, a young Glass Walker has been in covert communication with the Margrave. Through her he has learned that the Glass Walkers' silence has a deeper reason than normal intertribal hostilities: the Glass Walkers have their own problems. He now knows that the European Glass Walkers are on the verge of tearing themselves apart. Those resident in the Eurohub have come to identify with the Weaver to such a degree that they have lost the trust of their own tribemates.

The Margrave has yet to decide what to do with this information. Odds are, though, that he will find a way to twist it to his advantage.

While Alpha Acts, Beta Learns

Across the continent, Shadow Lord advisors are watching, learning and judging. They note those whose beliefs and temperament are likely to prove helpful to the Margrave's cause and quietly act as their patrons. Werewolves from other tribes who show a little too much insight or distrust of the Shadow Lords' overtures are quietly sidelined by a quiet word in the appropriate ear.

The Judges of Doom have been seen at more and more moots across the continent as they winnow the corrupt from the ranks. Konietzko wants only strong, true Garou in his army.

Other Tribes

Bone Gnawers

Once among the most numerous tribes in Europe, a great portion of the Bone Gnawers simply up and left for the New World back in the 1920s and 30s. The population has slowly been growing again since then, but generally the tribe is found sparingly in Europe's largest cities and in some of the larger, dirtier towns.

The one exception to this seems to be London. While Gnawers were quite numerous there until the

From the perspective of the European Garou, it seems absolutely clear that the Apocalypse is imminent. There are precious few wild places left. The Weaver has almost completely conquered the Wyld on the continent, and in turn the Wyrm continues to corrupt her power base. Konietzko feels that the time has come for the Shadow Lords to stop playing Beta to the Silver Fangs and usurp the Alpha tribe position that they have coveted for so long.

He may just be the werewolf to do it. Few associate this lean, dangerous man in his 60s with the more devious reputation that his tribe has gained. The Fenrir respect his lust for battle, the Furies his even-handed dealings with women and the Fianna his lust for life. It's fairly easy for outsiders to notice the ruthless intelligence that burns behind his grizzled face — not so easy to realize the implications.

The Silver Fangs are the weakest they have ever been on the continent. House Austere Howl is all but gone and House Gleaming Eye has grown paranoid and insular. They no longer present a significant threat to Shadow Lord ambitions in Europe. America, though, is another story. Konietzko knows that King Jonas Albrecht has started to rebuild the Fangs' position in America in the last few years. If the Margrave is to challenge his rise, he must do something soon.

Luckily, Albrecht's most notable achievement to date, barring attaining the Silver Crown, is the destruction of the Seventh Generation. Despite entering the Silver Record, this victory has had little impact on the rank and file Garou in Europe. Few had heard of the Seventh Generation before it was destroyed and even fewer realized the insidious nature of the danger it presented.

Konietzko's first step was to get the support of his tribe worldwide. Large numbers of Shadow Lords from other parts of the world have been making their way to Hungary to gather under the Margrave's banner. This has given him the troops to support the other tribes on multiple fronts, building up debts that he eventually intends to call in.

If Konietzko can now unite the tribes in Europe and do some significant damage to one or more of the many threats facing them, he might yet become a serious contender for Albrecht in the contest to be the one to lead the Gaia's Warriors into the Final Battle.

He feels that now is the time to start winning some victories that will boost his Renown. The vampires of Eastern Europe seem to be weakening for the first time in centuries. While he does not know the cause for sure, he suspects that it has something to do with the recent freeing of the demon Kupala, which was heralded by a series of storms and earthquakes that shook most of the region known as Transylvania.

Kupala is a threat that has to be dealt with eventually, but for the time being the demon seems to be leaving the werewolves well alone. It has yet to approach anywhere near any of the Garou's caerns in the area. In fact, it is almost as if it was purposefully avoiding them.

The Garou are well aware of its presence in the lands of Europe once more as its passage corrupts the very it earth it moves through. Still, for the time being Konietzko prefers to focus on some of the lesser threats. The distracted bands of Leeches seem to be an obvious immediate target, as does whatever has been birthed in the Balkans.

When they are dealt with, then he may have a band of followers strong and experienced enough to take down Kupala and thus hand leadership of the Garou Nation to him.

mid-1990s, the majority of them were wiped out in a battle with an awakening ancient vampire several years ago. The tribe's numbers in this city have never really recovered.

Paris, by contrast, has a strong and thriving community of Gnawers. The tribe has cordial, if not close, relationships with the plague of Ratkin living in the city's sewers and the two groups exchange information on a regular basis.

However, even more than the Glass Walkers, the tribe suffers from the strength of the vampires in Europe. Many of the ancient monsters were hunting Garou when the present generation of Bone Gnawers' great-great-grandparents were cubs.

Children of Gaia

The Children of Gaia don't receive a warm welcome in many European caerns. Far too many septs are constantly at war for the Children's messages to be heard or appreciated. This never stops the Children from trying, though. The relative peace between the Italian Get of Fenris and Black Furies

is largely the unaccredited work of a small pack of Children who spent several months fighting alongside both tribes in the area, gently pointing out the similarities between the two tribes' agendas for the region. However, the Children have two major European Septs of their own: the Sept of Mountain Springs in Switzerland and the Sept of Tolerance on the outskirts of Brighton, England.

The Children are well represented in Ireland and the UK. Their counsel has been invaluable in helping the warring parts of the Fianna find peace with each other, even as Northern Ireland itself moves towards a peaceful resolution of the troubles.

Anne Scott, warder of the Brighton caern has caught word of the in-fighting between the Silver Fang Houses Austere Howl and Gleaming Eye, when a solitary survivor of Austere Howl's Dover caern escaped the slaughter and fled to Brighton. She has yet to decide on a plan of action.

A few of the Children tried to take an active role in the Balkan crisis that has plagued the continent over the last decade, with little success. Few members of the tribe who either traveled alone into the area or who ran with the Black Fury (and, very occasionally, Shadow Lord) packs that have investigated have returned. Now that the alliance between the Furies and the Lords has started to push the forces of the Wyrm back towards Serbia, the Children are doing their best to cleanse the land and the people. However, the task the tribe has set itself is not an easy one.

Konietzko is counting on the tribe's help in his forthcoming moot to try and cement some of the alliances he has already forged. To this end, he has taken the unprecedented step of leaving his Carpathian stronghold and traveling to the Swiss sept twice in the last year. The members of the sept remain wary, though. While his intentions seem honorable enough, they cannot bring themselves to trust a man so intent on finding violent solutions to every problem.

Red Talons

The rage of Europe's Red Talons burns with an intensity their counterparts elsewhere in the world struggle to match. They have seen their Kinfolk systematically and ruthlessly hunted out of existence across the continent. They have seen the Wyld places systematically built on, ploughed into fields, turned into the Weaver-laced parody of nature that humans call gardens or bound under a web of roads and rail. The tribe clings to its few remaining caerns deep in the mountains of northern Spain, in the center of Italy and the very eastern fringes of Europe: Finland, Poland, Slovakia, Hungary and Romania.

Three years ago, all communication ceased with the few septs that the Talons had in the Balkans. With considerable effort the tribe opened an attack moon bridge to the one of their caerns, deep in Serbia. Not a single member of the packs that went through returned.

Hard on the heels of that blow to the tribe came another sign that they had to act soon or lose Europe forever. A year ago a lone wolf, striking out into Scandinavia from Russia or Finland somehow found a mate and started breeding. The new pack was sighted by humans, and received coverage in the local media.

The response of the locals was swift and brutal: they did their best to kill all the cubs and very nearly succeeded. One of the cubs underwent its first change as its brothers and sisters were slaughtered and tore the hunters apart.

The frightened and confused cub was found by a pack of Talons and taken in by a Finnish sept. Its parents and their further litters were watched and protected from afar by packs from the sept. After all, they were Kinfolk.

The elders of the tribe met in secret shortly afterwards. They received an emissary from the Shadow Lords, who spoke of the humans' reaction to the slaughter and their calls for the remaining wolves to be hunted down. The emissary also spoke of her own tribe's growing intolerance of the humans and their despoiling ways. She spoke of the war in the Balkans and the damage humans were doing once more to Mother Gaia. She offered the help of the Shadow Lords in recovering the Talon's Balkan caerns and she made a surprising suggestion. The time had come, she said, to reinstate the Impergium. The Red Talon elders, while approving of the sentiment, refused to ally themselves with a tribe so thoroughly infused with a human concept like politics.

Then came the destruction of the river Tisza. A small Talon caern near the banks of the river fell to the Banes unleashed by the cyanide pollution. The Talons, furious at this massive desecration of nature by man, accepted the Shadow Lords' proposal.

In the months since, villages in northern Spain, isolated parts of Scandinavia and the rural areas of Eastern Europe have been "culled" by the tribe. With each strike the tribe grows more confident but the Veil wears a little bit thinner. Folk memories of werewolves run deep in the people of Europe and it wouldn't take much for the persecution of the few wild wolves remaining to start all over again.

Silent Striders

The wandering tribe has never had much time for Europe. Their traveling Kinfolk have been persecuted by the natives repeatedly throughout history, which hardly endears the continent to the Striders.

That said, the tribe's more aggressive stance on the Leech problem in recent years has seen more and more Silent Striders spending brief periods with septs of other tribes. They stay just long enough to help the sept destroy a vampire or two and then move on. There is no home to be found for a Silent Strider in Europe.

Silver Fangs

The Silver Fangs are in terminal decline in Europe, and have been for centuries. House Winter Snow's attempts to dominate the Fianna and Get of Fenris in the 17th century nearly handed England to the Black Spiral Dancers and destroyed much of the tribe's credibility in the eyes of European Garou. The house's fall went largely unmourned.

With the Shadow Curtain in place, the European Fangs were cut off from their Russian homelands and their descent from power accelerated. House Austere Howl, which replaced Winter Snow in the UK, slowly rotted from within. Its Kinfolk, infected with blood from Spiral Kinfolk, bred werewolves with a marked tendency to fall to the Wyrm. Queen Mary, the young Scottish Ahroun who rules the house, eventually fled her caern in Edinburgh to Tara in Ireland to beg the Ard Righ of the Fianna's help. More of her house had fallen to the Wyrm than the few remaining members could hope to deal with, she claimed. Reports had already reached the Council of Song that the Fang's Dublin caern had fallen to corruption and Mary was able to confirm that fallen members of her own house were to blame. The remaining members of Austere Howl fought alongside the Fianna to cleanse the caern and it remains their last holding.

However, Mary did not tell the Fianna the whole truth. House Gleaming Eye, whose stronghold is in France, has become obsessive in its hunt for Wyrm-corruption. Having purged the taint within its own ranks, it turned on Austere Howl, and declared the whole house Wyrm-tainted. The Dover and Bath caerns fell to that house's onslaught. Mary is counting on the Fianna to protect her house from outright destruction.

House Wise Heart has all but disappeared from Europe. However, a few members have recently reappeared in Greece, pledging their support to the Black Furies in dealing with the Wyrm beast that many suspect is gathering strength in Serbia.

A World of Rage

Stargazers

The Stargazers of Europe are surprisingly numerous, especially when the tribe's scant overall numbers are taken into account. Indeed, few of the other tribes realize quite how many of them there are throughout the continent. It's an easy mistake to make: they hold no caerns anywhere on the continent and rarely stay long with any local sept.

Instead, the Stargazers choose to live in the cities of Europe, close to the spirits of the Weaver, which many members of the tribe see as the Garou's true enemy. Members of both the Klaital Puk and Ouroborans camps can be found throughout the Eurohub area. There they watch and learn the ways of their enemy. Few places on earth offer such an extensive area so calcified into the web.

The tribe does recognize the danger of so many of its members spending much of their time in close proximity to the Weaver, though. At least twice a year, all members of the tribe who can be contacted travel to one of the few Wyld places left in Europe. Once they have centered themselves fully once more, they return to their meditations in the great cities of Europe.

Uktena

An Uktena in a European caern is a rare sight indeed. However, these ever-curious Garou do travel the world, drawn by their desire for knowledge. A handful has traveled to Scotland and the Balkans, and serves as advisors to the Garou efforts to deal with the growing Wyrm-infestations in those lands. After all, few know Banes like this tribe and both lands have Banes aplenty.

Runs-the-Sky, an elderly Theurge, has been quietly collecting tales of the recent battles in Scotland from the Fianna and Fenrir Galliards and has made a worrisome connection. All took place after the red star, Anthelios, first appeared in the Umbral skies. What this portends, he doesn't yet know, but he intends to find out and is slowly winning the trust of packs in the area to further his aim.

Wendigo

It is doubtful that there have ever been more than two or three members of this tribe in Europe at the same time. What reason have the members of the Wendigo for visiting the homelands of the Wyrmcomers? They have their hands full fighting corruption on the other side of the Atlantic Ocean. Let the Europeans fight their own battles.

Other Changing Breeds

Europe was the primary battleground of the War of Rage. Here the Changing Breeds felt the rage of the Garou most keenly, and here most died. The Grondr, wereboars who were Gaia's cleaners and groomers, had their last stand on the continent.

One group of Bastet, the European Qualmi, was destroyed utterly. The few remaining Spanish Lynx show no trace of being Kinfolk to the tribe. Indeed, the handful that survive now teeter on the brink of extinction. The rest of the Bastet retired from the continent to safer lands elsewhere.

In the centuries since, the heavy presence of the Garou and the sheer number of powerful, old vampires prowling Europe's nights have been enough to dissuade the Changing Breeds from trying to return.

Only the Ceilican tribe returned to the continent, and then only for their annual Samhain revel on the Scottish moors. This may have proved their undoing, though. The last revel was disrupted unexpectedly by a huge force of Black Spiral Dancers and fomori. While the Ceilican fought with a fury that their wildcat Kin would be proud of, most died. A few were captured. Some of the captives chose to serve the Wyrm. Most died — eventually.

The European Gurahl were hunted down mercilessly long ago. Very few survived long enough to participate in the werebears' withdrawal from the world. Still, a very few Gurahl have started to emerge from their caves in the Alps, Pyrenees and even the Carpathians. Their numbers are even more limited than in other parts of the world and they steer well clear of the werewolves.

Perhaps the only other shapeshifters to be found in any numbers in Europe are the Corax and Ratkin. Corax are range across the continent, with a particular stronghold in London. The Tower of London has long served as meeting point for the children of Raven, as well as a point of contact between them and the restless dead.

The Ratkin, meanwhile, infest nearly every city on the continent. Deep under Paris, on the edge of the Eurohub, resides Madame DeFarge, the Great-Grandmere of Europe. From the sewers of the city she directs her children in their efforts to bring the chaos of the Wyld back to an ever more Weaver-ridden Europe.

Coyotes, of course, are never found outside zoos, but persistent rumors place a Nuwisha in Scotland. A few Corax have even claimed that he plays in a pipeband, but nobody believes a word of that.

The Forces of the Wyrm

The Wyrm recognizes no political boundaries in its relentless corruption of The Realm. While three principal regions of Europe are particular foci for its minion's efforts at the moment, they don't represent any grand scheme for the corruption of Europe. They are merely a few more pieces in a worldwide picture.

However, lest we forget, the continent was the scene of one of its great successes: the fall of an entire tribe of werewolves.

Black Spiral Dancers

"There's no place like home. There's no place like home. Soon, there will be no place like home."
— Mnn'ger, Scots Black Spiral Ragabash

The Black Spirals were born in Europe. While they are now so pervasive throughout the world that they have long left the concept of homeland behind, they have a significant presence all over the continent. Still, Scotland was the land of their birth and they have recently returned there in great numbers. This return has nothing to do with anything as sentimental as a desire to come home, though.

For months the greatest of their Theurges all over the world were granted recurring visions of a creature stirring under the waters of a great lake. Eventually they made the connection between that and legends of Cirigh the Crest-Headed, a great servitor of the Wyrm that the tribe summoned in the early days after it entered the Corrupter's service.

The combined efforts of the Fianna, the Silver Fangs and the Fenrir drove the malevolent creature, which they knew as Árd Cruimh Beithíoch, back to the Mile-Deep Loch more than 1,500 years ago. The Black Spiral's Theurges interpret the recent visions as signs that Cirigh is close to waking once more and that they should do everything in their power to help it.

Francesco, the tribe's representative on the Pentex board was able to press for aggressive Endron expansion into the North Sea oil industry. Packs from all over the world converged on Scotland to help the few Dancers who remained there — mostly Cluithi — take back two caerns they had lost centuries ago. These were the Gloom and Sorrow Caern, set between the two burns (a Scots name for river) of the same name in the Ochils and the long-abandoned Night's Eye Caern near Caithness. The bawn of the latter was being used on a yearly basis by a tribe of werecats, as it had been since the Spirals were forced to abandon it centuries ago. The name Caithness, ironically, means "cat people".

The next step, obviously, is to deal with the packs that keep watch on Mile-Deep Loch. The Spirals are

busy gathering the intelligence and numbers necessary to make their assault work.

The Balkans

The misery, terror and death that nearly a decade of violence has wrought in the Balkans has turned it into a breeding ground for servants of the Wyrm. Banes, from Kalus to Psychomachie, flocked to the area, drawn by the misery that the humans inflict on each other.

The despair the victims feel and the callousness of many of the soldiers on all sides of the conflict have driven many to fall prey to Banes and be reborn as fomori. A good portion of the desertions from the armies involved is the result of these new fomori transferring to serve under new generals in the Wyrm's legions.

A bigger problem faces the Garou, though. The centuries of conflict here have steadily been feeding Jo'cllath'mattric, a servant of Beast-of-War that was defeated millennia ago and bound deep in the earth of the land now called Serbia. The decade-long feast of suffering it has been served up has awakened it. It has sensed the birth of a new like-minded creature in the aftermath of the Tisza disaster and is attempting to contact it. The Tisza spirit has more than enough power to disrupt the millennia-old wards holding Jo'cllath'mattric.

When it does so, even Konietzko's nascent alliance may not be able to stand against it.

The Black Forest

The Get speculate wildly as to the reason the Black Spirals seem to be so determined to take the Sept of the Blood Fist. They little suspect the truth. Cratt'ath, a Black Spiral Ahroun, is the bearer of a Wyrm fetish called the Blightseed. This rotted acorn seed has the ability to turn even the most powerful caern into a Blight. It also torments the holder with visions that drive him to attempt to capture the nearest caern so it can fulfill its purpose.

What Cratt'ath doesn't realize is that it would give him similar visions of any caern he was in close proximity to. He hasn't strayed far from the Schwarzwald in the last five years and so he hasn't had the opportunity to discover this. He remains obsessed with the idea that the Wyrm wants him to take this caern at all costs, and he won't rest until he does so.

His reputation has spread far through the tunnels and Hives of his tribe, and he is rarely short of willing warriors to take part in this great crusade. It is only a matter of time before he is victorious.

Pentex

Where there is demand, Pentex will supply in its own, unique fashion. In Europe it has found a market of ever-growing demands. As an example, Europeans hunger for junk food just as much as Americans. O'Tolley's was quick to capitalize on that, expanding into the UK in the 1970s under the brand name Mr. Burger. From there it has made significant in-roads into mainland Europe.

The megacorporation's newest target is the emerging economies of the former communist countries on the eastern end of Europe. While still poor compared to most European countries, their populations hunger for western brands and goods as status symbols.

Indeed, the new commercial markets in Eastern Europe have proven to be a major business opportunity for Pentex, which has always found gaining a foothold in Europe a slow, frustrating business. Its subsidiaries have been quick to invest money where European companies have been reluctant to do so. Consolidex Worldwide's Real Estate Investment Trust has been pumping money into building developments such as new office blocks and shopping centers in many cities, including Budapest, Bucharest and Bratislava. The construction methods used in the building of these schemes seem to involve unhealthy amounts of chemicals being used to "seal the foundations." Still, the Americans must know what they're doing, right? They've been building schemes like this over there for decades and must know the best way of doing it.

A quick peek into the Penumbra quickly puts paid to that argument. The developments become the core of Blights, which rapidly spread to infect surrounding areas. Sometimes Weaver and Wyrm-spirits fight for control of the territory. More often, a twisted fusion of both emerges.

Endron Oil has invested heavily in the North Sea oil fields over the last few years, with predictable results for the aquatic life and the surrounding shorelines. The ever more frequent "accidents" which release crude oil into the sea have finally come to the attention of the Rokea, who are occasionally seen in waters around northern Europe.

Black Dog Games' products are sold mainly through specialty stores in the UK. However, they are even more popular on mainland Europe, particularly in France and Spain, where local companies sell translated versions and produce original material under license. Both of the companies, incidentally, are partially owned by Vesuvius, Inc., yet another Pentex subsidiary.

King Breweries products are brewed under license by many breweries across the continent. One brand of lager, King's Special, while a very small seller in the US, has become the drink of choice of football fans at soccer matches throughout Europe. The secret added extras that the license agreements with King specify as part of the production process might well have something to do with the hooliganism that afflicts many matches. Garou have certainly noted an unusual number of fomori who chant the names of football teams as they attack.

Leeches

The vampires are also an ever-present threat. Many are old and terrible compared to their New World counterparts. Europe's cities hold the lairs of vampires that were ancient when the oldest Elder Garou's great-grandparent was a pup. These canny and powerful monsters have centuries of experience in surviving and, on the rare occasions when they're forced into physical confrontations, more than enough raw power to back up that experience.

Several years ago a single vampire was able to destroy several packs of Fianna and Bone Gnawers in central London. Swift action by a pack of Glass Walkers that arrived on the scene just too late to participate in the battle dealt with the evidence, including nearly a dozen Garou corpses. Thanks to the Delirium, the few witnesses around Charing Cross Road in the wee small hours were left with memories of a particularly vicious fight between gangs of drunken football fans. The fate of the creature is still unknown and the Glass Walkers of the city are nervously making preparations for its reappearance.

It is incidents like this that cause most of the tribes to leave the cities to the Glass Walkers and Bone Gnawers. After all, there are plenty of other Wyrmspawn to be dealt with before these Leeches. This is, naturally, shortsighted in the extreme. As the cities grow, and many members of the urban tribes avoid picking fights with these ancient predators, the vampires are winning by default. Each new housing estate or out of town business park takes a little more territory from the Garou and hands it to the vampires.

However, even in the countryside one can't avoid the undead entirely. The Shadow Lords have been fighting a group of Leeches that live in and around the Carpathian Mountains for as long as they have been in the lands. Neither side has yet gained a clear advantage over the other.

As they finally destroy one vampire lord and his offspring, another seems to rise in another part of Eastern Europe. Skirmishes between packs of Garou

and gangs of twisted, vicious young vampires are common. Many rites of passage for young werewolf packs focus on dealing with such gangs by fair means or foul.

In the far north, feral vampires are common, many of whom wander through the forests and mountains of the region. The Get of Fenris take great delight in testing their strength and combat skill against them and even greater delight in tearing apart every last one they can get their claws on.

Russia

I cannot forecast you the actions of Russia. It is a riddle wrapped in a mystery inside an enigma.

— Winston Churchill

Massive in size and ethnically diverse, Russia's werewolf population is at once alien and recognizable to Western Garou. Long a bastion of the Wyld in a world increasingly enthralled by the Weaver, for centuries Russia's Garou succeeded in isolating the country from the changes in the West, maintaining its idyllic rural splendor far longer than any other European power. All this changed rapidly and with cataclysmic results over the last 80 years, however, making Russia one of the most polluted and Wyrm tainted countries in the world. The story of this fall is both tragic and immense in scope. With the appearance of the Shadow Curtain and the rise of Baba Yaga in the early 1990s, Russia's supernatural activities occurred behind an invisible wall, disappearing almost completely from the world stage — until now.

History
Beginnings

Slavic tribes first migrated to Russia from the West in large numbers during the 5th century AD. Scandinavian chieftains established the first Russian State during the 9th century in Novgorod and the Kieven Rus (modern day Ukraine). The first major figure to unify the Rus was a chief named Rurik, Kinfolk to the Fenrir. This caused conflict between the Fenrir and the Silver Fangs, who saw Russia as their domain, a conflict not resolved until many years later when Silver Fang Kinfolk ascended to the throne of the tsars. Rurik's descendant, Oleg, moved the capitol to Kiev, attacked Constantinople in 941 and subsequently signed a treaty in 944. This began commerce between the Rus and the Byzantine Empire and, not inconsequentially, opened Russia to vampiric powers from the West. From that time forth, much of Russian Garou history has found them at odds with the vampires, or *upyr* (to use the Russian name). The growing interna-

The Zmei

Some say the Zmei are the most terrible and destructive Wyrm-things to take physical form. The horrible thing is that this claim cannot be easily disproved. The Great Zmei are dragons of the Wyrm, monsters that were summoned into the world long ago to do battle with a hideously powerful enemy. There were seven of them then: Gregornous, Rustarin, Trevera, Sharkala, Shazear, Illyana and Goluko. Over the years, the Russian Garou were able to slay one — Sharkala — and bind the rest, although at great cost. The Zmei were — and are — that powerful.

And now, rumor has it, as many as four of the six surviving Zmei have awakened — and they seek to wake the rest.

Statistics for the Zmei are not given; even one of these monsters is capable of challenging, even destroying the Silver Pack itself. They should be exactly as terrifying as the Storyteller sees fit — they are, after all, the vanguard of the Apocalypse.

---

tionalism of early Kieven Rus also drew attention from the Shadow Lords in Eastern Europe and from among the Mongol hordes, who invaded in the 13th century. Finally, trade along the Dnieper River increased the size, opulence and sophistication of Russia's cities, opening the door for the Warders.

The decline of Kiev, and the rise of Novgorod as the center of Russian commerce and culture, did not significantly change the balance of power between the Garou tribes except to increase the Silver Fangs' hold on the most desirable Kinfolk. The Silver Fang Kinfolk Ivan IV, also known as Ivan the Terrible, was the first to officially hold the title of tsar in 1547. Ivan IV personified, to some, what later became an all too common conundrum about the Fangs themselves. Greatly expanding Russian territory and influence during his early reign, the madness of his later years killed over 50,000 people.

Peter the Great (1682-1725) extended the Rus and in 1721 founded the imperial dynasty. As Russia's greatness grew, and Peter accepted foreign ideas, a second wave of alien *upyr* sought to capture the aristocracy. Although the Warders benefited greatly from the Weaver's increased presence, the Wyrm too found a new and more commodious home in a modernizing Russia. Silver Fang influence continued to wane, culminating in ultimate disgrace when the vampiric pawn, Catherine the Great, ascended the throne. Seeing enemies at every turn and prey to

their growing madness, the Silver Fangs spiraled further and further out of control. Each successive regime became weaker throughout the remaining 19th century. Little did they know that it was a mere prelude for what was to come.

The 20th Century

Westernization and modernization spread throughout the Russian Empire during the 19th and early 20th centuries, but the imperial powers refused to change with the times, stifling such Western philosophies as democratization and limiting industrialization (largely due to Silver Fang influence). While this limited the Weaver, and hence the Wyrm's, growth during the 1800s, by the 20th century all bets were off. Major losses in the Russo-Japanese War of 1905 and the First World War weakened the tsarist regime and, with it, the Silver Fangs who sank into brooding inaction. Some believe that Rasputin, the mad monk who held the royal family under his sway, was a ghoul who became Embraced in the nights before or after his death. Since several vampires claim to be Rasputin, it is difficult to determine which, if any of them, is telling the truth. What is generally undisputed, however, is that his assassin, a noble dandy named Felix Yusupov, was Silver Fang Kinfolk. Before his death on December 16, 1916, however, Rasputin predicted that if he was murdered, the royal family would soon follow. This prophecy came all too true.

Revolution and Terror (1917-41)

In 1917 a series of revolts quickly lead to revolution and the abdication of Czar Nicholas II, ending 1000 years of Silver Fang dominance. A provisional government lead by Prince Georgi Lvov in April fell to the May government of Alexander Kerensky, followed by a Communist coup led by Vladimir Ilyich Lenin in November. The Bone Gnawers and Shadow Lords lost little time capitalizing on these events to the Silver Fangs' disadvantage. The Wyrm's minions, especially those among the Black Spiral Dancers, took advantage of the royal confusion to launch a series of attacks against Garou interests throughout the war-ravaged land. Pulling disparate tribes together, the Fangs launched some effective counterattacks but stumbled badly while raiding a Black Spiral caern at the Children of Gaia's behest. The werewolves fell afoul of the Zmei Shazear. The resulting carnage of this battle weakened many tribes for years to come and permanently damaged the House of the Crescent Moon's reputation as infallible war leaders. Some also believe that the Children of Gaia's role in unwittingly leading the Fangs into the Wyrm's trap sealed their fate.

Lenin's death in 1924 resulted in a bloody power struggle in which Joseph Stalin emerged triumphant. Throughout the late 1930s Stalin's growing paranoia led to a series of show trials, during which he purged the government, the military and civil society. This period, widely known as the Terror, resulted in millions of deaths. Stalin's brutality, combined with his determination to turn Russia into a modern mechanized society, virtually guaranteed that anything built by the Weaver would become fodder for the Wyrm.

The Great Patriotic War (1941-45)

Despite a 1939 non-aggression pact, Nazi Germany launched a massive invasion of the Soviet Union in June 1941. Early Nazi gains tore the poorly led Soviet army to shreds, killing or capturing millions of soldiers in the war's earliest months and coming within kilometers of Moscow. The Soviet army traded territory for time, at first giving way before the Nazi Blitzkrieg. Germany's military machinery soon encountered stiff Soviet resistance and ground to a halt in the Russian winter. The Garou had little decisive influence over the war's direction, their fortunes rising and falling along with everyone else's. Still, patriotic Garou played their part. It is a common truism that, during the 900 day Siege of Leningrad, people were reduced to eating shoe leather, rodents and the paste from wallpaper. Although thousands died of starvation, many more would have perished if the Bone Gnawers hadn't used their Gifts to make the food more nourishing. Similarly, though the Get of Fenris are often thought to have fought for the Nazis, Russian-Varangian Fenrir were among the fiercest partisans in the war and distrust the German variety to this day. Russian winter counter-strikes in 1941-42 and 1942-43, stopped the German advance. During the battle for Stalingrad (now Volgograd), the German 6th Army surrendered to the Soviet forces, ending Hitler's plans for Russia and marking the turning point in the war.

Cold War (1946-87)

After World War II the Soviet Union instituted the infamous "Iron Curtain" over Russia and the land gains they made during the war. The Soviet-Bloc included Poland, Czechoslovakia, Hungary, Romania, Bulgaria and Eastern Germany, all of which fell under Russian rule. Russia saw this as a much-needed buffer zone; many in the West saw it as naked aggression. Under cover of this expansion, the Russian Brujah were able to increase their holdings. The most notable development during this time from a werewolf perspective, however, was Stalin's explosion of an atomic bomb in Kazakhstan on August 29, 1949.

Howls of rage rose up from the werewolves of Russia, especially among the Red Talons, at such a Wyrm-fetid device being exploded on "Russian" soil. Instead of blaming the Wyrm or Joseph Stalin, however, they turned their collective wrath on the Children of Gaia, who had always counseled a path of coexistence with man. Few Children of Gaia now live in Russia; the survivors hide among the Glass Walkers and the Bone Gnawers. Silver Fang reticence to act at this crucial moment may have been, in part, a result of their own bad feelings toward the Gaians for their poor council in the Shazear debacle during the 1917 Revolution. Regardless, this became the final proof in many Garou's eyes that the Fangs were unfit to lead.

Nikita Khruschev replaced Stalin in 1953 and instituted a number of limited reforms. While actively seeking co-existence with the West, Khruschev continued to enlarge the Soviet Union's military stockpile. Deposed in a coup in 1964, Khruschev lost power to Leonid Brezhnev who held power throughout the 60s and 70s. Soviet power reached its apex and began its inexorable fall with the ill-considered invasion of Afghanistan in 1979 (often called "Russia's Vietnam"). Following Brezhnev's death in 1982, two

---

Kursk (1943)

While many in the West remember such battles as D-Day, the size, casualties and sheer scope of the Russian theatre dwarfed anything in the West. At the outset of Operation Citadel and the Battle of Kursk (July 1943), the German Wehrmacht had, in all, amassed almost 1,000,000 men, over 2,500 tanks and SPGs, 10,000 field guns and 2,000 aircraft. In a single battle all this was arrayed against 977,000 Soviets, 3300 tanks, 20,000 field guns and 3,000 aircraft. In total, over 7,000 tanks and other self-propelled weapons rolled into a 100 by 80-mile salient around Kursk, resulting in the largest tank battle in history and *the* decisive battle in the European Theatre. The Nazis' most elite tank corps, which had overrun the rest of Europe virtually unopposed only two years before, were mangled beyond repair in a battle which Hitler admitted made his "stomach turn over." Kursk also became famous to the Garou for a far different reason. Whether it was by coincidence or design, the battle raged over the Umbral prison/lair of the Zmei Gregornous. The combined bloodshed and the mystical machinations between two potent mages awoke the Zmei from his ancient slumber.

A World of Rage

lusterless politburo politicians took the fore in rapid succession (the timid reformer Andropov 1982-84 and the old-guard Chernenko 1984-85), ending with the ascension of Mikhail Gorbachev in 1985.

In 1987 Gorbachev inaugurated a series of reforms, including increased freedoms and democratization of the political process (glasnost) and economic restructuring (perestroika). He also reached a rapprochement with the West, effectively ending the Cold War. A number of old hard-liners — including the vampiric manipulators in the Kremlin — opposed these reforms. Major economic dislocation and ethnic unrest in the republics soon made Gorbachev's position untenable.

Having long since learned the secret of survival in the Soviet Union, Russian Garou were content to sit and await events. They did not have long to wait. In the late winter of 1990, Baba Yaga awoke…

The Terror 1991-99
Twilight (1991-93)

It began in the small hours of August 18th, 1991. While Gorbachev was on vacation in the Crimea, a clique of Soviet insiders placed him under arrest and attempted to gain control of the crumbling Soviet Union by force. Tanks surrounded the Russian White House and prepared to fire on the purge's resistors. Hordes of ordinary Russian citizens took to the streets to defend their new won freedoms. Unsure about firing on their own people, the coup-plotters' military units stood immobilized on August 19th as Boris Yeltsin stood astride a tank and declared that he, as the recently popularly elected President of the newly formed Union of Soviet States, was taking command of the military. Within two days the coup collapsed, leading to the arrest of the putschists, the ousting of Mikhal Gorbachev and the dissolution of the Soviet Union. Only three Russian citizens were killed in this near bloodless revolt. As dramatic as these events were, the clandestine revolution that took place behind the scenes was far more deadly.

An invisible horror stalked the night streets of Moscow. Visiting government dachas, fortified military and KGB strongholds, and public museums alike, the Baba Yaga and her minions purged almost every prominent upyr in the city in a matter of three nights. Russia's werewolves saw nothing of the struggle — but the adversary was not completely invisible. Early in the conflict the Silent Striders had seen the first clouds of the gathering storm and had warned the other tribes to little avail. Now, as they frantically scrambled to uncover the enemy's movements, the horror stalked them individually. By the end of the war the Striders would have made an invaluable contribution, but they would also pay a heavy price.

It was not long before Russian Garou began to realize that something was very wrong indeed. In early 1992 the Gauntlet became mysteriously stronger and more treacherous, largely cutting the Garou off from the Penumbra and the rest of the world. This barrier was quickly termed the "Shadow Curtain," and its effects were crippling. Certain caerns began to flutter, falter and die — although not all, to be sure, and not at once. While other caerns across the country were drained of their Gnosis and septs devastated by Bane attacks, the Glass Walkers and the Bone Gnawers went about their business, seemingly unscathed. This did not go unnoticed, especially by the Red Talons who were under increasing pressure by well-armed hunt teams consisting of both vampires and human mages. The whispered campaign against the Glass Walkers was at least partially traceable to the Shadow Lords, who could not resist the opportunity to weaken their urban rivals. The hostile tribes charged that the Glass Walkers, with their alien Weaver-spun ways, had sold out Russia's Garou and had made dark pacts with whatever power was draining the caerns. The Glass Walkers' relations with the Talons continued to worsen until the two were almost openly at war.

Night (1994-96)

After consolidating her power over the upyr and erecting her Shadow Curtain, the Baba Yaga now turned her baleful gaze upon the werewolves. Starting in 1994 she commenced a major offensive against those whom she saw as descendants of her hated enemies — the ancient bogatyrs. In a series of audacious lightning strikes, the hag decimated several of the weakened and divided septs. The attacks were methodical, concentrated and utterly effective, leaving dead in their wake many of Russia's best and bravest Garou. Where her forces encountered resistance, it was in small pockets that soon fell before the concentrated strength of her "armies." Loss after loss weakened the Garou Nation as several tribes bore the brunt of her fury. Despite their outward strength, Russia's ruling triumvirate of tribes — the Silver Fangs, Get of Fenris and Black Furies — quickly found themselves under siege. Hardly a month went by when each tribe didn't lose some valued member or another. The other tribes: divided, embittered by years of misrule or simply playing it safe, were reluctant to come to their aid.

Silver Fang leadership seemed to be comprised of a group not unlike one would have expected to find during the early times of legends. Chief among these were Chases-Street-Demons (heroic wielder of the Twin Swords of Lothair), Piotr Volk (legendary leader of the great Sept of the Crescent Moon) and Arkady (who possessed the purest blood and keenest claws the family had seen in generations). Also, with such allied military luminaries as Mother's Pride of the Furies, Anton Nordenskald of the Fenrir and Chien Sun of the Stargazers advising the Fangs and — other tribes prayed — monitoring their madness, the werewolves still had a reasonable hope of victory. Other signs were less hopeful. Arkady had miraculously escaped the

Baba Yaga, the Wyld and the Wyrm

Before the tsars, before the Kievan princes or even the earliest tribal chieftains, there was the Baba Yaga. Sorceress, teacher and healer, she was as one with Gaia and wandered the land, attending its manifold hurts and sicknesses. In the silent night of the early world, however, a shadow fell upon her, devouring her light and turning her mind to darker pursuits. Though still a creature of the wilderness at heart, she now found that those creatures and spirits who once listened to her song now fled before her in stark terror. In the hour of her despair a cool, sibilant and soothing voice told her how the Wyld would once more serve and adore her — for a price.

In the hag, the Wyrm soon found an ally every bit as amenable to its corruption as the early artificers of the Weaver. The Baba Yaga, however, was no mere pawn to be bent to the Wyrm's will. A truly ancient being with power nearing that of a Maeljin Incarna, she was a creature of the Wyld, corrupt true, but with her own vision of Russia's future. The Garou were, at least once, part of that future. As the hag's agents approached them, however, most violently rejected her overtures, seeing her as an abomination to Gaia. Since that time, the hag did not wholly give up trying to gather her errant "children" to her side, though those who refused her provoked her wrath. Creatures of Gaia as she once was, the Garou were nevertheless impediments to her vision of Russia. They would convert or die.

Shadow Curtain and sought aid among the American Fangs of House Wyrmfoe, only to be rebuffed. Despite the horrors he knew he would face upon his return, he dutifully came back to Russia with his sorrowful news. The Russian Garou could expect no help from the decadent families of the West; they were on their own.

In the time-honored tradition of Russian warfare, the Garou traded territory for time, losing several caerns and many lives as they sought to organize themselves into a cohesive fighting force. Defeats mounted, but by late 1995 the Fangs and their allies had built the foundation for survival and a counter offensive. Still, all was not well among them. The Wyrm of Corruption fed on the leadership's Harano and despair. Most deeply bitten was Piotr Volk. Ancestor spirits had spoken of the Firebird Crystal, a mighty tribal artifact reputedly lost to the Dark Umbra. Volk's every waking hour fixated on the item and he diverted some of his greatest warriors away from the war in search of the item. Many did not return, but eventually his niece Tamara Tvarivich, a potent Theurge and member of the Ivory Priesthood, returned with the Firebird Crystal. Volk proved unequal to the task of wielding the device, however, and was found a drooling imbecile in his inner sanctum. Control of the caern fell to his untested niece. Besides her leadership abilities and strategic sensibilities, the young Theurge had one other thing going for her: she was the direct descendant of the Silver Fang heroes who slew the Zmei Sharkala. In such times, pure blood like hers carried much weight with the demoralized Fangs.

Meanwhile other tribes found both victory and disastrous defeat while going it alone. The Wendigo, though geographically limited, bit into the hag's outstretched claw so deeply that her minions had to withdraw from much of Siberia by early 1995. This was, perhaps, the first true victory of the war and a sign that the hag could be beaten. Nevertheless, the actual damage to the vampire was negligible and her strikes throughout the rest of Russia went on unabated. The Wendigo leader, Blood-on-the-Wind, went on an embassy to the House of the Crescent Moon, but was ambushed and killed on the way. Blaming the Silver Fangs, the Wendigo refused to take any expanded role in the hostilities.

Weakened by past violence, the Children of Gaia had little to contribute save their wisdom and, with previous mistakes still remembered by both the Fangs and the Red Talons, they often found their advice unwelcome. Still, there were those who would listen. The Glass Walkers and Bone Gnawers had found a useful ally when they had taken the Children of Gaia into their caerns. For pacifists, the Russian Gaians had an astute tactical sense of the enemy's psychology and advised their two protectors with keen precision. In late 1996, much to the War Council's relief, the Glass Walkers were openly attacked. Though this served to finally diminish the taint of suspicion that hung around them and draw them actively into the conflict, the nature of the attack was devastating. In a move almost unprecedented among the cautious, oldest generation of vampires, the hag herself paid a visit to the Sept of the Learning Hall in Moscow. Of the 40 sept members, 17 were still in the vicinity at the time. Not a single Glass Walker, including the sept's leader (Boris Tsergov), left the city alive. If the Glass Walkers had not listened to the Gaians and moved most of their operations from Moscow to St. Petersburg, things could have gone a lot worse. Still, almost an entire fifth of Russia's Glass Walkers died in a single winter's night; the tribe was now at war.

Other tribes, too, saw 1996 as a low point in the war. The Uktena were determined to stay out of the war at all costs, despite direct pleas from both the Silver Fangs and the Red Talons. Now one of Baba Yaga's ambassadors arrived at their Spirit Stone Caern, bearing gifts and a proposition. The war was all but over, he said, but the Uktena and their darkling spirit magics intrigued the hag. They would rise fast in her service if they would show her how to reverse the Rite of Draconic Binding that held the Zmei Trevero beneath their caern. Such an overture showed, despite her ancient wisdom, how little the hag understood the Garou; the Uktena tore her legate limb from limb. In reply the Banetenders soon came under a fierce attack that left over a quarter of the sept dead, forcing their leader, Ut-Sala Ghost-in-the-Mist, to seek out hitherto unpalatable alliances among the European tribes.

The Shadow Lords, as always, presented another problem for the ruling tribes. Two major septs represented the Lords' interests in Russia: The Sept of the Brooding Sky, complicit in the Red Talons' slaughter of the Children of Gaia and suspected of Wyrm-taint, festered like a brooding sore in the Ukraine. Considered a viable war target by the ruling troika, the sept's leader — Eduard, Sun-Curser of the Society of Nidhogg — openly dared a Fenrir pack to storm his gates.

The Thunderstrike Sept (a Shadow Lord caern in the southern foothills of the Urals), however, was far more politic. Since the war's outset the sept leader, Alexander (Father Night) Volkav, continued with the tribe's usual snarling vitriol. The Shadow Lords had so successfully sown major dissent amongst the other tribes that, when they in turn were attacked, no one came to their aid. Initially suffering extreme losses, the

mysterious but timely death of Father Night opened the way for a new kind of leader among the tribe. Cagey and conciliatory, Volkav's successor was an up-and-coming Philodox named Anatoly Masaryk. His first move was to approach the Get of Fenris through an unexpected intermediary—Alyosha Lyubov, the leader of Russia's remaining Children of Gaia. The Get didn't know whether to be more dubious of the Shadow Lord's sincerity or the Gaian's, apparently, boundless propensity for forgiveness. They nevertheless dutifully passed the information along to the Silver Fangs; the Shadow Lords were on board.

Despite energetic leadership by Tamara Tvarivich, Garou confidence in their Silver Fang rulers continued to sink. The Get and the Furies, long their staunchest supporters, suffered greatly at the war's forefront. The rate of attrition had already depleted both tribes of over 1/3 of their strength. By year's end the Garou had weathered the worst that the hag could throw at them. The death toll had been horrific, but they had survived. Now, the time had come to go on the offensive.

In 1996 two ancient families represented the Silver Fangs in Russia. In the north there was the great though mercurial House of the Crescent Moon, while the Aral Sea contained an ancient but dying caern belonging to the level-headed Fangs of House Wise Heart. By the end of 1997 there would only be one family left.

Parry & Thrust (January — October 1997)

A cold 1997 January started out the year about as disastrously as possible. The Stargazers had made a contribution to the war effort far exceeding their meager numbers. The most important link in this chain was their leader, Chien Sun, whom his tribe called the Mountain Wind. Throughout the war, he had advised House Wise Heart, showing a supernatural ability to predict the enemy's movements. Unfortunately, his eyes were cast so far afield that he never saw the hand wielding the poisoned dagger that struck him from behind. A slow, dark Wyrm-toxin burned through him, despite the Garou's best healing arts. Kept alive in a state of stasis, he was out of the war at a time when his wisdom was needed most.

Despite this loss, throughout the opening months of 1997 the Garou launched a series of swift counter attacks. To the Wyrm-spawn, victory had been a seemingly foregone conclusion. Suddenly the Garou seemed to be everywhere, hitting at supposedly secret Black Spiral caerns or at *upyr* pawns, who considered themselves all but invulnerable in their urban citadels. Indeed it soon became an unclear whether the

Garou were prisoners within the Shadow Curtain with Baba Yaga, or if she was trapped inside with them. After six months of such audacity, the hag realized she had to go back on the offensive or face rebellion within her own ranks. Her eyes fell upon the Stargazers and House Wise Heart.

The Stargazers' Sept of the Crystal Mind and the allied Aral Sea Caern, maintained by House Wise Heart, had not seen a direct attack in over three years. In late October 1997 the hammer fell with all the subtlety of a thunderclap. After heavy fighting, at month's end House Wise Heart had fallen; not a member of the sept who had been in residence survived. A few remained scattered throughout the country, but the family's 1,000-year presence in Russia was effectively finished. Simultaneously the hag sent additional forces to deal with the Wendigo who had meted out her first defeat in Siberia. After fierce fighting which further depleted the tribe's membership, the Baba Yaga's operatives suffered a second bitter defeat in the frozen wasteland. The Stargazer caern survived by a hair through guerilla tactics and because Baba Yaga abruptly tried to re-deploy her forces (largely without success) to another hot spot. From all around the country, Banes, fomori and Black Spiral Dancers alike converged by moon bridge to one location — Kursk.

Kursk (November 1997)

The Garou knew that Kursk was once the prison for the entropic Zmei, Gregornous Deathwing, but subsequent observations reported that he had left the area since his awakening during the Second World War. Now, the Silent Striders claimed, the pigeon had secretly come home to roost. Although the Garou's last major confrontation with a Zmei had ended in disaster, the opportunity to destroy one of the hag's greatest allies in a single swoop was too good to miss. The leading tribes went about assembling the greatest fighting force of Garou assembled in Russia since the War of Rage — nearly every werewolf in all of the land. A sense of *esprit de corps* had taken hold among the tribes. The chaotic and dispirited tribal structure Baba Yaga had first attacked was now a disciplined and motivated army. Their backs against the Shadow Curtain, the Garou were now fighting for Gaia, their Motherland and their very survival.

The Silver Fangs had once met with bitter defeat when confronting Shazear; they had no interest in repeating the experience. Baba Yaga's tactics had been brilliant in their way, seemingly random and virtually unpredictable, but underriding them was a weakness born of fear and a fundamental misunderstanding of the modern world and Garou nature. Still, the attack on the Kursk nest was going to be an all or nothing strategy. The plan was to attack in waves, using potent fetishes and ancient rites to bend moon bridges in to the source, overwhelming the Zmei and any other Wyrm-spawn present with massive force. The strategy was elegantly simple, and the commanding council withheld it from the rank and file until the last moment to minimize the chance of a leak. Everything was perfect except for one problem — there was a spy on the high council.

On November 1st the werewolves made their move. Moon bridges opened onto the hilly salient among the wheat fields, under the no-moon sky which Garou seers had foretold as the most propitious time to attack. Gregornous had recently devastated a small Red Talon caern to the north and wisdom totems believed that the Zmei would be asleep. Using the Ragabash blackness to their advantage, Garou scouts used ancient signs, visible only to Gaia's allies, to find the Zmei's lair. The great necropolis was rife with the spirits of those who had died there in 1943, a ready food source for the entropic Zmei. As is often the case with such great Wyrm-beasts, the Zmei's lair also played host to a nest of lesser entities, including numerous Banes and a Black Spiral hive. Taken by surprise, the Wyrm's minions fell back before the well-organized barrage of teeth, bullets and claws. Gaia's wrath, summoned by rites seldom used, opened up rents in the ground beneath their feet, hurling the Wyrm-spawn to their doom. Similarly, the freezing November winds and cooperative Wyldlings kept the region's sparse human population away from the battle.

The Silver Fangs had learned much since their encounter with Shazear. The leaders of the three commanding tribes knew that the hag had eyes and ears everywhere. Thus, each commander laid part of his or her plans in secret. Many of the packs were mixed, cutting across tribal lines in a manner rarely seen before in Russia. The Garou now dominated the field, but there was no sign of Gregornous. Not lulled by the seemingly easy victory, the Garou had cast wards against the advent of Wyrm-spun bridges opening in their mist. So it was, when Baba Yaga sprung her trap, that her minions found themselves expected.

In truth, the hag had little time to prepare. Her quisling was aware of the attack only shortly before the moon bridges opened. Additionally, she found that many of her forces were tied down by the Stargazers in the south and by the Wendigo to the north. Expecting an easy victory similar to the ones they enjoyed in years past, the Wyrm-spawn suddenly found themselves thrust into the meat grinder. Initially out-numbering the werewolves by nearly five to one on the field, the arriving attackers confidently surged against Gaia's defenders. Fluid in attack and defense, the Garou fell back in retreat, drawing the hag's forces into a sporadic series of sorties. The Bone Gnawer leader, Nicholas Zukeine, and Silver Fang hunt master, Nicolai Predatelski, led one such attack into a darkened valley, though only the Silver Fang emerged alive. More and more moon bridges opened and new waves of Garou cut the enemy to pieces as attack abruptly turned to retreat. It was then that Gregornous Deathwing awoke.

Always the hag's most loyal among the Zmei, he may have awakened at Baba Yaga's behest or perhaps simply because his dreams grew outraged by the puny wolves who dared to breach the dragon's den. A creature of inky blackness, the Wyrm-spirit erupted into the moonless sky with a hurricane of spectral wings and a scream that withered life, leaving half a dozen werewolves dead before the battle was joined. As the blackness descended, additional moon bridges opened, disgorging even more Banes and Black Spiral Dancers. With 100 Garou present on the field, the hag's forces no-doubt thought that the Garou had tapped the last of their reserves.

But the Gaian werewolves' leaders had been waiting for this moment. Now the remainder of the moon bridges opened, revealing at last the tribes' true strength as the rest of their forces swept onto the salient, driving any opposition before them. An icy spirit-gale created a nearly impenetrable ceiling, pinning the Zmei to a low altitude above the field. Lightning strikes pierced its stygian blackness, revealing its skeletal structure as the Garou now aimed the majority of their attacks against the beast. The Black Fury leader, Mother's Pride, tore deeply at the creature's wing, sending it crashing to the ground, though the ichor that disgorged from the terrible rents also fatally poisoned the Ahroun. Silent Striders and Fangs of the Ivory Priesthood drained away the creature's Dark Umbral energies as Tamara Tvarivich and Anton Nordenskald of the Fenrir delivered the killing blows. Dismayed and demoralized, the remaining Wyrm-spawn fled the field, though few escaped to spread news of the hag's defeat. Over 50 Garou lay dead at the battle's end, but many times that number of the Wyrm's brood was destroyed. In all, the year 1997 had cost the Garou more lives than at any other time in modern history, but it was also the beginning of the end for Baba Yaga. The tide had turned.

The Death of Baba Yaga (1998)

Throughout 1998 the Garou were dismantling Baba Yaga's grandiose power structure brick by brick. Indeed, it is likely that her preoccupation with destroying the werewolves left her open to attack by her Leech enemies. Whether Russia's *upyr* pursued freedom or the hag's potent vitae, the Garou noted that more than a few vampires were turning up dead. A few even naively attempted to spin alliances with the werewolves, though most of these were killed out of hand. Attacks escalated against the Garou, but they were increasingly haphazard and without any guiding strategy. Many Black Spiral Dancers, disillusioned by the hag's increasingly erratic tactics, withdrew their aid. Although they were careful to maintain the illusion of subservience to Baba Yaga, it seemed that other agencies within the Wyrm's ranks now saw her as more of a liability than an asset. The more she lost, the more the hag lashed out, leaving a trail of death in her wake. But the thrashing she made was of something that was, itself, dying.

Baba Yaga was one with Mother Russia, but attempted to extend her influence beyond Russia's traditional boundaries. In these realms her knowledge and powers failed her, and throughout the war many of her foes evaded her in strongholds that eluded her lore. In the end, the Baba Yaga simply ran out of time and space. In truth, her power had been disintegrating for a year and a half before she met her final demise. Almost as much a prisoner of her own Shadow Curtain as the other supernaturals of Russia, she awaited her death with dark equanimity. From the Garou perspective, Baba Yaga's death was almost anticlimactic. The parry and thrust of war continued, but suddenly they sensed that their Wyrm-spawned enemies — overextended without the hag's backing — were suddenly bereft of will. Something dark, ancient and terrible beyond even Baba Yaga's ken had moved; the hag was dead, but probably not at Garou hands. And with her died the Shadow Curtain; Russia was free once again.

[Note: For the vampiric perspective of these events, see **Nights of Prophecy**.]

The Present

In spite of their great victory, there are those among the tribes' more informed leadership who see the negative fallout from the hag's demise. For all her corruption and power, the Baba Yaga was in many ways a high profile target and, in a sense, a knowable enemy. Whatever destroyed her is not. Despite her innate genius, potent blood and magics, the hag had been asleep for centuries and was ill equipped to grasp the realities of a world on the cusp of the 21st century.

Also, some Garou believe that, for all her Wyrm-taint, there was an aspect of Baba Yaga (part of her original nature) that was still friendly to the Wyld. Some wonder if the Wyrm withdrew its support because she had served its purpose and that now an even darker force waits in the wings. The Garou's traditional enemies — those Banes, *upyr* and the Black Spirals who served the hag — are by no means destroyed, though many areas are temporarily quiet.

Outside the Shadow Curtain, those who knew of the Baba Yaga's awakening saw the rise of this ancient vampire as, perhaps, the first step in the impending Apocalypse. Foreign luminaries among the world's supernatural population watched the Shadow Curtain with trepidation, expecting dark armies to come pouring from its inky borders at any moment. With Baba Yaga's apparent demise and the curtain's dissolution, many sighed with relief that the worst had not come to pass. Even the world's most prescient lords of order could do little to detect what went on within Russia's borders, but now believe that whatever happened in 1999 has diffused the situation. The werewolves who have battled Baba Yaga for the past decade, however, are not so sanguine. If Baba Yaga has died, but not at their hands, it stands to reason that whatever could destroy such an ancient monstrosity may well be even worse.

News of the Shadow Curtain's collapse has spread like wildfire. A small flood of foreign werewolves and other supernatural creatures have again entered Russia, seeking to capitalize on the power vacuum left by Baba Yaga's death. While some of these newcomers are friendly to the Russian Garou, others may prove to be new and potent enemies. Of course, those who seek to invade Russia from without would do well to remember the lessons of other would-be conquerors.

Vladimir Putin

A postscript of sorts: Shortly after Baba Yaga's death, another change occurred in Russia. On New Year's Eve 1999, Boris Yeltsin announced that he would step down from the Russian presidency. As Russian troops fought in the Chechin capitol, Yeltsin's successor, the 47-year-old Prime Minister Vladimir Putin stepped into the presidency. While many Garou believe that Yeltsin was nominally a pawn of the Baba Yaga's, it remains to be seen if his successor is compromised by similar supernatural entanglements. The enigmatic former leader of the KGB handily won the most recent elections on March 26, 2000; time will tell just what he'll do with his position.

A World of Rage

For now, the Russian werewolves enjoy a brief respite from over a decade of darkness. They have paid a horrendous price for this peace. Almost at half their pre-Terror numerical strength, the Russian Garou are still more organized, experienced and proud than they have been in centuries. Despite the obvious differences that still exist between them, the fractured tribes are, at least for now, united once more.

The Fate of the Armies

Despite her vast personal power, the Baba Yaga used agents to fulfill most of her ends. Many of these were pawns who had little idea that they served her designs. Some, however, served her directly and were used as either sledgehammer or a scalpel at her whim. In the wake of her demise, however, many of these agents died or were cast to the winds to fulfill their own designs.

The Army of Night

Mostly consisting of *upyr* agents, the Army of Night did much damage to the Garou during the early years of the Terror but seemed to go out of its way to engage foes other than the werewolves as the war progressed. Highly effective against dissident vampires and human mages, it was a major blow to Baba Yaga's power when the army's "general," an ancient Leech named Viktor, foolishly allowed himself to be caught north of St. Petersburg during the so-called "White Nights" (a period in June when the sun remains in the sky for two to three weeks). The Garou unearthed him and scattered his ashes in the Neva River. Little is known of what has happened to the rest of this army.

The Army of Conversion

The most loyal of Baba Yaga's forces, this army consisted of Banes, fomori and no few corrupted Garou. Led by a totem-spirit named Typhon, the Army of Conversion acted as the hag's "secret police," spying on her followers and ensuring their loyalty. Nominally subservient to Grandfather Thunder, in the wake of Baba Yaga's death the spirit (who appears as a black thunderhead with eyes of crackling yellow lightning) remains a totem in several Shadow Lord septs, including the Sept of the Brooding Sky. Despite the totem's survival, most of this army has been destroyed or dispersed in the wake of their mistress's death.

The Army of War

This was the Baba Yaga's primary combat force and its heavily armed soldiers took a serious toll on the Garou. Consisting primarily of tainted Garou and fomori, the army was often poorly led until it fell under the command of the Black Spiral Dancer, Snaps-at-Shadows. Between 1994-95 the Army of War accounted for more werewolf casualties than the rest of the hag's other forces put together. After 1996, however, command was split between the Black Spiral Dancer and a potent fomor named Gogol. The fomor's half of the army became increasingly unwieldy and was virtually destroyed at Kursk. Snaps-at-Shadows was the commander of the attack against House Wise Heart and has survived the hag's destruction, now ruling over the corrupted Hive of the Wasting Sea.

The Army of Despair

Consisting of the awakened Zmei, Wyrm creatures who have taken the form of dragons, the Army of Despair was Baba Yaga's most potent weapon during the Terror. Now, with her death, the remaining Zmei are free to do as they will. There were once seven of these mythic beasts, but Gregornous Deathwing died at Kursk and the Silver Fangs killed another, Sharkala the Cruel, centuries before. The five remaining Zmei are: Goluko, Illyana, Rustarin, Shazear and Trevero. Of these, only two (Shazear and Illyana) are currently awake. Trevero is trapped underground, tended by Uktena who keep him asleep. Rustarin awoke for brief periods with the Baba Yaga's aid, but with the hag's destruction she now sleeps more deeply than before, watched over by the Black Spiral Dancers of the Hive of the Wasting Sea. Goluko, horribly scarred by a nuclear test, writhes still in his bonds in the remote Taimyr Peninsula, despite repeated Black Spiral attempts to wake him.

The Army of the Arcane

Little is known about this chantry of magically bound mages. Responsible for the upkeep of the Shadow Curtain, it is obvious that they have failed in this task.

The Army of the Void

Summoned by Baba Yaga, it is believed that the demonic "Blood Angel" and his spirit minions have departed this plane and the nearby Penumbra. The line between the Wyrm and the infernal is hard to measure and Russian Garou know little about his role during the Terror, though most of his actions were subtle rather than overt.

Geography

Russia is the largest component of what was formerly the Union of Soviet Socialist Republics (USSR) and is the biggest country in the world. It extends from the Arctic Ocean in the north to the former republic of Kazakh and the People's Republic of China in the south, and from the Byelorussian and Ukrainian former republics in the west to the Pacific Ocean in the east. Russia covers an area of 6,592,800 square miles and has a population of approximately 146,393,000 people. In the northern areas of Russia, treeless arctic tundra is prevalent, while Siberia is predominantly composed of swampy, coniferous forests or "taiga." Southern Russia consists of steppes while its central portion contains a deep, forested belt. The Ural Mountains divide the country into eastern and western portions, with the eastern region containing the majority of Russia's territory. Russia's major rivers include the Volga and the Don to the west of the Urals, and the Yenisei, Amur, Lena and Ob to the east. Climactic conditions range from the subtropical shores of the Black Sea to the permanently frozen Arctic latitudes.

The Ukraine covers 233,100 square miles and has a population of 49,811,174. Part of the great East European Plain, most of the country is covered by an arable black soil perfect for the cultivation of grain. Its mountainous areas include the Carpathians in the southwest and the Crimean Chain in the south. Traditionally linked to Russia, the Ukraine too was covered by the Shadow Curtain and was the site for the great battle of Kursk.

Major Cities

Russia's capitol, Moscow, has a population of 8,368,449 (1995 est.). The next three largest cities are St. Petersburg 4,232,105; Nizhniy Novgorod 1,375,570 and Novosibirsk. Also frequently included in this list is Kiev, the capitol of the Ukraine, with a population of 2,630,000. Other Ukrainian cities include Kharkov 1,555,000 and Dnipropetrovsk 1,147,000.

Ethnic Groups

Russia contains numerous ethnic groups. Of these the Slavs are by far the largest, representing approximately 75% of the population. The second most populous group is Turko-Tartar, descendants of the 13th and 14th Century Mongol invaders. The Crimean and Kazakh Tartars live west of the Urals while the Baskir, Chuvasch, Tartar, Yakut, Oirot and Altai peoples are concentrated to the east. The third largest ethnicity includes the Japhetic peoples (Chechen, Kabardian, Balkar and Cherkess), while the fourth major group is the Finno-Ugrian group which shares cultural ties to the Turkish and Hungarian peoples. Other groups include the Jews, Mongolians, Greeks, Rroma, Koreans, Kurds, Chinese, Chezchs and Arabs. The Wendigo have found a home among the Chukchi in the northeast, a people related to the Native North Americans.

Caerns

There are a number of caerns in Russia, of varying power and influence, though after the machinations of Baba Yaga, there are considerably fewer than there once were. A mysterious draining destroyed some caerns outright while weakening others. Rumors of an artifact that might restore the caerns to life has raised some hope, but has so far come to no fruition.

Blood of the Sea Sept

Caern: Unpopulated region on the shore of the Black Sea.
Level: 4
Gauntlet: 3
Type: Wyld
Totem: Pegasus
Tribal Structure: Black Fury, but open to others by invitation.
Leader: Tatiana (Ahroun, homid)

Firebird Sept

Caern: The walled monastic city of Zagorsk, approximately 70km northeast of Moscow.
Level: 3
Gauntlet: 3
Type: Wisdom
Totem: Firebird
Tribal Structure: Silver Fang, commanded by Arkady.
Leader: Arkady (Ahroun, homid)

Sept of the People's Will

Caern: Gorky Park in Moscow.
Level: 3
Gauntlet: 3
Type: Visions
Totem: "Marx," a city father-like totem representing the more egalitarian tenets of Communism.
Tribal Structure: Open but currently administered by Bone Gnawers.
Leader: Power struggle between the street factions of Aleksandr Chesnokov (Ragabash, lupus) and the government faction of Gregor Tomsky (Galliard, homid).

White Sea Sept

Caern: Located on the shore of the White Sea, some distance from Archangel.
Level: 1
Gauntlet: 4
Type: Stamina
Totem: Unicorn
Tribal Structure: Children of Gaia, but open to Bone Gnawers and Glass Walkers. This caern was partially drained before the death of Baba Yaga.
Leader: Alyosha Lyubov (Philodox, homid)

The Sept of Fafnir's Brood

Caern: Unpopulated region near St. Petersburg on the shore of the Baltic Sea.

Level: 3

Gauntlet: 3

Type: Rage

Totem: Ancestral rage spirits of those who died in the siege of Leningrad.

Tribal Structure: Get of Fenris, though others are allowed grudging admittance. This caern was partially drained before the death of Baba Yaga.

Leader: Anton Nordenskald (Ahroun, lupus)

Sept of the Arctic Axe

Caern: Northern Coast across from Novaya Zemlya.

Level: 3

Gauntlet: 3

Type: Stamina

Totem: Boar

Tribal Structure: Get of Fenris, though others are allowed grudging admittance. This caern is constantly at war with the Black Spiral Pit of the Glowing Sea.

Leader: Yaroslav Silvereye (Theurge, homid)

Sept of the Kilakac'n

Caern: Satellite storage facility of the Hermitage museum in St. Petersburg.

Level: 3

Gauntlet: 3

Type: Wisdom

Totem: Cockroach

Tribal Structure: Exclusively Glass Walker

Leader: Boris Lavrosky (Theurge, homid)

The Falling Water Sept

Caern: A glade deep in the forests of northern Siberia.

Level: 3

Gauntlet: 3

Type: Visions

Totem: Griffin

Tribal Structure: Red Talon, but open to lupus of other tribes.

Leader: Tundra Runner (Galliard, lupus)

Thunderstrike Sept

Caern: Located in the western foothills of the southern Ural Mountains.

Level: 3
Gauntlet: 3
Type: Strength
Totem: Grandfather Thunder
Tribal Structure: Shadow Lords
Leader: Anatoly Masaryk (Philodox, homid)

Sept of the Brooding Sky

Caern: An out-of-the-way corner of the Ukraine.
Level: 4
Gauntlet: 3
Type: Visions
Totem: Typhon
Tribal Structure: Shadow Lords.
Leader: Eduard Sun-Curser (Philodox, homid)

Sept of the Crescent Moon

Caern: Hidden in the Ural Mountains.
Level: 5
Gauntlet: 2
Type: Kingship
Totem: Falcon
Tribal Structure: Silver Fangs, but open to others by invitation.
Leader: Queen Tamara Tvarivich (Theurge, homid) of the Ivory Priesthood.

Sept of the Crystal Mind

Caern: A crystal grotto beneath a mountaintop temple, near the Mongolian border.
Level: 2
Gauntlet: 4
Type: Enigmas and Wisdom
Totem: Chimera
Tribal Structure: Stargazer, but open to others by invitation. This caern was partially drained before the death of Baba Yaga. It is still sinking faster after her death and many associate this with the illness of its leader, Chien Sun.
Leader: Chien Sun (Galliard, homid) is currently in a coma. The acting leader is Lungtok (Philodox, homid) from Tibet's defunct Sept of the Snow Leopard.

Sept of the Spirit Stone

Caern: A small Yakut village located in the Siberian taiga.
Level: 3
Gauntlet: 3
Type: Gnosis
Totem: Uktena

Tribal Structure: Uktena ward this; it is closed to all others except Stargazers.
Leader: Ut-Sala Ghost-in-the-Mist (Theurge, homid)

Sept of the Siberian Wilds

Caern: Hidden deep within the arctic northeast, roughly 70 miles inland from the Bering Sea.
Level: 2
Gauntlet: 4
Type: Will
Totem: Wendigo
Tribal Structure: Exclusively Wendigo
Leader: Sakha Silver-Water (Philodox, metis)

Sept of the Winter Forest

Caern: A glade deep in the northern Siberian forests.
Level: 4
Gauntlet: 3
Type: Fertility
Totem: Stag
Tribal Structure: Red Talon, though lupus Garou of other tribes may occasionally enter.
Leader: Redjak (Philodox, lupus)

Black Spiral Pits

The Dancers have used the hag's power to gain several formerly Gaia consecrated caerns and to strengthen others. If any have benefited from Baba Yaga's reign of terror, it is the Black Spiral Dancers. Although many of them ultimately broke faith with her, her death came too suddenly for her to fully punish their treachery.

The Hive of the Glowing Sea

Caern: A sunken nuclear sub off Novaya Zemlya.
Level: 4
Gauntlet: 4 (Slightly higher than normal because of heavy Weaver presence.)
Type: Enigmas
Totem: Kraken
Tribal Structure: Black Spiral Dancers and other Wyrm-creatures.
Leader: Sergei Kozyrev (Ragabash, homid)

The Hive of the Unleashed Atom

Caern: The Chernobyl nuclear reactor in the Ukraine.
Level: 3
Gauntlet: 4 (Slightly higher than normal because of heavy Weaver presence.)

Type: Toxins
Totem: G'louogh, the Dance of Corruption
Tribal Structure: Black Spiral Dancers and other Wyrm-creatures.
Leader: Ivan Balefire (Theurge, metis)

Vzrozhdeniye (Renaissance Island)

Caern: Renaissance Island is in the Aral Sea on the border between Uzbekistan and Kazakhstan. It is a former base for the Soviet biological weapons program and the world's largest anthrax burial ground.

Level: 3

Gauntlet: 3

Type: Organism

Totem: The Green Dragon

Tribal Structure: Black Spiral Dancers and other Wyrmish things.

Leader: Nicolai Predatelski (Ahroun, homid), Silver Spiral traitor to the Silver Fangs.

The Hive of the Wasting Sea

Caern: The Aral Sea coast.

Level: 5

Gauntlet: 2

Type: Enigmas

Totem: G'louogh, the Dance of Corruption

Tribal Structure: Black Spiral Dancers and other Wyrmish beasts. The Shadow Curtain swallowed up this former House Wise Heart caern in 1997 and it fell to the Black Spiral Dancers. For more on the corruption of the Aral Sea Caern, see the **Silver Fangs Tribebook**.

Leader: Snaps-at-Shadows (Ahroun, lupus)

The Players

With the monolithic threat of the Baba Yaga gone from the scene, Russia is once again open territory for the Garou, *upyr* and other supernatural creatures.

Tribes

Smaller in number than at almost any other time in their history, Russia's Garou are nevertheless among the most battle-hardened in the world. Tested beyond all endurance, even formerly hostile tribes have found common ground. There are, of course, still splits and suspicion among the tribes. In a land where even the Red Talons show a cunning grasp of political acumen, it is little wonder that the situation between the tribes has been rife with intrigue. For now, however, they are more cohesive than they have ever been.

Black Furies

Originally enforcers of the Impergium, their status among Russia's tribes, and particularly with the ruling Fangs, has always been high. Maintaining a presence in many caerns belonging to other tribes, they served as both warriors and advisors. Over the past decade, the Furies have dared, lost and gained much. Loyal supporters and advisors to the Silver Fangs, they now stand to reap great rewards in victory. And, indeed, the fact that there is now a queen, rather than a king, sitting on the Silver Fang throne has served to smooth over some of the few remaining rough edges in the relationship. As leaders during the Terror, the Furies found themselves in a position to greatly aid the other tribes and gained a new sense of self-confidence tempered by Russian pragmatism. During the war they even reached something of a rapprochement with their rivals, the Get of Fenris, though some mistrust remains between the two tribes. The tribe's former leader, Mother's Pride, was among the Garou slaughtered by Gregornous at Kursk. The new leader, an Ahroun named Tatiana, is new to the position but hardly untested. She has breathed new life into the tribe and proved an apt stateswoman, as well as an able warleader.

Bone Gnawers

Russian Bone Gnawers claim areas of rural and urban squalor throughout Russia and are particularly numerous in Moscow, St. Petersburg and Kiev. They have always spoken out for Russia's downtrodden. Such egalitarian sentiments have won them much credit over the centuries, though during the 1917 Revolution, many of them made dangerous alliances in order to overthrow the nobility (i.e., the Silver Fangs) and create a workers' paradise. During the Soviet era the Bone Gnawers actually took hold of some of the party machinery, gaining real political power for the first time in their history. Bone Gnawers of this vintage are better fed, and generally cleaner and more circumspect than their brethren in other parts of the world. Since the fall of the USSR, increased poverty has swelled the ranks of the poor in Russia. Many Gnawers have reverted to the streets, resembling their Western relatives more and more.

After the loss of their longtime leader and father figure, Nicholas Zukeine, the Bone Gnawers fell into a period of chaos that persists into the present. Two new leaders have risen to the fore and battle for dominance of Moscow's Gorky Park Sept. One is a Ragabash named Aleksandr Chesnokov who supports the street faction, while the other (a Galliard named Gregor Tomsky) represents the party style Gnawers and has connections to organized crime. While the two were able to set aside their differences during the Terror, since then their rivalry has become increasingly heated, spilling over into violence and at least one death.

Children of Gaia

Situated in a secret caern on the Shores of the White Sea near Archangel is the remaining caern belonging to the Children of Gaia. With their near destruction at the claws of the Red Talons, the remainder of this once honored tribe scattered throughout Russia, sometimes finding refuge in Bone Gnawer or Glass Walker Caerns. The nominal ruler of the remaining Russian Children of Gaia is a spiritual seeker named Alyosha Lyubov. Despite the oft held opinion that the Children of Gaia are through in Russia, this wise Philodox played a pivotal role in unifying the tribes during the darkest days of Baba Yaga's Terror. Now, in the wake of the hag's death, however, Alyosha is nowhere to be found.

Fianna

This tribe has never been much of a factor in Russia and holds no caerns there. If the itinerant Fianna could be said to have a leader in Russia, however, it would be the Galliard named Dagger's-Edge. Well-connected and respected, this cagey propagandist cleaved his own path through the war, keeping Garou morale high while at the same time calling their leaders to accountability through his blistering yet subtle social commentary. In fact the Fianna gained one potent sponsor in the person of the Shadow Lord Anatoly Masaryk of the Thunderstrike Sept. Dagger's-Edge has done much to reshape the Russian Shadow Lords' image and has taken on some of their imperious ways. He has nevertheless used these contacts to aid other Fianna that pass through the country.

Get of Fenris

The Get of Fenris have long carried a heavy burden. Loyal thanes to the Silver Fangs throughout the centuries, they watched with dismay as the once proud tribe fell to madness and decadence. Taking up much of the burden of rule in the Fangs' name, they held the Garou nation together through ice and fire. Through this the Russian Fenrir have learned such lessons as forbearance and political strategy, qualities not always admired by Get in the West. Now, that the Silver Fangs have — at least temporarily — risen above their madness, the Fenrir have been largely content to reap those rewards given to a loyal and valued general, and to stand aside and let the Fangs reassert their leadership. The longest-lived leader and one of the oldest Garou in Russia, the Ahroun Anton Nordenskald survived at the forefront of the war against the Baba Yaga the same way he survived his previous two wars. Whether fighting the Nazis at Leningrad or the Wyrm during all the years since, the "Grey Wolf of the Baltic" proved himself one of the keenest strategic thinkers in Russia and a Garou who inspires loyalty among his own tribe and others. Having struck one of the two fatal blows against the Zmei Gregornous, he has also become something more — a legend.

Glass Walkers

As in many other countries, the Russian Weaver tribe has always been highly suspect by the more Wyld-oriented Garou. Seemingly invulnerable at the beginning of the Terror, the Russian Glass Walkers at first benefited greatly from the Baba Yaga's early purges. With their *upyr* competitors largely destroyed or in disarray, the urban tribe was briefly able to extend their influence into a host of new government and business venues — overextend, as it soon turned out. At the brink of what they saw as a new age, they soon lost almost everything. Their Moscow caern drained, their long-time leader (Boris Tsergov) along with many of their best operatives murdered, and forced to retreat to a lesser caern in St. Petersburg, the Glass Walkers found themselves under assault from every direction. Under their new leader, a young Theurge named Boris Lavrosky, the Sept of the Kilakac'n became a center for the urban resistance. Protected by the Cockroach Totem, its ability to survive was to amaze and encourage Garou throughout the nation.

During these bleak years the Glass Walkers formed a technological firewall that proved nigh impenetrable, even to the hag's sewer dwelling information gatherers. This advantage allowed the werewolf resistance to pass on information virtually unhindered while at the same time gathering intelligence on the enemy's movements. Strongly allied with the Bone Gnawers, Silent Striders and the remaining Children of Gaia, the Glass Walkers made the most out of these connections to improve their reputation among the other tribes — only the Red Talons remain truly hostile. Taking advantage of their new situation, the Glass Walkers now enjoy, for the moment, the high ground in the Russian world of commerce and technology.

Red Talons

If the other tribes sense a certain degree of bitterness among the Red Talons, it is because no tribe has suffered as much as they. The Talons have lost more caerns and more wolves than any other tribe. In part because of their bravery against nearly suicidal odds, throwing themselves against Baba Yaga and the Wyrm, it is also due to their intransigence when dealing with the homid dominated tribes. The Talons' warleader, Tundra Runner, was a divisive figure to say the least. A staunch advocate of a return to the Impergium, his ability to turn allies into enemies did not help the Red Talon cause, despite his bravery in battle. Disgusted with what he saw as abandonment by the other tribes, Tundra Runner led a pack into the Umbra, braving the Shadow Curtain to open a way back to the tribe's home realm. Pursued by a pack of Black Spiral Dancers, he has not resurfaced, even a year after Baba Yaga's death.

No less coddling toward humans than his predecessor, the Red Talons' new leader, Redjak, is nevertheless mindful that tribal survival lies in papering over their differences with the other tribes. During the Terror, the tribe gained invaluable assistance from the Get of Fenris in saving their potent Winter Forest Sept. The Talons still remain largely outside of Russian Garou society, though they have warm relations with the Wendigo and a reputed "understanding" with the Get. Tundra Runner believed that the tribe's true future lies in returning to Pangaea, while others in the tribe wish to stick things out. If Tundra Runner ever returns from his mission, this debate may again divide the tribe.

Shadow Lords

If the Shadow Lords have not won trust in Russia, they have at least earned some respect. There are, essentially, two extant factions among the Russian Shadow Lords, typified by their two main septs. The Sept of the Brooding Sky is under Eduard Sun-Curser, a priest of the Society of Nidhogg; this faction seemed little concerned throughout the war and evidence of the sept's collusion with the enemy continues to grow after the end of the war. The Thunderstrike Sept (southern foothills of the Urals), however, is far more politic. By taking some of the most dangerous missions against the Baba Yaga and her Wyrm-spawned allies, the Shadow Lords of this sept suffered heavy losses but gained more political cachet than they could have in a hundred years of subtle manipulation. Their new leader, Anatoly Masaryk, continues to play ball with the other victorious tribes and has even, as far as they know, kept his word on every occasion. Among this tribe are at least a few of the Eastern Lords who are widely perceived to have real honor. The Silver Fangs and Black Furies are waiting for the other shoe to drop, but many in the other tribes see this as sour grapes.

Silent Striders

Always few in number, the Silent Striders nevertheless proved to be a constant thorn in Baba Yaga's side. Masters of hit-and-run tactics, their main value was in passing along information in a manner almost impossible to detect, even by Baba Yaga's best agents. The hag considered them pernicious sneaks and spared no little effort in hunting them down one by one. Although their already small number dwindled even further throughout the Terror, the Silent Striders never faltered in their mission. Largely independent, if the Russian Striders have a leader, it is the enigmatic Ragabash named Natasha Moon Chaser. Although the Striders have no caerns in Russia, they held their first great moot in the wake of Baba Yaga's death. What occurred here is unknown, but the Striders whisper of an even greater enemy than the hag on the horizon. The war with Baba Yaga depleted almost half of the Russian Garou Nation's membership and the Striders fear what is to come next.

Silver Fangs

Over the past millennium there were two Silver Fang families who determined the fate of Russian Garou society: The House of the Crescent Moon and House Wise Heart. Now, after the Terror, only one remains. Arguably the oldest and most notable of the

Queen Tamara Tvarivich

The dying House of the Crescent Moon has found a new lease on life with the ascension of Queen Tvarivich. While little is truly known about this Theurge of the Ivory Priesthood, her bravery and political acumen were undeniably instrumental in winning the day against the Baba Yaga. A pragmatic warrior with mystic leanings, Queen Tvarivich remains — along with her fellow Zmei slayer, Anton Nordenskald — the most potent symbol of Garou unity in Russia. Recent communications between the new monarch and her counterparts in other Silver Fang houses since the war's end have been successful in some cases and less so in others. The bad blood between the Russian house and other European families is steadily improving, though some distrust remains between the Crescent Moon and the House of the Gleaming Eye. Accusations and incriminations now fly freely, however, between the Russian family and the American House Wyrmfoe. The American Fangs accuse the Russian Sept leader Arkady of consorting with the Wyrm and an attempt on the life of King Albrecht, while many in the Crescent Moon accuse the American house of abandoning them in their hour of need. While publicly defending her kinsman Arkady, the queen has quietly gone about investigating House Wyrmfoe's accusations.

Silver Fang families, the House of the Crescent Moon has held power since the earliest times. Its former greatness, however, proved little protection against the madness and Harano that faced them in the 20th century. The Silver Fangs fell far and fast over the past hundred years and if they appear to have gotten their act together for the moment, the house's long term prospects still remain in doubt. Propped up by the loyal Get of Fenris and the politically astute Furies, the Fangs staged something of a comeback under the command of their new Queen Tamara Tvarivich.

After the war ended, several prominent Fangs were accused of complicity with the Wyrm. Not least among these was hunt master Nicolai Predatelski. Once exposed, Nicolai fled the scene and remains in hiding after the war. Disgraced and damned, he has sought refuge with his allies and taken his place among the Silver Spiral. The Bone Gnawers hate him especially and accuse him of treacherously murdering their leader at Kursk. Despite the vitriol aimed at him, some knowledgeable Garou believe that he was only the *second* highest-ranking traitor in the high council. Arkady led the Firebird freehold against Baba Yaga with distinction, but now with the Shadow Curtain's fall, disturbing rumors have swirled around him. No less a personage than King Albrecht of House Wyrmfoe has publicly accused Arkady of consorting with the Wyrm. Displaying no sign of such taint, Arkady has returned the accusation and sought to rally family support. The hope for reconciliation between the two houses seems remote.

Stargazers

Never numerous, during the Terror the Stargazers nevertheless exerted an influence far out of proportion to their numbers. After the near destruction of the Children of Gaia, the Stargazers took on their role as the voice of moderation on the Garou Council. Mystics and philosophers, their voice counts for much as advisors to the other tribes' leaders. House Wise Heart particularly valued them and was especially open to their advice. Despite their losses during the war, the tribe's numbers actually increased when survivors from the great Sept of the Snow Leopard in Tibet dared the Shadow Curtain to join their brethren in the Sept of the Crystal Mind. Now, however, the Stargazers face a major threat. With the destruction of House Wise Heart they lost much of their influence over events. Even more troubling, their leader, Chien Sun "Mountain Wind," lies dying, and his caern fails around him. The oldest Garou in Russia fell victim to a poisoned dagger at the heart of his own monastery. Tribal healers have determined

that the poison came from the Zmei Trevero, but do not have the ability to reverse its effects. The sept's acting leader is the accomplished former leader of the Snow Leopard Sept, Lungtok. Although highly knowledgeable, he is no more able to prevent the caern's slow dissolution than the native Stargazers.

Uktena

Located to the far north among the Yakut peoples of Siberia and the Mongolians in the Far East, the Uktena have been a part of the Russian scene since the beginning. Near the commencement of hostilities against Baba Yaga, the eastern Sept of the Evergreen went up in flames under attack from an unknown Zmei. Fifteen Uktena died and only one escaped to tell the tale. The Spirit Stone Caern in Siberia is located above the resting-place of the Zmei Trevero (also, not coincidentally, the site of the 1908 Tunguska Blast); the Uktena have the dubious honor of tending the Zmei to keep him asleep. The tribe's new leader, Ut-Sala Ghost-in-the-Mist, is a puissant Theurge who has walked dark airts unknown to even the wisest of other tribes. Although this has benefited his tribe greatly, it has also made him security conscious to the point of paranoia. This paranoia was justified when minions of the Baba Yaga attacked the caern to free the Zmei Trevero, thereby forcing the tribe to become active in the war and ally with the European tribes. Having left the Garou Council in the 1500s over a disagreement about trapping, these Uktena are only now entertaining thoughts of rejoining greater Garou society.

Wendigo

Ages ago, when it was still possible to cross between North America and Eurasia over the Bering Strait land bridge, members of the Wendigo tribe returned to Siberia. They spread across the land, breeding with wolves, and the indigenous Yakut and Chukchi people. The Wendigo remained geographically isolated, but strong and proud in their traditions. This ended with the 20th century and expansion into these lands by the Soviet industrial machine — and the Wyrm. As with the Red Talons, the Wendigo found themselves under attack by wolf hunters who used special ammunition, supplied by the "people." The Wendigo's numbers have dwindled precipitously over the past 80 years. Forced to retreat farther and farther into the Siberian wilds, the tribe only retains one caern by the Bering Sea. The Wendigo have become far more adept at protecting themselves over the past decade, however, and their aggressive attacks took even the Baba Yaga's most hardened minions by surprise. During the war their leader, Blood-on-the-Wind, was killed while on a mission to the Silver Fangs. Although the Wendigo's new leader, Sakha Silver-Water, allowed other tribes limited access to their caern during the Terror, they are now more insular and suspicious than ever.

Other Players
Black Spiral Dancers

The Black Spiral Dancers have never held as much power in Russia as they do now. Not a major factor until the 20th century, during the 1917 Revolution they took advantage of renewed pressure upon the Garou by the *upyr*. Attaching themselves first to the Brujah, then Pentex and the Baba Yaga, the Black Spiral Dancers have spread across the country like a cancer. And if they ultimately betrayed each of their erstwhile partners, what of it? None of *them* have survived in Russia, but the Black Spiral Dancers are still here. Pentex may be staging a comeback, but there is no need to hurry. If the Spirals choose to ally themselves with the corporation again, it will be on their own terms.

Perhaps the most potent of the Black Spiral Dancers in Russia is the ancient Theurge Poison Tooth. Constant rumors contend that Poison Tooth is an Abomination given the "gift" of vampirism by Baba Yaga herself, and fortified by near-complete domination by one of the Maeljin Incarna. One of the few Black Spiral leaders to remain completely loyal to the hag throughout the war, Poison Tooth has made enemies among his own kind. A dark figure, even among the Black Spiral Dancers, he is an avatar of the Wyrm of Corruption and travels from hive to hive delivering the Wyrm's will to its followers. It remains to be seen, now that he is free of his bond to Baba Yaga, what he will do next.

Other major hive leaders include Snaps-at-Shadows (aggressive warleader of the Hive of the Wasting Sea), Sergei Kozyrev (enigmatic "captain" of the Hive of the Glowing Sea) and Ivan Balefire (Weaver maddened overlord of the Hive of the Unleashed Atom). Most hated of these creatures, however, is Nicolai Predatelski, Silver Spiral traitor to the Silver Fangs who has taken over control of the Vzrozhdeniye (Renaissance Island) Hive.

Vampires

The war between vampire and werewolf has burned far hotter in Russia than in most parts of the world in recent years. Through loyal servitors and witless pawns,

And the Siberakh?

It's mildly ironic that the fabled Siberakh, sometimes quietly mentioned as a possible "savior tribe" that could deliver Russia from the Baba Yaga, have had little to do with the fall of the hag's armies and nothing to do with the death of Gregornous. A few members of this minor Wendigo-Silver Fang "mixed tribe" did fight alongside their Wendigo relatives in the recent battles for Siberia, and it's even possible that one or two were anonymously at Kursk. But as far as being "Russia's best hope" — they have yet to live up to that wishful thought. As with so many other places around the world, Russia's *true* best hope is a united Garou Nation — battered, bloodied and sadly few in number as it is, but filled with werewolves who aren't willing to give up without a fight.

Baba Yaga used Russian Leeches as one more tool in her schemes to wipe out her Garou opposition. The werewolves have destroyed many vampires in their war against her and, as a result, native vampiric hatred for the Garou now far surpasses the blasé attitude frequently held by Leeches in other parts of the world. When the two sides clash, neither asks for, or receives, any mercy. There is evidence that potent foreign vampires are coming in to fill the power vacuum left by Baba Yaga's death and the destruction of the Brujah.

Pentex

Until a few years ago, Russia had no corporate base of its own. Starting in the late 1950s, the Communist government benefited greatly from the hard currency and knowledge brought in by the capitalist conglomerate, which was also all too happy to aid the Soviet military in its bioweapons research. Then, in late 1990, the whole thing fell apart. For reasons the company couldn't understand, the Black Spiral Dancers revolted. Between this rebellion, growing pressure from the Garou and competition from vampiric corporate predators, the company began to disintegrate. By 1992 it had lost contact with many of its operatives behind the Shadow Curtain and watched as unknown "investors" snatched up its holdings. Now, with Baba Yaga's death, the megacorp is trying to buy its way back into the country. It has to move cautiously, however. Still not knowing the exact nature of the Black Spiral revolt and wary of *upyr* rivals, it will be some time before it is up to full strength again.

Chapter Three: Africa and the Middle East

Africa

War in the Sudan

A week and a day after Black Tooth's death, some twenty dark brown wolves trekked across the As Sudd of the Sudan, moving at a slow trot, carrying themselves with the purpose of predators on the hunt. They shimmered in the heat like fever dreams, ghostly visions of a bygone era lost to the mists of time. From their wallows in the nearby banks of the Nile crocodiles watched, their unflinching stares taking in all before them. The wolves paid them no heed, for it was other concerns which brought them here this day. Presently they slowed their pace, then stopped altogether, sniffing the air and sand, eerily silent as they searched for signs of their prey. At some unseen signal they looked up, then turned toward a point on the horizon; cautiously at first, then with ever-increasing boldness, they slid deeper into the swamp, tracking their quarry in some way the crocodiles could scarcely fathom. As soon as they had come the wolves were gone, and silence reigned once again on the banks of the Nile.

An hour passed, then another, and then another. The watchers heard cries of battle, snarls of rage and howls of terror. The unyielding heat of the day continued unabated, forcing the crocodiles into the coolness of the river. Still they watched, waiting for the wolves' return. At last, near dusk, a wolf appeared in the distance, looking haggard and worn.

He trotted toward the riverbank, and the crocodiles allowed him to drink his fill. Another wolf came, and then another, each seeking the stream's life-giving waters. Some were injured, hobbling toward the river only with the aid of their packmates. Most were whole, though weary. At the last, the leader of the pack emerged, and the crocodile knew by the way the alpha walked that he had seen this wolf before.

Walks-With-Might drank deeply, washing away the trials he and his pack had endured in the past few hours. His thirst slaked, the leader gathered his pack around him. The wolves rested, ignoring their surroundings as they recovered from their ordeal. As twilight fell upon the great swamp of the As Sudd, the wolves' leader locked eyes with the crocodile in his place on the bank. *The Ahadi is sealed,* was the message they exchanged. Old wounds and older hatreds were forgotten. It was time to begin anew.

Walks-With-Might broke the stare, rousing his pack for the long journey home. The temple that was the target of their wrath was broken, but not destroyed. This nest, like so many others, would rise again. But for now the Mokolé and their Kin were safe, and that was enough. For now, all of Gaia's children acted as one.

For eons, African culture has been rich with tales of beasts who walk as men. They speak of great dinosaur kings who walk within the confines of the Congo basin, and Mother Spider who gave life to the world. They tell us of wise Lion who kills those who forget their place, and of Hyena, who knows the secret of death but will not share it with foolish Man, who cannot pass her tests. More than anywhere else in the world the animals here walk with men, and man and beast experience the world as one. So it is with Gaia's children, the shapeshifters. The wounds of the War of Rage bleed freely throughout much of the world, but here in Africa the battles fought were but distant peals of thunder, never quite reaching the borders of the Dark Continent. While there is much in the way of mistrust between the Garou and their siblings, the abject hatred so characteristic of Europe and the Americas is all but absent here.

Much of this solidarity is due to the deranged Simba Bon Bhat, Black Tooth, who has captured the attention of all of Africa's supernaturals for a decade and a half. He is gone now, vanquished by a coalition of Bastet, Garou and Mokolé who chained his magics and scattered his pride to the four winds. That alliance bore lasting fruit in the form of the Ahadi, a covenant among the shifters pledging mutual aid and support in all efforts against the Wyrm and its minions. Though not all of Africa's shifters have joined the Ahadi, the union has nonetheless become a potent force in supernatural affairs throughout the continent. No longer can vampires and minions of the Wyrm move freely among the populace, feeding where they like and destroying according to whim. The Changing Breeds have declared war, and they're moving with enough force and organization to keep their opponents on the defensive.

All is not well, however. Black Tooth's death woke something darker still, and that force stirs within the shifting sands of the Kalahari, the jungles of the Congo, and the teeming masses of humans in Egypt, Nigeria, and South Africa. What this force is, and the rhythm of its movements, is unknown. Its presence is nonetheless undeniable, and the changers who know of it seek answers even as they slaughter their foes.

East Africa

There is a place on Earth where it is still the morning of life, and the great herds run free. Life streams across a land suspended in time, last refuge of the greatest concentration of wildlife remaining on Earth — the Serengeti plains of east Africa.

— James Earl Jones, Africa, the Serengeti

Thank you, friend. It's good that you've agreed to sit with me and listen. So few do, these days. And these last few years, I've seen so much. Ah, where to begin...?

I do not think it possible to convey the beauty and grandeur of East Africa using words alone, for it is a vast, timeless place, filled with hope even as it reeks of death, and there is no other place on Earth which matches its magnificence. Once, all the world was as Africa is now; a place of life and prosperity, guided by cycles at once cruel and kind and populated by all manner of man and beast that people of the western world have all but forgotten. Slowly, under the heel of the whites in Europe, the barbarians in Asia, and the tribes in North America all this changed. The glorious elephants and buffalo were crushed to extinction, as were the legions of cats and hyenas and other creatures we cannot even name anymore. Only in Africa has a semblance of this diversity remained, and even here humans of all races seek to butcher it in the pursuit of their own livelihoods.

The children of Luna and Helios have done what they can to quell this loss of Gaia's legacy to us, but their own conflicts and indecisiveness have stymied their efforts at every turn. The Simba strike at the British colonials in Tsavo, while the Mokolé snap at the heels of the Egyptians in the lower Nile. The Bagheera prowl the outskirts of Nairobi, seeking to put fear into the hearts of men, as the Swara shift to and fro in the Umbra, doing all they can to aid the others without losing themselves in the process. All for naught, for this is not what these children of Gaia are meant to do; they are not Her warriors. They are Her spies, and Her memory, and Her messengers, and Her assassins. For all their power, it is the task of the Mokolé to remember the events of the world, not struggle against the tides of fate. And though they live in prides, the Simba are by nature solitary, living as they do out of necessity rather than by choice. The Bagheera are mighty, but usually work alone. The Ajaba are clever and relentless, but they lack the raw power needed to prevail against the Wyrm. And the Swara are swift, but they cannot be everywhere at once.

No, of all of Gaia's children, it is only we, the Garou, who may truly lay claim to the title of Her warriors. Similarly, it is we who have forsaken this vast place — a decision born of wisdom and pride, which has at once been our greatest failing and our greatest victory. I will tell you, now, of how that came to be undone. I will tell you of how the hyena-kings came back to Kilimanjaro, and how the Simba and the Bagheera embraced their roles as Africa's defenders, and how the Garou made all of this possible. And I will tell you to tread carefully here, for there is death in Africa now, and life as well, as there has always been. The rest of the world is ours, but this place belongs to others. Pay heed to these words, cub. Listen carefully, and learn.

Kenya

What place is this, where a man becomes a man only when he has killed a lion? Who alive has the courage to hunt elephant with nothing but a single great bow? I do not know who might rightfully be called Kenya's kings; are they men, or lions? Small wonder, then, that the Simba choose to breed with both. Whether Maasai, Wakamba, or Waliangulu, or any of the hundreds of other tribes in the region, the Simba have their pick of warriors from whom to choose their mates. Some will tell you that these tribes have been here forever, but they lie; most have been here only since shortly before the various European powers began their colonization efforts. Before that time there were others, and before them yet others. Even moreso than Medieval Europe, East Africa is a place of continual change. One constant, however, seems to be the oppression of the native tribes by outsiders, be they Arab or European. Following the explorations of Joseph Thompson through Maasailand in the mid- to late 1800s (a dangerous area due to the presence of the aggressive Maasai) a solid trail was established between Lake Victoria and the Kenyan coastal strip. The route began as a path for the ivory trade, as Europeans and other foreigners traveled to the interior to hunt and kill long-tusked elephants and then enslaved Africans to haul the ivory to the coast. Here, both were then sold to Arab merchants, to be distributed throughout the Middle East and Asia.

The dissolution of the slave trade put an end to this incarnation of the ivory market, but the conquest of Kenya was only just beginning. The Europeans sought to master the land, as did the Garou who traveled with them. Control and stability were key issues at the time, and mastering this land would lead to great political leverage back home. Vying with the Germans and the French for domination of Africa, the British set to creating a trans-Kenyan railway to better solidify their hold on the land and ease the trade of goods throughout their colonies. The rail represented, in a way other developments did not, the true conquest of Africa by the Europeans, and it was the final straw for Africa's shifters. The Simba reacted violently, tearing into Garou settlements with such speed and ferocity that the werewolves could not even begin to react. One pair of Simba in particular, who would gain great fame among the humans years later, did what they could to stem the growth of the rail, choosing as their battleground the aptly named Tsavo, the place of slaughter. They killed hundreds of workers and frightened off the rest, which forced the British to temporarily halt construction of the railway. Eventually, the lions fell to a soldier's bullets, but not before they'd left their mark. While the conquest of Africa continued unabated, the Garou as a whole soon pulled out of the European colonies, leaving the land to the shifters who'd fought so hard to protect it.

And what of the Maasai? The rail invaded their homeland, and for a time they fought the ever-increasing British presence in their lands. The conquest they were witnessing was hard for them to understand, and much of this confusion stemmed from a view of life and the world that is completely alien to most Europeans. To the Maasai, there are no such things as "wilderness" and "civilization." The realms of man and beast are but parts of the whole, and they cannot rightly be separated. And yet, that is exactly what the British set out to do here in Kenya. Acknowledging, in their way, that the lands of the Maasai and bountiful wildlife were being swallowed whole, they established reserves for Africa's wildlife and native peoples which would keep populations of each in existence for all the world to see. So it was that the northern and southern Maasai reserves were created, places which had less to do with tribal homes or wildlife movements and more with places in which the Europeans had little interest. The reserves bordered the railway to the north and south, and their creation accompanied treaties with the Maasai, which would let the British continue on their way unabated.

It is a hard thing to make an African understand that he is not to kill an animal. To him, the wildlife are as cattle are to whites, and his right to take them as he sees fit as God-given as ours to feed on the meat we raise. Such was not the way of the Europeans, however, and so wildlife reserves came to be created one after another in the years following World War II. The first of these was Selous, a massive park in Tanzania established by Constantine Ionides shortly after the War and consisting of an area three times the size of New Jersey. Kenya followed suit soon after, establishing parks of its own in Tsavo, Amboseli, Nairobi, and a variety of other areas. As the 1970s rolled around Selous became home to fully a tenth of Africa's elephants, though their fortune was the natives' tragedy. Forced out of the park, they became enemies to the wildlife they'd once lived with so harmoniously; similar policies of expulsion were adopted in Kenya. The settlers blamed them for the decline of East Africa's wildlife, cheerfully overlooking the fact that it was whites who ate up the animals' habitats, and who went on safari, and who brought guns into Africa in the first place. Africa's tribes became scapegoats for colonial shortsightedness and greed, and they began to look on the wildlife they'd traditionally counted as neighbors with hatred and resentment. All the while, the Simba sat back and laughed, for the Europeans were undermining their own interests in the region far more effectively than the Simba ever could.

Given this state of affairs, revolt was all but inevitable. It happened at different times in different areas; in Kenya, it happened during the 1950s, finally resulting in Kenyan independence in 1963 (but only after 10,000 or more peasants had died for the cause). Kenya was under new ownership, and it would change the way wildlife management was done forever.

Today, Kenya remains a place filled with darkness and light. Her wildlife was slaughtered mercilessly during the horrible ivory wars of the 1980s, offshoots of Black Tooth's silent reign of terror which held all of Africa paralyzed for fully a decade and a half. Those Simba and their Maasai Kin not allied with Black Tooth held the borders of Amboseli, striking deals with the Bon Bhat to keep the wildlife therein safe. However, they could not avoid a confrontation forever and eventually they, like all of Africa's shifters, were dragged into the war to bring Black Tooth and his allies to heel. The battleground for this conflict was to be the Serengeti plains, and it was a conflict that shook the very heavens themselves.

Tanzania

Situated to the south of Kenya, Tanzania has much in common with its more famous neighbor. Like Kenya, it is filled with a bounty of wildlife unrivaled anywhere on the planet. Also like Kenya, it paid for its independence from European control, in this case Germany, in blood. From Dar Es Salaam to Ngorongoro crater, and from the crystal clear waters of Lake Tanganyika to the blood-soaked plains of the Serengeti, Tanzania is a microcosm of everything that is Africa. In the years following independence many wildlife sanctuaries, such as Lake Manyara National Park, were formed; for every park so formed, thousands of Africans were forcibly removed from their homes. Selous and Serengeti became names etched in blood, and while radical shifts in conservation policy through the 1960s and 70s helped erode the imperialism at the heart of the new administrations, things would get much worse before they got better.

This state of affairs was doubly true for Tanzania's Changing Breeds. While the Mokolé feasted on the annual wildebeest migrations at the border of the Serengeti and the Maasai-Mara reserve in Kenya, they found their animal Kin dwindling in number and range; the Bastet found themselves in a similar situation. The wildlife crowded within the parks, fleeing human poachers outside and exhausting the land within. Those who remained outside were shot, either as vermin (in the case of large cats and crocodiles) or for money and sport (in the case of large game such as elephant and rhino). The pattern was the same in all the African colonies, regardless of ownership; wildlife dropped like flies as the land was reshaped in a form the Europeans found appealing. Some of Gaia's children, however, refused to lie down and suffer such indignities. One such individual was a Simba from Zululand in South Africa named Black Tooth.

As the ivory wars began in earnest during the latter part of the 1970s, Black Tooth put together a pride of Simba which lashed out at all of the European interlopers, be they supernatural or mundane in nature. There were vampires here, and he subjugated them. There were mages as well, redefining the nature of reality, and he expunged them. The ghosts who danced within the elephant graveyards were exorcised, leaving the land silent. He was not selective in his efforts; all who trod upon African soil were subject to his whim, and those who opposed him were eliminated. Most of Africa's Bastet supported him, as he fought against the oppression of the colonials. On the Serengeti, however, there was one group which refused to yield, and refused to die — these were the Ajaba, called by many the Choosers of the Slain. They opposed the Simba at every turn, slaughtering his allies and undermining his support. They knew the secrets of death, and no matter how Black Tooth beat them he could never permanently drive them off. However, as is often the case here, the Ajaba were betrayed by one of their own. In 1984 Black Tooth learned the truth of the Ajaba's Yava, and he used it to slaughter them in the Hyena King's court in Ngorongoro crater. The tribe's numbers went from thousands strong to less than a handful in the span of a single battle, and with their defeat Black Tooth ruled the continent from the Sahara to the Kalahari.

The Ajaba slaughter forced the other Bastet in the region to sit up and take notice of their ally's excesses. The Bagheera, watching from their perches deep within the Congo River basin, judged that the great Simba had gone too far, and formed a war party to stop him. They failed, fleeing home to lick their wounds and imagine their losses were a matter of mere chance. They made another attempt three years later; this sortie ended in failure as well. They had not the numbers to strike at him directly, for his powers were mighty indeed. He could not be surprised, and he could weave magics gifted to no changer before or since. None could take him alone, and so the Bagheera called a moratorium on war parties until they could figure out what to do.

At this point in the story, you might legitimately ask where the Garou were during this whole mess. After all, Tanzania was colonized by the Germans, and Kenya by the British; one might expect to find some Get of Fenris, or Fianna, or Silver Fangs lurking in East Africa somewhere, able to help. In truth, while there are indeed members of these tribes here, their numbers

A World of Rage

and influence are small indeed. We Garou make our protectorates slowly, and we do not blindly follow our Kinfolk everywhere they go. There are times when we immigrate in large numbers, settling or conquering new lands, but this only happens in wild places, or in places where the native Garou have been judged unfit to rule. We did this in America, and we did it in Australia, damning ourselves in the process. But Africa was never our land, and the Bastet, Mokolé, and Ananasi never yielded so much as an inch to any werewolves who thought to come here. Some Garou *do* exist here in force, but they are a strange and alien breed to us; I will speak of them later. For now, though, let me continue with my tale.

Now, where was I? Oh, yes; Black Tooth. What he overlooked was the fact that his power had made him arrogant; he was not nearly so thorough with the Ajaba as he might have imagined. Some fled to the four corners of the world, making whatever pacts they needed to survive. Some fell to the Wyrm. But others stayed here, seeking refuge with the Mokolé along the banks of the Zambezi, or with their hyena Kin, or even with the other Bastet tribes. The leader of the Ajaba remaining in Africa was a queen named Kisasi. It was she who engineered the peace with the Mokolé, and it was she who began coordinating a resistance move-

ment against Black Tooth, using the limited resources of the Ajaba and other Bastet to weaken the mighty Bon Bhat's position. Most importantly, however, it was she who discovered the African Garou.

We don't know much about the Kucha Ekundu; they are a lost camp of the Red Talons, and they have wandered much of Africa for quite some time. Decades ago, they sought out the Mokolé-mbembe, and begged them to help the Garou survive in this alien place. They came to help set right the short-sightedness of the Garou thousands of years before; they came to help, not on their own terms but on those of the Mokolé. The Mokolé, noting the declining numbers of African hunting dogs due to human persecution, took the Talons' request at face value, and gave them a test. If they could learn to take the shape of the hunting dogs, the Mokolé would help them. The Talons took up the challenge, and ever since they have roamed all of sub-Saharan Africa wearing the bodies of these painted wolves.

In the late 1980s, Kisasi made contact with these elusive Garou, entreating their aid in her battle against Black Tooth. Skeptical at first, and in no way convinced of Kisasi's own worthiness, they ignored her pleas for a decade and a half. Finally, just two years ago, they assented. What they did, however, was nothing like what the canny hyena had in mind.

Chapter Three: Africa and the Middle East

As her sphere of influence increased, Kisasi began recruiting allies from all over the continent. The Swara of Namibia helped form her stronghold, and the Simba of the Kalahari gave her a rallying point for those lions unhappy with Black Tooth's rule. The Mokolé of the Mara River pledged their unconditional support to her in hopes of restoring the balance that had long marked the Serengeti ecosystem. The Bagheera worked to solve logistical problems, using their global networks to stay ahead of the Endless Storm; stealing weapons shipments bound for military units in the Democratic Republic of the Congo didn't hurt, either. Her cleverest move was yet to come, though. She convinced all of her allies to call upon the Garou for aid, and to bury the grudges they'd held against us for so long. Malignant though he was, Black Tooth turned out to be the one threat that could make us focus on the present instead of obsessing with the past. We heard their plea, and we responded. As a result, we Striders taught the hyenas tactics, and undermined Black Tooth's vampiric support. In working together, we shifters maintained a running guerilla war against our enemy, always avoiding his claws by means of superior mobility and cooperation.

Eventually, three things happened which set up the final, apocalyptic conflict that forever changed the face of Africa. First, the Kucha Ekundu's canine Kin were struck by an outbreak of distemper, which gutted their ranks. Turning calamity into advantage, they spread the plague through the lion populations of the Serengeti, laying waste to all of Black Tooth's feline Kin. At the same time, an upset in the vampiric power structure left many packs of the things vulnerable, a vulnerability which we Silent Striders exploited and which left the Endless Storm without its allies. Finally, Black Tooth discovered the Mokolé involvement in Kisasi's uprising, and defiled their nests along the banks of the Zambezi River. This was the Bon Bhat's fatal error, for he assumed that the Mokolé's preference for inaction meant they were incapable of coordinated, sustained battle. He was wrong. Calling upon the Bagheera to coordinate their efforts, the Mokolé exploded into action, hunting the Endless Storm no matter where they fled, and slaughtering them to a man. Key to breaking their power was the mighty Spear of Mokolé-Mbembe, found at long last deep within the Congo basin. I am unclear as to the details of its discovery, but I believe the Kucha Ekundu were somehow involved. Regardless, the Endless Storm was shattered, and Black Tooth was on his own.

Then it came to pass that a mighty roar shook the Near Umbra, grasping the souls of all it touched and rending them with talons of fear. A great silence followed, deafening in its intensity, and we knew, all of us, that everything had changed. The Storm was over. The darkness had passed. Victory was ours. And yet, each of us who heard that sound knew that on that day, at that moment, something terrible was born.

I do not know how Black Tooth died; perhaps it was the Bagheera, raining fire upon him as they chained his magics and tore at him with their claws. It is their way to judge those they find unworthy, and they might well have found the justice they have sought for so long. Perhaps it was Gaia's warriors, the forgotten Garou we refer to now as the Kucha Ekundu. I do not think they could destroy Black Tooth alone, but they have hidden strengths, and we have underestimated them before. And then there are those who judge the rest of Gaia's children, even though common wisdom says they are long extinct. Did they come here, ending Black Tooth's reign with a serpent's tooth? The truth may never be fully understood. What is known is that Black Tooth, or what was left of him, was found strewn about the basin in Ngorongoro crater, his crushed skull staked on a long spear outside of the Hyena-King's court. Whoever killed him, they had a deep appreciation for irony.

The fallout from Black Tooth's death has been enormous. The Striders were badly bloodied by their wars with the vampires, and while it led to improved relations with the Bubasti it will nonetheless take them quite some time to recover. The Kucha Ekundu have lost most of their canine populations, with the bulk remaining in Selous game reserve in Tanzania and the Okavango in Botswana, and the rest scattered to the four winds. The Ajaba, Gaia's morbid laughter, have been redeemed, though their numbers remain low. Hakimu, the Mayi'o Simba king, has taken his place in Ngorongoro, though the Amadu'o who remain chafe under the new leadership, and plot against the smarter southern prides. Hakimu is wise and crafty, though, and so manages to evade Amadu'o treachery when it crops up. He fights with Kisasi constantly, but it is a good fight; their hatred for one another is strong, but softened by grudging respect. The Bagheera lost many in their fight with the Endless Storm, but they have taken their role as judges quite seriously; they have established a peace accord among all of the Changing Breeds, and they now work together as they do in few other places in the world. The architect of the Ahadi was a Bagheera called Kiva, and she speaks for the majority of her kind in East Africa. The Mokolé of the Zambezi have lost their legacy, but not their heritage; they will breed again, and until that time they wallow in the banks of the river. The Mokolé of the Congo celebrate their rebirth in the aftermath of the discovery of the Spear of Mokolé-Mbembe; their power is unquestioned, and their influence grows by the

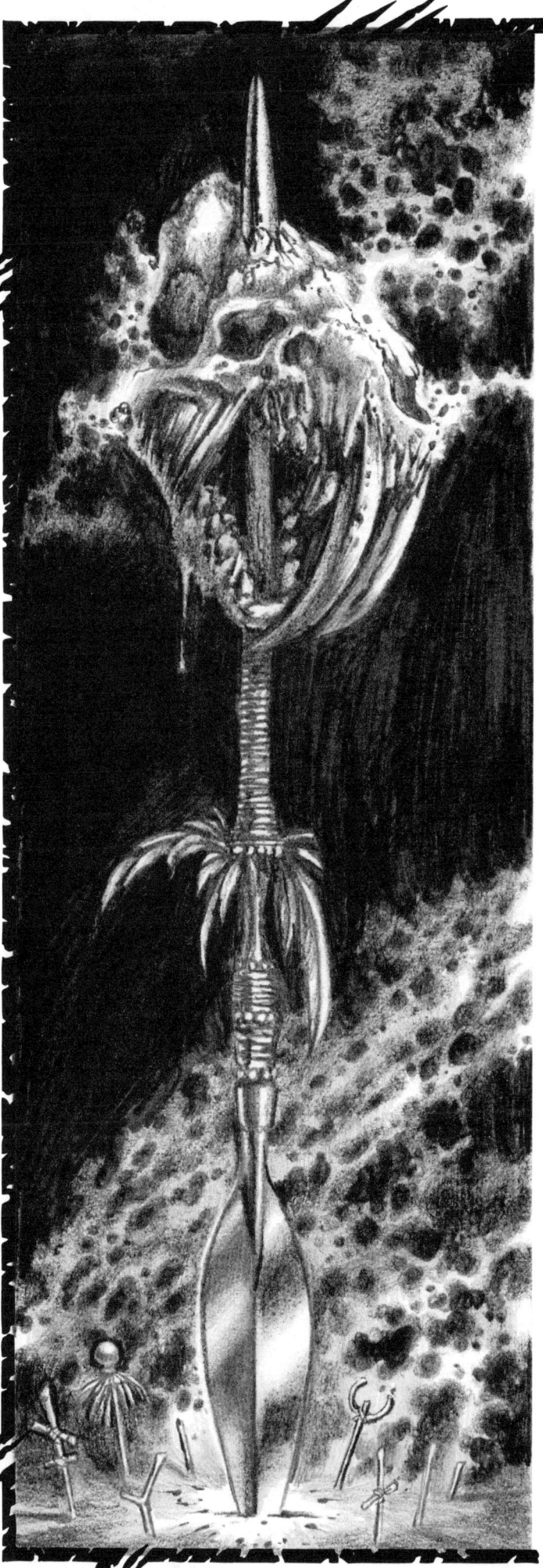

On the Nature of Lion Cooperation

One of the greatest misconceptions floating around in the world of the Discovery Channel is the notion that lions hunt cooperatively, and form prides to enhance their hunting ability. This is somewhat misleading, since lions (or rather, lionesses, as it is they who hunt) tend to break up, singly and in pairs, when they hunt, and enjoy their greatest success rates when few lions are involved in such endeavors (as discussed elsewhere, however, there are exceptions to this rule). Why, then, do lions stay together? Well, as the game offered by an area increases, the number of predators the land can support increases as well. Eventually, a threshold is breached and it becomes advantageous to forego individual territories and put up with sharing one's resources with others instead. Hence, lions stay together because living apart carries with it far too many costs.

The same is true of the Simba. It is a mistake to think the Simba fight as a coordinated unit, striking with the speed and finesse of a werewolf pack. This is true of Bagheera war parties as well; though they fight in numbers, they fight as an aggregate of individuals, not as a team. This is a limitation the werecats have great difficulty in overcoming, and it is why they fall to threats like the Garou in the world outside of Africa. The reason behind the Endless Storm's terrifying effectiveness, then, lies in the fact that these Simba managed to overcome their solitary nature and fight as a highly coordinated team. The combination of the Bastet's terrifying Gifts and the pack mentality normally restricted to the Garou, not to mention the various magical and vampiric abilities Black Tooth stole from his victims, are what made the Endless Storm a threat that simply could not be faced openly. No matter how good the PCs are, they're not *that* good, and the Storyteller is encouraged to convey this fact to the player characters.

day. The Swara have become the messengers they were always meant to be, serving as intermediaries between the Bastet courts and the Silent Striders to the north and the Kucha Ekundu to the east and south. The alliances formed during the battle with the Endless Storm remain, and we Striders worked with the Bagheera to craft the Ahadi, an agreement among Africa's shifters to aid one another in their battles with the Wyrm. Gaia's children have found their true path once again.

The most extensive consequences of the Endless Storm's passing, however, have come from the power vacuum Black Tooth left behind. Despite his barbarity, his success at keeping the minions of order from conquering Africa cannot be denied, and the iron control he exerted over the vampires of sub-Saharan Africa was enviable. Both of these forces now have free reign to do as they will, and while the vampires have been wounded by their own internal politics and the efforts of the Silent Striders only a fool would assume their influence is permanently removed. Worse still, the Dark Lord kept innumerable Wyrmish foes at bay, forcing their stench from his home as a thing which offended him. Now, these forces seek to return to the great plains, corrupting Gaia's bounty there despite the Bastet's greatest efforts. As I have said, they are not Gaia's chosen warriors, and as such they cannot do what the Garou can do. The Ahadi aside, they can do little more than identify the threats facing them, forming intermittent war parties to deal with the dangers as best they can. If the Kucha Ekundu recover, they might be able to help; they're losing Kin fast, though, and they have their own problems to face. The same holds true for the Silent Striders to the north; their vigilance is reserved for their ancient vampiric foes, and they have no time for the problems of Africa. The Bastet have thus traded one immense problem for innumerable smaller ones, and these may do what Black Tooth could not. Only time will tell.

Rwanda

To the west of Kenya and Tanzania lies one of Africa's most troubled states — Rwanda, a land subject to atrocities on a magnitude only rarely seen in the whole of human history. During the colonial period, the minority Tutsi tribe found favor with first the Germans and then the Belgians, dominating positions in both education and employment until the modern era. In 1959, the majority group, the Hutus, overthrew the Tutsi monarch, butchering hundreds of Tutsis and driving tens of thousands into exile. By 1990 the Tutsis had rallied, beginning a civil war which culminated in the deaths of more than 800,000 Tutsis and moderate Hutus. Despite their losses, the Tutsis prevailed, forcing some two million Hutus into exile. During the late 1990s the refugees began to return, but the civic upheavals had devastated the nation's fragile economy.

We Silent Striders have known our share of suffering. We have known exile and hatred, and we have tasted the bitterness of mistrust from the other tribes. Our Kin were slaughtered in the Second World War, then ignored and spat upon in all the decades since. The words "never again" hold special meaning for us; we know better than most just how selectively they are applied. We have seen the troubled places where they ring pathetically hollow. Never again? Hah! Time and again! Look across the land of Rwanda, cub, and you will see the face of genocide staring back at you. This is the Wyrm's legacy to us. This is the full measure of its power. Fomori and Urge Wyrms are trivial by comparison; it is the shackles on our souls, born of hatred and rage and indifference, which show us its awesome, unfettered might. Our failure, and the humans' damnation, lies in the fact that we have stood by and allowed such things to happen over and over again. The Impergium was a game of tag compared to this; I'm sure the Red Talons were quite pleased with the way things turned out.

But then again, perhaps not.

I once wondered why the Kucha Ekundu threw themselves so fervently behind the cause to rid the world of Black Tooth. After all, he was a force of destruction, annihilating the fruit of human labors throughout the whole of Africa. This is the Talons' most heartfelt goal, is it not? But something happened here, in Rwanda, which put the lie to any claims one might make about the inescapable taint of humans. Even now I fail to comprehend how it occurred, but I was there. I bore witness to it with my own eyes, and it is as real as anything in the world. It began in a game reserve to the west, on the border of what was then called Zaire, and what is now the Congo; the place was called Virunga, and it was home to the critically endangered populations of highland gorillas made famous by biologists such as Dian Fossey. The reserve was evacuated once hostilities broke out; the researchers there had to flee if they were to survive, and their equipment was subsequently stolen or destroyed by rebel forces. Somehow, the gorillas survived the days of war, and that in itself is nothing short of miraculous. However, the true surprise was yet to come. After the hostilities had died down the scientists studying the gorillas returned to the highlands and found, to their amazement, that some rangers had remained to protect the gorillas even amidst all the hostilities. These were not soldiers, and they persevered for months on end with no money, no reliable sources of food, and no supplies of any kind. Such relentless dedication to the survival of non-humans simply cannot be ignored, and I think the Talons, or at least these particular Talons, considered this act of sacrifice and made a conscious decision to give humanity another chance. Humans are a brutal, murderous lot, but they are also capable of acts of astonishing selflessness. Do not forget this, cub, no matter what you see in the world.

With its return to stability, Rwanda's doing its best to recover. Some 35% of the nation's land is arable, and some astonishingly innovative farming techniques developed before the civil war are proving sufficient for maintaining an extremely high population density without additional stress on the land. The government is

A World of Rage

highly progressive, embarking on ambitious reconstruction efforts with the help of the World Bank and seeking to re-establish its (mainly subsistence) agricultural base. Among shapeshifters, I've heard that there are some Black Furies in the area attending to the needs of disenfranchised women, as they suffered from the fallout more than any other single group. I think there were some Kucha Ekundu here once as well, and I know they have visited; but their animal half has been extirpated, so they've mostly moved to the east or south. There aren't any Bastet or Mokolé here, either; the only wildlife that survives is that in Virunga, and the star attraction there is the gorillas. Still, it is a place of hope. Though it has been crushed in the Wyrm's coils, Rwanda fights to recover. I can only wish them the best of luck.

Southern Africa

Unlike much of the rest of Africa, Southern Africa is typified by its diversity. Whereas North Africa is dominated by the expanse of the Sahara, East Africa by its savannas, and West Africa by its expansive forests, Southern Africa has a little bit of everything. From the Okavango to the Kalahari and the Cape of Good Hope to the Transvaal, Southern Africa is home to just about everything. This diversity applies to Gaia's children as much as anything; one can find Swara, Bagheera, and Simba here, as well as Mokolé, Garou, Ananasi, Ratkin, and Rokea. Gaia's enemies are legion as well: vampires infest the governments, even though their influence has lessened in recent years, they prowl the lands searching for victims. The minions of the Wyrm slaughter the wildlife here, gutting the land of its lifeblood. As is often the case, however, the greatest evils are perpetuated by humans, as are the greatest goods.

South Africa

It is of course a truism that Black Tooth and the Endless Storm did not exist in a vacuum, nor did they spring forth whole cloth. They came from the oppression and destruction of South Africa, playing upon the fears and hatreds of the innumerable tribes who suffered the wrath of the whites. For eighty years and more less than twenty percent of South Africa's population ruled the land, using semi-slave labor and a doctrine of institutionalized racism to strip the Transvaal of its incredible resources. Finally, in the 1980s, in response to the riots and rebellion coursing through South Africa's veins, and in the wake of the total eradication of all large predators from the countryside, Black Tooth and his pride erupted. They represent the greatest destructive force Africa has ever known, but the true evil lies in the hearts of the men who thought it their duty and their privilege to first invade, then conquer and rule a land that was not their own. Everything here was about control — the Africans were forced to obey, the rich mineral resources were coveted and stripped from the Earth, the predators were expunged, and the remaining game animals culled to fit the European ideal of stability. I wish we could blame the Wyrm for such things. I wish we could say they were the fault of Black Tooth, or traitorous Ajaba, or demented Garou. Such was not the case, however; these things were the doing of human beings, unaided, unfettered, and unafraid.

There are Garou here, in South Africa. Their power is weak, weaker than they would have you believe, because they have thus far been unable to establish lasting caerns or networks of power. Before the abolition of apartheid the vampires had the government locked up tight, and now… well, most of the Garou are whites, so you can imagine how far they get. These are mostly Get of Fenris, and they are divided into two groups with radically divergent philosophies. One group supports the racist ideologies of apartheid, viewing the black Africans as backward and superstitious, and undeserving of our respect. They are the ones who called for the extermination of the lions of the Transvaal, since their views extended to the Simba as well as their native Kin. The other group wanted apartheid torn down from the beginning; apartheid coddles the weak, they said, denying the strong their chance to stand and face the jaws of the Wyrm. I have to believe this was the majority view of the tribe. The alternative is too disgusting to imagine.

Anyway, as with the rest of Africa, Southern Africa's nations revolted; Swaziland, Botswana, Lesotho, and many others paid for their independence with blood, but the colonial government in South Africa remained strong until the 1980s. Finally, even it fell, again without much in the way of supernatural intervention. The shifters were doing their part, though; if I understand correctly, some of the most effective demonstrations were staged by nothing other than Bone Gnawers, and the Mayi'o Simba had to have had a hand in apartheid's fall. However, any such contributions were purely mundane in nature, since most shifters had more immediate problems to deal with. They had to protect what Kin they could from being slaughtered, and this alone proved to be a Herculean effort.

Today, Southern Africa is a haven for the cheetah and leopard populations of Africa. Outside of the Serengeti, these animals have few other places to call home; they survive here despite constant pressure from Afrikaner farmers and ranchers, who shoot them on sight as threats to their herds. It is only in the parks that they are safe, and it is only there that some semblance of the diversity South Africa once knew remains. Kruger is the largest of these parks, and it is one of the last refuges of the Amadu'o Simba. However, it is the Swara who dominate here, breeding readily with the humans of neighboring Swaziland, which shares the southern border of the park. The Bagheera, too, lay claim to this area, and they use it as an anchorhead for extending the influence of Gaia's children into Southern Africa. Ultimately, however, it will be left to the Swara alone to police this area; all of South Africa's other Bastet Kin have fallen to human predations. Perhaps this trend will be reversed in the years to come; lions have been seen leaving the confines of Kruger, and they are being allowed to do so. It is, perhaps, a false hope, but it is all we have.

With the abolition of apartheid, an unexpected shift has occurred within the politics of our most reclusive cousins — the Rokea. Since the Table Bay oil spill in 1983 some sixty kilometers from Cape Town, the weresharks have exhibited tremendous interest in the growth of human industry in these areas. However, movement on land, whether to attack industrial complexes which require or move crude oil or simply as a means of exploration, had been largely limited by the South African Group Areas Act, which curtailed the movements of Africans throughout the nation. Do you see how this happened? Since they make no particular distinction between humans of different skin color, the human laws were rather confusing to the Rokea, who found themselves hounded by Afrikaner police when they came ashore as wearing the skins of native Africans. With the change in government, their movements on land are much less restricted, and as a result attacks on industrial complexes have increased dramatically. These attacks, once fairly sporadic, have become more coordinated of late. A terrified Rokea has told me that the source of this uncharacteristic coordination is a huge Karkha called Shreds-the-Surface, though many shifters in South Africa simply call him Shreds. He is not Wyrm-tainted, but he'll tear anyone he encounters on land to pieces anyway. While his efforts to stop the Wyrm are commendable, his extremism is dangerous, particularly when Africans find themselves forced to turn to forests for fuel wood because a power station has been destroyed. Avoid him if possible.

Here's pure rumor for you: The new regime has also, so I've heard, affected those Rokea born of humans, or who choose for whatever reason to live on land. They have allegedly been making alliances to save themselves from war parties launched by their oceanic brethren — I don't know why they're fighting in the first place, but I can only assume it's a surfeit of Rage — and some of these alliances have been strange indeed. I've heard tales of shark-people acting as enforcers for Black Tooth in the last years of his reign; makes sense, as his magics could hide their location from their pursuers. With his fall, rumor has it, they have made contact with and begun talking to the Swara about the Umbra, and how they might negotiate it to escape their fates. The Swara have little aid to offer thus far, but they know well what it's like to be hunted, and so they hide the in-betweeners when they can. Sadly, I believe some weresharks have thrown in their lot with what few vampires have managed to thread their way throughout the government, using their influence to stay a few steps ahead of the ocean dwellers. Such individuals are threats to us as much as anyone, so don't shed too many tears if you find yourself forced to kill one.

Namibia

Though the status of the Swara's cat Kin once looked bleak, they are now on the rebound. Proof of the more positive aspects of humanity is now irrefutable, for it is humans who set themselves the goal of preserving the cheetah in the wild. In Namibia, South Africa's neighbor to the northwest, some 90% of all cheetahs roam on private farmland, and they are shot for their transgressions. Humans seeking to save them, however, have endeavored to work closely with the owners of these lands, using cheetah psychology to control their travels and make the prospect of coexistence somewhat more tenable. As it happens, the cheetahs are deathly afraid of dogs; some Striders I've talked to speculate that this is a remnant of the War of Rage, but I think it's just because cheetahs are weird. No matter the reason, biologists seeking to save the cheetah found that by giving dogs to the ranchers of Namibia they could save the cheetah populations from extinction at the hands of humans. It is ironic and laughable, but it works, so who am I to argue?

When most people think of Africa they think of Third World nations, poor in all things. Not so in Namibia; the roads are good and the economy even better, and the government has done well for itself since it won its independence from South Africa in 1990. It's urbanized enough that things like lions just won't do, and as such they were eradicated long ago. Cheetahs aren't well liked either, but they're harder to kill because they're a bit more secretive. The resemblance between the cheetah's plight here and that of wolves in North America is uncanny; the fact that much of their conservation boils down to figuring when they can be shot is eerier even still. The Swara seem to have things well in hand, though; Wyrm-things come here, seeking to gain a foothold in the wake of Black Tooth's destruction, but the Swara have proven surprisingly effective at warding off such interlopers. Much of this is due to a colonial Swara named Tinus Grellman. Though cat-born rather than homid, he was raised by Afrikaner Swara Kin, and he knows as much about how humans work as any human. He's quite striking in Feline form, having the rare king cheetah morph, and his ability to traverse the worlds of animal and human, and physical and spirit, has brought him tremendous success in organizing defenses against Wyrm threats. He's a good ally, and open to working with others so long as they show the proper respect.

Despite Grellman's efforts, it is only a matter of time until the vampires reestablish themselves; with so many Swara running around, though, that may be a long time coming. I know many of the Leeches have taken huge losses with the change in South Africa's government; the recent shakeup in their ranks might have unsettled them even further, so some might be getting desperate. I've talked to Grellman about this, and he's pretty concerned about it; he hasn't asked for help as of yet, but I think he will soon have no other option.

Botswana

To the north of South Africa lies the Kalahari Desert, one of the least hospitable pieces of land in the entire world. This place covers Botswana, swallowing up some 75% of the country, before yielding to the magnificent Okavango delta to the north. Here, the waters of the Okavango River empty into the flat desert and create a paradise of islands and lagoons that summon wildlife in droves. This rich, bountiful land is home to the Mayi'o tribe of the Simba, and it is here they made their first alliances with the Kucha Ekundu camp of the Red Talons.

The Okavango is a sanctuary and haven to a staggering array of wildlife species; elephant and hippo lounge here annually, and lions, hyenas, and hunting dogs hunt as though they stood in the gates of Heaven itself. Where the Serengeti is famous because of its diversity of wildlife, the Okavango is famous for its diversity of ecosystems. It is the stuff of fever dreams, and yet it is entirely real.

Botswana is in many ways southern Africa's success story; it has an incredibly stable economy, relying almost exclusively on its mineral reserves for its continued success, and has been ranked higher even than South Africa in terms of development. Since most of the country is dominated by the Kalahari, and thus subject to frequent drought, agriculture is nowhere nearly as extensive here as it is in the rest of southern Africa. Instead, cattle ranching is more the norm; crops are grown mainly for immediate consumption, instead of for their market value. Botswana's infrastructure is also impressive; highways have been built to link regions across the desert, and while its railways are limited they nonetheless form a critical link in the African railway system. Air links between urban areas are impressive, and the country boasts three international airports.

Though tourism is a small industry at present, it is growing in economic significance. The Okavango delta, Savuti, Gemsbok, and Chobe national parks, and the Kalahari itself draw tourists in the thousands, and rightly so; few places in Africa can best Botswana's incredible wildlife reserves. Chobe, a stone's throw from Namibia, Zambia, and Zimbabwe, is thick with elephants, and Savuti has some of the most audacious lions in the world — while most are content to feast on wildebeest and the occasional zebra, these make water buffalo their standard fare, and occasionally take juvenile elephants. A number of Garou assume such kills are the Simba's doing, but this is not the case. Indeed, the Mayi'o revere Savuti's lions because of their ferocious audacity, siring cubs within the prides to strengthen their bestial halves. The continual war between Savuti's lions and hyenas, though, is almost certainly a product of Simba aggression. Though it isn't clear where Kisasi and her supporters originated, Savuti is a good bet; it is only here that the hyenas exist in numbers strong enough to rival those of East Africa.

Despite its success, however, Botswana is now a land of suffering. Cattle suck the land of its limited plant life, and their overgrazing is destroying what little arable land the region holds. The Kalahari's tides encroach upon the land at every turn, and in the months since Black Tooth's death it has become apparent that he was holding darker powers in check deep within the shifting sands of the desert. Whether this was a manifestation of the Wyrm or something even more alien is unclear, but it is spreading, claiming all the land it touches. But, desertification is only the beginning; whatever this force is, it is fouling Botswana's water supplies as well. At one time up to 93% of the country's inhabitants had access to fresh water, but no longer; now, supplies have been shrinking rapidly, and the effects of drought are magnified every year. Hakimu is trying to organize a party to investigate the issue, but there is so much posturing between his supporters and those of Kisasi that his efforts have proven less than successful. Soon, we will have to establish contact with the Kucha Ekundu, gaining their trust and using them to help us identify this piece of Wyrm-taint and expunge it. That is, of course, far more easily said than done.

Central Africa

Central Africa is dominated by the Congo River basin, one of the most remote and least explored areas on Earth and counted as a stronghold of many of Gaia's children. Though the land is torn by strife, this place is the seat of the Ahadi and forms the foundation for many shifters' war to take back Africa from the chaos that consumes it now. Strange things, terrible things were awakened here by Black Tooth's death cry, and Central Africa's Changing Breeds are only now learning of the many things he kept at bay while he terrorized the land. In addition, vampires and other supernaturals are taking advantage of the civil wars, which now have a stranglehold on the continent, and the Mokolé and Bastet are waging a ferocious campaign to annihilate their influence once and for all. They come perilously close to rending the Veil, but we stand ready to aid them in any way we can.

Congo River Basin

It is an odd thing, perhaps, to find in a place so plagued with drought and strife as Africa a region of unconquered life. When contrasted with the vastness of the Sahara to the north, or the teaming herds in the rolling plains to the east and south, it is somewhat disquieting to find a place of such incredible richness as the Congo nestled in the crook of the western African coast. Reaching from Nigeria to Angola along the coast, and from the coast to Rwanda in the interior, the Congo River basin is deceptively vast. The Congo is home to the greatest concentration of Mokolé in the world, and it is their ancestral homeland. Similarly, the Bagheera live here in numbers unmatched throughout the world. They and the Mokolé are kings here, and this is a place where others will not follow. Unfortunately, it is also a place of slaughter and destruction; this is its tale.

Four and a half centuries ago, the Portuguese arrived here to find a kingdom as orderly and well governed as their own, with a system of courts and kings and vassals and a bureaucratic organization analogous to that of Europe. For a time, the Kingdom of Kongo and the Portuguese they took as neighbors lived in peace, exchanging ambassadors, religious missionaries, and methods of government. It was a peace born of conquest, though, as the Kongo people could teach the Europeans a thing or two about the nature of subjugation; they traded slaves with the Portuguese, furthering the global slave trade as they learned about the European ways. As such, the Portuguese respected the Kongo's sovereignty for a time, both out of desire and of necessity.

The Bagheera and Mokolé-mbembe of the river basin looked on these events with distress, as they found their Kin being stolen from them at a terrifying rate. While it is true that the most central and least accessible areas of the rainforest were largely untouched by the slave trade, the defilement of den-

realms and nests alike was still extensive. They fought as best they could, but were overwhelmed by numbers and supernatural threats lost to the mists of time. They did the only thing they could do in such a situation: they pulled back and waited, watching for a time when they might reclaim their ancestral birthrights.

The accord between the Kongo and the Portuguese could never last, of course; while the Kongo rulers were happy to export subjugated tribes as slaves, the voraciousness of the Portuguese was such that the kingdom found its ranks thinning rapidly. Growing concern over the state of affairs strained the relationship between the Kongo rulers and the Europeans, but it made no difference. Eventually, the region was partitioned up between France, Belgium, and Portugal, and centuries of revolution and strife followed, which continue, even to this day. Only the Mokolé could tell you for sure how much they and the Bagheera were involved in this disruption; it is unquestionable that they were active, but the history of the area is so chaotic that the full extent of their activities may never be known.

The modern day Congo River basin is split between two countries: these are the Republic of the Congo and the Democratic Republic of the Congo. Of these, the more significant to the Garou is the Democratic Republic of the Congo, known until very recently as Zaire. The country occupies an area fully a quarter of the size of the United States, and it has a population in excess of 50 million people. The potential for this region in all respects is unimaginable, but it suffers from constant conflict and heavy influxes of refugees from every quarter. The country's infrastructure is poor, the government is rife with corruption, and murky economic policies and stillborn foreign aid efforts stifle the economy. The greatest strain on the region, however, comes in the form of refugees spilling over the borders from neighboring countries. In the wake of genocide in Rwanda, nearly a million refugees flooded into the country, only returning when the Congo civil war erupted in 1996. In addition, hundreds of thousands of Angolans, Burundi, Sudanese, and Ugandan refugees now call the Congo home, and there is nothing the government can do to help them. Renewed hostilities between the national and rebel forces in 1998 haven't helped matters, resulting in yet more displacement.

The Congo is the last hope for some of Africa's shifters, particularly the Bagheera and the Mokolé-mbembe. While the leopards and crocodiles are being slaughtered as vermin throughout much of Africa, here they still exist in the hundreds of thousands. They are not safe, but their numbers are strong, and the shifters who rely on them are likewise fairly well off. Since recovering the Spear of Mokolé-Mbembe, the greatest weapon of his kind, Swims-in-Mbembe's-Wake has roused the Mokolé to action; how they will choose wield their influence remains to be seen, but they are unquestionably more active now than they have ever been before. The destruction of the forests is their main concern, and they combat the industry that fuels its destruction. The refugees that crowd the Congo's borders are proving especially problematic; although they are not by any stretch of the imagination Wyrm-tainted, they are nonetheless destroying huge areas of rainforest in their quest for fuel wood. They are a problem with no simple solution, for they cannot simply be expunged or killed. The Mokolé recognize this, and do what they can to aid them. However, the Mokolé are not the only ones who take it upon themselves to aid the refugees; tales have leaked out about displaced men and women who were treated to stays in magnificent estates within the forest borders, areas which do not exist on any map. Solitary though they may be, the Bagheera are doing their part.

Black Tooth's death cry swept through the whole of Africa, and with its touch everyone changed. His final roar was heard deep within the Congo jungles, and as a result even the mysterious Ananasi have become more active than is their wont. They have ventured out from their ancient homes, striking at vampires throughout the Congo with incredible ferocity. The reason for this upswing in their activity is unclear; they had no part in the eradication of the Endless Storm, and are not a part of the Ahadi as far as anyone knows. For whatever reason, though, the werespiders have become a force to be reckoned with. The Bagheera and Mokolé tend to avoid them.

There is one other shifter network in the Congo basin, but we don't talk about it much. This is the Umbral tunnel network of Lord Ebola, a Ratkin of some repute. Like the Ananasi, he refused to become part of the Ahadi, and he showed no interest in helping us deal with Black Tooth or his minions. In point of fact, he might even have been a silent ally of the Dark Lord. Regardless, he now seems content to snipe at the human refugees fleeing about, earning him the enmity of both the shifters native to the Congo and the few werewolves visiting the region. Interestingly enough, however, there seems to be an underground underground of sorts, where rats of modest station take it upon themselves to sort out ties with their Gaian neighbors in response to increased Wyrmish activity deep within the jungle. On at least one occasion I saw a pair talking to a Kucha Ekundu and I've heard that their networks extend to ancient places even the Mokolé have forgotten. This is nonsense, of course, but the extent of their tunnels is broad indeed, and if they could be courted as allies our mobility would increase tenfold.

The Congo's shifters take no part in the human politics of either the state or the other nations sharing its borders; they are sick to death of the slaughter which characterizes this part of Africa, and they are determined to see it end. Taking advantage of curfews and martial law to sneak into cities and cull those they deem unworthy, they are proving amazingly adept at seeking out and destroying vampires, mages, and a variety of other independent supernatural types. None are truly insulated from their wrath; whether rebels or government forces, humans or Wyrm-spawned pawns of puppet dictators — all are falling to their teeth and claws, and they will see peace and stability in the Congo if they have to slaughter every pretender to rulership to do it.

There are Garou here as well, but make no mistake: these are not hospitable lands for them. The Mokolé and the Bagheera treat them as outsiders, and there are few enough here that they cannot coordinate effectively. It is only by granting the crocodiles and panthers immense respect that they are permitted to stay, and even then few remain for long. Contrary to what you might have heard, the influence of the Black Furies here is actually quite limited. They have two permanent caerns deep in the basin, but their septs are small and ever-changing. These are currently used as bases of operation for coordinating relief efforts among the multitude of refugees pouring over the borders daily; they haven't the influence to do much else, and now more than ever they bow to the will of the Mokolé and the Bagheera. As for other werewolves, there are rumors of Glass Walker activity near the borders, dealing with improving the infrastructure of the area, but I've yet to meet any who would admit to such things. Such deeds come close to breaking their vow to the Nation, and that's something I don't think they're prepared to do.

The Ahadi aside, recent events deep within the Congo are making the Mokolé and Bagheera rethink their policies on the Garou. Ancient evils once again walk the world, traversing the nearly transparent gauntlet within the basin to wreak havoc on the surrounding lands. The Black Furies were the first to sound the alarm, and the Mokolé have not forgotten this. Several of the werewolves have joined the native shifters in battle against these new threats, and some have even died in the defense of nests and den-realms. The Mokolé and Bagheera do not forget such things, and they pay their debts. What this will mean for Garou operating in the region is unclear, but relations among all concerned are fairly stable at the moment. Perhaps we'll get it right this time around.

Central African Republic

It seems that if anything can go wrong in the Central African Republic, someone will find a way to make it happen. Though once hailed as one of the last great wildlife refuges in Africa, widespread poaching has shattered that reputation. Constant military uprisings — to the tune of three mutinies of the armed forces in 1996 alone — have contributed to the political instability that characterizes most of central Africa. Extensive deforestation to the south and harmattan winds from the north strain the environment to the breaking point and beyond. The constant political turmoil has destroyed many businesses in the capital, which is actually a good thing from the point of view of the few Bagheera who can tolerate the place. The fighting slows the raping of the land considerably, but the price is hordes of vampires who consider the place a happy hunting grounds, so torn up politically and economically that no one is safe from their tender mercies.

Oddly enough, the government never seems to stabilize enough for true corruption to set in; social unrest is the norm here, and that makes travel throughout the region exceedingly dangerous. This is unfortunate, since the country is home to Bamingui-Bangoran and St. Flores National Parks, which are possibly the most pristine national parks in all of Africa. Everything from pygmies to elephants lives here, and one can even find lowland gorillas on a good day. Poachers, mostly from Sudan, have gutted most of the diversity these parks once enjoyed. The Dzanga-Sangha Reserve to the southwest is much more interesting in an ecological sense, as it is home to some of the country's last remaining virgin rainforest. There are secrets aplenty to be found here and in neighboring Cameroon, if one is brave enough to seek them.

Simba, Bagheera, and Mokolé can all be found here, though none in significant numbers. I do know of one Mokolé who acts as a guide in Bamingui-Bangoran; he's a friendly little pygmy named Henry (though his Mokolé name is Seeks-Wonder) who's very approachable about most things. Just be sure you don't get him riled, though. It's tough to do, but when it happens, watch out. Some of Lord Ebola's brood might be lurking around as well, as his tunnels reach throughout the Congo, which neighbors the CAR to the south. Pickings are good here if you're a wererat, but the risks involved are disgusting.

West Africa

When the European powers pulled out of Africa in the 1960s, West Africa suffered for it more than any other region on the continent. While other areas were more or less prepared for independence, or at least demanding it, West Africa crumbled into a multitude of smaller nations, each suffering from many of the same maladies. Poor economies, corruption, drought, deforestation, desertification, and territorial disputes characterize much of the region, and it has become a breeding ground for industrial exploitation and supernatural corruption on a massive scale. Emblematic examples of such countries are described below.

Nigeria

Still recovering from its civil war three decades ago, Africa's most populous nation remains a land deeply divided in every way imaginable. Religious tensions have been on the rise since the adoption of *sharia*, or Islamic law, in many predominantly Christian areas, and the conflicts between the affluent oil companies and the poor populating the delta have led to demonstrations and riots leaving thousands dead. It should come as no surprise, then, that Nigeria is a rich feeding ground for manifestations of the Wyrm, nor that these in turn draw Gaia's children in droves. Garou of all sorts come here, particularly Glass Walkers, seeking to slow the development of the country's oil industries. While Pentex has many tendrils in Africa, none are so strong as those strewn about the Nigerian coast, and the city Garou undermine their efforts at every turn. The Bagheera reveal their cosmopolitan nature here, often working in tandem with the werewolves to disrupt Pentex operations on an international scale. The Rokea strike at Lagos from the coast, and the Ratkin foul crops from within, sowing the seeds of famine on a massive scale (I'm not sure whether these are connected to those in the Congo or not; I think not, but nothing would surprise me). The country is one step away from Impergium, and the shifters are less interested in natural areas or national stability than they are in corporate sabotage and culling the growing human populations. Some with humanitarian concerns protest such extremism, but their worries are swept aside by the urgent need for action.

While much of Africa is involved in bloody civil wars, Nigeria is the poster child for unchecked population growth, and the situation there is spiraling out of control. Once an exporter of food, the country is now beginning to suffer for its lack of resources to feed its people. The government is highly corrupt, and bribery and abuse by both officials and members of law enforcement runs rampant. Vampiric influence increases nightly, particularly with respect to the illegal drug trade; Nigeria serves as a waystation for heroin shipments bound for Europe and Asia, and so operations here are intensifying. The Silent Strider presence in the coastal cities has increased in response to this, and in fact we use Lagos as a waypoint to the Amazon and the war fought therein. The ties, both corporate and supernatural, between Nigeria and Brazil are strong indeed.

Nigeria gained independence from the British in 1960, and promptly fell victim to inter-tribal strife which culminated in a painful civil war lasting from 1966-1968. The peace that followed the war was eagerly embraced and more-or-less lasting, though the government fell to corruption quickly. Nigeria's potential influence on the rest of Africa is immense, in both economic and political terms, and its role in African affairs would be great indeed were it not so hobbled by political instability and poor macroeconomic management. The Glass Walkers can take some credit for this, but not much; internal strife in Pentex caused a lot of it, as did plain old human corruption and incompetence.

The Kucha Ekundu used to have Kin here, in Kainji Lake National Park and contiguous Borgu Game Reserve. They haven't been sighted for awhile, though, and are probably extinct, mostly due to the intense poaching common throughout the area. The lake itself was the source of some significant turmoil a couple of years ago, much of it Pentex related. Due to poor maintenance, the Kainji Lake dam gave way to torrential rains, flooding a fair number of settlements downstream. A lot of people died that day, and there was no one there to stop it from happening. Pentex won that round, but payback's a bitch and the Bagheera and Striders are seeing to it that they get what's coming to them.

On a bright note, the Mokolé in Ibadan have a different perspective on the situation in Nigeria than most. They are responsible for the city's inclusion in the UN-sponsored Sustainable Cities Program, an endeavor meant to enhance the city's facilities such that the people therein are less subject to impoverished conditions. As tropical Africa's largest indigenous city, Ibadan was an ideal candidate for the project. The Mokolé here fight the Wyrm in the subtlest manner possible: they seek the well-being of the humans under their care in such a way that their needs do not conflict with those of Gaia. Though this is not a battle which can be won with claws and teeth, I do know of a few Black Furies who have become involved in the project; since conflicts from Lagos occasionally spread as far as Ibadan, the extra protection probably doesn't hurt.

There's an awful lot of intrigue going on in Nigeria. Lots of politics, lots of drugs, lots of problems, lots of folks trying to take advantage of it all. If you have to travel there, take friends, and watch your step.

Cote d'Ivoire

Home to what were once the largest forests in all of West Africa, the Ivory Coast has long been an area of minor interest for the Garou, as well as other supernaturals of all sorts. Gaining independence from

France in 1960, Cote d'Ivoire has been trying for years to turn its economy around, all to no avail. While it is fairly stable politically, its economy seems to shun diversity, leaving it a bit player at best in the international scene. The devaluing of the Franc Zone currencies in 1994 helped set the stage for a comeback, but despite an initial spurt of growth low prices continue to bog the economy down.

In truth, the slow development of Cote d'Ivoire's economy doesn't bother the few shifters native to the area one little bit. The country is home to Comoé National Park, the largest natural reserve in West Africa, and the few Bagheera who live here are content to watch over the remaining wildlife herds as the country around them stagnates. More adventurous types find plenty to keep them occupied in the cities, particularly the capital of Abidjan, as they are minor transition points for the heroin trade. In addition to guaranteeing a fair amount of international hijinks, particularly from the US and Latin America, this also brings various denizens of the World of Darkness out of the woodwork. The vampires here are fairly bold, using their servants to take victims even in broad daylight, and their presence has drawn some packs of Silent Striders to the country in pursuit. When coupled with the extensive criminal networks based here, this makes the Ivory Coast a place to be avoided unless absolutely necessary.

But we find many of our own interests here as well. Taï National Park is proving to be silent battleground between ghostly Banes and the Bagheera who make this their home. The Taï is home to some of the last rainforests in West Africa, and the flora here is truly astonishing — there are trees here that tower 150 feet above the ground, and the air is rich with ancient power rarely seen elsewhere in the world. However, a feeling of desolation holds fast in the Taï, and just being there brings with it a feeling that is somewhat eerie, almost haunted. It's hard to pin down, but despite the beauty and majesty of this place Garou who visit usually can't wait to leave.

Only the Bagheera can stay for long, and they have recently seen evidence of Wyrm-possessed wildlife even deep within the sanctuary. What is happening here is unclear, but it merits further investigation. That's what the Bagheera do, though, so if you hear from one about this, be ready to act. The park is further threatened by the influx of refugees from Liberia, following the civil war that began in 1989. Of the three hundred and fifty thousand who've trickled over the border in the last decade some 85 thousand remain, and they use the forest for fuel wood when the need arises. The Bagheera fight this as well, though their focus is shifting more and more to their more Wyrm-heavy problems by the day.

Liberia

Though it shouldn't come as a surprise to anyone given the strife it's seen lately, Liberia is an ecological nightmare given form. On the land rainforests are lost at a frightening rate, and their loss leads to a concurrent loss of biodiversity and degraded soils which make the land more vulnerable to flooding and other ecological catastrophe. Not content to stop with the land, however, Liberian industries contaminate the sea as well, pumping raw sewage into coastal waters and caring not a whit about the oil residue that contaminates the country's territorial waters. Endron is doing quite well for itself here, as it came into the country to help rebuild the place and set up shop shredding the trees for development concerns and polluting the waters to foul aquatic habitats off the coast. In the meantime, they maintain strong ties with vampire-infested markets for heroin bound for the Middle East and cocaine bound for Europe, keeping connectivity high between operations in South America and those scattered throughout West Africa and Southwest Asia. Not many in the Pentex hierarchy can claim to be so efficient in their destruction, and Endron is soaking up status like mad.

Extensive though its environmental problems are, the Liberian government is more interested in rebuilding the country after seven years of civil war than it is in playing nice with the environment. Resettling refugees is one of their main concerns, and violent political squabbles have hindered the reconstruction process. Though rich in natural resources of all types, Liberia's economy will only survive with the aid of foreign investors; having Endron show up on their doorstep in 1997 must have seemed like a reprieve from God. They're on their way to rebuilding, but they've no idea of the serpent they've allowed into their midst.

I can sympathize with the concerns of the government; after all, it's only rational to look after your own people before you begin to focus heavily on the environment. Unfortunately, the Rokea are not so forgiving as I. Some call this part of Africa home, and they've seen enough oil and sewage to last them a lifetime. Choosing to make their displeasure known in the most direct manner possible, they've taken to invading the shores of Monrovia and sabotaging the industries based there, killing any unfortunates who happen across their paths. They've managed to pick quite a fight with Endron, and they haven't bothered to communicate with the rest of us as to their intentions or desires. I wish them the best of luck, but there's little we can do for such loose cannons when they won't deign to coordinate their efforts with those who would be their allies.

North Africa

If there is any place in Africa we Garou might call our own, it is the deserts of North Africa. This is the homeland, if such can be said to exist, for the Silent Striders, and it is from here we wage our war against the vampires, who seek to corrupt the oldest cultures of humanity in the world. Save for the banks of the Nile the presence of other shifters here is nigh-undetectable; the cats have all been butchered over the years, the streams choked to death by the desert, the quiet places where spiders roam blown away by harmattan winds. Only we persevere, and in the wake of Black Tooth's death we have begun to strike at our ancient foes in wars of annihilation which seek to cleanse their very presence from the land. The Ahadi has given us a renewed sense of unity and purpose, and we have been transformed from beleaguered soldiers on the cusp of extinction into relentless warriors who will stop at nothing to free our land from the coils of the Wyrm and the bonds of our ancient curse. Let the world beware, for we are reborn.

Egypt

Perhaps more than any other land on Earth, Egypt is a place of secrets. Weaving through long-sealed tombs, shifting sands, and urban alleys, the lore here is ancient and vast, and this is true of its inhabitants as well. More populous than any other country in Africa save Nigeria, Egypt is home to a bewildering array of humans and those who prey on them, all shrouded in secrecy and packed into an astonishingly small area. In recent times the place has grown even more crowded, and correspondingly more dangerous. It is a hunting ground, in a very literal sense, and its legacies haunt Gaia's children even now. Sometimes it is we who are hunters; we strike with speed and secrecy, using our magics to guide us as we learn our secrets and strike out at old foes. Mostly, however, we are prey, for despite our great power even we fall to force of numbers, and numbers are the one thing the drinkers of blood have on their side.

The importance of Egypt in Africa and the Middle East cannot be underestimated. It controls the Sinai Peninsula, which links Africa and the rest of the Eastern Hemisphere, and the Suez Canal, the shortest link between the Mediterranean Sea and the Indian Ocean. It is situated opposite Israel, which establishes its role in the Middle East, and its status as a waypoint between North and South, East and West makes it a potent lure for supernaturals of all sorts.

The Nile River, once Edenic, has lessened in significance in the last century, due to both the gradual drying of North Africa and the construction of the Aswan Dam. This latter development has radically altered the lives of Egypt's Mokolé populations; once they ruled the land, but the dam changed everything. They have since fled upriver into the Sudan, though they return to help the Bubasti on occasion when asked. The dam has had other effects as well; without periodic flooding, the banks of the Lower Nile have dried up, turning to desert and destroying the agricultural base on which the people have depended for so long. Industry powered by the dam results in oil runoffs that pollute coral reefs and marine habitats, damage that is compounded by pesticides and the dumping of raw sewage into the river. In simplest terms, the river is a mess, and cleaning it up will be even messier. The more I think about that, the more I wonder if we shouldn't count ourselves lucky to be forever exiled from our ancestral home.

Corruption is rife here in Egypt, but it is subtle. I cannot tell you who, or what, or where, or when, but you can taste it all around you. Those who come here give up on fighting overt battles quickly, as they find there is nothing to fight. Only the Bubasti can hope to break even in such games, and even they find themselves suffering for it more often than not. Some would have you believe that all that transpires here is supernatural in origin; for example, the rise and fall of Egyptian governments has been attributed to vampiric clans, or shapeshifter Kin, or magical influence, or any number of other things. In truth, though, Egyptian history has been mostly human in origin; the supernaturals only take credit after the humans have done their dirty work. I do not know the details of otherworldly involvement, here. However, I can tell you that nearly every supernatural in existence has some ties here, and that the information networks in and around the major cities tend to be quite extensive. You'll have to find the specifics on your own, though; I am to tell you of the Wyrm and Gaia's children, not the other denizens of the world. Pay attention, then, for this is what they are up to.

Long ago, vampires fought for control of this place, and we have been dealing with the fallout ever since. Our expulsion from Egypt by Set so long ago has left the others skulking in shadows, fighting an ever-growing enemy as their own numbers dwindle to nothing. The Bubasti have been waging a protracted war with the ancient ones for centuries, but their efforts have always been solitary in nature. They have recently set to changing this, however. Years ago, I encountered a Strider who spoke favorably of the Rite of Dormant Wisdom. He rambled on at length about vampire warlocks and the secrets they might hold, and while I thought him mad I let him pass; his death was his own business, and I want no truck with one who

engages in such obscene rituals. Now, years later, I have encountered Harbingers who speak of the Bubasti with respect and eagerness; indeed, they speak of the mystics with awe. I cannot say what exactly the Bubasti have done to earn such esteem, or even what role the Eaters played in their plans; in truth, I think I'm better off not knowing. But I do know this: Bubasti knowledge of magic and spirit is unparalleled among Gaia's children, and so perhaps the rumors of the weakening of Set's ancient curse hold true.

As for their own kind, the Bubasti skirmishes with the vampires infesting Egypt continue unabated. They fight the Leeches beneath the city, within the walls of pyramids, and across the desert to Alexandria and beyond. As members of the Ahadi they have called upon aid from Silent Striders on a few occasions, using us to clear out dug-in nests of vampires when their own magics prove insufficient for the task. We perform these tasks gladly, for they further our own goals as well reinforcing allegiances with the cats.

With the ratification of the Ahadi, the Silent Striders have gone on the warpath. In the wake of Black Tooth's death and the recent shakeup in vampiric society Walks-With-Might has been leading his pack on more and more raids throughout Africa, cutting a bloody swath from Riyadh to Cairo, to Casablanca and Lagos, to Cape Town and Nairobi. Their efforts have even taken them to Colombia and Brazil, chasing their vampiric foes around the world. Common wisdom holds that the vampires will always have an advantage, since they can sire a dozen Leeches in a single night, but that's not stopping Walks-With-Might and his pack. The vampires are nothing without experience, and even the old ones are on poor footing when confronted with a highly trained and well-coordinated Garou pack. In addition, Walks-With-Might helped engineer the Ahadi, and now he uses it to demand aid from any shifter he encounters in the pursuit of his goals. Any who might suspect his motives put aside their suspicion when he treats them with respect, honors their homes, and bows to the will of the spirits guiding them. As such, the Bastet share secrets with him and the Mokolé teach him long forgotten things, which make him and his pack all but unstoppable. Precious little can stand before him, and because of this he *is* Africa as far as most Garou are concerned. One day or another his luck will run out, but not before he's delivered his share and more of vampires to final death.

Morocco

Situated between the worlds of Europe and Africa, Morocco has always had a fairly unique flavor about it. Many Silent Striders consider this country their second home, as it is fairly stable and a good substitute for their roots within Egypt. One of the most powerful and famous caerns in the world, the Wheel of Ptah, can be found in Casablanca, and the Barbary Coast to the north is a place of great social significance for both normal humans and the denizens of the World of Darkness. There are some political issues here, ranging from administration of the Sahara Desert to land disputes with Spain, and the issue of native peoples is one which receives a fair amount of attention, but the country's status as a crossroads and its reputation for openness make it quite attractive nonetheless.

Environmental issues in the area are as significant as they are anywhere else, but there are no real crises brewing; the Striders work to keep things accessible, and this means keeping a low profile and avoiding protracted conflicts when possible. The caern is seeing an awful lot of use lately, mainly from Walks-With-Might and his allies, but for the most part traffic hasn't been adversely affected much. With the advent of the Ahadi, other shifters have begun to make entreaties for access to the caern; such requests have not yet been honored, though the subject is one which has engendered some debate among the Garou who know of it. No one wants a werecat prancing around the sept, but on the other hand there's also no reason to alienate newfound allies, particularly ones that are proving useful in battles against the vampires which infest the rest of Africa.

A strange sort of détente exists between the vampires occupying Tangier to the north and the Silent Striders of Casablanca. To call this arrangement a truce would be an exercise in absurdity, but it is nonetheless true that the werewolves don't habitually hunt down and dismember the vampires, while the vampires in turn do their best to keep their habits under wraps and their faces out of sight. These Leeches are apparently of a different sect than most on Walks-With-Might's hit list, so that no doubt helps. The fact that no one wants to bring war to the crossroads of the Old World doesn't hurt either.

Middle East

If favor now should greet my story,
Allah must receive the glory.
— Aaron Shepard, *The Enchanted Storks: A Tale of Old Baghdad*

The Middle East forms a crossroads between Europe, Africa and Asia. Traditionally, the Middle East includes those areas of North Africa — Morocco, Algeria, Tunisia, Libya and Egypt — which share linguistic and ethnic identities with the Islamic Arabian Peninsula. Occasionally, Afghanistan is also included as part of the region. For purposes of this book, however, these countries are covered under the African and Asian sections rather than this one.

Although there exist several significant differences among the Middle Eastern region's countries, most acknowledge certain similarities: the entire area is arid to some degree, the dominant religion is Islam and all but three countries (Iran, Israel and Turkey) speak Arabic. Additionally, the countries of the Middle East have, in recent times, crossed over the brink into modernity, yet still struggle with maintaining traditional and fundamentalist values. With a few exceptions most of the region's countries have fought to attain their independence and establish themselves as sovereign territories. Further, the political and social aspects of the Middle East have been irrevocably changed, and at times determined, by the presence of the abundant oil found there.

As wolves do not adapt well to desert climates, the Middle East typically has few "native" Garou. Silent Striders make their presence felt in Egypt and other North African regions, but travel only rarely on the Arabian Peninsula. The Children of Gaia once helped guide early civilizations in the region. In recent years, they, along with several individuals from other tribes, have gravitated to the ecological disaster area around Iraq, Kuwait and Saudi Arabia left in the wake of the Gulf War of 1991. A few Glass Walkers already lived in the region overseeing oil production and lobbying for more natural drilling options and responsible ecological policies.

Geography

The Middle East is bounded by the Mediterranean, Black, Caspian, Arabian and Red Seas, while the Persian Gulf thrusts up between Iran and the rest of the eastern edge of the peninsula. The Arabian Peninsula (land mass two-thirds the size of Alaska) and the Levant (the area along the Mediterranean between Turkey and Egypt) serve as a land bridge between Europe, Asia and Africa.

Though most people visualize blowing, wind-scoured dunes, such sand deserts form only a small part of the region, being found mostly in Saudi Arabia. Even there, rocky plains predominate. Nonetheless, the Dasht-e-Kavir or Great Salt Desert of Iran claims the distinction of being the largest area in the world with no vegetation whatsoever. High plateaus and mountains form much of Turkey, Iran and Yemen, where most of the terrain lies above 1000 meters. The highest mountains of the region are the Damavand in Iran, Mount Ararat in Turkey and Jabal an-Nabi Shu'ayb in Yemen. The Tigris and Euphrates Rivers, often called the cradle of civilization, flow from the Anatolian highlands through Iraq to the Persian Gulf. With the exception of a few rivers in Turkey and northwestern Iran, waterways flowing year round to the sea are rare in such an arid climate.

Climate

Ironically for a region surrounded on all sides by water, aridity, the severe lack of water and rainfall, determines the climate and lifestyle of the people of the Middle East. In some regions rainfall is so light as to be practically nonexistent; southeastern Saudi Arabia and western Oman may see years pass without rain.

Mountain ridges and two moist climate systems guarantee that some parts of the region receive great variation, though. The coastal regions of Syria, Lebanon and Turkey see significant amounts of rain from the Mediterranean, while Northwestern Iran boasts a strip of rain-washed land and cyclonic storms extending along the Black Sea. Monsoon rains from the Indian climatic system affect the southernmost portion of Saudi Arabia and southeastern Iran, while annual rainfall in Yemen's mountains reaches significant amounts as well.

The temperature varies widely in different locations and different times of year. Summer is hottest, with the low-lying coastal lands on the Red Sea and the Arabian Sea and Persian Gulf showing Farenheit temperatures from the high 90s to well into the hundreds and with humidity up to 70% on most days. Night brings little relief with temperatures in the 80s.

In the higher altitudes, the temperature drops significantly. High plateaus that are hot during the day may reach freezing temperatures at night and snow-capped mountains can be found in Turkey, Iran and occasionally Yemen.

History of the Region
The Cradle of Civilization

Along with the Nile Valley, Mesopotamia's Fertile Crescent lays claim to some of the earliest known societies. About 5000 BCE the Al-Ubaid culture appeared in Mesopotamia (modern day Iraq). Their influence spread to what is now the coast of the Persian Gulf. Stone Age artifacts also prove the existence of people in Israel's Negev desert and on the West Bank near Jericho. The Umm an-Nar culture settled along the Gulf in the area that is the modern day United Arab Emirates around 3100 BCE. while the Canaanites and Amorites held power in the Levant and Sumer, the world's first great empire, came to power in Mesopotamia. Around 3200 BCE. the powerful trading empire of Dilmun arose on the island of Bahrain.

A World of Rage

While the Silent Striders kept their domain in Egypt, the Children of Gaia went among the great leaders of Mesopotamia, teaching them and encouraging humankind's progress while trying to instill into them the notion that they should be the caretakers of the sacred land and its creatures.

Sargon of Akkad, a Sumerian king, conquered much of Mesopotamia and the Levant in the late 24th century BCE. He strove against Dilmun, but that mighty kingdom lasted for nearly 2000 years.

Other great leaders born in Mesopotamia were Abraham, the Hebrew patriarch, born in Ur on the Euphrates River, who migrated from Ur to Canaan around 1800 BCE and Hammurabi, the Babylonian king, famous for his code of laws. The Children of Gaia claim credit for helping him to codify and publish the laws so all could know and abide by them.

Rise of Empires

In the following centuries, the biblical kingdom of Israel rose and fell within a century, splitting into two parts — Israel and Judah — after the death of King Solomon. The 7th century BCE saw the rise of the Medes, first of many great Persian empires in the area now known as Iran. Conquered by Cyrus and ruled by his successors over the next 60 years or so, the Persian Empire conquered Babylon, Egypt, Asia Minor and parts of Greece. In 331 BCE Alexander the Great concluded a series of conquests that took in Asia Minor, the Middle East, Persia and part of India, crushing Persia with the sack of Persepolis, its capital city.

After Alexander's death, his generals carved his empire up among themselves. Byzantines and Sassanians squabbled for control, with small client states caught in between. The nomads of the desert and the frankincense kingdoms of southern Arabia remained independent, with the rulers of what is now Yemen achieving untold wealth through their control of the trade routes north. Divided into bickering kingdoms, each vied for control of the frankincense trade. By the 3rd century CE, the frankincense trade had declined to the point where Arabia became of marginal importance to the rest of the world. Nevertheless, the Byzantine-Sassanian wars had drained the kingdoms, making them ripe for conquest from an unexpected quarter.

The Coming of Islam

The term "Middle East" was given to the region by Europeans both because of its location and its position as a center for trade during the days of caravans. Camel trains met here and markets grew up around the lucrative trade in spices, pearls and other exotic goods. Here also, as traders met together, they discussed cultural and religious ideas. Judaism, Christianity and Islam flowered in the region and shrines sacred to each arose.

In the year 570, the prophet Mohammed was born in Mecca, in western Arabia. He received divine revelations that he preached until his death at Medina in 632. So compelling was Mohammed's message that it literally swept away other religions in the Arabian Peninsula.

In the 7th century, following the teachings of the Prophet Mohammed, Arab culture, language and government burst forth into a conquering army, creating a great Islamic Empire stretching from Spain through North Africa, across the Middle East and deep into central Asia. The prophet's companions governed the empire, but a dispute arose over who should be caliph (the leader of the Muslim community, literally meaning "successor" or "lieutenant"). This led to the present day division between the Shi'ite and Sunni Muslims.

The Modern Age

Successive empires followed the split between Sunni and Shi'ite, leading eventually to the Golden Age of Islamic culture and society. Guided by the few remaining Children of Gaia, the Abassid caliph Harun ar-Rashid led an invasion against Byzantium, almost reaching Constantinople, where ancient vampires ruled the night, and reigned over a great upsurge of arts, medicine, science and literature. His successor created the House of Wisdom, a Baghdad academy that translated Greek and Roman literature, science and philosophy into Arabic, thus preserving such works for posterity when they were lost during Europe's Dark Ages.

The decline of the Islamic Empire left a vacuum that European and other foreign powers tried to exploit. European states were avid to spread Christianity and to gain control of trade routes in the region during the Crusades. Ultimately defeated, they nevertheless left their mark on the region, particularly in the Levant and the holy city of Jerusalem. By the early 16th century, the Ottoman Turks ruled the region as part of their great empire. With that empire's decline, European powers began colonizing the Middle East, first with Portuguese, then British traders. (The British were curtailing French aspirations at the time.) Many Children of Gaia struggled along with their Kinfolk to achieve nationhood and throw off the yoke of colonialism.

After years of struggle against the colonial powers, some countries began to gain independence. The region was of minor importance during World War II, yet in the wake of that conflict, the British were under great pressure to allow unrestricted Jewish immigration to the area that would become Israel. Already European Zionists, calling for the Jews of the world to return to Palestine and become self-sufficient there,

Founded by Mohammed and based on divine revelations he received, Islam grew from its humble beginnings in 613 to become the dominant religion of the Middle East, North Africa, and parts of Europe and Asia. Islam's adherents believe that the Jewish Old Testament and the teachings of Christ are valid, but unfinished, whereas Islam is the perfected revelation of God. The words given to Mohammed as revealed by the archangel Gabriel were written down in the Qur'an (Koran). The writings (the name means "recitations") have never been changed and translations are considered to be introductions to the Qur'an rather than definitive texts.

After Mohammed's death, the new religion split into different sects due to a dispute about who should be his successor. Thus were born the Sunni and Shi'ite sects. Of the two, far more Muslims are Sunni than Shi'ite, thought the latter are dominant in Iran and form significant minorities in Iraq and a few other nations.

Islam rests upon what are known as the Five Pillars of the Faith: the Creed, Prayer, Alms, Fasting and Pilgrimage. These five observances help all believers to remember that Islam calls for both men and women to be equal in their total submission to God. The term Islam actually means "submission," while the word Muslim literally means "submitter."

The Creed: The Creed stands at the center of Islamic belief and simply states "There is no God but God and Mohammed is the Prophet of God." Anyone stating this in the presence of two reliable witnesses is considered to be a Muslim. Muslims believe that Mohammed was the last in a line of prophets, each of whom added to God's revelations, thus they accept the writings of Abraham, the Torah, David's psalms and the teachings of Christ. They do not, however, accept Christ's divinity.

Prayer: Every Muslim prays five times per day — sunrise, noon, late afternoon, sunset and night. The muezzin calls the faithful to prayer and they perform a ritual of body movements, recitations of prayer and portions of the Qur'an intended to express the believers' submission to and humility before God. All face Mecca, holy city of Mohammed's birth, to make their prayers.

Alms: All Muslims should pay out one-fortieth of their yearly income as *zakat* or alms for the poor. This generosity thus purifies the person's wealth and also shows his sense of responsibility to those less fortunate.

Fasting: During Ramadan, the ninth month of the Muslim calendar, all Muslims (with the exception of those too weak, young, old or ill to participate) abstain from eating, drinking, smoking and sex from sunrise to sunset. Extra prayers during this time are encouraged as the fasting is intended to bring the faithful closer to God and to each other as each shares the experience at the same time. During this time, life changes for all Muslims as daily routines are held to a minimum. Many look forward to Ramadan, however, for many feast during the night and hold celebrations that may go on all night after the participants sleep through the afternoon.

Pilgrimage: Each Muslim who can afford to do so should make the pilgrimage to Mecca at least once during her lifetime. Such a pilgrimage made during Zuul-Hijja, the last month of the Muslim calendar, rewards the participants by the forgiving of all past sins. Saudi Arabia restricts the number of pilgrims per year via a quota system so those wanting to make the *hajj* pilgrimage do not overwhelm the facilities. Nearly two million Muslims make the pilgrimage each year.

---

had been bringing in settlers and buying land. With the horrors of the Holocaust made clear, the world supported the idea of a Jewish state. Meanwhile, Palestinians who had lived and worked in the region for generations suddenly found themselves turned off the land their families had traditionally tenanted. Proposals were made (assisted by powerful appeals from noted Gaian speakers) to create two states — one Jewish, the other Palestinian. Britain, left unable to govern the area by its losses in the war, turned the problem over to the United Nations. The state of Israel emerged while the Palestinian homeland never took root. To the Jews, their return to Israel means they are occupying land God gave to them, while the Arabs see the Israelis as usurpers and colonizers much like the crusaders. The conflict became even more heated by the discovery that the Middle East could satisfy the world's craving for a substance it cannot do without — oil.

The Politics of Oil

The Middle East's strategic importance in the modern era has emerged only with the discovery of its oil reserves. The oil industry of the Middle East began in Persia where oil was discovered in 1908. Next, substantial quantities were found in the Kurdish region in northern Iraq and in Bahrain. By the time of World War II, the Middle East, especially the Gulf region, was known to have some of the richest oil fields in the world. Today, oil is the main economic factor in Iran, Iraq, all the Gulf states, Syria and Yemen. Even those countries not blessed have some dependence on it as workers from those states often send home part or all of their wages to sustain their families. Oil-rich countries also derive income from investments made with some of their oil revenues.

At one end of the spectrum of riches lie the small, oil-producing countries such as Kuwait and the United Arab Emirates, whose per capita income rivals that of the richest westerners. At the other end are those who have no oil, have large populations or who suffer from the aftereffects of years of turmoil and warfare.

Oil has made the Middle East a playground for interference by the rest of the petroleum-hungry world. No country in the Middle East remains untouched by foreign interests and no country can determine their own direction without a thought for the policies laid upon them by various superpowers.

While the United States prefers Israel's democratic system and shares many of its cultural values, its need for oil makes it essential to have friendly relationships with at least some Arab states — even those that are dictatorial. The US supports Israel due to agreements and treaties made with it at the country's inception, yet finds itself faced with the hatred of the surrounding Arab states who view it as both a manipulative colonial power and an irreverent bully. While it existed, the USSR made inroads into the Middle East by supporting various nationalist movements hoping to further their aims toward world communism. Their interference in the region was as shameless and self-serving as the United States.

Thus when Iran succumbed to a fundamentalist Islamic revolution in 1979, frightening their neighbors into believing such revolts were imminent in their own countries, not only Saudi Arabia, Kuwait and other Arab states, but also the US backed Saddam Hussein in his attempt to contain the fervent religious fundamentalists. Funded by its rich neighbors and using war material from the USSR and America, Iraq fought a costly and deadly war with Iran for eight years (ending in 1988), and successfully blunted any general uprising the Islamic Movement might have engendered.

Despite being saved by Hussein and Iraq's sacrifices (perhaps a million killed on each side, the countries devastated), Kuwait refused to forgive Iraq's war debts, demanding repayment of the funds they had loaned Hussein's forces for the war effort. The US and Britain threatened enemies of Kuwait who might be tempted to seize the rich, but tiny country, yet the US had not fought a war since its defeat in Vietnam.

Hoping to seize Kuwait's oil for his destitute country and reopen ports the Kuwaiti had closed to him, Saddam Hussein invaded Kuwait in 1990, believing that no one would seriously impede him. To his regret, Saudi Arabia and the Kuwaiti leadership in exile convinced the United States to assist and the Gulf War was fought under the auspices of UN Peacekeeping forces – not for the sovereign rights of Kuwait, but to protect their oil interests in the Gulf. Defeated, yet still filled with hatred for what he saw as a betrayal by Kuwait, Hussein vowed that if he could not have Kuwait's oil, no one would. His retreating army stripped Kuwait's oil fields of every piece of equipment, then set explosives around the wells, setting them afire and unleashing both the largest, most destructive oil spill in history and the poisoning of the atmosphere in the region for years to come.

The Role of the Garou

While they have had a presence in the area and acted as teachers, advisors, business partners, patriots and even avengers, at times, the Garou of the Middle East have rarely had the numbers or the luxury of making a major difference there. Economic concerns have always held precedence over ecological ones and Garou entering the area don't have a true commitment to it and often don't understand the issues facing either the people or their fellow werewolves in the region. Those who do come hoping to make a difference often find themselves lost amid the strange customs. Garou females find the attitudes toward women in many Middle Eastern countries both insulting and impossible to ignore.

They cannot then turn to their wolf Kin for company either; there are no wolf packs in the region who aren't either in zoos or held on hidden private reserves by Kinfolk or werewolf packs. Often, the native Garou, mostly Children of Gaia, a few Silent Striders and Glass Walkers, resent the intrusion of foreign Garou and behave with as much hostility toward them as the most fundamentalist regime toward Americans. This has only recently begun to change as werewolves journey to the Gulf states hoping to aid in the cleanup efforts there.

Ecological Disaster

The Gulf War left an ecological disaster in its wake that brought dozens of foreign Garou to the area to offer assistance to the region's native werewolves. They arrived in hell. Fleeing Kuwait in 1991, Iraqi soldiers pumped millions of gallons of crude oil into the Gulf, then blasted open the control mechanisms and set fire to every Kuwaiti oil well they could find. The result was

Other Shapeshifters

With the exception of a few Bastet drawn to the region in search of secrets and the occasional Nuwisha found traversing the deserts, the only other shapeshifters in any numbers besides Garou are the Rokea found in the Persian Gulf. A very few Mokolé may still frequent some of the less populated coves, though most prefer the Nile in Egypt. Once every few years a Corax may travel through part of the region. Aside from these few, however, the area is almost bereft of Gaia's children. Even the werewolves are few and scattered, with no real contact between groups. And the other shapeshifters try to keep contact with the Garou to a minimum, if indeed they allow themselves to meet Gaia's warriors at all.

over 700 uncontrolled oil well fires, leaving rivers of burning crude oil trailing across the sands of Kuwait's oil fields, and blackening the skies with oily soot, which then carried on the winds and fell to earth, coating everything it touched. This miasmic cloud covered Kuwait, Qatar, Bahrain, much of the United Arab Emirates, all of southwestern Iran, most of Iraq and the eastern half of Saudi Arabia. When the smoke began to clear in November of 1991, the landscape of those areas revealed swamps and lakes of crude oil mixed with salty brine brought to the surface along with the oil by the explosions. Throughout 1992 the oil congealed, becoming more impossible to clean out of the soil and most now believe that it is impossible to ever completely rid lakes of the oil and soot in them, killing fish and other marine life as well as any other creatures dependent on their waters. Further, as the oil followed the path of least resistance, it drained down wadis and into fields, destroying the most fertile lands and burying them under crusted asphalt-like layers of oil.

Iraqi mines and unexploded ordnance from the allies make it a dangerous undertaking to even try to reach some of the most devastated lands. Further, the combustible chemicals present in crude oil can turn what seems to be a gooey, but traversable desert landscape into a raging lake of fire in little more than a minute's time.

The oil pumped into the Persian Gulf constitutes the biggest oil spill in history, fully the equivalent of twenty-five to forty *Exxon Valdez* spills, flowing down the coast of Saudi Arabia and beyond. These coastlines were still recovering from the spill of two million barrels released from Iranian offshore platforms when Iraqi missiles hit them in 1983. At that time, 7000 barrels a day flowed into the Gulf for ten months. In contrast, the Gulf War spill gushed an average of 150,000 barrels a

day in the period of a few weeks. Smothering every living thing, the oil also bound itself to coastal sediment, making it extremely hard to cleanse, and its chemicals caused damage to fish, shellfish, birds and other creatures in the region. Tidal movements leached some oil out of contaminated sediment for over a year, sending it deeper into the Gulf. Due to the flatness of the land, high tide can move over half a mile or more inland, leaving tidal flats and salt marshes coated with inches thick crude oil, destroying habitats of fish, crabs, worms and birds and the sea grasses that provide food for the area's animals. Since such habitats are given little value in the affected countries, while the oil industry is of paramount importance, the main emphasis has been on recovering what oil they can and ignoring the damage done to the coasts.

The damage done to the smaller fish and sea creatures has had a marked effect on the larger food fish usually found in the Gulf, and most notably on the ten species of shark and the bottlenose dolphins who inhabit its waters. The Rokea native to the area seem to have declared war on all and sundry, perhaps in response to the deaths of many of their Kinfolk. They welcome no one's help and bitterly resent the lack of effective clean-up intended for their coastal homes.

Four species of marine turtles, the green, the hawksbill, the leatherback and the loggerhead nest on Gulf islands now coated in oil or make their habitats in southern areas along the Gulf. Listed as "threatened" and "endangered" by the World Conservation Union, they may become extinct here due to the pollution. Though some preliminary cleanup managed to salvage the turtles' breeding season just after the war, inches of tarry oil remain in the sands of their breeding grounds and attention has shifted elsewhere.

While predictions of a nuclear winter scenario brought on by Kuwait's oil fires has not materialized, the oily, sooty clouds have caused damage in far-flung locations. On April 30, 1991 Bangladesh received a terrible beating from a devastating cyclone that roared up from the Bay of Bengal with 150-mile an hour winds and waves over twenty feet higher than normal high tides. The death toll reached almost 200,000. In June, central and eastern China experienced unbelievable rainfalls leading to massive flooding along the Yangtze and Huai Rivers. About 3000 people died and over 200,000,000 people — one-fifth of China's population — were affected by the floods. In the winter of 1991-92 Israel, Jordan, Syria and Lebanon were pounded by winter storms so fierce that they caused terrible floods, avalanches and the collapse of buildings under the heavy load of ice and snow. Hundreds died. A mission report from the space shuttle Atlantis in March of 1992 stated that the earth's lower atmosphere was shrouded with a cloak of dust and smoke. Though some of it has been attributed to the eruption of Mount Pinatubo in the Philippines, scientific testing has shown that these storms of the century have had at their root the smoke engendered by the Kuwaiti oil fires.

Now, almost a decade after the war, human agents and Garou still struggle to contain the damage done to the Persian Gulf and its surrounding lands. Ironically, Iraq remains one of the worst hit areas suffering from respiratory illnesses and other diseases brought on by the contaminants released during the hostilities. A few Garou, notably many Ahroun, rage against the decision not to oust or kill Saddam Hussein and have grouped together with the intention of secretly entering Iraq and slaying him. Others agitate for more money to be spent on reclaiming lands and seacoasts despoiled by the war's aftermath. Still, the business of the Gulf is money, money made through oil, and in the Gulf, it remains business as usual.

The Countries

Bahrain

An emirate in the Persian Gulf, Bahrain encompasses one large and 32 small islands (mostly uninhabited), and covers the same land area as Memphis, Tennessee. Its population of 400,000 contains two-thirds native Arabs, mostly Shi'ite Muslims, and one-third foreign workers. Its capital is Manama. Though Arabic remains the official language, English is widely spoken. Since its birth in 3200 BCE Bahrain has been a center for trade. It was once the seat of the Dilmun Empire, one of the great trading states of the ancient world that flourished for over 2000 years. In its decline, Bahrain was absorbed by Babylon. Successive foreign empires and rulers held the country until it gained its independence from Britain in 1971.

It never completely lost its importance in trade, with its pearl fisheries bringing it great wealth. Just after the pearl market collapsed, oil was discovered there and the Bahrainis were the first in the region to enjoy increased education, health benefits and other modern conveniences. Due to their head start, Bahrain was able to act as brokers for Saudi Arabia, Kuwait and Qatar when those countries' oil boom occurred.

The ruling Khalifa family, themselves Sunni Muslims, suspended the country's national assembly in 1975 amid leftist and Shi'ite attempts to overthrow their rule. Yet Bahrain is a major refining and industrial center. Its aluminum smelting plant and major banking and telecommunications center make it otherwise the picture of modernity. Since 1986 Bahrain has been linked to Saudi Arabia via causeway.

Though the country traditionally disliked Iran (due to Persian rulership earlier in its history), relations with that country have improved as Shi'ite fundamentalism has backed off somewhat. Conversely, Bahrain's relations with Iraq have taken a decided plunge in the wake of Saddam Hussein's ordering of a missile attack on them during the Gulf War (though the missile landed harmlessly at sea). For now, their main interest to Garou is as a staging area for the Glass Walkers' economic attempts to garner clean-up funds to save the Gulf Coast from annihilation.

Iran

This Texas-sized nation consists mostly of numerous mountain ranges (and one volcano) and deserts, with the Great Salt Desert and the Great Sand Desert occupying the eastern portion of its main plateau. Most of the land is parched and dependent since ancient times on clever underground irrigation channels called *ghanats*. Its capital is Tehran and its official language is Farsi or Persian. Sometimes called the easternmost country of the Middle East, Iran is a non-Arab state, settled by Aryans (the ancestors of the Persians, the Aryans gave the country its name) in ancient times. Of its approximately 64 million people, almost 70% are of Persian descent. Nonetheless, there are large Arab minorities in the southwest and Turks in the northwest. Its culture follows that of survivors of the desert who offer hospitality to those in need, and strangers often find that this is so even when they are from the "Great Satan" (America). Despite their fundamentalist leanings, most Iranians hate the American government, not its individual citizens.

Persia took shape as a country in the 6th century BCE under Cyrus the Great. His successors, Darius I and Xerxes, expanded the empire to India in the east and the Aegean Sea in the west. After being conquered in turn by Alexander the Great, the region came under Sassanian control. Wracked by conflicts with Rome and Byzantium, the Persians easily fell to the Arabs and the spread of Islam. After 600 years, they were supplanted by the Seljuk Turks, who ushered in an age of literature, science and art and marked by such worthies as the poet-mathematician Omar Khayyam. The Seljuk influence collapsed under Mongol invader Ghengis Khan. Again in 1380, Tamarlane invaded and successive rulers came and went, up into the 20th century.

In 1926 Reza Khan Pahlavi, a Cossack officer in the imperial army, took over the throne and founded the Pahlavi dynasty. He was forced into exile in World War II and his son, Mohammed Reza, succeeded him. At the end of the war, the United States helped him rid his country of invading Russian forces and firmly allied him to the west. Though his government was repressive, the shah rapidly modernized Iran, reducing illiteracy, emancipating women and improving health services and government industrialization. When the price of oil rose precipitously, the shah wasted his newfound millions on shaky development schemes, unneeded weapons arsenals and courtiers who caught his fancy. Meanwhile, the people suffered as prices for everything rose beyond their means to pay for them. Smoldering resistance to his rule broke into violence, which the shah answered with repression. Leftist students found themselves allied with right-wing fundamentalists in the attempt to overthrow the shah. The movement then found a guiding force in the form of Grand Ayatollah Khomeini. Exiled to Turkey, then eventually to France, the Ayatollah became the spokesman for the forces opposing the shah's rule. For his part, the shah underestimated how sickened the people were by his excesses. Seeing the destruction of much of the natural habitat and the deleterious effects on both the people and the creatures by the shah's expenditures and oil policies, many Iranian shapeshifters supported the revolution, with its promise of a return to sanity.

In 1979, in an initially near-bloodless coup, the shah was overthrown and the Islamic Republic of Iran was born. Then came a period of bloodbaths as people disappeared and executions took place after brief, spurious trials. When the air cleared, the country found itself under the leadership of Ayatollah Khomeini, who assumed the title of supreme spiritual leader. It was written into the Iranian constitution that the government must answer to a supreme jurist, a cleric who could interpret and enact Islamic law in order to keep corruption out of the governance of the country. Iran then began a program designed to institute old Islamic laws and effect fundamentalist revolutions in their neighboring countries.

Within a year, Iran found itself at war with Iraq — ostensibly over an old border dispute, but in reality as a means of keeping the Iranians from "infecting" other Middle Eastern nations with their revolutionary ideology. Saddam Hussein intended to blunt Iran's capacity for military expansion, and he did so with eight years of warfare that saw a return to trenches and the use of poison gas by Hussein's forces. Because it had taken American hostages during its revolution, Iran suffered from an international embargo on arms shipments and could not acquire the material it needed. Finally, Iran accepted a UN cease-fire agreement in 1988. After Khomeini's death in 1989, Iran curtailed its extremist attitude and began to cautiously rebuild its relations with outside powers. Nonetheless, it remains dogmatically fundamentalist, with 95% of its population being practicing Shi'ite Muslims. Despite its mistrust of the Great Satan, it supported the allies against Saddam Hussein in the Gulf War.

Garou have found it difficult to really affect Iran in significant ways. While some supported the revolution, most remained neutral, especially those females who resented the return to outmoded and repressive laws meant to restrain women. Nonetheless, many natives, as well as well-meaning foreign Garou, have banded together in the wake of the Gulf War. They seek to clear the air (and the land) of the soot and particles that now cover the southwestern fourth of the country, legacy of the oil fires set by Hussein's forces as they retreated from Kuwait. No one is really certain yet whether the air is fit to breathe, the water uncontaminated and the land usable for food production. The stunted growth of the animals and vegetation occupy many Theurges seeking ways to cleanse them and call forth eloquent condemnations against further warfare in the region from the Philodox.

Iraq

The Sumerian civilization of Mesopotamia is credited with being the first to cultivate the land and conceive of writing, to invent the wheel, counting and calendars — all accomplishments some Children of Gaia claim occurred because of the tribe's guidance and influence. Trade routes established the great city of Ur and made the Mesopotamian region, which lay between the Tigris and Euphrates Rivers the Cradle of Civilization. Eventually, though, the great civilization collapsed, giving way to successive states.

In 1700 BCE Hammurabi, king of the small town of Babylon, reunited the land and renamed it Babylonia. His code of laws — also said to have been formulated with the assistance of a renowned Child of Gaia Philodox — became the basis of modern law. After his death, Babylonia fell to the Assyrians. Under Nebuchadnezzar II, however, the kingdom achieved its most glorious age. The city of Babylon became famous for its Hanging Gardens, considered one of the Seven Wonders of the Ancient World.

After a series of conquests by different invaders, the Arab Muslims captured the country in 637 CE. The Abbasid emperors, descended from the Prophet Mohammed's uncle, moved the capital of their empire from Damascus to Baghdad, which lies near the convergence of the Tigris and Euphrates Rivers. Mongol invaders destroyed Baghdad in 1258.

In the 16th century, Turks conquered the region, adding it to the Ottoman Empire, which collapsed during World War I. Under British rule, Iraq was created from three former Ottoman provinces, giving it a landmass slightly larger than that of California. The area contains rich archeological sites as well as lucrative oil fields. The British made Iraq a kingdom under King Faisal and in 1932, Iraq achieved independence, with its capital at Baghdad and its official language Arabic.

In 1958, King Faisal was killed in a military coup and Iraq declared itself a republic. The Sunni dominated Ba'ath Party came to power while skirmishes among potential leaders and rebellions by the Kurds in northern Iraq kept the country unstable.

The Arab-Israeli conflict in 1967 pushed Iraq toward the Soviet Union as they saw America's favoritism toward Israel. Though bad relations with Iran over a border dispute were ostensibly settled in 1975, Iraq built up its army and war materiel, appealing to the Soviets while denouncing the United States for its policies supporting Israel.

In 1979 Saddam Hussein became president of Iraq. The Islamic fundamentalist revolution in Iran posed a great threat to Iraq's Sunni government. Fears of revolutions breaking out in Iraq and Iran's other neighbors ran high. Believing that he acted on behalf of all threatened Arab nations, Saddam borrowed money from Kuwait and Saudi Arabia and took the offensive. Eight years of trench warfare and the use of illegal chemical weapons drained both countries to exhaustion and in 1988 the UN helped establish a cease-fire.

In 1990 relations with Kuwait soured as they oversold their quota of oil, thus reducing prices and depriving Iraq of much-needed funds. Further, Kuwait refused to grant Iraq access to islands at the mouth of the only usable river leading to the Gulf, thus making the cost of transporting Iraq's oil to market prohibitive. Finally, the tiny country refused to forgive Iraq's war debt to it. Enraged because his country had suffered eight years of war only to have those who also benefited from Iraq's sacrifices apparently betray him, Saddam invaded and annexed Kuwait.

Many other Arab nations condemned Saddam's actions and Saudi Arabia, fearing they were next, opened their country to the United States and United Nations troops to repel Iraq's invasion of Kuwait. Hoping to bring allies to his side, Saddam sent SCUD missile attacks against Israel, assuming they would retaliate. They did not do so as a favor to the United States. The bombing of Baghdad and of Saddam's forces in Kuwait followed by a short ground offensive forced Iraqi troops into retreat. As they left, they set fire to Kuwait's oil wells and dumped millions of barrels of crude oil into the Persian Gulf. Rather than following up on their victory, the Allies allowed Saddam to remain in power once he retreated from Kuwait and agreed to comply with disarmament and UN Security Council resolutions. Rebellions by Kurds in the north

and Shi'ites in the south were savagely repressed and Iraq was closed to foreigners. Today it remains under trade embargo and in isolation, victim of its own scorched earth policy.

Although the Children of Gaia maintain a presence in their ancestral lands, it is not known whether they supported or opposed Saddam's political maneuverings. What is certain is that they must now be dealing with the aftermath of the Kuwaiti oil fires. If they plan any punishment for this assault on Gaia, they have not shared their plans with any others — or perhaps they no longer exist at all. They may have perished attempting to defend their Kinfolk; they may have somehow been corrupted. Until an outside pack can enter Iraq and discern the truth, their fate remains a mystery.

Israel

Israel, or Palestine as it was called until recently, sits atop a spit of land that links the Middle East with Africa, making it a much sought after prize for both strategic and trade reasons. Although a Jewish kingdom existed there about 2500 years ago and lasted approximately a century, the land was successively conquered by the Assyrians, Greeks and Romans. Despite Jewish rebellions, the country did not again surface as a Jewish state until after World War II.

Palestine became part of the Ottoman Empire alongside the rest of the Middle East. It was freed with that empire's collapse after World War I. The Zionist movement in Europe, which encouraged Jews to move to Palestine and learn to be self sufficient by farming the "promised land," had already made its influence felt and the British Mandate encouraged such settlements.

Because of its history as the Hebrew Promised Land, the birthplace of Jesus and Jerusalem's status as a holy city sacred to Muslims, members of all three religions flocked to the region on pilgrimage. As more Jewish settlers bought land and took up farming, they displaced Arab Palestinians who had worked the land as tenant farmers for generations. Pilgrimage became dangerous as skirmishes between the *Yishuv* — the mostly European Jewish settlers — and the Palestinians clashed. With Europe becoming ever more hostile to Jews on the eve of World War II, more Jewish settlers poured into the region.

At the end of World War II when the horror of the Holocaust became common knowledge, Europe's Jews banded together under the Zionist banner, declaring that they would form a Jewish state. Never again would Jews meekly go to the slaughter; they would create their own country and defend themselves from all aggressors. The British, reeling from the aftereffects of years of war, could no longer effectively govern the region and also feared to alienate the Arab states who controlled the oil Britain needed. They turned the problem over to the United Nations, who declared that two states would be created — one Jewish, the other Palestinian.

In May of 1948 the country of Israel, the dream of a Jewish homeland, became reality. About the size of New Jersey or Belgium, the tiny country immediately erupted into war as the Palestinians appealed to their Arab neighbors for support against these new "European colonials." Somehow, the Palestinian state never came into being, perhaps because the land they were promised, now known as the West Bank, ostensibly belonged to neighboring Jordan.

Despite its relative size, Israel proved a match for its neighbors. Utilizing excellent intelligence, conscription of all 18-year-olds for military service and decisive, short-term military strikes, Israel gained more territory to create defensible borders or trade back for peace. Israel's determined and outnumbered people (650,000 people against several million Arabs) won that war and the wars that followed, as the Arab states repeatedly tested their hated neighbors. The West, notably the United States, has supported Israel in its wars with various Arab countries of the region, especially in 1956 and for the Six Day War in 1967, mostly to oppose the Soviet Union, who had ties to Egypt and several other Arab nations. In response to attacks and keenly feeling the need for greater security, Israel annexed the Gaza Strip and West Bank and the Golan Heights, the latter of which had provided Syria with a strategic high ground from which to launch attacks against Galilee lying below.

In 1973, however, it cost the United States much as the Arab nations raised oil prices precipitously and declared a boycott on exporting oil to anyone supporting Israel, letting the western world know that they controlled this essential commodity and using it as leverage in political maneuverings. The October War in which Egypt and Syria banded together to attack Israel was initially successful, but when Israel recovered and defeated them, the Soviets threatened to intervene, causing the United States to go on nuclear alert and the UN to order a cease-fire. Such wars proved a grave drain on Israel's economy.

Operation Peace for Galilee in 1979 saw Israel's attempt to destroy the PLO (Palestine Liberation Organization) by invading southern Lebanon where Palestinian refugees were encamped. Though a success in military terms, world opinion turned against Israel when it was discovered that Christian troops attached to the Israeli forces massacred Palestinian families.

During the Gulf War, Saddam Hussein launched SCUD missile attacks against Israel trying to goad them into joining the war. Had they done so, the Arab allies would most likely have broken off their support and joined with Hussein in what would then have become yet another Arab-Israeli conflict. Luckily, cool heads prevailed.

While Hebrew is the most widely spoken language in Israel, many Jews and Arabs also speak Arabic. English is widely known as well.

Jerusalem is a holy city to Muslim, Christian and Jew alike and control of the city is one of the main topics in peace initiatives. Arabs still live in Israel, though most live in the "occupied territories" of the West Bank and Gaza Strip. The *Intifada*, a Palestinian uprising against that occupation began in 1987 with strikes, graffiti, thrown rocks and boycotts. They have closed schools and driven the economy of the area into ruin and given rise to a militant resistance movement called Hamas.

Despite recent peace initiatives and attempts to meet with Palestinian representatives to return some rule to them, the conflict continues. As more Russian Jews immigrate to Israel, those newcomers settle more land and Israel's government becomes less favorably disposed to returning the land to the Palestinians.

Garou occasionally find themselves embroiled in disputes between their Palestinian and Jewish Kinfolk, but there are so few of each that this remains more individual spats than a concern affecting many. A few werewolves traveled to Israel to study the anomalous storms that occurred in the wake of the Gulf War, while some others speak of dreams of something incredibly foul and Wyrm-tainted lying beneath the soil near Jerusalem.

Jordan

The Jordan River Valley is considered one of the earliest places of settlement on earth. During the epipaleaolithic era (200,000-8000 BCE) people were not only hunting large and small animals but also domesticating and herding goats. By the eighth millennium BCE a Neolithic culture had settled in parts of what would become Jordan at Jericho and along the Jordan River's east bank. Amman, Jordan's capital, is one of the most ancient cities known and was set among seven hills. It has now grown to encompass sixteen hills. The area has long served as an important stop along the land route between Africa and Europe.

The Neolithic people who settled the Jordan Valley eventually evolved into the Israelite tribes. After slavery in Egypt and an exodus from that country back to their "promised land" they were conquered by Saul in the 11th century. David became king after Saul, and David's son Solomon, after him. With his death, Israel split into two countries, Israel and Judah (or Judea). While Israel fell to the Assyrians, then to a series of conquerors, Judah experienced the influence of several groups, including the Nabataeans, who built the city of Petra, carved into the cliffs of reddish sandstone in the Jordanian highlands.

Rome conquered the area and made the region into a province of the empire. Eventually the Byzantine Empire, as the eastern representatives of the Holy Roman Empire, took over rule of Jordan. In the sixth century Arab caliphs, followers of Islam, defeated the Byzantines. When trade shifted to the sea routes rather than overland travel, Jordan lost its importance to the rest of the world. Taken by the Ottoman Turks and made part of their empire, Jordan gained independence from the Ottomans as Transjordan after World War I.

At the end of World War II, the UN divided the area from Israel along the Jordan River, the Dead Sea and Wadi al Jayb down to the Gulf of Aqaba. The Arab League Council opposed the creation of Israel and attacked. Jordan had control of the eastern half of Jerusalem, including the Dome of the Rock (Muslim), the Church of the Holy Sepulcher (Christian) and the Wailing Wall. They gained the area west of the Jordan River known as the West Bank. They also gained several thousand Palestinian refugees who had fled to that region. From Jordan, the Palestinian Liberation Organization staged raids into Israel, eventually becoming thought of as the quintessential terrorist group. Israel retaliated and eventually, during the Six Day War, recovered all of Jerusalem and the West Bank. More refugees flooded into Jordan, making Palestinians over half of Jordan's total population.

Although Palestinians continue to live in Jordan, King Hussein ousted the Palestinian Liberation Organization from the country in 1970, disapproving of the bad press their terrorist actions garnered and fearing that they were trying to take over the state.

Nonetheless, Jordan supported Iraq in the Iran-Iraq War and gave nominal support to Saddam Hussein during the Gulf War. To do otherwise might have touched off a revolution among the Palestinians living in Jordan.

About the size of the state of Maine, Jordan's population is mostly Arab with a sizeable minority of Circassians. About 50% of the population are Palestinian and still registered as refugees. Bedouins number about 40,000. Most are better educated than many other Arabs are and the country is highly westernized, though women still remain behind men in professions. Arabic is the official language and over 90% of the population are Sunni Muslims. The country is noted for its friendly people and its attempts to remain on good terms with their Arab neighbors and the rest of the world. Jordan has set aside several nature preserves, the result of encouragement from its native werewolf population — mostly Children of Gaia — and a few Black Furies drawn to the area by the plight of its female refugees. The Jordanian Garou have also noted the Wyrm presence near Jerusalem and have opened a cautious dialogue with their Israeli counterparts to decide how to combat it. As a final note, there seems to be something in the vicinity of Jericho that's of particular interest to the Ananasi, for recent years have seen werespiders gathering in the region for some unnamed purpose.

Kuwait

Much has already been said regarding Kuwait, a tiny emirate that rests at the tip of Iraq and to the east of Saudi Arabia. The country was not settled until 300 years ago. In the 1700s, a few tents surrounded a fort that also served as a trading post. The Al-Sabah family, now the rulers of Kuwait, became responsible for keeping order and administering the law. The town grew quickly, establishing itself as a thriving trading port by the 19th century. The Ottomans held a claim to the emirate even after the country came under British protection. In 1899, Mubarak the Great signed an agreement stating that in return for the British navy's protection, Kuwait would agree never to give away territory to or accept protection from or negotiate with any other foreign powers without British consent.

After war with Al-Saud, founder of modern Saudi Arabia, the British forced Kuwait to give up two-thirds of their claimed land to Al-Saud in return for a guarantee of independence. Despite trying to keep Americans out of Kuwait, Britain finally had to agree to a joint British-US oil concession and the first wells were opened in 1936. Kuwait's riches soon became apparent and after World War II, its oil made Kuwait fabulously wealthy, improved every citizen's standard of living and paid for health care and advances in education. A national assembly convened, but fearing the leftist candidates in it (and challenges to his own authority) the emir suspended the constitution and dissolved the assembly. A series of changes and demonstrations ensued, culminating in a pro-democracy movement in 1990.

Such considerations were put aside as Iraq invaded Kuwait. With Iraq's withdrawal, Kuwait began repairing the damage, concentrating on restoring Kuwait City and their oil wells. A New National Assembly was convened in 1992. Kuwait, along with Saudi Arabia, now boasts the greatest number of Garou in the Middle East, drawn there to assist in the clean-up efforts. Although several tribes are represented, it is difficult for the "foreigners" to be accorded respect among the natives of the region, which slows recovery efforts. Nonetheless, progress is being made and talks of creating a diversified permanent sept are proceeding — if they could only agree upon a sept leader.

Lebanon

This tiny country, somewhat smaller than the state of Connecticut, suffers from its mixed population and their differing goals. The largest group, Shi'ite Muslims live in the south and the interior Biqa' valley. They have never been able to gain any actual power in the government of Lebanon. In Beirut, the capital, Maronite Christians form the largest group and hold most power. Sunni Muslims also live in Beirut and inhabit Tripoli, while Greek Orthodox and Druze (an offshoot of Islam) make up the rest of the populace.

When the PLO moved its headquarters to Lebanon after its expulsion from Jordan in 1970 pressure against the right-wing Christians increased as the PLO gave new heart to leftist Muslims. Civil War erupted in 1975, only quelled by Syrian intervention in 1990. Lebanon expelled the PLO in 1982. A series of wars, hostage-takings and assassinations followed, with Israel, then UN Peacekeepers and again Israel taking part of South Lebanon to protect Israel's borders from incursions. Over the years, group has fought group in a tangle of conflicts too twisted and complex to explain without devoting an entire book to it, while Beirut, once the banking and intellectual center of the Middle East, has been bombed into rubble.

Despite efforts to bring calm to the area, it remains a region where religious and cultural differences could break into new warfare at a moment's notice. Werewolves in Lebanon are almost all Glass Walkers and a very few Bone Gnawers drawn to Beirut when it reigned as a capital of commerce.

Oman

Settled in the third millennium BCE, Oman became wealthy and important due to its control of frankincense, one of the most precious and sought after substances in the ancient world. Its long history encompassed both Portuguese occupation and the formation of an Omani empire. Civil war to determine control of its own interior and a policy of isolationism led Oman to be cut off from most of the rest of the world. Slowly, the Sultanate is emerging from its self-imposed segregation. Though tourists and visitors are now allowed, Oman is still slow to accept outsiders, mostly in an attempt to keep its unspoiled beaches and pristine mountains as well as its culture untouched. Few Garou have found reason to go to the area — except to spot check for oil damage along its beaches in the wake of the Gulf War.

A World of Rage

Qatar

The thumb-shaped Qatar Peninsula juts northward between the Persian Gulf and the Gulf of Bahrain on the eastern edge of the Arabian Peninsula. The land is mostly flat and rocky with no natural vegetation. Sandstorms in Qatar are a common occurrence. Since the 18th century, when Qatar established itself as a pearling center, the Al-Thani family has dominated the country. Aside from pearls, Qatar remained without much to offer and was terribly poor until its oil boom after the Second World War. Because the pearl market collapsed and the country was so poor, Qatar suffered under widespread poverty, malnutrition and disease. Qatar's emirs were uninterested in the everyday running of the country and Khalifa Bin Hamad Al-Thani became deputy ruler and Prime Minister. After years of virtually ruling the country, he took power in a coup approved by most of the male members of the ruling family. Qatar briefly considered becoming part of the United Arab Emirates, but when Bahrain pulled out, so did Qatar. Instead, it gained independence in 1971. It looked on the Iranian Revolution with alarm and its policies tend to echo those of Saudi Arabia. Of Qatar's over 250,000 people, two-thirds are foreign workers, though Garou find little reason to visit Qatar.

Saudi Arabia

Largely desert, Saudi Arabia is more than twice the size of Texas and occupies most of the land area of the Arabian Peninsula. Settled along the Gulf coast area since the 4th or 5th millennium BCE by people from what is now Iraq, they were a part of the Nabataean civilization. In the 18th century, the Al-Saud family, the royal house of modern Saudi Arabia ruled as sheiks in the Najd near modern day Riyadh. The first Saudi Empire grew from an alliance between them and Mohammed Bin Abdul Wahhab, a judge who preached a strict, unadorned form of Islam. This religion remains the officially recognized form of Islam practiced in Saudi Arabia today. They conquered and converted first the Najd, then most of the rest of the peninsula. Though driven out and forced to flee to Kuwait, the Al-Saud recouped their losses, drove the Ottoman forces out of the area and turned their attention to the interior.

Oil was discovered in the 1920s, but not truly exploited until after World War II. Profligate expenditures such as grand palaces and Rolls Royce cars led to the 1964 ousting of Saud by his younger brother Faisal. One of his first acts as king was to outlaw slavery and begin modernizing the country. During the 1960s great wealth accrued from Saudi oil holdings, yet they were as nothing compared to the money which poured in when the Arab-Israeli War led to the region's oil embargo and price hikes in the 1970s. Suddenly, Saudi Arabia's income went from 4 billion dollars to 36 billion dollars a year. Yet Saudi Arabia's leadership worked to stabilize and lower oil prices to a moderate level, realizing that if they broke Europe and the Americas' ability to pay for oil, their country would also suffer.

During the Iranian revolution, Saudi Arabia deepened their ties to Britain, France and the United States. When Iraq subsequently invaded Kuwait in 1990, King Fahd requested that troops from those countries help defend Saudi soil from Iraqi invaders. The result was a force of over 500,000 encamped on Saudi soil and the ousting of Iraq from Kuwait. While Saudi Arabia has since appointed a Consultative Council, the royal family shows no signs of surrendering any real power. Nonetheless, when important matters are considered, discussions with the royal family, advisors, and business and religious community leaders are held before announcing a decision.

Today, despite its modern veneer, Saudi Arabia remains strictly Muslim. Neither alcohol nor pork is allowed within the country, women are expected to dress modestly and be accompanied by male relatives and chaperones, at prayer time shops close and no theatres or cinemas exist in the country. Most people (except in highly westernized areas such as large hotels in main cities) do not smoke. Non-Muslims are not allowed inside mosques and no one who is not a Muslim may come within 25 kilometers of the city of Mecca. All of this is enforced through the *matawwa* or religious police, who seriously patrol and bring in offenders.

Most Garou remain on the outskirts of Saudi Arabia, notably along the horrifically damaged coastline that is the legacy of the Gulf War. Despite their fringe activities, Saudi Arabia boasts what is probably the largest number of Garou in the Middle East. Some few venture into other areas, especially as rumors of a great gathering of Wyrmspawn in the Empty Quarter (the southern desert) gain credence.

Syria

Syria once encompassed the entire Mediterranean Arab world, including Jordan, Israel, Lebanon and the lands that comprise its modern borders. An important Phoenician trading post, its strategic position made it ripe for conquest by the Romans, Persians, Egyptians and Babylonians. As part of the Ottoman Empire, the region gained its independence, which was taken away when France received its governance after World War I. Despite its colorful past, Syria's population is 90%

Arab and Arabic remains the official language. During World War II France agreed to Syria's independence, which came about in 1946.

A number of military coups later, the Ba'ath party gained control. Syria briefly entered a United Arab Republic with Egypt, but this proved unpopular and was abandoned in the 60s. In 1967 the Six Day War with Israel and in 1970 the Black September hostilities in Jordan weakened the country severely. Defense Minister Hafez al-Assad then seized power.

Syria gained a reputation as a haven and training ground for terrorists and suffered economically because of the US listing of them as a country supporting international terrorism (a claim made more immediate by the suspicion of their involvement in the 1988 Pan-Am air explosion over Lockerbie, Scotland. Syria began amending that reputation by its support of the Allied forces in the Gulf War and its participation in the Peace Initiatives begun in Madrid in 1991.

A little over the size of Italy, Syria holds a fertile coastal strip, a mountainous border with Lebanon, cultivated steppes where such important centers as Damascus and Aleppo are situated and a stony desert in the south-east. The Sept of the Bloodied Moon lies within the inhospitable Jebel an-Nusariyah mountain range. Its members seem highly out of place in the region, as only a few (those who usually deal with outsiders) are Arabs. The majority of the sept consists of Fianna, Get of Fenris and Shadow Lords who originally came to the Middle East to learn terrorist tactics for use against such foes as Pentex. They still accept a few trainees whom they train to perform precision strikes against the Wyrm's agents all over the world.

Turkey

Just the names of Turkey's cities and sites conjure up visions of ancient times and faded glories. Constantinople (today's Istanbul), the Golden Horn, Anatolia, Cappadocia, Mount Ararat — all resonate with an almost-mythological recognition of their place in history. Anatolian Turkey's earliest known civilization was that of the Hittites. In 330 CE the Roman emperor Constantine made Byzantium his new imperial capital and renamed it Constantinople. It became the center of the Byzantine Empire for 1000 years. During the European Dark Ages, this last vestige of Roman civilization kept Western culture alive.

Threatened by the Persians, Turks, Arabs and jealous European Christian powers. The empire's decline came with conquests by the Seljuk Turks who took most of Anatolia. IN 1095 Pope Urban II called for crusaders to bring holy war to the Levant. To reach the Holy Land, they had to pass through Constantinople and in return for allowing them passage, Emperor Alexius Comnenus demanded that any territories won from the Turks be returned to the Byzantine Empire. The Fourth Crusade, however, took and sacked Constantinople, and the Byzantines were unable to recover it for almost 60 years. The Seljuks were displaced by the Mongol invaders and the new Turkish states arose as the Ottoman Empire and in 1453 conquered Constantinople.

A century later the Ottoman Empire reached its greatest extent both in power and cultural accomplishments. The Janissaries, the first modern standing army gave the Turks an enormous advantage and allowed them the military conquests they needed to maintain their empire. Their westward expansion was halted at Vienna in 1683 and by the 19th century, their time was essentially over. Nationalist ideas reigned and other powers defeated the Turks, carving up the empire among many and leaving the Turks with almost nothing by the end of World War I.

Mustafa Kemal, later called Ataturk, became the father of modern Turkey. He repelled the Anzacs at Gallipoli and masterminded Turkey's war for independence. Soon thereafter he began a modernization program, establishing a democracy, de-emphasizing religion in government, adopting Latin script and European dress as well as equal rights for women. He also moved the capital from Istanbul to Ankara. Today Turkey is an economic power of the Mediterranean, providing manufactured goods and engineering expertise to its Arab neighbors. As the bridge between Europe and the Middle East, Turkey is actually more European than Arab in outlook despite its populace being 99% Muslim. Though Turkish remains the official language, many others are spoken as Turks work in several European countries during part of the year. Its many ancient cities and warm-water coasts make it popular with tourists and serious scholars alike.

Many Garou of different tribes congregate in Turkey as a staging area for forays into Eastern Europe and the Middle East. Led mostly by Shadow Lords and Silver Fangs, these quick-strike packs travel to remote regions where they deal with incursions by Pentex and ecological emergencies brought on by industrial neglect or the incessant warfare that seems to plague the region.

United Arab Emirates

Despite early settlement similar to other Middle Eastern countries and Greek settlements, the Middle Ages saw the region become important as part of the Kingdom of Hormuz that controlled the entry to the Persian Gulf. The Portuguese held the territory until British naval power displaced them. When the British

A World of Rage

Empire dissolved after World War II, seven hereditary emirs occupying lands that together comprise an area about the size of South Carolina banded together into the United Arab Emirates. In 1971 they declared independence. Abu Dhabi has emerged as one of the most modern cities on earth and Dubai is an incredibly busy trade center. Oil is the chief (and sometimes only) export of the UAE. Only about 40% of the population are Arab. The rest are foreign workers, generally male, most from India and Pakistan. Few Garou visit the United Arab Emirates except to track Wyrm-tainted oil magnates to their vibrant modern cities where they occasionally attempt to discredit or assassinate them.

Yemen

From its long history (settled 1000 years BCE) as a trade empire based on frankincense and coffee (shipped from the port of Mocha) and its subjugation by Britain, the Ottomans and Imam Yahya's brief kingship, Yemen emerged in its modern configuration of the Yemen Arab Republic and the People's Democratic Republic of Yemen. In the 1980s, the two warring countries agreed on a fourteen-month plan of unification. Yemeni subjects who worked in Saudi Arabia were expelled from that country during the Gulf War because Yemen sympathized with Iraq.

Subject to monsoons and geographically diverse (coastland, mountains, and fertile plateaus), Yemen's highlands remain volcanically active with hot springs and earthquakes. Several Garou have recently taken advantage of Yemen's new policy allowing visitors to the area to search for a rumored Black Spiral Dancer hive located in the empty desert regions running from Saudi Arabia's Empty Quarter to the sea.

Chapter Four: India and Asia

India and the Subcontinent

India begins in the north where Tibet, Nepal and Bhutan leave off. The Himalayas stretch across northern India, the border between 100 and 200 miles north of the mountain's foothills.

An enormous flood plain stretches south of the mountains. The Ganges River and its tributaries flow south and then east, emptying into the Bay of Bengal; Bangladesh owns the lower reaches of the river, and quarrels constantly with India over water rights. The Indus River flows southwest; tributaries that originate in India cross over the border into Pakistan and drain down to the Indian Ocean. The Brahmaputra River flows east along the *northern* slope of the Himalayas, then curves around the edge of the range and runs southwest to join up with the Ganges. Along the way it crosses from China into India and thence to Bangladesh. The flood plain supports some of the highest population densities in the world — eroded topsoil has washed down from the mountains for thousands of years, enriching already fertile land below.

A high plateau, the Deccan, occupies most of the Indian peninsula. Low mountain ranges and steep valleys criss-cross it. Mountain ranges border it along the shores. The Western Ghats, facing the Arabian Sea, fall very sharply from 3000 feet to sea level. The Eastern Ghats only rise half that high and there's a thin coastal plain, the Coromandel Coast, between the Eastern Ghats and the Bengal Sea. The Nilghiri Hills stand in the southern tip of the peninsula, somewhat separate from the Deccan.

Mountains form the core of Sri Lanka, with two plateaus surrounding them. The northern part of the island slopes down into a dry coastal plain.

The lowlands all share a similar climate. The southwestern monsoon winds blow from June to November, bringing constant warm rain. In the Western Ghats, the annual rainfall exceeds 125 inches in places where steep slopes force thunderheads to shed their rain. In the interior, up against the Himalayan foothills, the rainfall declines to 50-60 inches a year. Malaria flourishes along with pulmonary infections and exuberant growths of molds and fungi. From December through February, the northeastern monsoons carry air off the Himalayas, bringing drought and chill, punctuated by occasional wet storms that dump snow in the highlands and frigid rain elsewhere. In between the monsoons, the still, humid air grows ever hotter; in May, it routinely hits 120° Fahrenheit in inland valleys. Lowland temperatures seldom rise over 100° on the coasts, and almost never get below 70° anywhere below the mountains.

The high interior plains and mountains get snow in the winter, with extremes of summer heat as well. There's more diurnal variation at higher elevations. The plains often experience 20 degrees or less change from high noon to the middle of the night; in the mountains and plateaus, the temperature often changes 40 degrees or more in the course of a day.

People and Beasts

India has one of the most ethnically diverse populations in the world. Successive invasions (some violent, some peaceful) over thousands of years created an amazingly diverse mix of features. Skin tone, for instance, ranges from as light as many Europeans to darker than most Africans.

Half of Indians speak Hindustani as their primary language. About a quarter of the population, mostly in southern India and Sri Lanka, speak Tamil or another of the Dravidian languages. Thousands of minor languages flourish, or at least remain somewhat current, in various parts of the sub-continent. English serves as a second language among the edu-

cated classes. Eighty percent of Indians follow Hinduism in some form; about ten percent practice Islam, with smaller groups adhering to Sikhism, Jainism, Buddhism, Christianity or any of the other religions that have come in through the ages.

India supports at least 2000 wild wolves, mostly in the plains and hills in the western part of the country. Recent surveys find the wolf population much more widely spread and much less cut off into isolated pockets than they'd imagined. This means the wolves enjoy a better range of genetic variation than anyone expected, and conservation measures make it likely that the wolves can move further away from their endangered status. The last decade has seen a dramatic rise in the rate of wolf attacks on human beings, beyond the increase expected from simple increase in population near wolf habitats.

Half the world's wild tigers live in India: between 3000 and 4000 Bengal tigers. Unlike the wolves, tigers do inhabit severely fragmented territory, mostly nature reserves and parks that dot the mountains, flood plains and the Western Ghats. Inbreeding leaves isolated populations vulnerable to hereditary disease and illness, so the total number of tigers fluctuates wildly. Conservation efforts are always vulnerable to political pressure — as highly visible symbols of national achievement, they become targets of partisan squabbling.

Around 4000 mugger crocodiles live in slow-moving streams, marshes and irrigation channels throughout India and Sri Lanka. Like tigers, they suffer from fragmented populations, and the crocodile isn't as photogenic or cuddly. When sufficiently desperate for habitat, mugger crocodiles sometimes walk several miles over high and dry land in search of wet places a little more protected than the homes they're losing. A handful of Australian saltwater crocodiles live along the shores of the Bay of Bengal, facing even more habitat disruption after the Week of Nightmares (see below). The gharial lives in fast-moving rivers, mostly in the Himalayas and upper reaches of the flood plans. It nearly became extinct in the 1970s; conservation efforts have brought the total population up to about 1500.

No ravens live in India. The subcontinent does have large, healthy populations of spiders, rats and foxes.

A Very Quick History

The Indus Valley includes some of the oldest known permanent settlements in the world — civilization arrived early. Archaeologists dispute how much early Indian civilizations interacted with peers on the Iranian plateau and elsewhere. Harappa and Mohenjo-daro became cities several millennia before Christ, at about the same time the first cities arose in Mesopotamia. Priest-kings ruled over stratified populations in cities built of black stone, trading far and wide. Unknown forces undermined the Harappan culture around 2000-1700 BCE. Some Garou claim (with varying degrees of plausibility) to recall past lives in which they helped topple the society for reasons ranging from impiety to offense against some prominent Garou leader. Skeptics point at known phenomena like drought.

The Aryans moved down from the north, filling the vacuum in leadership. After a few centuries of chaos, urban civilization returned, and spread south with the new arrivals. The Vedas, the oldest Indian scriptures, took on something like their current forms between 1500 and 800 BCE. They combine historical chronicles with religious inspiration. Kingdoms larger than and not directly connected to clan structures emerged in the centuries immediately before Christ, the era of the epic poems, the *Mahabharata* and *Ramayana*. The caste system took on its current form at the same time, its development echoes in the sacred poetry.

In about 325 BCE, Canda Gupta Maurya started building the first subcontinent-spanning empire. He drove back the frontier of Alexander the Great's empire and united almost all of what's now India. At the end of his life he converted to Jainism, abdicated in favor of his son and deliberately starved to death in Jainist fashion, purifying his spirit of all fleshly contamination. (Indian Stargazers claim a now-lost totemic spirit was responsible for some conversions like Canda's.) Canda's grandson Ashoka extended the empire further and his conversion to Buddhism marked the new faith's vindication as a lasting force in Indian society.

In time, the Mauryan Empire fell like all others. A fresh era of turmoil began about 150 BCE. About 320 CE, the Guptas built a new empire in northern and central India. It didn't reach as far as the Mauryas' claims did, but culture and technological progress flourished under Gupta rule, and it remained a model for Indian princes long after the dynasty itself failed, around 750. Elsewhere in India, short-lived kingdoms continued to come and go.

The Turks arrived around 1200, and swept away all resistance in northern India. Their invasion was one of the major factors in disrupting the Silk Road, ending regular land trade between China and Europe for several centuries. The Mamluk dynasty lasted until 1526, and united the northern half of the country under Muslim rule. The challenge forced more unity on the southern Indian kingdoms, with successive dynasties uniting almost all non-Turkish-dominated India for generations at a time.

In the 1520s, the new Mughal dynasty, led by Turkish peoples from central Asia, displaced Turkish and Indian rulers alike. At its height, the Mughal Empire included all but the southern tip of India, and lands both east and west of current Indian borders. Akbar the Great consolidated early conquests and laid down the foundation for all later Indian government, formalizing religious and social roles. Regional forces weakened the empire's coherence in the 18th century, creating the cracks into which colonial powers poured with increasing strength. Efforts to drive out the British, who emerged as the new rulers, culminated in the doomed great revolt of 1857-9. In the wake of mass executions of rebels, no further meaningful challenge to British rule rose for almost a century.

The Portuguese set up the first European settlements in India, in the early 16th century. Other European powers followed, with Britain arriving relatively late but backing its efforts more seriously. By the end of the 1700s, English occupiers had displaced their competitors as well as securing control over the native princes. When the Maratha dynasty surrendered in 1803, the British East India Company controlled every major kingdom and most minor ones on the subcontinent.

To the British, India was a place to make money. The government gave little or no official sanction to missionary and cultural efforts, though some governors acted on their own against *suttee* (widow-burning) and other practices. Much of the country came under the control of absentee landlords, who really didn't care what their subjects did as long as the rent came in on time. Day-to-day management of farms, estates, factories, railroads and the like became the province of working- and middle-class young men. They exercised far more practical power than they ever could have at home; the successful ones went back to the British Isles to take official positions, while the less successful ones stayed close to their power and far from the law.

In some parts of India, the local hierarchies remained intact. In others, radical dislocation set in. In Bengal, for instance, territorial enforcement of harsh forfeiture laws stripped nearly everyone of ancestral property claims, and a huge number of families remain landless to this day. People without assets feel less reluctance to rebel. Somehow the British seldom connected punitive practices on their part with violence among the people. By the turn of the 20th century, opposition to British rule became almost universal. The examples of Canada and Australia moving peacefully to self-government set an example of what could be done. In 1915, an ethnic Indian lawyer born in South Africa — Mohandas K. Gandhi — moved to his homeland, first to take part in and then (to his surprise) to lead the independence movement.

British control weakened slowly in response to a unique pair of ideas. Gandhi's emphasis on nonviolent resistance earned very favorable press for the would-be seceders. Occasional British massacres of protest marchers looked very bad indeed in the eyes of the world. In addition, Britain's leaders genuinely thought of themselves as decent people, and while their colonial subjects (and their own lower classes) might disagree with that sentiment, the fact remains that the British government refused to use means at its disposal. There was no systematic genocide or even wholesale destruction of native-owned resources, only the uncoordinated fits of violence by local authorities, who almost always faced harsh punishment for their acts.

World War II made Indian independence possible. Britain could no longer afford the empire and had to let it go, on whatever looked like favorable terms. The last viceroy of India, Lord Louis Mountbatten, agreed to separate the subcontinent into primarily Hindu and primarily Muslim territories. Unfortunately, the facts of population distribution made this tricky. Muslims mostly lived in the extreme west and the extreme east of the flood plains, making it necessary (so planners thought) to establish the single Muslim country with two parts separated by the width of the new Indian nation. Muslims trying to enter the areas that would become Pakistan and Sikhs and Hindus trying to move out crossed each other in enormous numbers. At least ten million people moved in 1947-48. The move didn't go smoothly: at least 250,000 people died in religious and ethnic battles, and possibly several times that number.

The partition took place, and India and Pakistan (in two parts) came into being in 1948. Gandhi found that his powers of persuasion failed when it came to reconciling the disparate members of his own nation. A Hindu fanatic assassinated him early in 1948, but Gandhi would have died soon of illness and despair in any event. Pakistan instituted the rule of Islam, while India adopted a strictly secular and strongly socialist constitution. The first prime minister, Jawaharlal Nehru, tried to deal as closely with the Soviet Union as possible without risking condemnation by the West as an actual Soviet ally.

India and Pakistan fought a war in 1965 over the predominantly Muslim territory of Kashmir (which remains part of India) and another in 1971 over East Pakistan (which became the independent Muslim nation of Bangladesh). Tensions continue to run high, with regular border skirmishes ever since. Indira Gandhi became Prime Minister in 1966. When her own Sikh bodyguards assassinated her in 1984 for her decision to use troops against Sikh activists, her son Rajiv became Prime Minister. Tamils, inhabitants of Sri Lanka seeking independence, assassinated him in 1990. India struggled along under the burden of massively corrupt central planning in constant conflict with ethnic, religious and regional ambitions to advance one group at the expense of all others.

India Now

Atal Bihari Vajpayee of the Bharatiya Janata Party holds the Prime Minister's chair now. The BJP is vigorously pro-Hindu in its nationalism, and supports the suppression of other religions. India's huge Hindu population makes this a feasible platform, even though by no means all Hindus endorse it. The BJP also tries to balance economic liberalization with the tricky business of ensuring constant favoritism for the right creeds. BJP ministers of culture try diligently to keep out Western influences, without much luck. A unified opposition could oust Vajpayee, but at the moment he enjoys widespread support thanks to (in reality) his firm line against Pakistani influence in the west and (in the World of Darkness) his enthusiastic denunciations of Bangladeshi responsibility for the Week of Nightmares. India's resources, including its store of nuclear weapons, rest in the hands of leaders who glory in burning mosques and openly speak of their rivals as sub-human creatures.

Just under a billion people live in India. 82% of them are Hindu, 11% Muslim, the rest an assortment of Sikh, Christian, Buddhist and other faiths; Hindi is the most common native language, English almost universal, with hundreds or thousands of other languages spoken in different parts of the country. Extremes of wealth and poverty coexist, not just in different territories but in the same block in many cities. The sum total of competing Western, Soviet and traditional ideas is a cultural hash, in which almost any excuse to ignore or abuse one's neighbor may do. In the suburbs of New Delhi or Calcutta, professionals, programmers and the like live in a style indistinguishable from suburban New York or Paris. Over the next hill, people huddle in shanties built on garbage dumps, thousands of homeless people crowded together, looking for the spots that aren't quite as thoroughly toxic as the other places they might live.

A World of Rage

The Week of Nightmares

Through thinning ozone,
Waves fall on wrinkled earth —
Gravity, light, ancient refuse of stars,
Speak of a drowning —
But this, this is something other.
Busy monster eats dark holes in the spirit world
Where wild things have to go
To disappear
Forever

      — Bruce Cockburn, "If a Tree Falls"

See **Time of Thin Blood** for the full details. In brief: one of the world's oldest and most powerful vampires woke up. Hungry and insane, it slaughtered its way across the landscape for several days, finally collapsing in the face of supernatural and technological assaults. The effort cost the lives of countless innocent bystanders, dozens or hundreds of veteran shapeshifters and three of the most powerful *Kuei-jin* on the planet. Nobody within the World of Darkness knows the whole story. Here's how they see it….

In the first week of June 1999, India and Bangladesh came within minutes of nuclear war. Something happened on the border between the countries, in the Ganges Delta, and nobody seems to know just what. A massive typhoon, unprecedented for so early in the rainy season, blasted through the area, unleashing tidal waves and flooding which killed hundreds of thousands of people. That wasn't all, though. Some unknown party used a variety of exotic weapons, apparently indiscriminately, on people and property across a swath dozens of miles wide. Hallucinogens in airborne form gave everyone in the region bizarre visions while poison gases inflicted horrible deaths by a sort of instant exsanguination. Whoever the attackers were, they'd apparently stockpiled mutagens for some time, as the wildlife of the area — nearly all dead — showed massive mutations and deformations.

Conflicting early records suggested the use of one or more tactical nuclear weapons, some modified form of neutron bombs developed for use in the European theatre during the 1980s. There were also strange, unaccounted for atmospheric phenomena. Meteorologists have yet to explain regional fluctuations in solar intensity, and military analysts suspect that some of the gas weapons must have created lensing effects in the upper atmosphere on their way to dispersing.

At this point, detailed investigation seems unlikely. Top-level meetings and exchange of secret data made it clear to the Indian and Bangladeshi governments that neither side initiated the bizarre situation — at least, not on central orders, though both sides worry about whether some of their forces acted independently — and the threat of war faded. Clean-up gave way naturally to cover-up. Whoever it was out there who killed thousands (or perhaps many more) of innocent bystanders along with some of the best-trained and best-equipped warriors the countries could muster for border duties, neither side really wants to know until and unless they can do something about it. Terrorists? Fanatical elements within the military? American, Russian or Chinese provocateurs? The assailants made no demands and left behind no clues at all as to their identities. So the authorities on the spot hope that the attackers fell to their own weapons.

The world at large doesn't care, either. Media attention quickly moved on, in part thanks to impassioned pleas from world leaders not to exacerbate the tensions through sensationalistic coverage. The press sticks to more manageable catastrophes. Intelligence agencies probe and fail to find clues the Indian and Bangladeshi investigators missed. Only kooks and extremists continue to wonder or worry much about it.

The Garou Nation and the Beast Courts know a bit more than the public at large. Something of almost unimaginable age, power and malevolence woke up in the delta, after countless centuries of slumber. Some vampires the Beast Courts captured and interrogated

Who's Covering It Up?

Everyone. Every homid shapeshifter with connections in influential organizations pulls strings frantically. Every shapeshifter with useful allies exploits them to the full. On one memorable August evening, a Glass Walker spy encountered two magicians, two vampires and a ghost possessing a security guard, all removing documents from adjacent offices in New Delhi, the Indian capital. They somehow avoided a fight, finished their business and departed in various directions. Several groups independently arrived at the notion of planting incomplete, partially destroyed forgeries that implicate Indian or Bangladeshi officials in plotting the June attack. The people framed have strong motivation to cover it up, of course; by the time they finish their work, so much real evidence about the attack's nature is also gone that nobody could establish the truth of the situation.

Similar forgeries planted in government offices and news agencies around the world help inspire opinion-shapers to keep it all quiet.

later that summer said that the being was one of their greatest, oldest elders, the guardian of a lineage who set out to slaughter its heirs. Other vampires deny this and profess themselves as baffled as everyone else, and thorough testing shows them to have told the truth. The few *Kuei-jin* who speak regularly with hengeyokai say that the force was some being outside the Middle Kingdom, and that its defeat came primarily at the hands of three of their elders. Glass Walkers and other technophilic changers hear garbled accounts about secret factions within the world's armies and spy agencies using previously unsuspected weapons.

The Changing Breeds know for sure that during that week, several entities ripped massive holes in the Gauntlet. The Gauntlet literally ceased to exist for several days, in various spots scattered over almost two hundred miles. Spirits, ghosts and strange things all poured into the world. Caerns, other sacred spots and the paths of power that hengeyokai call "dragon lines" all suffered: the rips drained normal concentrations of spiritual resonance utterly dry. After three days of that, somebody did indeed use battlefield nuclear weapons, with a unique set of enhancements. Some sort of enchantment boosted the spiritual damage the bombs inflicted. Miniature maelstroms continue to rage in the battle zone, pockets of chaos that extend from Umbral heights deep into the lands of the dead. Most of the Gauntlet healed up, leaving behind assorted mundane and monstrous carnage.

The total affected area is about three hundred miles across. It runs from the Bay of Bengal north to where the Ganges' main channel crosses the Indian/Bangladeshi border. The Indian city of Calcutta lies on the southwestern edge of the storm zone, and the Bangladeshi city of Dhaka lies on the northeastern edge. The intervening lands were nearly completely depopulated, and the respective governments underwrite massive resettlement efforts now that they feel the contamination has all been cleared up.

In terms of game mechanics, the Gauntlet rating throughout the area ranges from 3 to 5, even at points where it would normally rise much higher. Nightmares continue to haunt the dreams of nearly everyone in the area. Spirits gain 2 extra Rage while in the area, and manifest uncoordinated, violent tendencies. Every ghost in the area is consumed by a mad, mindless desire to slaughter the still-living members of its family and anyone else it was attached to in life — exorcists of all kinds run themselves ragged trying to deal with the problem. (Perhaps fortunately for hapless mortal targets, massive storms in the Underworld slice most unprotected ghosts into mere ribbons of angry memory, incapable of action.)

Inside the Umbral storms themselves, everything collapses into raw chaos. The clouds are each about five to ten miles across, and drift throughout the blighted area at about one mile per hour. Nobody really knows what's inside them. The rain that falls out of them does three dice of aggravated damage each hour to anyone it strikes. Inside the storms, the damage comes faster. Observers report seeing their packmates venturing forward only to dissolve into a fine mist of blood and bone. Totemic spirits say that when they try to venture in, they encounter similar levels of damage, and that they choose not to venture in. Perhaps an Incarna could learn more, but none seems interested in the trip.

Fortunately, the storms are slowly weakening. They no longer manifest physically as anything more impressive than bad weather, with their remaining power concentrated in the Umbra. Each month they shrink about 10%; in another year they'll be gone. The boundaries of the blighted area creep in at a few miles per month. In a few years the zone may collapse altogether, or it may stabilize around the particularly intense damage at its core. In the meantime, all the sorts of supernatural being who can deal with various aspects of the unseen world do their respective parts to keep the forces inside from spreading. There have been some (fortunately poorly coordinated) Wyrm-spawn attacks on cities inside the area, including one successful enough that the authorities had to manufacture a cover story involving oil tanker explosions at a waterfront refinery to account for all the apparent deaths by incineration and strangulation. Packs of shapeshifters navigate the area very cautiously; the

Was It Worth It?

Anyone who looks at the total damage created by the Week of Nightmares and its aftermath must wonder: was it worth it? Certainly the Garou whose comrades gave their lives in the battle do. Prayers to their totems, to the powers of the Tellurian and to Gaia herself all generate a consistent answer. Yes. It was worth it. Bad as things are, they would have been far, far worse if that ancient evil thing had survived to continue its rampage. Particularly potent dreamers wake with visions of the whole world charred and exsanguinated, while perhaps a dozen monsters like the one in Bangladesh shuffle through the ruins, hunting each other as the last remaining sources of nourishment. A few Theurges around the affected area haven't been able to dream since.

most prominent guide among them is Ashoka's Eye, a Red Talon Theurge who is doing her best to contain the spiritual damage. Unfortunately, she has sustained horrible wounds on both sides of the Gauntlet, wounds that refuse to heal properly. Her friends fear that she is not much longer for the world, but she continues to press forward with her attempts to heal the land.

The Beast Courts and Western shapechangers negotiate very, very carefully with *Kuei-jin* about joint efforts to curtail and clean up the mess. Shapeshifter diplomats know how much they don't know about the souls who've drawn the Second Breath. *Kuei-jin* politics combine theology with territorial claims, personal bickering and other matters, and conflicts flare up for incomprehensible reasons. The most enthusiastic Cathayan vampires rush in and do some good, then plunge into the heart of the storm and find painful destruction. Their more cautious associates do a remarkably good job cleansing spiritual corruption around points and lines of power, applying principles that shapeshifters generally don't grasp. In turn, few Cathayans know as much as they think they do about the powers that the shapeshifters serve. Both sides try to stay out of each other's way, to avoid accidentally breaking a healing in progress, and try to work out territorial boundaries that make sense in both physical and spiritual terms.

The Land Between Kingdoms

Western and Eastern shapeshifters each claim India as part of their sphere of influence when they want to take credit for something. When they want to criticize something Indian shapeshifters do, then of course India is someone else's

responsibility. In truth, India's shapeshifters form communities of their own, some tied to the outside world and some wholly independent.

In the half-century since India gained its independence, Indian shapeshifters have argued constantly about the true nature of their legacy and duties. A minority view, growing more popular every years, holds that the Impergium and Concord were both mistakes. Gaia did not appoint her children to slaughter humanity, but neither did she charge them to adopt and defend human cultures. With apocalypse imminent, the Camp of Shiva teaches, Gaia's children have literally and precisely no responsibilities to humanity whatsoever. The shapeshifters will fight the foes of the world, and let humanity get in the way or flee as it chooses.

The Philodox in the Camp of Shiva point out just how bad the legacy of three thousand years of "peaceful engagement" with human society in India is. No quantity of spiritual wisdom stopped the custom of burning widows alive, or abolished the abuses possible under the caste system, or persuaded farmers to use land in renewable and sustainable ways. The spirits did not save India and its neighbors from religious war after independence and did not stop the Week of Nightmares. Shivans feel compelled to defend the world (or at least the subcontinent) as a whole, not to make nice with this culture or that.

The wolf attacks in western India show Shivan ideals in practice. Lupus packs of Black Furies, Children of Gaia and Shadow Lords have joined Red Talon septs. The rest of the camp watches to see what happens. If the wolves can make humanity flee, fine. If humanity rallies, homid Shivans will help the wolves move. Shivan Glass Walkers and Silver Fangs maneuver carefully to keep wolf-hunting efforts disorganized, unsupported and portrayed unfavorably in the mass media. Gujarat province is, for the Shivans, a laboratory for their ideas.

Other shapeshifters haven't (yet) organized in response to the Shivans. Different dissenters pursue their concerns in various ways. The most numerous group of anti-Shivans work around the blight created by the Week of Nightmares, showing in action that Garou nature makes them fit to save and heal humanity as well as the world. Shiva the Destroyer is not the Wyrm — the Garou who oppose the Shivans know better than to make facile comparisons like that — but anti-Shivans also recognize the risks of sliding from venerating Shiva into venerating the Wyrm. Vishnu and Krishna, Creator and Sustainer, also matter to the world, and responding to human (and monstrous) destruction with creation strikes many Garou as a fine idea.

Indian shapeshifters find the East Asian notion of "fortress courts" interesting. The Indians want more time to see how the concept works out before adopting it themselves. The closest Indian parallel is the push to unite the habitats of endangered animals, particularly the ones who provide Kinfolk to various Changing Breeds, so that cross-Breed councils can act on behalf of them all. Southern changers seem to have more success at this, forming fairly extensive sanctuaries in the Eastern Ghats and along the Coromandel Plains.

The Southern Indian Co-Development Association, staffed by well-meaning humans as well as changers and Kinfolk, works with local industries to ease the economic dislocations that follow sanctuary creation. Glass Walker connections are essential here, since more advanced technology often reduces pollution problems while increasing efficiency — 1950s factories do much more damage to the world in almost all cases than their 1990s replacements. Increased profits (particularly ones distributed through profit-sharing plans managed by outside accounting firms less prone to graft) and reduced resource requirements or wastes to dispose of make manufacturers happy enough to cooperate. The most prominent figure among them is the accountant Gopalsingh Alagh, Stargazer Kinfolk and a rising force in Indian politics. Alagh is becoming very heavily involved in global summit meetings, WTO conferences and the like; his voice is a constant call for localization efforts. Alagh's ambition is to overcome the various Western-created barriers to modernization and help his country modernize in sustainable ways that will benefit both the population and the land.

Eastern Asia

Westerners like to speak of Asia and its people as "exotic," "mysterious," or simply "other." These labels free observers from having to pay attention to details; indulging in flights of fantasy supported by the vaguest generalities certainly takes less effort than looking at real complexities. In truth, the countries at the eastern edge of Eurasia hold neither super-enlightened mystic masters, guardians of absolutely every truth and the rightful leaders of every decent human being, nor barely human little brown brothers, unfit for modern technology and in need of perennial stewardship. Asia is inhabited by people, some better than others, whose societies differ in some ways from those elsewhere and which share many points in common.

The same truth applies to all the supernatural inhabitants of the region. Ancient creatures of vast power do know secrets forgotten elsewhere, but in turn the elders of other continents know things that their Asian peers lost long ago or never knew. The twin veils of over-enthusiastic awe and unfounded condescension make it hard for Westerners to see Asia as it is, just as the peoples of Asia tend to see the West through a variety of falsifying lenses. These illusions never did any good, and as the world lurches toward Apocalypse, mutual unwillingness to see the truth may be one of the best weapons of all in the arsenal of the world's would-be destroyers.

The Middle Kingdom

Some inhabitants of eastern Asia, both mortal and supernatural, refer to the whole region as the "Middle Kingdom." The term reflects an important cultural truth: every nation from the steppes of inner Asia to the Pacific, from the icy plains just south of Siberian tundra to the jungles of the Vietnamese peninsula, owes a major cultural debt to China. Chinese civilization developed first and influenced all the lands around it. However, insofar as the term leads people to think of the whole region as one continuous realm, it leads them astray. Many distinct cultures flourish within China itself, and each of the nations around it contains multitudes of its own. It's easier to claim primacy over all than to make it mean something in practice.

Many members of the Beast Courts, along with many individuals of Western Breeds who live in Asia, do call their territory the Middle Kingdom. So do a great many elder Western Garou and other shapeshifters, drawing on terminology that dates back centuries in European thought. The smart ones realize that the Middle Kingdom is a concept rather than an actual entity.

An Overview
Walls and Trunks

Every generalization about eastern Asia fails at some point. A billion people simply don't all think the same way, and the land changes substantially from one end of its three thousand mile expanse to the other.

Mountains define the natural boundaries in eastern Asia. The Himalayas form a nearly impenetrable barrier between western China and the Indian subcontinent; it took modern technology to make warfare between China and India possible. The Tien Shan Mountains and the deserts around them make the land routes from China to Russia almost as difficult — the Silk Road of medieval times dried up partly literally, with climatic changes ruining vital oases. The Tunnan Sheng Mountains of southeast China don't rise as high

as the Himalayas to their west, but they offer steep slopes and treacherous ground for anyone seeking to cross into Burma or Thailand. Thick, unhealthy jungles clutter the relatively narrow lowlands that connect China to Vietnam.

To the east, there's a single large border: the Pacific Ocean. Island chains make it possible to sail southeast, to Polynesia, Indonesia and the lands south of them. The massive ocean due east yielded seldom, if ever, to explorers before the industrial age, and those who may have found answers to some of its secrets seldom returned to tell of their discoveries.

On the mainland, the mountains and the sea shape the weather for the whole area. In winter, high-pressure systems in central Siberia emit bone-chilling winds that blow all across Mongolia, Korea and the northern half of China. Drought extends beyond the reach of the winds themselves. In the summer, warm moist winds blow in from the ocean, creating cyclones and monsoons.

Mongolia, Manchuria, Korea and China's Yellow River valley all share a similar climate: scorchingly hot and often very humid in summer, as cold as -50° Fahrenheit and parched dry in winter. Flat lands tend to be arid plains and fields, with the few remaining forests clinging to steep mountain slopes. The only exceptions to the usual winter drought occur relatively close to the ocean, where ocean winds can run into nearby mountains and shed their rain — this gives Korea dense forests, as China used to have before demand for timber denuded large swaths of land millennia ago.

The Yangtze River valley of southern China, with tributaries reaching far into the interior, experiences very different weather. It also gets hot and wet in the summer, but stays wet in winter, and most of the valley seldom, if ever, experiences frost. The southern reaches of the valley shade into jungle and tropical mountain slopes. Fields, marshes, and forest groves make up most of the valley, at least where it hasn't been developed.

Mountains take up most of Japan, with lowlands generally occupying only a narrow strip at the base of the mountains. The few broad plains hold the largest cities, and have been fought over from the days of earliest human settlement. The climate ranges from nearly tropical in the south to almost arctic in the north; most of the country has temperate weather comparable to the middle latitudes of America.

The Tibetan plateau is similar to interior China: dry all year, hot in summer, bitterly cold in winter. Some fertile lands exist around the lakes and mountain rivers, and more has been carved out from the terraced hills. Long ago, the plateau was densely forested, but the region's inhabitants cut down nearly all the trees for firewood and shelter centuries ago. Modern efforts at reforestation proceed slowly and erratically at best.

People and Beasts

Outsiders (and most natives) look at eastern Asia and see sprawling cities and crowded fields. They see the truth… but only part of it. More than 90% of the people in these countries live in less than 20% of the land. Years may go by between one sighting of a human being in a distant desert or swamp and the next sighting. In earlier ages, the Beast Courts and other changers lived among humanity. As the Sixth Age, the sorrowful Age of Iron, rushes down like a black tidal wave, more and more of Gaia's chosen retreat to havens far from humanity and enter human lands only when absolutely necessary to deal with Kinfolk.

Defining ethnicity is an art, not a science. The facts of degrees of relationship exist in the world at large; the importance people attach to various ties exists only in the minds of observers. Even in the World of Darkness, where powerful spiritual forces reflect shared belief (and sometimes shape whole cultures), the boundaries between this group of people and the next are soft and flexible. Exceptions exist for every generalization. The borders drawn here reflect how most of the people involved define themselves, not necessarily the conclusions any other student of the peoples might draw.

The vast majority of Chinese people identify themselves as Han. Within this broad category there are several important subgroups: Hakka in the east, Cantonese in the south, Wu in the north, smaller groups spread throughout the region. The Chinese government recognizes more than a hundred other ethnic groups, mostly nomadic and semi-nomadic peoples along the borders. To China, of course, Tibet is another province of minorities, however much the Tibetans think of themselves as their own people in a conquered land.

Ethnic Mongolians comprise 85% of Mongolia's population. Smaller tribes, some with only a few dozen survivors, exist as they can around the fringes, competing for scarce resources. Mongolians are also one of the big minorities in China — by some estimates, more Mongols live in "autonomous regions" within China than in Mongolia itself. A single ethnic group accounts for virtually the entire population of both North and South Korea, apart from a few tribes both governments wish would hurry up and vanish, to simplify their record-keeping.

Japan's population consists almost entirely of ethnic Japanese, but includes more than a million ethnic Koreans along with the Ainu people of the northern island Hokkaido. In recent years, genetic and other studies showed Ainu heritage to be far more pervasive in the general Japanese population than anyone had expected. The news meets the sort of welcome that white supremacists in America feel upon finding they have African-American ancestors.

The total wolf population of eastern Asia is in the tens of thousands: less than 100,000, possibly less than half of that. China holds a few thousand (all in the Yellow River valley and north of there), Tibet another few thousand. At least 30,000 wolves live in Mongolia, where much of the environment remains undeveloped even if polluted at a distance by massive Soviet and Maoist industrial enterprises. The last known Japanese wolf sighting occurred in 1907; a move to reintroduce Chinese wolves remains stalled in negotiations.

A few hundred wild Siberian tigers still roam the forests of eastern Siberia, northeastern China and northern Korea — more exist in zoos than in the wild. Almost two thousand Indochinese tigers occupy the forested mountains that straddle southern China, Burma, Laos, Vietnam and Malaysia. Less than 50 South Chinese tigers exist in the wild reaches of the Yangtze, with about the same number in zoos. Alligators used to exist in large numbers along the Yangtze River. Now they're almost extinct, hiding among relatively undeveloped areas. Unfortunately for them, the sorts of low plains they like best also attract the densest human settlement. Spiders and rats, of course, flourish everywhere. A wide variety of poisonous snakes live in the warm southern parts of the region, and a few particularly venomous species farther north. A handful of wild bears exist in remote mountains, though their Gurahl kin all died or fled long, long ago.

The Nomads

Tribes of people who may or may not accept the authority of any nation-state move across the lands claimed by Russia, Mongolia, China, Tibet and former Soviet republics. The word "nomad" refers to several quite different ways of living.

Full-time nomads maintain no permanent settlements of any kind. The people ride horses and tend herds of cattle, goats and sheep. They may spend a few weeks at a particular oasis to pick fruits and vegetables, then they move on again. Most nomadic tribes establish regular routes, whether they circle around in the course of a year or spend several years in extended arcs. Complex negotiations settle most disputes about who gets access to grazing land and other resources at any given time. (Wars settle the rest.) Whatever possessions these nomads have must go on saddles and carts.

Even full-time or "pure" nomads often set up camps for women who are pregnant or raising very small children. A few men usually act as guards. The rest of the tribe comes by from time to time with supplies. Elderly members of the tribe may stay with settled women, or may simply die once they can no longer move regularly. Few nomadic peoples get the luxury of extended compassionate care for sick and ailing tribe members.

Semi-nomadic peoples spend part of the year in one place as a tribe. Usually this means wintering in some particularly promising spot, with good grazing and shelter for the animals and convenient places for the people to dwell away from the worst of winter storms. Once spring comes, the tribe moves on again.

The larger a tribe grows, the harder migration becomes. Particularly large tribes, like the Mongols were in their heyday, don't really migrate at all. They make seasonal moves from winter to summer quarters, often wrapped in rituals to evoke a proper feeling of ties to the ancestral spirit of migration in the participants. The nomadic heritage takes on ceremonial and nostalgic value rather than mattering in practical existence.

At the start of the new millennium, various tribes practice all these ways of living. Small tribes confound census takers (and tax collectors) in a dozen countries, while some big successful tribes of Mongols and Uighurs don't look any different from the self-professed farmers of other peoples.

In the World of Darkness, fully and semi-nomadic peoples make wonderful Kinfolk. Their movements let them remain in contact with isolated populations of endangered species. Kinfolk nomads tend to regard sedentary societies not just as weak and ripe for looting, but as tools of Weaver, Wyrm or both, making the occasional sack and pillage a religious duty as well as a valuable supplement to income and tribal resources. For their part, Kinfolk in national governments fear that dark forces seduce nomads into serving the impending Sixth Age, and want to make all the nomads stay put for proper education.

Mongolia: A Distant Home

Most of Mongolia is a plateau, from 3,000 to 5,000 feet above sea level. The Gobi desert stretches across the southern part of the country, cutting off most lines of travel to China. The Altai Mountains likewise block off most routes north to Siberia. Major rivers flow north into Lake Baikal (across the border in Siberia) or northwest into Lake Uys, Lake Hyargus, Lake Hovsgol and several smaller lakes.

More than three-quarters of the land serves as pasture for grazing herds. Two and a half million people

---

Status and Rights

The notion of equal rights that apply universally to all citizens of a nation, let alone to foreigners and everyone in the world beyond, simply doesn't occur in any of the major philosophies of eastern Asia. Individuals hold rights and responsibilities based on their social ranks, which in turn depend on the individual's own moral worth and the virtue of the family. Until Western ideas spread, peasants don't revolt in the name of equality, but for the authorities to exercise the wisdom and justice they're supposed to possess. No imperial Chinese or Japanese scholar would give a moment's thought to the idea that an outsider could have a fundamentally worthy new idea. Debate raged over whether all barbarians were hopelessly doomed to ignorance, or whether some might be educated so as to be the equivalent of slow children in civilized lands.

Few ideas occur to only one person. Ancient philosophers in various lands do teach that heaven regards all people as equals, possessed of some unalienable rights. It's just that their teachings remain marginalized, influencing neither official popularity nor popular views.

Garou and other shapechangers find this sort of status system very congenial, at least in principle. They live themselves in a strictly ordered hierarchy endorsed by Gaia, and usually approve of a comparable order among humans. Leveling breaks down the social distinctions that should naturally accompany distinctions in birth, gifts and achievements. Many eastern Asian changers look favorably on traditional revival movements, which restore an awareness of hierarchy to human society.

---

live in Mongolia. 90% are Mongolian in ethnicity and language; the remaining 10% includes Kazakh, Chinese and Russian communities plus a mix of smaller groups. Somewhat more than half the people live in cities, while the other half spread thinly, with an average density of five people per square mile. More than 95% of Mongolians practice some form of Tibetan Buddhism, even if some local practices would horrify scholars of the pure faith. Most of the remainder hold to some form of Islam. In practice, of course, religious boundaries ebb and flow, and people mingle elements of many faiths of past and present. (Until the fall of the Soviet Union, nobody was officially anything but atheist in the Marxist-Leninist vein. Even today, many Mongolians don't talk about their beliefs except to people they know very well.)

The Mongolian People's Revolutionary Party holds a solid majority, and seems likely to continue to do so. The Great State Hural, the legislature, appoints cabinet officers, and the parties represented in the Hural put forth candidates for President. Mongolian law combines ideas from Russian, Chinese and Turkish traditions, overlaid with native innovations. The Hural appoints judges, and unlike most Western governments, Mongolia makes no provision for judges to overturn the actions of the other branches.

Corruption runs rampant at all levels, with the real law being whatever people last paid for. Officially, the MPRP embraces free trade, restrained government spending and social liberties. In practice, petty tyrants of the Communist era cling vigorously to their fiefdoms, and "free" trade is usually free only to the parties with the best bribes. The loss of Soviet aid in 1991 nearly destroyed the industrial sectors of the economy, and they remain struggling today. Most mines remain closed, and almost none run at capacity. Without ore, refineries don't work, and without refined metals, factories don't work. Foreigners with money for new enterprises encounter a mix of welcome (it's a job!) and suspicion (did they set this up to enslave us?).

Lake Hovsgol: The Court of the Walled Lake

Lake Hovsgol National Park surrounds Lake Hovsgol, fourteenth largest lake in the world — a full one percent of the world's fresh water sits here, in a steep valley in the Sayan Mountains. The lake itself runs 85 miles north to south, and up to 23 miles east to west. The park's irregular borders add a few more miles of protected space all around the lake, and an extra east-west expanse up against the Siberian border.

In reality, the national park suffers badly. Overgrazing, illegal logging and poaching deplete the animal and plant life of the region, while fuel spills and toxic waste dumping foul the lake. In the World of Darkness, it's even worse. In 1998, in fact, it gets so bad that the government closes down the park completely for an indefinite period. Various scientific and commercial groups work to restore the park to something like health, but without expectation of success anytime soon.

At least, that's what the world thinks.

The lake and its environs do suffer. They're also getting healing attention from the new inhabitants: a major new court for the children of the Emerald Mother. Mongolia makes sense as a gathering spot for the hengeyokai. Here live more than half the region's wolves. Their territory overlaps that of remaining tigers (along with lynx and other great cats). Rats and ravens go everywhere, of course, and foxes find sufficient prey in the forests. The land and

lake are too cold for most great lizards, so some of the "restoration facilities" include extensive hothouses. All of the Changing Breeds who wish to participate in the life of the Court of the Walled Lake may do so.

The court's biggest advantage is its remoteness. The great crises of the new millennium don't touch it. The environmental problems threatening the lake and park are very real, but not news; they're part of the legacy of a vanished era of industry-obsessed dictatorship. Nothing like China's Three Gorges Dam, Korea's famine and constant near-war or Tibet's active conflicts loom over northern Mongolia. Here the beasts can consider their actions with the benefits of distance. The courts close to the scene play vital roles, of course, coordinating observation and activity on the spot. The Court of the Walled Lake is in the process of becoming a new center of contemplation and shared wisdom, a haven for those wearied by battle and a school for those ready to step forth.

The Court also acts the primary embassy for meeting with Sunset People. The Beast Courts know the risks of treachery; sad events in recent years confirm that some of Gaia's children still reject honesty and integrity. The Court of the Walled Lake exists far from the places the hengeyokai act most directly. If worst came to worst and it fell to attackers, the battle against the evils of the age will still continue. Sunset People come here and see the glories of the Beast Courts arrayed for peace and study: ancient libraries and even more ancient scholars working alongside this generation's leaders and this year's cubs. The court's designers hope that perhaps strangers may feel a touch of shame at their own barbarian ignorance. It's safer this way.

Hengeyokai critics of the new court describe it as a bubble of irrelevance, a dream of a lost age at a time when the Green Mother needs Her children to face the dark future. Skeptical Sunset People say that the hengeyokai write themselves out of the story of the Apocalypse, leaving the battlefields to Gaia's more serious and motivated children. The court's advocates respond that action without consideration is merely stupid, and that wisdom takes time to accumulate.

China: The Ailing Parent

China matters to the region and the world. Of course it matters: a billion people who share one culture (sort of), one language (or at least several closely related ones) and a legacy older than any other existing society can scarcely be ignored. Their decisions necessarily affect everyone around them. Unfortunately, China's actions at the start of the new century aren't those of a strong general or wise emperor but of an old parent stricken with confusion, no longer quite sure where the arms and legs all go, whose eyes see

A World of Rage

past glories rather than present trouble. Some hengeyokai scholars say that the Sixth Age begins with the decline and fall of the "Mao Dynasty," and both Eastern and Western students of the Prophecy of the Phoenix find signs of its fulfillment here.

Chinese history runs back thousands of years before the beginning of the Christian era. Only the Zhong Lung know for sure which of the dynasties attributed to prehistoric times existed, and they don't care to argue the matter with human scholars. Scientific evidence definitely confirms the Shang dynasty, from the 18th to 12th centuries BCE, and provides partial confirmation for the Xia dynasty five hundred years before that. Anything earlier is the stuff of tales. The Shang dynasty and its successor the Jou dynasty set the pattern of Chinese culture. The I Ching, the classic book of oracles, dates back to this era, as do some early poems and prayers. In the millennium before Christ, rival dynasties conquered more and more of their neighbors, and in 221 BCE, Qin Shihaungdi united all of what we now think of as China. His short-lived dynasty, the Qin, gave its very name to China.

Careless or exuberant Westerners speak of an unbroken continuity in Chinese civilization. They're wrong. The truth is a complex pattern of integration, collapse, conquest and reintegration. After Qin came the Han dynasty, which gave its name to the people of China and set the pattern for all its successors. Four hundred years of civil war followed the Han's collapse in 220 CE, with nomadic conquerors ruling some parts of the old kingdom and petty tyrants grasping at the west. The Sui and Tang dynasties brought the country together again from 581 to 960, and then chaos returned in the period of Five Dynasties (in the north) and Six Kingdoms (in the south). The Liao, cousins to the Mongols and Manchus, ruled the north for two hundred years, and the Jurchen, another nomadic people, rule for a century after that.

In 1264 the Mongols under Qubilai Khan completed their conquest of all of China. A century later they declined into ineffective decadence and native opposition rose, culminating in the Ming dynasty, the first ethnically Han dynasty to rule the country in four hundred years. In turn the Ming became overconfident and lax, and the Manchus swept down to seize the whole country by 1644. Lacking the legitimacy of being Han, the Manchus compensated by striving for the legitimacy of orthodoxy. They so successfully adopted classical Chinese patterns that they couldn't respond at all to the rising tide of Western presence, suffering defeat after defeat until their final collapse in revolt and civil war in 1911. In the somewhat more than two thousand years of the Chinese imperial system, Chinese emperors presided over unified kingdoms scarcely half the time.

Changes kept happening. Sun Yat-Sen's well-meaning, liberally organized Chinese republic struggled along until gangster Chiang Kai-shek came to power. He made the republic an instrument of personal enrichment, much like the biggest protection racket ever, and fed rebellious anger which Mao Zedong and his Communist forces exploited brilliantly. Civil war began in earnest in the 1930s. The outbreak of hostilities with Japan slowed but didn't stop the war; in 1949, Chiang and his retainers fled to Taiwan to found a reduced version of the republic. Mao consolidated the mainland under the rule of the People's Republic of China. In the 1960s, Mao unleashed the Cultural Revolution, an attempt to purify the country ideologically that destroyed most of the leading intellectuals of a generation and created unresolved injustices whose consequences last to this day. The Chinese Politburo continued after Mao's death in erratic, drifting efforts to perfect Communism, create a distinctive Chinese grand synthesis or simply muddle through.

China Now

In theory, China remains a Communist nation, committed to Mao Zedong Thought as the mature expression of Marxism-Leninism. In practice it's certainly centralized and totalitarian, with political philosophy that draws on Confucian and (particularly) Legalist traditions of the imperial era as well as modern ideas. Supreme power is a matter of personal domain; every time the supreme leader dies, power struggles break out at the top, and no institutional process, no equivalent to free elections or even simple hereditary kingship, guides the transition. The lines of power on

---

How Do You Say That?

Wherever possible, this chapter uses the pinyin rendering of Chinese names. It looks weird but is actually much simpler than alternatives. Nearly all the consonants sound just like they look, with three key exceptions: "z" sounds like a very soft "dz", as in "adze"; "x" is a very soft "hs" sound, almost like "shoe"; "q" is a particularly hard "ch", as in the German "ach" or the Scottish "loch". The vowel "a" is as in "watch"; "e" is very much like the short "u" in "gun"; "i" is short, as in "pig"; "o" is long, like in "go"; "u" is long, like "flu." The Chinese stacks of vowels sometimes look intimidating: "iao" is almost like "yow" as a single, short syllable; "ei" is the vowel sound in "way"; "ou" is the vowel sound in "Joe." Some of the details get complex, but these rules get you quite close almost all the time.

paper, running up through the national congress and executive branches to the president, have little to do with who actually makes decisions. The chairman of the Chinese Communist Party, who isn't anywhere on official charts, makes the real decisions. Sometimes the chairman *is* the president, like now: Jiang Zemin holds both positions. That's not always true.

Nor do organizational charts account for the role of the People's Liberation Army. In the 1980s its senior generals clashed with Deng Xiaoping, who slashed their funding. They responded by going into business, and the PLA is still the largest business owner in the nation, despite repeated attempts by the central government to cut this economic independence. In addition, local and provincial authorities balance power within their territory in a wide variety of ways; some amount to nearly independent lords who can ignore almost all directives from the capital in Beijing. A leader as strong as Mao might pull the country back together, almost certainly into a new age of tyranny. More likely, the existing tensions will escalate until the whole regime collapses in the face of a credible outside alternative. If Mao was the emperor who founded a new dynasty, what comes next is more likely to be another era of interregnum and splintering than a glorious new unity.

The Ambassadors

Changers who recall past lives in China look at the current political situation and think about dynastic collapse. For all the Communist regime's effort to free itself from outdated imperialist dogma, social patterns don't change overnight. One of the new "fortress courts" maintains no fixed location at all. Instead, the Court at Large, or the court of the Ambassadors, sends its packs wherever they suspect they may find allies. The Court at Large aims to build a network of humans, animals, changers, spirits and *shen* ready to act when the government collapses. Instead of generations of chaos, the Court at Large hopes, only a few years of disorder need follow. Some visionaries of the Court dream that they can make China so strong that it can fend off the Sixth Age altogether; others hope more temperately to secure some strongholds for all until the Wheel of Ages starts turning upward again.

The Court at Large prides itself on diversity. Its critics call it "mongrel" and "motley." The elderly Zhong Lung and Khan who founded the court in the 1970s accept with good humor their role as troublemakers. They provide shelter to hengeyokai and Western changers with more fondness for dealing with outsiders than most changer communities approve of. The court aims to put that curiosity to use. Sometimes it works,

sometimes not. Some troublemakers get themselves killed or wounded for their troubles. But sometimes the court wins a valuable success. The court seeks out anyone and everyone who might help preserve China: all sorts of supernatural creatures, human magicians, normal humans of good will and even (a very few) vampires who share a love for the Middle Kingdom. Their ambassadors are a varied lot, including Ten Thousand Eyes, an orphaned Ananasi who was raised by the court rather than his own kind, and was trained in the arts of negotiating with Kumo; Fallen River, a Silent Strider under exile from the Garou Nation who seeks to prove himself by understanding and dealing with Yin-oriented *Kuei-jin*, and Bandit-Eater, a scholarly Hakken elder who has dedicated his efforts to understanding and reasoning with the Namebreaker mages.

One of the more unusual groups within the court is the Firehair Family. In the 17th century, Spanish and Irish sailors of Celtic ancestry took part in trading missions to China, and a few settled down. Their ranks included a handful of Fianna. The changers married into local families, and in a few generations their ethnic identity vanished altogether except for a recessive tendency to bright red hair. The Garou retain their tribe's affinity for creatures of dream and spirit. The Firehair Family lives in and around Beijing, and recently discovered that they get along splendidly with the *hsien*, the mysterious "Eastern Changelings," of the capital. The Garou don't really understand the issues that confront the Jade Mandarin of Beijing, but it's clear to each side that the other means well, and together they may yet crack some holes in the wall of rigid formalism and impending death.

Hong Kong

See **World of Darkness: Hong Kong** for a much more detailed history and coverage of the state of affairs there. This section provides a quick overview and updates the events of the present moment.

Before the 1700s, Hong Kong was merely a set of barren islands inhabited by a few thousand fishermen. The opium trade made Hong Kong suddenly useful as a port, and by the time the British seized the island in 1841, it was a regional trade center. The population went from thousands to millions within three generations as Chinese and foreigners alike swarmed in to pursue wealth. Britain's extremely *laissez-faire* social policy allowed gross injustices to prevail, but also preserved local culture even as the Chinese Republic and the People's Republic set about stamping out tradition. In the mid-20th century, industry started growing along with trade, though the territory itself remained (and remains) extremely resource-poor.

Hong Kong Now

In 1984, to almost everyone's surprise, the British government agreed to return all of Hong Kong to China in 1997, when the lease on the New Territories would run out. In 1997, the changeover happened very peacefully. The Chinese government pays lip service to the notion of respecting Hong Kong's system of social order, forcing its changes on the territory in piecemeal fashion. The chain reaction of currency collapses and Asia-wide depression has done as much harm to Hong Kong's economy as the flight of so many wealthy (and not-so-wealthy) inhabitants to Canada, the US and other havens.

Hong Kong is technically a "special administrative region" of the People's Republic. The PRC appoints three of the thirteen cabinet officers, including current Chief Secretary Anson Chan. The Legislative Council includes members elected directly, appointed by election committees and selected directly in parliamentary fashion. Independent councilors outnumber all the parties represented, and at this point debate is very much a struggle each against all. PRC-backed investigations have swept much of the old-time organized crime influence out of the police... and created many new openings for the gangs that the PRC or the Army favors. Everyone knows that the tanks *could* come rolling in just as they did in Tiananmen Square. Nobody knows what outsiders would do, and so far nobody's been willing to push it far enough to find out.

The Mother of Peach Trees Caern

The Sept of the Council for Universal Trade emerged from factional fighting within the Warders in 1898. Its members and their Kinfolk played small but significant parts in stabilizing British-Chinese relations. They couldn't stop any of the wars of the 20th century (though they tried, and some died valiantly in an effort to slay warmongers before it became too late), but they did protect Hong Kong from the worst disruptions. In the early 1980s, the Sept offered tours of Hong Kong's quiet spots to British diplomats contemplating their response to Chinese proposals on handling the island after 1997. The caern's guardians believe that the opportunity to ponder in peace, largely free of Wyrm and Weaver corruption, contributed to sound decision-making in 1984.

The turnover itself created no problems for the caern or sept. Unfortunately, the bad news came not long thereafter. The sept discovered that while they'd done a fine job policing their own Kinfolk and the businesses adjacent to the zoo in which the caern rested, they'd overlooked problems elsewhere. A purge of anti-Communist Triad influence in the police department stripped the sept of many valuable contacts. Comparable internal security investigations in the civil service led to the dismissal on grounds of psychological instability of some of the sept's best-placed Kinfolk and other allies. By the start of 1998, the caern lacked official ties to protect it from the press of development.

Ambitious officers in the People's Liberation Army set up front groups to seize control of the shopping mall and film company adjacent to the zoo. Sept leader Jo Wu found herself facing economic aggression on all fronts; her decision to concentrate on the properties close to the caern cost her the opportunity to defend her assets elsewhere. Sept elder Wok Wok Rik is in failing health and may lose controlling interest in his film company at any time. The zoo itself suffers from neglect and pollutants. The new government would prefer to build a series of smaller zoos, and distribute the construction favors to their allies. The ministry of public works turns a blind eye to waste dumping in the hills around the zoo as long as the kickbacks keep coming in, and the resulting poisons rot the land both physically and in the Umbra.

Divisions run deep within the Hong Kong werewolf community. Mainland supporters like Glass Walker Theurge Wu Tong press to close down the Mother of Peach Trees Caern altogether, so as to sever a tie to the old imperial era. Stargazers trying to get close to the ruins of Shigalu Monastery and the region-wide debates over their tribe's fate crowd the city, threatening to alert the general public to a new supernatural presence; long-time residents resent the influx. So far only minor brawls punctuate heated arguments, and greater violence remains (for the moment) a worry rather than a reality.

Similar divisions afflict the other Changing Breeds. Khan police officer Ling Chu, once the darling of honest Hong Kong citizens, quit the police force after repeated quarrels with his new Communist superiors (and, less publicly, with a new rival — a mainlander Khan with Communist sympathies). He now works as a private eye, and as a covert operative for Interpol. Some of his Kinfolk see him as a traitor, others as a hero. Only the Ratkin flourish. The city's crowded nature hasn't changed, nor has their determination to meet the Apocalypse on their own terms.

The Western Lands

China's western provinces don't look much like the east. The Takla Makan desert sprawls across Xinjiang province, with actual sand dunes

just like in the movies, along with utterly barren rocky and earthen hills. The Himalayas and Tien Shan mountain ranges converge like eyelids, poised endlessly before blinking. Rivers descend from snowy heights to go nowhere, literally. They drain into the desert and vanish before connecting to lakes or rivers that flow out of the desert. The Tarim Basin, which includes some not-quite-so-desolate plains around the edges of the desert, started drying up before the Christian era. Forests gave way to steppes and then to desert. Life now clusters around the remaining oases and underground rivers. In the summer, temperatures get to 130° Fahrenheit and more, while in winter they descend to -60°, plus gale-force winds.

The Uighur nomads, related to both Turks and Mongols, live here. China calls the province the "Uighur Autonomous Territory" and treats it much like an American Indian reservation. Chinese inspectors generally treat the Uighurs like developmentally disabled children who might someday carry out orders well but who certainly can't function as part of the modern world. Ambitious Uighurs find ways to garner wealth surreptitiously, often in the drug and arms trade that weaves across the borders between former Soviet republics, China, India and Pakistan. Extremes of illicit wealth and imposed poverty coexist with persistent tribal life.

Xinjiang also hosts a unique population of Garou. Wolves flourish in the mountains, at least where Stalinist and Maoist factory complexes (now nearly all abandoned) didn't blight everything for miles. The mountain wildlife and the human communities of oasis dwellers and herders provide small but stable populations of Kinfolk for both homid and lupus Garou. The Tarim Basin is closer to the Black and Baltic Seas than to the Pacific Ocean. While the routes here are rough and often dangerous, the survivors find it worthwhile.

This is where the outcasts of the Garou Nation come. Metis gather in caves and villages around almost-dead oases. Children with parents of different tribes live in extended networks of informal kinship, among fellow Garou who'd all just as soon not talk about their ancestry. Visionaries, heretics and defeated would-be rulers try to rally their fellow outcasts, or simply plot revenge on their enemies. The basin lies far enough from zealots for Garou purity that few crusades interfere with the eccentric, passionate rhythms of outcast life.

The Beast Courts take no official notice of the outcasts. A few missionary-minded Kitsune and Tengu attempt to recruit the Western outcasts to superior Eastern ways. They find few willing audiences; after losing out to one set of rules, the outcasts generally prefer their own anarchy to someone else's authority.

The Takla Makan Penumbra holds a mystery that few scholars probe with any success. Low clouds cover the spiritual sky, and a red glow suffuses them. It looks like there are cities burning, somewhere just over the horizon from wherever an observer is at the moment. Archeology provides no evidence of ancient cities in the region, and neither human nor changer folklore includes lost civilizations. A pack of sages who once made the trip across the Himalayas to India consulted Mokolé about the matter. The lizards professed to find no clue about it in their racial memories. Since the appearance of the Red Star, some prophets claim that the red nights offer a glimpse of the future, a sign of the destruction that the star or its servants will soon unleash.

Taiwan

An ethnically mixed population of Pacific Islanders first settled Taiwan ten thousand years ago. For a very long time they had little contact with the outside world: they fished and hunted in their territory, and others passed them by. The island is sub-tropical, with dense forests surrounding steep, high mountains, and offers few incentives for pre-industrial traders and conquerors. Except in the highest mountains, the weather ranges from hot and rainy in summer to warm and rainy in winter. It very seldom gets under 60° Fahrenheit even in mid-winter.

European traders in the 1500s found the island useful enough to bother with. An early Portuguese outpost fell to Dutch invasion. In 1626, the Dutch built a capital at Tainan, the first permanent modern settlement. In the 1660s, the recently triumphant Manchus evicted the Dutch and then fended off an attempt at Ming revival. Mainland immigrants poured in once Taiwan became securely a part of the Chinese empire. Japan seized the island in 1895 and held it until the end of World War II. Taiwan returned to Chinese control only briefly; the fleeing remnants of the Chinese Republic settled in Taiwan. The Kuomintang nationalist party declared Taiwan the new seat of the Chinese Republic; they moved the capital to Taipei, nearly on the opposite end of the island from Tainan. They still scarcely acknowledge the PRC's control of China, just as the PRC's leaders prefer to regard Taiwan as a rebellious subordinate unit soon to yield to central control.

President Lee Tenghui, of the Democratic Progressive Party, opposes the Kuomintang line of eventual reunification (with Taiwan leading the mainland rather than vice versa, of course). The DPP accepts the schism as a fact of life and favors a fully independent Taiwan. Few governments elsewhere in the world care to support such an assertion in the face of China's persistent claims.

Several times in the 1980s and '90s, the US found itself facing the threat of war with China over US defense agreements with Taiwan. The Taiwanese government gets less recognition from the United Nations than dozens of would-be independent states and even non-governmental organization. Pacific regional defense treaties carefully avoid saying too much about Taiwan.

The current balance of power looks even worse than usual for Taiwanese who dream of real independence. In the aftermath of a devastating earthquake in September 1999, the mainland government demanded that relief workers earn PRC approval before entering Taiwan. Almost all foreigners complied, happily or grumblingly but with few serious objections.

Taiwan Now

For the first two generations after 1949, Taiwan was a one-party state, owned and operated by the Kuomintang. Lee's DPP successfully challenged that supremacy in the 1980s, and today several smaller parties also hold enough seats to count in crucial elections. The Legislative Yuan includes some representatives chosen by councils of overseas Chinese and some selected by the aboriginal tribes of the island, in addition to the majority of representatives elected by the island's Chinese population.

The 1999 earthquake only worsened economic hardships endemic to the whole region. The Taiwanese economy last experienced overall growth in 1997. Some sectors, like parts of computer manufacturing, do fairly well, but even there the picture isn't rosy. (The real-world situation includes more good news; as always, in the World of Darkness good news moves slowly, while bad news speeds everywhere.) Rising standards of living in Taiwan make cheap labor of less developed countries look appealing to manufacturers, just as Taiwan itself did decades ago. Taiwanese concerned with their independence think that it's a close race to see whether China collapses into chaos before or after it can reach to grab a weakened Taiwan.

Taiwan's environment suffered badly after the Kuomintang exodus. Would-be liberators of China couldn't be bothered with the fate of a few trees or monkeys. Today, half the island's drinking water suffers from waste contamination, while toxic levels of heavy metals blight the rice crops. The DPP does strongly support an expansive system of national parks, which protect habitats but can scarcely repel air- and waterborne contamination from elsewhere. The list of extinct species is small, the list of endangered species much longer. Lee's administration backs efforts to import replenishing populations from elsewhere. So far few of these programs show much success, though at least they don't noticeably make things worse.

The Court of Five Chambers

On the eastern side of Taiwan, the mountains plunge down steeply into the sea, with cliffs dozens to hundreds of feet high. This wild land now enjoys park status, and the rigors of the terrain keep casual visitors away. One of the new "fortress courts" preparing for the Sixth Age flourishes in a network of caves around a small, beautiful cascade. The rising sun shines directly into the central caves through the waterfall on the solstices; the court's inhabitants take this as a mark of the Green Mother's delight in Her own creation and feel themselves blessed to gather here.

The outermost ring of chambers stays almost completely undeveloped, to avoid creating anything that would attract sea-going tourists. Successively deeper rings show more elaborate decorations. The Court of Five Chambers isn't the first Beast Courts presence here — disease and attacks from Wyrm-creatures destroyed previous courts, whose legacy includes extensive mosaics illustrating the history of the ages. To these, the new inhabitants add tapestries, statues, even computerized displays evoking the best of the fading Fifth Age. The deepest chamber, where the elders gather to debate the weightiest questions, echoes to music created by rescued spirits who sing to each other in the small crevices that bring air into the caves. The Court of Five Chambers includes war sentai that specialize in breaking through the hideously complex Weaver and Wyrm snares set around the island; the elders hope to assemble an army of allies for coming battles.

Long tunnels run inland to concealed entrances out of sight of the sea. A few tunnels sink down deep, into flooded chambers where the elders very, very cautiously negotiate with independent Same-Bito who show signs of listening. Nobody on either side really expects anything to come of it… but something useful might yet emerge, and both sides agree that talking now does no harm.

North and South Korea

Organized kingdoms developed on the Korean peninsula almost as soon as in China. Chinese principalities conquered parts of the peninsula a few centuries before the Christian era. The Koguryo tribes most successfully resisted, and became the dominant ethnic group. Tradition refers to the Three Kingdoms, though in fact there were four for centuries: Koguryo (the kingdom sharing the name of the people governed in it and the other three kingdoms), Paekche, Kaya and Shilla. All four emerged between 57 BCE and 42 CE.

Buddhist missionaries entered the peninsula in the fourth century. The rulers of Paekche and Shilla found the new teachings quite compatible with warfare, and by the middle of the sixth century, only those two kingdoms remained. Armies of Tang dynasty China invaded in 660. They crushed remnants of the defunct kingdoms, then found their progress halted — one of the very few serious setbacks the Chinese armies experienced on their eastern borders. Shilla conquered all its rivals and drove out the Chinese in 668. In the wake of the Chinese retreat, a united Korean kingdom governed for the first time. The smaller, weaker kingdom of Parhae stretched from the northern edge of the Korean peninsula into Manchuria.

Shilla culture set the pattern for Korea, much the way Han culture did for China. Buddhism spread everywhere, seamlessly incorporating folk beliefs, blunting the kingdom's military edge and encouraging social stability as a side effect of seeking long-term perfection. It didn't last forever, of course. In 935, conflicts between the king and regional princes escalated into civil war. The suppressed rival kingdoms emerged again for a few generations, and Parhae influence extended further south. (Parhae itself collapsed under late Tang invasion in the middle of the 10th century, sending refugees rather than would-be rulers into the peninsula thereafter.) Generations of inconclusive war followed.

In 1022, the king of Koryo reached a peace accord with the Liao dynasty then ruling northern China (one of several dynasties founded by nomadic invaders). The peace gave Koryo time to recover and then to expand on Shilla cultural developments, including the creation of art styles that remain popular today. Sectional rivalries early in the 13th century weakened the kingdom and the Mongol invasion nearly destroyed it altogether. The dynasty recovered, sort of, and staggered on through minor revolts and occasional competing kings until the end of the 14th century.

Neo-Confucian revival displaced Buddhism as a governing philosophy. In 1392 the Choson dynasty took the throne, and Choson kings continued to rule until 1910. Early Choson kings sponsored the development of a new alphabet distinct from Chinese, to help distinguish their kingdom from China. Korea fended off a Japanese invasion in the late 1500s and two Manchurian invasions in the early 1600s. The next round of invasion, at the end of the 19th century, succeeded because Japan's modernized military simply overwhelmed the less sophisticated Korean defenses. By 1905, Japanese troops controlled all of Korea. The last Choson king officially abdicated five years later.

Japan attempted to systematically stamp out Korean culture. The occupation government outlawed the Korean language and Korean family names, forcing Japanese names on everyone. All mid- and upper-level government positions went to Japanese officials brought over from Japan for the purpose, as did many managerial positions. Japan reserved the right to veto any transfer of land, and routinely confiscated the assets of troublemakers for distribution to more cooperative Koreans and Japanese immigrants. The occupation lasted until 1945. In the waning months of World War II, when it became clear that the Allies were determined enough to invade even Japan itself if need be, Japanese troops systematically burned and looted Korean businesses, infrastructure and personal property, so as to tie up Allied resources on the way to Japan.

The Allies agreed that the Soviet Union would accept the surrender of Japanese forces above 38 degrees north latitude, the Americans below it. Neither side imagined that the border would become permanent; each country presumed that a unified Korea on their favored terms would soon emerge. The current governments of North and South Korea were both imposed by their respective occupiers in 1948. Two years later, the Soviet-equipped North Korean army poured across the border in an effort to overwhelm all southern resistance. Seoul, halfway down the peninsula, changed hands four times in the first year. Gradually the South Korean army, backed by the UN, forced the invaders back, and until war's end in 1953, fighting concentrated in bloody pitched battles along the 38th parallel. The two Koreas each lost half a million people; China lost almost a million soldiers, the US 33,000, the UN 16,000. Half of all industry and a third of all housing in both countries were destroyed in the war.

Hot war gave way to cold war. The Demilitarized Zone along the 38th parallel became a permanent fixture. North Korea became the family dynasty of the Kim family, run on strictly Stalinist lines; South Korea drifted through half a dozen different constitutions, all promising liberty and offering economic opportunity without much political choice. Massive industrial subsidies paid off as South Korean goods found markets worldwide.

The south creeps along toward something like democracy, balancing fears of renewed chaos against the proven risks of sustained tyranny — one president ended his term when a disgruntled citizen assassinated him, and mobs take to the streets when official oppression grows too strong.

North Korea perches on the brink of collapse. Kim Il Sung's death in 1994 left a power void his son Kim Jong Il cannot completely fill. Famines caused by bureaucratic mismanagement and corruption are now routine, and as many as half the people suffer from malnutrition each year. China's internal turmoil reduces an already-weak commitment to support North

Korea, leaving a paranoid set of authorities unwilling to risk change and unable to keep doing the same old thing. For the time being, they successfully run an international extortion racket. The US and other governments pay them in food and supplies to back away from threatened invasion or use of nuclear weapons.

South Korea has 46 million people, the North 21 million. Combined with the increasing disparities in income and well-being, Northern envy grows every year. Bribes can only work so long. Nobody knows just when the North will snap and try another invasion, but many South Koreans fear it won't be long.

Japan

See **World of Darkness: Tokyo** for an extended history of Japan and particular attention to the role the *Kuei-jin* play in shaping Japan's politics and culture.

Japan's first settlers were a mix of seafaring peoples; scholars continue to argue over the exact of ratio of pre-Han Chinese to Polynesians and other contributing cultures. Around the start of the Christian era, the last major migrations concluded. Thereafter the main islands' ethnic mix stayed much the same.

The Yamato kingdom first united most of Honshu around 300 CE, through a combination of conquest and diplomacy. Central power never lasted long, and the kingdom flourished or lapsed into chaos depending on the personalities at any given moment. Buddhist monks brought their religion to Japan in the 6th century. At first priests of Shinto, the dominant native religion, objected vigorously. Careful negotiations, study and compromise led to a reconciliation in which Buddhists presented Shinto deities as manifestations of the Buddha. Buddhism became the state religion. Unlike most losers in the battle for state endorsement, Shinto remained tolerated and widely practiced, simply not officially sanctioned.

At the end of the first millennium, the Japanese kingdom stretched all the way north to Hokkaido, conquering the Ainu while keeping them separate from the populace at large. *Samurai* as a social class, warriors in feudal relationships of mutual oaths of commitment between superiors and subordinates, bound by tenets of honorable warfare, emerged in response to the Fujiwara family's control of the central government. The Fujiwaras spent several generations monopolizing power and indulging their taste for corruption. The Taira family led a successful revolt, only to fall in turn to the Minamoto family in 1185. The Minamotos formalized the role of *shogun*, the supreme military leader who acted (in theory) on behalf of the emperor, controlling the resources of the kingdom.

During the next five centuries, rival families seized the shogunate for a generation or more, only to lose it in a fresh cycle of chaos. Japanese defenders turned back Mongol invasions in the 14th century, at the cost of many of the country's best troops and most of the chain of command. Toward the end of the 16th century, increasingly effective shoguns brought warring families back under central control. Tokugawa Ieyasu defeated his last major opponents in 1600, establishing the Tokugawa family as supreme warlords for the next two and a half centuries. During the era of disorder, Christianity arrived with European traders. At first the Japanese nobility tolerated it as a minor nuisance. When it proved quite popular among both the lower classes and the aristocracy, tolerance turned to persecution. The Tokugawas banished all Christians to a handful of cities on pain of death, and hunted down converts trying to live anywhere else.

The Tokugawas did not escape the laziness and corruption that brought down their predecessors. Unlike the rivals of earlier shoguns, however, Tokugawa opponents didn't aim to set up a new shogunate. Instead, a small cabal of warlords, generals and intellectuals forced the last Tokugawa to step down and restored real power to the emperor. Emperor Meiji embarked on an ambitious program of modernization. Japan had never totally isolated itself from the outside world, despite some shoguns' wish for solitude. Now the country's leaders embraced Western technology while trying to keep much of Western culture at bay. Competent (or at least strong-willed) samurai became business managers; their less effective peers became flunkies and trust-fund recipients.

Along with modernity, the Meiji Restoration brought a renewed sense of manifest destiny. Japan went to war with China in 1894 and Russia in 1904, winning both times in short order and annexing large holdings on the mainland. Japan joined the Allies in World War I but stayed mostly out of the conflict. Under Emperor Hirohito, Japan invaded Manchuria in 1931 and China itself in 1937. The Japanese invaders committed mass slaughter, created slave labor camps and (in remote areas of Korea and Manchuria) facilities for conducting torturous experiments on human beings. Legal and moral responsibility for these acts remains a hotly contested subject six decades later. The Japanese concluded an agreement with Hitler's regime (earning the Japanese the status of "honorary Aryans") and attacked the United States in 1941. Eventually, exhausted resources — of both war materiels and manpower — combined with overwhelming Allied assets to drive Japan into defeat. American use of atomic bombs on Hiroshima and Nagasaki made the implicit defeat explicit.

Since the militaristic approach to modernity had proven so thoroughly unsuccessful, more peaceful approaches gained popular and official support. During the American post-war occupation, Japan's major industries shifted to peacetime production. Many suspected war criminals remained ensconced at the heads of their corporate boards thanks to American concerns about the Soviet menace. At a time when Soviet troops were actually rolling through small, defenseless nations all around the Soviet Union, US leaders had no interest in creating turmoil in Japan. Former Japanese warlords gave their support to American military bases and intelligence operations in exchange for help concealing unpleasant secrets.

Japan Now

Japanese manufacturers put Western notions of mass production and consumer marketing to use far more thoroughly than most of their Western rivals, and won enough economic influence in the lands of their former enemies to spark a fresh round of paranoid fears. In truth, the worldwide gains came at the expense of social and economic stagnation at home. When a few key parts of the Japanese economic system weakened in the 1980s, a decade of general depression soon followed. Even the most ruthless backroom manipulators can only take their power so far: the Liberal Democratic Party, which had ruled since the end of the war, lost control of the government in 1993, though an LDP Prime Minister returned to power in 1998.

At the end of the century, 125 million people live in Japan. The population is barely growing at all; without immigration it would shrink, since the native birth rate is well below the level needed to balance out the death rate. The factories of Chinese and other Pacific Rim nations compete very effectively against Japanese industries, and Chinese immigrants face exactly the complaints about stealing native jobs that Asian immigrants encounter in the West. Government debt chokes off a huge fraction of the country's wealth and there's no plausible way to reduce it without completely overhauling government ties to industry. Contrary to Western mythology, many of the most successful companies are precisely those that

refused to submit to central management of economic development. It's the followers and copiers who rely on the government to pay their bills.

As at the end of the Tokugawa shogunate, many Japanese feel a pervasive sense that things just aren't right. Some turn to traditional religious revival: the ranks of devout, practicing Buddhists and Shinto grow every year. Some turn to new and heterodox religions, and a handful of these make violent efforts to topple

the status quo. Some Japanese choose to immigrate, or at least to affiliate themselves with foreign companies run on un-Japanese models so as to escape the pressures of Japanese conformity. So far no visionary offers a future popular enough to draw major support, and nobody can guess what vision might take hold. Japan experiences nothing like the overt return to warlord days that plagues parts of China, but Japan too suffers for want of a sense of direction.

The atomic bombs unleashed potent Wyrm forces into Japan's Penumbra. It's unclear now whether the bombs themselves tore holes into dark realms, or whether perhaps preexisting powers drained the bombs' energy for their own ends. In any event, the soul of Japan sickens year by year. Even the most remote wilderness suffers eruptions of Wyrm creatures and (more insidious) a general reduced vitality. Mighty caerns grow weak; small new caerns rot prematurely. Courts in other countries report finding Japanese hengeyokai, and even Sunset People with substantial Japanese ancestry, more brittle, more prone to quarrel, more given to extremes. At least some of this is projection, but there seems to be some core of truth to it. Particularly discouraged Theurges talk about needing to abandon Japan altogether, while particularly outraged Ahroun discuss depopulating the islands to starve the Wyrm-spirits.

The War of Six Faces

In recent years the ongoing conflicts between factions in the Japanese underworld have turned strange. Chinese Triads looking for new markets they don't have to share with the People's Liberation Army pour in, sheltering among the laborers who work in Japanese sweatshops. The grandchildren of World War II warlords, bored with life as shareholders in interlocking directorates or minor ministry posts, decide that peaceful expansion is for losers, and plot a new era of Japanese empire starting in the underground. Supernatural beings of many sorts pursue their own agendas as well.

A secret war rages for control of Kyoto. Human politicians started it, though they don't know it (yet), with their talk of perhaps moving the Japanese capital back to Kyoto. The move to Tokyo symbolized a change in postwar Japan; a return to Kyoto would mark a fresh acceptance of older notions of Japan's destiny. The move would also put the capital right in the middle of the Kanto plain, home to many of Japan's biggest industries. Some unknown wit compared it to a famous Noh play in which anthropomorphic versions of the six elements that compose I Ching hexagrams fight it out until heaven freezes them in their current forms. The name stuck.

Tiger Toranaga, a Japanese Khan, leads the effort by an alliance of Tokyo yakuza families, to secure Kyoto's underworld for themselves. He won early successes, impressing some of Kyoto's criminal elders and forcing others into subjugation.

Now he finds the going slower. He finds that some of the people he deals with, and particularly the Kinfolk, are more prone in recent months to psychological abnormalities. He doesn't yet know that they've become victims of Bane-tainted candies manufactured by a *Kuei-jin* industrialist, Harada Tetsuo. For most of this century, *Kuei-jin* Yoshida Shimazu has manufactured Japan's best candies and used his factory complex to help purge the Wyrm-taint that afflicts his homeland. Harada began as one of Yoshida's protégés, but found the lures of dealing with demons tempting. To hide his new associations, Harada moved across the country to open his own factory, packaging his wares to look as much like Yoshida's as trademarks allow. Eventually, someone will notice the cursed nature of Harada's candies, and it's possible that Toranaga and Yoshida will fight together long enough to fix the problem.

Toranaga does know that anti-Communist Chinese immigrants underwrite the costs to import Chinese military weapons and fomor soldiers: the immigrants hope to start a new Sino-Japanese war.

Tibet

Tibet's history begins at the same time as China's. Scholars trace rivalries in pre-dynastic times, with tribes sharing dragon totems pitted against tribes sharing phoenix totems. The dragon tribes won out in the east and became the forerunners of modern Chinese civilization. The victory came only after sustained struggle: Shang dynasty chronicles make no mention of victorious westerners, but the capital moved more than a dozen times apart from occasions with documented explanations like flood or famine. It took centuries for the Jian people, the ancestors of modern Tibetans, to give up their efforts to control the west.

The Jian show up repeatedly in Chinese records during times of trouble. Whenever the ruling dynasty became slack, the Jian moved in to seize their share of loot. In calmer times, the Jian practiced herding. In the 4th century CE, the Jians first fought against and then intermarried with nomadic peoples from further west. The kingdom of Tibet emerged over the next two centuries as an entity with fairly stable borders and culture. The united armies of the new kingdom won enough battles against their Chinese opponents to secure treaties acknowledging the kingdom's eastern borders. In 641 CE, an inter-dynastic marriage between the prince of Tibet and the daughter of one of China's leading generals confirmed the status quo.

Throughout the Chinese imperial era, Tibet's borders stretched out when China was weak and drew in again when China strengthened. The two nations competed for control of oases and trade routes. In particularly triumphant moments, Tibet ruled over almost as many people as China, with claims running from the eastern edge of Turkey to deep inside what's now China. At other times, the kingdom included even less land than now comprises the "administrative region."

Buddhism came to China in the 8th century, and found ready acceptance among a people well aware of existing on the margins of their known world. Buddhist teaching helped formalize an emerging serfdom system. Ninety-five percent of the population were thereafter peasants, not allowed to change their social situation; small lineages of hereditary priests and bureaucrats administered the kingdom. All of this, the sages said, was the result of karma, and any peasant who was truly good, completely submissive to authorities and in all ways accepting of his lot might hope for a better life next time around. Changing people's condition in a single lifetime would tamper with the manifest fruits of karma and jeopardize the universe.

The triumph of Buddhism didn't lead to stagnation; Tibetan culture continued to change just as Chinese culture did. In the 9th century, a series of kings tried to drive out Buddhism and revive earlier tribal religions, and lost much of the kingdom to Chinese conquest in the midst of civil war. Buddhism returned to official favor, but retained influences from Bon, the leading native belief. Traditional Tibetan quietness in the face of outside hostility supported court commitment to a more "closed" style of Buddhist practice than prevailed in India. Tibetan Buddhism favored meditation, the use of mantras and the belief that the truest wisdom cannot be shared or taught. A grand convention of competing Buddhist schools in 1076 hammered out a consensus on essential doctrines, including the reincarnation of sages and their repeated appointment to power across lifetimes.

The Tibetans surrendered to the Mongol horde and received generous terms, which allowed Tibet to preserve its culture during the centuries of outside rule. China conquered Tibet outright during the Ming dynasty, in the late 14th century. Tibetan nobles grew very rich on the trade in tribute, exploiting every loophole they could find to collect fees and levies along the way. In 1409, angry monks convened and founded a new school of Buddhist thought. "Yellow Hat" Buddhism reaffirmed a strictly ascetic approach to holiness, with wisdom coming only through the denial of material impulses and the classes doing physical labor encouraged (or required) to support monks and nuns. The new sect foundered for two generations, before winning support from Mongol converts, who proclaimed the sect's leader of the time the Dalai Lama, supreme leader. Mongol troops backed Yellow Hat nobles' efforts to drive out the Chinese.

Tibet spent the next several centuries in legal limbo. In practice, Mongol princes ruled over Tibetan nobles. In theory, depending on who said what at any given time, Tibet belonged to China, which allowed Mongols to rule on the emperor's behalf. During the Qing dynasty, the Chinese intervened repeatedly to protect the Dalai Lama, who usually cooperated readily, from rebel movements. After a 1747 uprising, the Chinese abolished the kingship altogether. They replaced it with rule by gexia, academically-trained bureaucrats subordinate to the Dalai Lama and the Amban, chief protector of the temples.

Nepalese troops invaded Tibet several times at the end of the 18th century. In 1793, the Amban responded to the crisis with a declaration of complete de facto power for himself and his heirs and future incarnations. Thereafter, all government decrees bore his imprint. The Dalai Lama could write to the emperor only through the Amban. Even the confirmation of the Dalai Lama's new incarnation depended on the Amban, who oversaw a lottery system to select from candidates. Unsatisfactory Dalai Lamas all tended to die early, unless protected by the Chinese authorities. Every aspect of Tibetan life came under the Amban's scrutiny, and remained there until 1911.

As the Qing dynasty collapsed under the weight of corruption and change, European presence touched Tibet for the first time. British troops marched across the Himalayas several times; in 1904, the troops massacred more than a thousand Tibetans who tried to resist. The 13th Dalai Lama fled to Mongolia for personal protection. In his absence, the Chinese struck a deal with the British, including outright bribes. The new Republic of China organized Tibet and the western provinces of China into a single province, abolishing the Amban's authority.

The next forty years passed in mutual confusion for everyone involved. The Republic of China lacked resources to do anything effective with its new province of Xikang and in general tried to ignore it. The army garrison in Lhasa revolted, captured the Amban and settled into protracted skirmishing with Tibet's main military force, the New Army. The armies provided the only existing civil authorities; the monks scattered, no quantity of wisdom apparently sufficient for the needs of a people dreaming of improvement in this life while suffering fresh chaos. The Dalai Lama tried to avoid fueling sympathy for independence, always dealing with China in a carefully subordinate role.

Tibet Now

In 1950, rivals to the Dalai Lama led a revolt against the new People's Republic of China. They failed badly. China imposed a military dictatorship, which remains to this day. Tallies of the Tibetans killed in the early years of occupation vary: somewhere between 2% and 10% of the 600,000 people then living in Tibet were executed or killed in battle by 1959. The general in charge of the Tibetan military zone gained all the old powers of the Amban and more. In 1959, the 14th Dalai Lama, only recently confirmed in his position, fled to India. Shortly thereafter, China and India went to war, with control of Tibet one of the issues. China triumphed decisively in 1962; the Dalai Lama remains in exile.

Today more than two million people live in Tibet. All but 70,000 of them are Tibetan. The minority includes Han Chinese (including the occupation troops), Mongols, Turks, Uighurs and members of many smaller tribes. In places where the occupation forces and the local authorities cooperate, life goes as well as it can under occupation. The Chinese government spends many millions of dollars every year to renovate damaged temples, pay for education, improve public works and the like. Where dissent flares, local authorities become too greedy or the occupation commander simply feels like being harsh, matters get much worse. Some villages are now completely empty, their people shot, penned in prison camps or exiled. In the World of Darkness, the People's Liberation Army allows use of chemical and biological weapons in "controlled" circumstances, so some particularly obstinate valleys are now simply sterile earth and rock.

The Dalai Lama remains a popular worldwide symbol of Tibet's collective wish for independence. He gracefully manages to avoid discussing just what sort of system he thinks Tibet should have, since a message of renewed permanent serfdom would alienate Westerners. He focuses on a message of personal enlightenment and lets others fill in the gaps as they see fit. China, for its part, propagandizes on behalf of its success stories and denies the existence of atrocity zones. No resolution to this war of symbols seems likely to occur any time soon.

Shigalu Monastery and Afterwards

For almost a thousand years, the Sept of the Snow Leopard held court in Shigalu Monastery, in southern Tibet. The Stargazer tribe has little formal organization, but insofar as any group led the tribe, Shigalu's residents did. Many of the key developments in Stargazer philosophy happened here, and spread around the world thanks to traveling students. Through countless changes of political power over Tibet's human population, the monastery endured, assisted by a combination of serene wisdom and cunning intelligence carefully applied.

Serenity and cunning sometimes fail. In 1998, the monastery's good fortune ran out.

In the real world, the Chinese occupation of Tibet is a complex, ambiguous process; simple slogans don't do justice to the issues. In the World of Darkness, some matters are more clearly focused. The southwestern department of the People's Liberation Army includes willing servitors of the Wyrm as well as unwitting dupes, all the way up the chain of command to the provincial offices (and possibly all the way to Beijing). It's not just mortal men and women who revive the ancient war of dragon against phoenix; it's also creatures bent on destruction. Shigalu's elaborate defenses crumbled when fomori scouts pinpointed the monastery's location and called in the troops.

Officially, in the early hours of June 2, 1998, a "tragic failure of communications" led to the accidental release of nerve gases destined for safe disposal at a remote incinerator site. The Chinese government deplores the calamity, paid handsome reparations to the relatives of people in the three villages destroyed by the leaks and invests large sums in improved monitoring and disposal facilities. Nobody outside the chain of command sees the raw panic that holds sway as colonels try to figure just what the hell happened in that valley. None of the troops who marched up to Shigalu monastery survive; most of them didn't even leave corpses behind.

Banes possessed an entire regiment. The now-fomor major forged orders instructing him to depopulate the monastery and vicinity, and everyone set forth. The special weapons units emptied their stockpiles for the purpose, while ground troops worked on each other to shape improvised weapons in flesh and bone. The humans and Garou found themselves facing an unprecedented force, and no quantity of Gifts or supernatural martial arts sufficed to hold back the invaders. By noon, only a few dozen survivors clustered in the deepest caves beneath the monastery, and by sunset, they were all dead. The troops then turned on each other, leaving behind empty uniforms drained of blood and ichor. Less than a dozen Garou escaped into the Umbra to bring word of the defeat to the outside world.

In the wake of the caern's loss and desecration, Stargazers around the world debate the causes of the

tragedy and their course of action now that the tribe's heart lies still. One faction of Stargazers — led by Tara, former Keeper of the Land at Shigalu and one of the highest-ranking survivors — argues that the monastery brought its doom down for insufficient attention to its own teachings. Tara speaks with the fire of a recent convert when she says that yes, indeed, the Weaver is the real root of the world's suffering, and that the Tibetan Buddhism so congenial to many of the changer monks is itself a great tool for the Weaver. Karma freezes the world every lifetime, justifying the continuing power of some men and women over others, she points out. The new Camp of the Ten Thousand Things dedicates itself to attacking the Weaver's webs throughout human society: everything must change, or perish.

The Beast Courts take note of the loss, and the sages of the Court of the Walled Lake have their own ideas about what to do next. The very terms of the Stargazer debate show a maturity rare among Sunset People. Sympathetic Mirrors always argued that the Courts should accept more enlightened outsiders than the Courts traditionally do. Now their arguments carry more weight. In the Sixth Age, the Green Mother needs all the wise and loyal children She can get in one place with one accord. The Court of the Walled Lake now formally invites all members of the Stargazer tribe to join with the Beast Courts.

Most of the Garou Nation shrug their shoulders at the news, if they hear it at all. Tibet is so peripheral to their concerns, and the battle against Apocalypse so pressing everywhere. Who can take the time to worry about a bunch of monks?

The Strikers and Hand aren't having much success rousing their fellow Garou. Would-be crusaders find plenty of targets closer to home. The uncertainties surrounding Albrecht's status and the overall condition of his tribe require attention; the Amazon always needs warriors; countless local issues press in. More than a year after the monastery's fall, only a handful of packs now roam the mountains, destroying Wyrm-tainted soldiers and weaponry as they can. It's not nearly enough to make a difference; if anything, such small-scale action feeds Chinese fears of terrorism and alienates the Tibetans who will face the reprisals.

Chapter Five: Australia and the South Seas

Australia and New Zealand
History of Australia

Long ago, long before Gaia called the three tribes to the Pure Lands, the ancestors of the aboriginal Australians arrived on the island continent. They found a land shaped over 3,500 million years before, yet separated from Gondwanaland for only 50 million of those years. Australia's unique animal and plant life attest to its separation from the rest of the world since that time. The aborigines are relative newcomers, crossing from New Guinea around 50,000 BCE. Dingoes, wild canines with whom some Garou tribes now breed, came to Australia about 2,000 BCE, probably brought there by seafarers. Still, despite the occasional sighting of the land or an isolated visitor, most of the land remained empty of human occupants.

Until white men came to settle in the late 1700s, the aborigines lived in harmony with nature and the spirits of the Dreamtime. The aborigines bred with the Bunyip, who also, thanks to the use of a rite, bred with the marsupial "wolves" of Australia. Because the aborigines kept Gaia's laws and made no permanent disfigurement of the land, the Bunyip never enforced the Impergium in Australia. Over 300,000 aborigines

speaking some 500 different languages existed in Australia prior to white settlement. Today less than 200,000 remain — recovering from a far lesser number — most of whom are of mixed descent.

European explorers found Australia in the 1600s, though the first settlement was a British penal colony at Fort Jackson (later renamed Sydney). Free settlers arrived and the port became an important whaling center. Europeans spread to Tasmania in 1803 and to the west, colonizing all six of the modern states of Australia by 1859.

And werewolves came with the Europeans to Australia, some even aboard convict ships. The Bunyip felt that the newcomers were touched with taint and greed for caerns and wanted nothing to do with the European werewolves. As the settlers treated the aborigines, so too did many Garou treat their Bunyip kin. As they did in America, the invaders sought to take caerns for themselves, to claim sovereignty over pristine lands and to discredit Gaia's native children. In what has been called the worst crime of the Garou Nation, Europe's werewolves eradicated all the Bunyip, led astray by a Red Talon's rage for vengeance and a

Black Spiral Dancer plot which convinced the Europeans that the native werewolves were Wyrm-tainted. This act of genocide, known as the War of Tears, turned the spirits of the land against the Garou, making it difficult for them to oversee their stolen protectorates or to keep Wyrm-spirits from corrupting the Dreamtime. And as a final blow, the Tasmanian thylacine was wiped out, leaving the newcomers little choice other than to breed with dingoes or import wolf Kinfolk and hide them in their various protectorates.

By repeated attempts to atone and through quests and great deeds to cleanse the lands, the European werewolves have won back some of the spirits. In many places, however, the spirits remain angry and obdurate and Garou control of those areas is tentative at best.

To prevent more bloodshed between tribes claiming protectorates, the Garou set up the Jindabyne Council, a multitribal decision-making body to oversee and coordinate Garou activities in Australia. Despite its goals of protecting the physical and spiritual environments of the country, the council is fraught with rivalries, jealousies and attempts by some members to undermine the authority or standing of other members. Some believe that the council is on the verge of fracturing.

History of New Zealand

New Zealand's known history begins with the arrival of the Maori (pronounced Mau-ree, *not* Mayor-ee), a Polynesian people who probably originated on the Southeast Asian mainland. Traveling in marvelously designed open outrigger ships, the Maori came to new Zealand between 700 and 1100 CE, bringing with them families, plants, seeds, and even rats and dogs. Needless to say, some Garou and a few Ratkin came with them as well.

The first part of their new homeland that they saw were mountains wreathed in mist. Thus they named it Aotearoa, "land of the long white cloud." Their stories of the land told that the great hero Maui fished the islands up from the bottom of the ocean (not such a bad explanation of the development of many islands from underwater volcanoes). The northern island was called Te Ika a Maui or Maui's fish, while the southern island became known as Te Wake a Maui or Maui's canoe. Already fabulous boat crafters, the Maori became great carvers, decorating the prows of ships and the gateposts of villages and producing *tikis*, fertility symbols out of greenstone (nephrite or jade). Many Maori were ritual cannibals, eating the dead and the vanquished in war. By 1600, however, the Maori had turned from hunting and fishing to agriculture. Still they were a proud and ferocious people.

In 1642 Abel Tasman, searching for the fabled southern continent cartographers and scientists theorized must exist, found New Zealand and made contact with the Maori. They killed four of his crewmembers and he sailed away after mapping part of the coast. The Dutch for whom he was working named the land Nieuw-Zeeland after their own southwestern province. In 1789 Captain James Cook and his crew circumnavigated the islands. Eventually Cook established good relations with the Maori. Soon Australian, British, American and French whalers and seal hunters built stations on the islands coasts

In the 1830s Australian sheep ranchers bought land from the Maori in New Zealand. Working class Europeans fleeing the Napoleonic Wars and missionaries immigrated to New Zealand. British citizens also began colonizing and Britain annexed the islands, making New Zealand part of its New South Wales colony (before making it a separate colony altogether). Though the Maori resisted, like the aborigines in Australia, they lost most of their best land to enormous sheep stations (ranches). In 1851 a gold rush brought even more people and trade to both Australia and New Zealand.

Despite England's attempts to control settlement, the South Island's hilly, open country proved perfect for grazing sheep and it soon boasted enormous exports of wool, lamb and mutton. In the north, the dairy industry thrived. Though still considered sparsely settled, the land began to feel too small to the Maori as more settlers arrived and pressured them into selling lands they wished to keep. In 1860, their resentment flared into open war. Increasing numbers and support for the settlers' claims proved too much for the Maori and by 1872, the wars were over.

Part of and yet apart from the conflict were the Garou, the Ratkin and the few Rokea whose shark Kinfolk had long remained hidden off the eastern coast of North Island. The werewolves who arrived with the Maori were Silent Striders and Stargazers, but a handful of Children of Gaia, Bone Gnawers and Fianna came later with English and Irish settlers. The Ratkin, who usually confine their activities to New Zealand's large cities, claim a bloodline reaching back further than the islands' settlement by the Maori — and never let the European Garou forget it. Once found, the Rokea have fought a losing battle against those who hunt their Kinfolk (and themselves) for food and for sport. Most hated are those who indulge in the cruel practice of "topping" or "finning." Such fishers catch a shark, cut off its fin for use in shark's fin soup or other delicacies and throw the shark back into the water to slowly bleed to death or starve (removing the fin interferes with the shark's ability to swim).

Rather than forming a council and allocating different areas of the islands to specific tribes, the Garou of New Zealand have pinpointed several points of interest they all hold in common. Septs guard certain lands, especially unspoiled and unsettled wilderness, but the leaders of all the septs come together at Grand Moots to discuss problems that face them all and to assign trouble-shooter packs to areas where their skills are most needed. Of course, fights *do* break out — especially with the Striders, Stargazers and Children of Gaia generally uniting to oppose the Fianna and the few other Europeans who have immigrated in more recent years, most notably Black Furies, Glass Walkers and Silver Fangs (the Bone Gnawers can be more frequently found near Ratkin territory than with the other Garou). Such disagreements are never quite as heated or filled with personal animosity as those among Australia's werewolves, though. Pauluawa Ear-Torn has attributed this to the formation of septs across tribal lines and the fact that New Zealand's spirits aren't angered by the mere presence of European Garou. Though the country moves toward ever more manufacturing, Garou influence has helped it to maintain and set aside lands, coastal areas, fjords and volcanic regions as protected parklands. Working in concert with the spirits, they accomplish far more than the beset Garou of Australia who must ever convince hostile spirits of their good intentions. Nonetheless, incursions from Wyrm-tainted companies as well as attempts by Black Spiral Dancers to pollute and corrupt several sacred Maori sites keeps New Zealand's Garou more than busy.

Modern Times

Australia became an independent commonwealth in 1901, while New Zealand became a dominion of the British Empire in 1907. Both lands' troops fought in World War I as the "Anzacs" (Australian and New Zealand Army Corps), with over 8,600 of them dying at Gallipoli in Turkey. They also fought in several places in World War II, gaining a reputation as a rough and ready crowd of determined fighters. After World War II, New Zealand became a force speaking for smaller powers in the United Nations.

Australia began a campaign to attract immigrants from Europe. Though they excluded their nearest neighbors at first, by the 1980s almost a third of all immigrants were Asian. Both countries plan for complete independence from Britain by 2001 and each courts the Asian countries nearby, seeking to link their economies so both may profit. In many areas, people have begun to appreciate and respect the Aborigines. Most native people now live in and around cities and towns, though some maintain some features of tribal life — particularly those in the Northern Territories and Western Australia.

While the Maori people of New Zealand are more integrated into daily life in the cities (by 2015 approximately 30 percent of New Zealand's population will be of half-Maori descent), they still labor under misunderstandings, higher unemployment and difficulties with the law. Further, they seek to reclaim lands belonging to them from the British government. This land constitutes about one half of New Zealand and its offshore fisheries, making it less than likely this suit will be settled in the near future. Garou currently wrestle with this alongside the Maori people in an attempt to atone for atrocities committed there as well.

Australia's Geography

It has been said that Gaia carved a piece from the bottom of India and set it adrift so that the corruption infecting the mainland would not take root there. As the land floated along, it split again, breaking into more manageable pieces. One of the largest became Antarctica. Another became Australia and the smallest piece New Zealand. The placement of each of the latter two lands is told in the Garou epic "Badfoot and Warning-Howl's Race" which tells the tale wherein each of these Ragabash stood on the land and paddled their way eastward. Just as Badfoot (who was then known as Swiftfoot) gained a significant lead a great Wyrm creature rose from the bottom of the sea and bit off a big chunk of his land, taking his leg along with it. The force of the bite was such that it cracked the remaining land in three pieces. Those islands later became New Zealand.

Australia's advanced age shows in its landscapes. Rather than lofty, snow-covered peaks with breathtaking gorges, its mountains are rounded and blunted or folded and craggy, like an ancient, weathered face. Millions of years of wear have worn the mountains down, making this continent the flattest in the world. Australia and the island of Tasmania constitute a single continent. Most of it is low, flat, dry plateau with very little vegetation. It is the largest island in the world, being approximately the size of the continental United States, and the only continent comprised of a single country.

Australia is large enough that it has six different climatic zones ranging from tropical in the northern part to a mild marine climate dominated by the ocean currents on the southeast coast, where most Australians live. The interior, by far the largest area, is arid or semi-arid. The three great natural regions of Australia are the Great Western Plateau, the Great Dividing Range (also called the Eastern Highlands) and the Central Lowlands.

Considered one of the most spectacular sights of the natural world, the Great Barrier Reef, longest coral formation in the world, graces Australia's northeastern coast. Now in terrible danger from oceanic peril as well as pollutants and tourism, the Reef's over 600 small islands are home to the region's Rokea.

The Great Western Plateau

Some three to six billion years old, much of he interior of this region is desert. Encompassing the Great Sandy Desert, The Gibson Desert and the Victoria Desert, it also contains the "gibber" plains, a vast barren land covered with pebbles and spiky bushes. Within the plateau rise rock outcroppings, the best known of which is Ayers Rock, called Uluru by the aborigine tribes who hold it sacred. Scenes from Aboriginal (and Bunyip) legends grace the walls of the rock's caves, painted there thousands of years ago. Part of the plateau receives enough rain for farmers and ranchers to work the land or use it for grazing. As with the rest of the continent, the plateau is divided into several protectorates.

The Central Lowlands

The central lowlands contain some of Australia's finest pastureland. It contains within it the Great Artesian Basin, almost 700,000 square miles where deep underground water is found. The basin catches water from the rivers that run inland from the east. Lake Eyre in the southern part of the lowlands is a deep depression filled only with salty dried mud and dinosaur fossils. South of the lake lies the rugged, yet beautiful Flinders Range, whose rocks are a billion years old.

The Eastern Highlands

Consisting of plateaus, hills and low mountains, the eastern highlands are commonly known as the Great Dividing Range. To its east lie Australia's great cities and main population areas — Sydney, Brisbane and Melbourne. It serves as the continent's main watershed, with long, inland rivers snaking sluggishly across the interior, while short, swift rivers flow to the east or south and the coast. The range includes the Blue Mountains west of Sydney and the Australian Alps near Melbourne.

The island of Tasmania, separated from the mainland by Bass Strait, though counted a separate state, is actually an extension of the Australian Alps, with a mountainous interior whose many streams and rivers are harnessed to generate electricity.

Flora and Fauna

Australia's isolation over millions of years allowed species that became extinct elsewhere to live and flourish without competition. Nearly half its native mammals are marsupials, such as the now-extinct thylacine. Thylacines, though called tigers because of their stripes, actually bred with and were Kinfolk of the Bunyip. This remarkable feat was made possible by a rite allegedly given to the Bunyip by the Mokolé, a rite that allows a shifter to change his breed form — for instance, from wolf to thylacine. Forty types of kangaroo, the koala, the echidna and the duck-billed platypus are some of the best known unique animals of the continent. Others include the emu, the black swan and the lyrebird. Not so long ago, there was great concern that lumber production might decimate the eucalyptus trees upon whose leaves the koala exclusively feed. In more recent times an aggressive policy of reforestation has helped lessen that concern — a victory for conservation. Many Australians now recognize their unique species and have made moves to protect them, yet many remain endangered.

Of course, there are also plenty of non-marsupials in Australia, many of which are Kin to shapeshifters. The saltwater crocs of the northern swamplands are the breeding stock of the Gumagan, the Australian Mokolé. Some werewolves have been able to successfully breed with dingoes, although the odds are very poor (and, in the case of even partly domesticated dingoes, impossible). Poisonous snakes abound in Australia, which hints at a possible Nagah presence. And, of course, the imported rats make life easier for Australia's Ratkin.

Current Issues

Though there are more issues and happenings among the shapechangers of Australia, the following are of most immediate concern:

The Barrier Reef

Despite the Garou focus on land issues, the most critically endangered ecosystem in Australia is the Great Barrier Reef. Its fragile coral is home to more than 1000 species of fish, manta rays, moray eels, lobsters, sharks, starfish, sea urchins and other marine life. It provides breeding grounds for humpback whales as well as green and loggerhead turtles. Besides mangling from divers, boating accidents and the runoff of pollutants, the reef is currently under attack from millions of crown-of-thorns starfish, which clamp onto the coral and spit digestive juice out to eat the polyps, leaving large expanses of the coral bleached and dead. While debate has raged over how to rid the reef of the starfish (which is notoriously hard to kill as it regenerates from small pieces), the Rokea have become increasingly hostile. More of their habitat dies each day and their Kinfolk with it. Chakara

Teeth-in-the-Enemy, an implacable wereshark of hot temper and bold courage has taken the unprecedented step of seeking out Garou who might be sympathetic to her people and their plight. Because Cairns is one of the most used points from which day trips to the Great Barrier Reef are made, she currently seeks help there. Soon, however, she may attempt to contact the Red Talons of the Cape York Protectorate. She has also heard rumor that a Mokolé may be found somewhere in the swamps of the area and wonders if she might make common cause.

The Ghost Tribe and the Rainbow Serpent

Though the thylacines are forever gone from Australia, their spirits continue to roam the Penumbra. And much to the dismay of the immigrant werewolves, so too do the spirits of the Bunyip.

The ghost Bunyip are creatures of spirit alone, able to manifest in the real world only by means of the Materialize Charm. They are solitary beasts, given to roaming the most lonely and desolate reaches of the spirit world. Their coughing cries are able to induce Harano in those who listen, and they are experts at navigating moon paths. It's said that they feed on the death-energies of the Dark Umbra, and are thus able to persist. Whatever maintains them, though, it's clear that they are driven by a desire for revenge. The Council is continually beset by tales of ghost Bunyip attacking living werewolves, or driving them mad as they wander the Penumbra.

Many Australian Garou have thrown themselves into finding a way to set the angry spirits at rest. So far, the most promising sign has been the rescue and purification of Ngalyod the Rainbow Serpent, the totem of the lost Bunyip. This rescue came at the height of an extended battle with Black Spiral Dancers, during which the lives of many Garou, Gaian and otherwise, were lost. The sacrifices made have strengthened Ngalyod somewhat, and the Rainbow Serpent has begun some sort of journey across the Dreamtime to see what has happened to its land and people. Reports of ghost Bunyip attacks continue to filter in, but Australia's Garou wait with bated breath to see if Ngalyod will be able to bring healing and peace to the lost spirits. Of course, the Rainbow Serpent is still much weaker than it should be, and there's the dire possibility that the Dancers might take advantage of its wounds to strike again. Currently, the Council is in the process of drafting packs to go out into the Penumbra, find Ngalyod in the course of its travels, and ensure its safety.

The Question of Mamu

Recently, Mamu, leader of the Pilbara Protectorate's Red Talons and their representative to the Jindabyne Council by right of conquest, found himself discredited by the spirit of Wolf himself, the Progenitor, for attempting to lead a genocidal assault on the Gumagan crocodile-shifters. When his pack rejected his leadership in order to pursue a potential peace, Mamu, confused and angry, wandered away from the Gumagan lands and Pilbara Protectorate alike. He hasn't been seen since, and his lieutenant Rage-In-The-Streets has assumed the role of Pilbara sept leader.

Now rumors are starting to filter in that Mamu has defected to the Black Spiral Dancers. The most recurrent tale speaks of a massive black hound that has attacked wayward Garou, defeating them without killing them and dragging them away. In particular, this monster seems to be attacking Red Talons, for already five of the remaining 44 Talons in Australia have gone missing. Rage-In-The-Streets fears that Mamu may be taking prisoners for forcible conversion, although she remains hopeful that the rumors are false, and that Mamu has retained the strength to throw off the Wyrm's blandishments.

Whatever its actual identity, *something* now stalks the fringes of the Pilbara Protectorate. Humans living in the region have been attacked and killed, their corpses half-eaten. Their homes have been ransacked and wrecked, their livestock driven off or killed and left to rot. Strange rumors persist of mines that the Red Talons have not been able to close down emitting terrible sounds from deep within their twisting shafts. It surprises no one that the whispers originate with the Uktena. If anyone would recognize Wyrm-taint, *they* should.

Other voices claim that Mamu did in fact murder some Mokolé, but don't claim to know the reason or whether Wolf has indeed repudiated the Red Talon leader. They call for Mamu to come to the council to explain his actions. These voices suggest that Mamu is consulting with the other Red Talons to decide what his course of action should be and whether he can still lead them or remain on the council. Less naïve council members sneer at this interpretation, reminding everyone that thinking and contemplation aren't Mamu's strong suit.

The other Red Talon leaders have *not* approached the council nor have they answered messengers sent to them asking what is happening with Mamu and whether he still speaks for them; Rage-In-The-Streets doesn't want to spread any more dishonor than Mamu might deserve. This may change if Chakara succeeds in finding Marindi, leader of the Cape York Red Talons, and persuades him to help her. Marindi is not above seizing on Chakara's troubles as an excuse to show himself in a good light to the council and cutting out his rivals without having to best them in battle.

Meanwhile, as the council stirs and stews in agitation and indecision, Mamu might be corrupting the western reaches of the country — or he might not. Those Garou who have felt hamstrung by the council's lengthy deliberations in the past are seriously considering declaring the whole council incompetent and mounting their own expedition to find the truth. And some werewolves, sick of the whole mess with the council, hostile spirits and the guilt of being in a land whose guardians their forebears murdered, have begun to turn jealous and acquisitive eyes toward their more peaceful neighbor New Zealand.

Return of the Bunyip?

One council member has paid little attention to the uproar concerning Mamu. Cernonous, Child of Gaia Theurge and renowned geneticist has finally achieved his dream only to find himself enmeshed in nightmare. Following what he believed to be Gaia's wishes, Cernonous has worked unstintingly to find some sign of the survival of the thylacine. Sneaking into the unexplored wilderness of Tasmania's southwest region, he combed ravine and forest looking for some sign of their survival. Despite some evidence that they might still exist, he could not get near any of them; in fact, he never even spotted any fleeing. Because the thylacine had once been Kinfolk breeding with the Bunyip, Cernonous hoped that he might find some traces of the Bunyip bloodline in them. If he could, he would then use science to clone them from DNA taken from the thylacine. Giving up after his fruitless search, he returned home.

Two days later, a special exhibit came to a nearby museum. Supposedly it was the bones and partially preserved skin of a thylacine recently discovered on Tasmania. Seeing his chance, Cernonous didn't hesitate. He broke in that night and stole some of the bones and skin. Back in his lab, he feverishly sought for the precious DNA, using spirit-fetishes to detect what science couldn't see. He discovered something… *not* thylacine.

Hardly daring to breathe, he processed enough to create twelve clones, ten females and two males. Over the next months he watched as they took shape and grew. He watched them as they developed, making certain they received the proper nourishment and petitioning the spirits for information about the Bunyip. They remained strangely silent. He paid no attention to that except as an annoyance and a hindrance to his great work. He even provided special pouches for them to spend the last months of development in, to make it more like what they would have experienced in the wild.

Then they emerged. Smaller than he thought they would be, the newborn cubs were a light brown striped with a darker sable color. Even so, all the cubs smelled like werewolves, even if their scent was a bit... off. He has taught them the Garou tongue, which they quickly mastered, as well as English and the Aboriginal words he knows. Rather than waiting until adolescence to begin their First Change, they began doing so within two months after they were born. They also seemed almost immediately to form into a pack with the largest of the females leading them.

Cernonous is beginning to worry, however. He has not confided his great triumph to anyone, yet he wants to bring the "children" before the council and get them integrated into chosen packs so they can learn how to be Garou and accept the others as their sisters and brothers as fully as their "littermates." Yet, his Bunyip clones seem inordinately aggressive, far more brutal in some ways than is needed when they make a kill. They seem to enjoy the hunt and the meat, but are even more taken with the terror and pain of the killing itself. They have become secretive when he's around and gather in a group to whisper in voices too low for him to hear.

He desperately wants to let others know about his "children" and is trying to find a time to introduce them when they won't be overshadowed by lesser concerns that are given too much attention. Meanwhile, they keep growing... and growing. Their tempers become less certain and if he weren't too proud of having produced them, he'd surely notice the madness in their eyes....

New Zealand

In contrast with Australia's landscape, New Zealand's islands are largely mountainous. Somewhat larger than the United Kingdom in size, the islands all boast different beginnings. North Island formed through volcanic activity while three-quarters of New Zealand harbors sedimentary rock some 500 million years old. New Zealand's climate, much like that of southeastern Australia is mild, with few days of subfreezing or temperatures above 90 degrees Fahrenheit per year. New Zealand harbors large areas of grazing land and together with Australia has more sheep than any other two nations worldwide. The country consists of three main islands — North Island, South Island and Stewart Island — and several smaller ones, not all of which are inhabited.

The South Island

New Zealanders refer to South Island as the Mainland. It is the largest and most varied of the main three. Dominated by the Southern Alps, a massive mountain chain running down its west coast, South Island has magnificent alpine views with snowfields, lovely glacial lakes and glaciers that flex downward through rain forests almost to sea level. Mount Cook, the country's highest mountain is located in one of New Zealand's seven national parks. The Maori call this mountain Aorangi or "cloud piercer."

Below the Alps deep fjords indent the southwestern coast, making the area reminiscent of Norway. Also made into parkland, some of the fjordland remains unexplored by humans. Garou maintain a sept there on one of the mountains rising straight out of the sea. Sutherland Falls, the fourth highest waterfall in the world graces this area. From the Alps' foothills to the east coast is the region known as the Canterbury Plains. Christchurch, New Zealand's third largest city, is set in the Canterbury Plains.

Stewart Island

Foveaux Strait separates South Island from the 600 square mile Stewart Island. Known to the Maori as the Isle of the Glowing Sky, Stewart Island has fewer than 600 inhabitants. It remains a peaceful, unspoiled spot whose beaches and forests provide refuge for wildlife. The Garou usually keep an observer or two posted there, but rotate the duty, as there is little need for their intervention most of the time.

The North Island

Dramatic geography is part and parcel of North Island. Slicing across the center of the island is a complex, active volcanic region. Tongariro National Park includes Mounts Tongariro, Ruapehu and Ngauruhoe, three active peaks. To the west lies Mount Egmont, over 8000 ft, extinct for 250 years and often compared to Japan's Mount Fujiyama. To the north the Waitomo Caves, enormous limestone grottoes, are filled with stalactites and stalagmites lit by thousands of small glowworms, while further north lies a region of geysers, boiling mud pools and spouting steam. Lake Taupo, New Zealand's largest, is located almost in the center of the island. The east coast also provides seaside resorts that offer deep sea fishing for tuna, marlin and shark — which doesn't endear it to the Rokea there. Wellington, New Zealand's capital and second-largest city and Auckland, the largest — and still fastest growing — city lie on the southern and northern tips of North Island, respectively.

Flora and Fauna

Like Australia, which lies some 1200 miles away, New Zealand harbors several unique species. Best known among these is the kiwi. This flightless, long-billed bird is New Zealand's' unofficial national bird. Keas, large green parrots, are another recognized 'Zealander. Among the plants native to the country, the giant kauri has almost been wiped out, surviving in only a small area. The pohutukawa has brilliant scarlet flowers and is sacred to the Maori and the rata twines around other plants for support while it graces them with fragrant, brightly colored blossoms.

Current Issues

Though they usually get along well, Terroa Color-of-the-Sand, an albino Stargazer, and Ferlenya Deathclaw, an enterprising Black Fury, are almost at each other's throats, for each seeks the honor of establishing a new sept in New Zealand. Both argue for that sept to be on Stewart Island, pointing out that it's a prime target for exploitation that would ruin its pristine wilderness areas and that recently a marvelous place for a caern has been found. Neither will surrender her pride of place to the other and each is lining up supporters among the other Garou to further her cause. Unknown to either is that Gunnar Strikes First, an Australian Get of Fenris, has been moving throughout the islands drumming up support for an extended contest between the two to see who is better suited to lead. He has convinced each sept that it should devise a trial or deed to test each candidate, thereby bringing them all into the choosing process. Gunnar himself doesn't think either of the females is fit for the role of Sept leader. He just wants to delay either of them from making a claim on the area where the caern is to be. While the New Zealanders posture and bicker, he plans to move others of his tribe who are tired of Carla Grimmson's leadership here to establish their own Sept. Once they are in place, just let the others try to take it back!

The South Seas: Indonesia

The South Seas are the domain of the Rokea. Though a smattering of Gaia's other children live in the region, here the weresharks are the most numerous of the Changing Breeds. They make their homes in and around the various islands of the South Seas. Though Rokea most often choose lairs near uninhabited islands, many can be found walking the streets of great cities such as Jakarta. In Indonesia, the Khan's main concerns are the forests of the islands while the few Garou hope to prevent any more damage than has already occurred. The Rokea fight to save the entire ecosystem of the

world's third largest coral reef — much like their Australian cousins do with the Great Barrier Reef.

History

Indonesia is the largest and arguably most important country in Southeast Asia. Though Westerners tend to dismiss the island archipelago, thinking of it as small and distant, it has the fourth largest population in the world (it was fifth when the Soviet Union was still extant). Indonesia's history stretches back over 4000 years from the time when people called Indonesians crossed from the Asian mainland from southwest China. Coastal Malay followed, as did trade with China at least as far back as 100 BCE.

Even earlier, trade with India had led to settlers and by the seventh and eighth centuries CE Sumatra and Java had become kingdoms with a Hindu-Indonesian hybrid culture that lasted even beyond the coming of Islam. While the Indians brought Hinduism, Chinese traders imported Buddhism. During the eighth and ninth centuries, Indonesian architecture flowered, especially in the building of magnificent Buddhist shrines and temples. Nevertheless, throughout its history Indonesia has always combined one religion with another, with old beliefs coloring new ones and new ones lending vibrancy to old.

A year or two before Kublai Khan planned an invasion of Java, Marco Polo visited the islands and noted that the people in seaports, especially the Strait of Malacca, were converting to Islam — brought to them by Saracen merchant traders. Along with the traders traveled a Silent Strider called Abdul Sees-the-Night-Clearly. He was the first known Garou on the islands and visited as many islands as he could, seeking places for others of his kind to establish Kinfolk populations. It is said that Abdul uncovered the secret lair of a Wyrm-creature bent on conquering and enslaving the people and animals of the islands and slew it by grasping the foul thing and dragging it with him into one of the active volcanoes that dot the islands.

Though Kublai Khan originally intended to punish an upstart king, his troops instead helped one of the claimants to the throne establish the powerful Majapahit Empire. Some say this was a favor he paid to a native of the islands, a great Khan warrior known as Soft-Walker who had once saved his life.

Known as the Spice Islands, Indonesia produced pepper, cloves, nutmeg, rare herbs, scented woods and exotic oils. The riches to be gained from a single voyage were such that Europeans turned covetous eyes toward conquest of the prized islands. First came the Portuguese. Their mistakes included an unreasoning hatred of Muslims and contempt for the native people. Though both Britain and Holland made their presence in the islands known, the Dutch were given an unexpected boost when the British defeated the Spanish Armada. Without Spanish ships preying on them the Dutch established a lasting trade empire in the Spice Islands. A few adventurous Fianna and Get of Fenris sailed with the Europeans.

When the Dutch arrived, the Indonesians thought of them as allies against the Portuguese. Soon enough, they discovered that the Dutch were as bad, if not worse, masters. After scrambling with the British for control, Holland maintained control in Indonesia for over two centuries. They introduced the concept of large plantations devoted to producing one crop, producing coffee, palm oil, chinchona (used for making quinine) and rubber. The story of Dutch rule in Indonesia is one of brutality and negligence. Their own reformers noted that the Dutch used "forceful pacification" to acquire new territories, broke treaties, helped promote the trade in opium, encouraged slavery and brutality against the Indonesian people and neglected the education of these people who were supposed to be Holland's wards. The werewolves soon became disgusted with Dutch brutality and policies of stripping the land of its native plants to force-grow cash crops for European exploitation.

Though the Indonesians — aided by an outraged Khan and the three Garou who had come to Indonesia with the Europeans — staged small, scattered rebellions, the Dutch were not displaced until the Japanese invaded in 1942 during World War II. While the Japanese insisted that they supported Indonesian independence, they actually wanted to claim the islands for themselves. The Communists tried to gain a foothold and maneuver the Indonesians into declaring independence under their protection. The Indonesians fooled both sides by declaring independence themselves in 1945.

A Dutch military action to retake Indonesia and an attempted Communist takeover both failed. Dedicated leaders and the will of the people have led Indonesia out of terrible economic straits and assured their continued independence. They have reclaimed lost lands and made themselves one of the most important countries in Southeast Asia. Though over 200 indigenous languages are spoken throughout the country, it is unified by its official language Bahasa Indonesia, a dialect of Malay. This language came to the fore and acted as a catalyst for the revolution in 1945. It, along with the new republic's Five Principles, have helped the Indonesian people persevere. Those principles are: Belief in God, Nationalism, Humanitarianism, Democracy and Social Justice.

Geography

Consisting of over 13,600 islands, of which 6000 are inhabited, Indonesia rests along the equator and touches upon the Indian and Pacific Oceans and the South China Sea. The islands make a natural barrier between the Pacific Ocean and the Indian Ocean, forming straits that are strategically important as well as making the islands centers for trade. Though many islands are tiny, Kalimantan (once called Borneo) is the third largest island on earth.

Indonesia's closest neighbors are Malaysia, Singapore and the Philippines to the north and northeast and Australia to the southeast. The myriad islands are most easily categorized in four groups. The Western Islands consist of Sumatra, Java and Kalimantan. The Lesser Sunda Islands stretch from Java toward Australia. Irian Jaya is the western part of the island of New Guinea. The Eastern Islands, consisting of Sulawesi and the Maluku group, found spread out over a thousand miles of ocean between Australia and the Philippines, make up the rest of Indonesia's island chain.

Often called the most beautiful and fruitful land in the world, Indonesia's landscape revels in the dramatic — active volcanoes, cindered cones from extinct ones, dense green jungles, fertile plains and teeming swamps. Bamboo, papaya, coconut and banana trees share space with rice paddies and terraces, teak, sugarcane, rubber trees and palms. Overall, the islands show a riot of green accented with brilliant flowers and leaves. Here are found wild orchids and banyans, lianas and flowers as tall as a man.

The land supports an amazing array of animal life — monkeys, thirty-foot long pythons, crocodiles, tigers, rhinos, a few elephants and a myriad of small animals and brilliantly feathered birds, including the fabulous bird of paradise.

Bali and the Lesser Sundas

Part of the Lesser Sunda chain, Bali is considered paradise by some. Balinese architecture, dance and costuming are world famous. It is the only part of Indonesia that still follows Hinduism. The other islands in the chain, Lombok, Sumbawa, Sumba, Flores, Timor and a slew of smaller islands, have no large cities and host about 8.5 million people.

Sumatra

This thousand-mile long island features mountains along its western side, near the shore while in the east the land slopes downward ending in savanna and marshland. In the south are located great plantations with rubber, sugar and other commercial crops. The island is one of the major oil and natural gas producers in Indonesia. Approximately 30 million people live on Sumatra.

Java

One of the most lush and densely populated places on earth, Java boasts 95 million people and hosts four of Indonesia's five largest cities. Rice terraces and plantations of coffee, rubber, tea and sugar dot the land while a chain of volcanic mountains runs the length of the island. Jakarta, the capital, is located on Java. With 6.5 million people living in Jakarta, it ranks as one of the largest cities in the world. Its mix of cultures gives it a cosmopolitan air, while its trade in traditional Indonesian crafts, such as batik cloth and carved teak wood items keeps it firmly a part of its own culture. Notably, a single European Bone Gnawer lives in the slums surrounding Jakarta with her Kinfolk husband, a Jakartan fisherman; this young Ragabash, named Teresa Loosejaw, is often the first contact for visiting Western Garou.

Kalimantan

This is the Indonesian side of the island that used to be called Borneo. Forested and hilly, Kalimantan is a major exporter of timber. Oil and rubber also provide export goods, while there is farmland in the west. There are few cities on Kalimantan and fewer than seven million Indonesians living there. Of those, many are Dayaks who have their own language and live by hunting, fishing and nomadic farming.

Sulawesi and Maluku

Once thought by traders to be several small islands, Sulawesi is instead a single mass with oddly shaped arms that thrust out in several directions. Animals and plants found on Sulawesi include varieties found nowhere else in the world. Gidra Sulanongga, known to her tribe (the Stargazers) as Rain-caller, lives on Sulawesi and tries to prevent the exploitation and extinction of these rare flora and fauna. Once famous for the smuggling and outright piracy that occurred here, the main city of Ujung Pandang now serves as a center for communications and trade between East and West and for education. Maluku, formerly known as the Moluccas, the quintessential Spice Islands, produces the fabulous spices that caused a trading rush not unlike the excitement that overtook California during the gold rush. At one time, they were the most important trading center in the world.

Irian Jaya

Easternmost of the islands, Irian Jaya consists of the western half of New Guinea. The eastern part of the island is Papua New Guinea, formerly held by

Australia. Though the area has a rich culture, some parts of this region remain unexplored. Some tribes living here still subsist through primitive agriculture, hunting and fishing, living only slightly more advanced lives than their Stone Age precursors. Among them live a Fianna and a Child of Gaia hoping to build a new Kinfolk base and to import a few wolves to see if they can adapt to the equatorial conditions here.

Shapeshifters in Indonesia

Though Garou helped instigate independence movements and fought guerrilla actions to oust various oppressors, they are too few in numbers to have a major effect on Indonesia's continuing government and development. They decry the country's oil and natural gas industries despite their positive effects in providing much needed cash for the country. So far, they have fought a holding battle against Pentex and its subsidiaries, which have tried time and again to insinuate themselves into Indonesian businesses. The lone Khan who lives on Irian Jaya fights to keep the rain forests from being destroyed and has attempted (so far unsuccessfully) to form a breeding relationship with one of the few native tigers left in Indonesia. Both the Garou and the few remaining Khan support Indonesia's continuing efforts at conservation; conversely, the many Ratkin scattered across the islands continue to do their best to "manage" the human population. A few Gumagan frequent the swamps on isolated islands, and one wallow is notable as a place where Mokolé from all four streams commonly meet to exchange tales and memories. The Rokea, the most numerous changers in Indonesia, did not pay enough attention to the build-up of industry and housing on the various islands believing their seas weren't threatened. Too late, they have discovered that the all-important coral reefs were bleaching and dying.

Conservation

The Garou and other shapeshifters living in Indonesia have found that they have greatly benefited from the people's own love of nature and conservationist leanings. In general, the country has had a good record regarding the preservation of their rare plants and animals. In the seventh century, a king declared certain lands off limits to show his Hindu reverence for all life, especially that of the lush island of Sumatra. Other kings through the ages set aside protected lands where one-horned Javan rhinos, tigers and other rare creatures could freely roam. Even under European rule, some lands were made into nature reserves. In 1928 the country's first national park was founded.

Nevertheless, saving lands and species became of minor importance to a people battling for their freedom from colonial powers, then trying to dig out from under economic disaster. In the quest for stability after independence, sacred mountains were mined and rainforests plowed to create more farmland. Land around ports also suffered through industrialization, while the seas soured under pollution and warming from factories. A radically growing population also added strain to lands pushed to the limit to sustain them.

In the 1970s conservation efforts again came to the fore. Of its first five national parks, each protects an irreplaceable species. Ujung Kulon in West Java hosts the last Javan rhinos, while Lorentz in Irian Jaya has the only glacial area in Southeast Asia. East Java has Baluran, a savanna where the banteng live. Gunung Leuser, located in northern Sumatra is home to the Sumatran rhino, orangutans and the extremely rare *rafflesia* flower. Finally, the island of Komodo is world famous as the last refuge of the Komodo dragon. While tourists wishing to visit these parks bring wealth to Indonesia, some are off-limits to visitors due to the fragility of the ecosystem and the rarity of the species found there. Both the Garou and the Khan support this even against other conservationists who argue that more access will reap more money and allow the country to dedicate more space to protected lands.

The same care has not been taken with Indonesia's coral reefs. Like the Great Barrier Reef of Australia, the archipelago's reefs suffer from industrial pollution, which clouds the water, killing the coral reefs that provide shelter for the sea life all around them. Further, excess heat from industry dumped into the waters to cool is changing temperatures in the seas. Both these factors bleach, then kill coral, leaving those fish, plants and animals that depend on them for shelter with nowhere to live, procreate and eat. Those fish that serve as food for the larger species are being taken at an alarming rate by commercial fishers. Some fishers even use poison and dynamite to assure themselves of a large enough catch. Even the smaller species are netted and taken to Japan and other Asian countries for use as human food. Without that food source, the sharks that frequent the tropical waters die — and those sharks are Kin to the Rokea. The weresharks care very little for preserving Indonesia's land. They want something done to stop the destruction of the coral reefs. A few have tried to reason with Indonesian officials, and at least one, Lone Tooth, has urged his kin to meet with and try to coordinate with the Garou. Thus far, the other Rokea have proven to be reluctant to involve the wolves. The most radical, such as Uga Longfang, argue for more *biting* methods of encouraging official support for reef protection and if no progress is made soon, she may persuade the others to adopt her point of view.

Antarctica

The land retains an identity of its own, still deeper and subtler than we can know.
— Barry Lopez, *Arctic Dreams*

Geography

As large as Europe and the United States put together, the continent of Antarctica, the coldest, highest, windiest and most icy place on earth, lies at the southernmost tip of the globe. Gondwana, once a supercontinent, broke apart sometime in the late Jurassic period. It split apart in several stages, one of which loosed India, Australia and Antarctica from East Africa. Australasia and Antarctica then separated, with the latter drifting into chill waters and temperatures, eventually taking up its position at the pole and losing its forests to the frigid climate. Now separated from the other continents by a changing, floating sea of pack ice and the ever-stormy Southern Ocean, Antarctica rests 600 miles from South America, 1550 miles from Australia and 2500 miles from the tip of Africa. The continent is divided into two regions, Lesser Antarctica, a peninsula and trailing arm that stretches toward South America, and Greater Antarctica, where an enormous ice sheet rises steeply from the ocean and flattens into a plateau some two and a half miles above sea level. At the dividing line between the two rise the Transantarctic Mountains, one of the world's great mountain chains, stretching over 3000 miles. In many places, the range disappears, submerged beneath the ice except for high peaks appearing as isolated mountains in a sea of white. Unlike Greater Antarctica which forms a solid block, Lesser Antarctica consists of three fragments held together and to the Greater portion by the mass of ice that overlays it. The ice raises Antarctica's average height to well above sea level, higher than any other continent's average height. However, the weight of all the ice also depresses the rocky surface to well below sea level. So heavy is the ice that it deforms Earth's shape, making our world pear shaped as it flattens at the pole. If the ice were removed, the land it holds below sea level would rise above the surrounding water. Glacial movements still shape the continent, which contains still-active volcanoes as well.

Winds may blow up to 200 miles per hour, causing whiteouts when blowing snow makes land and sky impossible to tell apart. Though little snow falls in this frozen land, temperatures that can drop to more than -100° Fahrenheit causes snow to turn to ice. In some places, ice and snow reach more than two miles deep. Mountains, steep valleys and glaciers make travel difficult at best. At midwinter the sun never rises, making the continent dark twenty-four hours a day, while at midsummer, the sun never sets.

Touched by the Atlantic, Pacific and Indian Oceans Antarctica is nevertheless surrounded by ice. Salt water and ocean currents usually keep seas from freezing, but Antarctic air and water are so cold that in winter the ice often covers an area almost as extensive as the continent itself. In warmer weather, chunks of ice break off and float as icebergs throughout the region. In such climes, almost no plants grow and few animals exist. The land has no trees or shrubs, and few animals can live in its frigid climes.

The Inhabitants

The blue whale, the largest mammal on earth, frequents Antarctic waters and feeds on three tons of krill per day. Humpback, bottle-nosed, finback and sperm whales also hunt the Antarctic with its plentiful food. Whales used to be more plentiful here until whale hunters killed most of them, bringing some species near extinction. Later, hunters also sought and killed millions of penguins and seals for their fat. When the hunting eventually stopped, seals and penguins returned, but the whales have become a rare sight.

James Ross, Crabeater and Weddell seals are all found here, as are fierce leopard seals that eat krill, penguins and other seals and have been known to attack explorers. Elephant seals and Antarctic fur seals were almost wiped out by hunters in the 1800s yet maintain a fragile existence here.

Antarctica plays host to several types of birds as well. Skua, large brown gulls, eat the eggs of other birds (and have a reputation for eating almost anything), while petrels, small robin-sized seabirds nest among rocks and skim the ocean. Several types of albatross call the Antarctic home, while the Arctic tern raises its young in the Arctic, then flies more than 10,000 miles to live in Antarctica. The best known birds of the region are penguins, whose flipper like wings and tuxedo coloring give them their charm. Though penguins cannot fly, they are champion swimmers and can swim underwater for up to half an hour at a time before surfacing for air. The Adelie, chinstrap, and emperor penguins are best known.

The Known History

Unlike the Arctic, where Eskimo tribes settled thousands of years ago, no people have ever settled

A World of Rage

Antarctica. No cities exist there and no country owns it, the result of a treaty that keeps any country from claiming the continent. Most visitors to the region are scientists.

In 1772 Captain James Cook sailed from England searching for a southern continent. His ship was not strong enough to break through the ice and 150 miles from Antarctica he was forced to turn back. In the 1800s, English and Americans sailed in the seas near Antarctica to hunt seals and whales, but failed to find the continent itself. In 1838 Lieutenant Charles Wilkes of the U. S. Navy sailed along 1500 miles of the Antarctica's coast, proving the continent's existence. In 1895 the Antarctic, a Norwegian whaling ship made the first landing on the icy shores, and in 1911 a race to see who would be first to reach the south pole began. Norway's Amundsen reached the pole first, followed four months later by Englishman Robert Scott. Scott's expedition ran out of food and froze to death, but exploration continued. One of the best known explorers was Richard Byrd, who led his first expedition in 1928. He led four more before his death in 1957.

During the 1950s many countries constructed buildings for their scientists and military personnel. Squabbles over rights ensued until a peace treaty was signed giving all the interested parties certain rights to the land (or forbidding them from actually claiming the land as their own—the wording is ambiguous). As a result, no wars have been fought in Antarctica, and efforts have been made to minimize the effect of those who come there. The land seems remarkably unspoiled as a result. Nonetheless, efforts may have come too late and be too little.

Exploitation and Dangers

Even before Robert Scott's ill-fated expedition, commercial whalers and seal hunters were exploiting the region's inhabitants. This only ceased when one species after another was annihilated, making it uneconomical to continue the effort. Today, the fish, especially krill, upon which whales, seals, and other fish depend for food, may fall to man's greed as well. It is already being marketed as food for humans in Japan and other places and more will assuredly be harvested in the future. Seabirds of all sorts, seals and whales all eat krill and a disruption in the food chain could prove disastrous to all of them.

Mineral wealth abounds in the Antarctic. Iron and what is possibly the world's largest reserve of coal have been discovered in the Transantarctic Mountains, as have some traces of gold, uranium, tin, copper, cobalt and titanium. The latter have been found in the few ice-free areas thus mapped (which constitutes only the tiniest percent of the continent). Offshore deposits of both oil and gas have been found and in some places drilling has already begun.

Constant watch must be kept to preserve what is left. Despite its isolation, Adelie penguin eggs show traces of DDT and the coast is sometimes littered with plastic trash. Most seriously, it is possible that oil and minerals may be found in "commercial" quantities either in the sea or underground, prompting its exploitation. The seas are so rough and the danger of icebergs so prevalent, that there exists real dangers of spills and industrial pollution either from platforms or tankers. Any oil spill would be almost impossible to clean up under the conditions present in Antarctica. Oil would coat the ice-free coasts where seabirds, seals, and penguins nest, feed and live, killing the krill and possibly almost every animal dependent on it. Onshore facilities needed to process any oil and gas found would cause even more disruption and pollution than the current scientific bases do. They would also provide competition with the wildlife for snow-free areas and probably disrupt not only feeding, but also breeding behavior. Nevertheless, the Antarctic Treaty Consultative Parties (over twenty countries with an interest in the region) currently discuss *how* to do it rather than *if* it should be done at all.

Not actually exploitation *per se*, but a danger nonetheless is the hole in the ozone layer that appears over Antarctica during the three months of darkness every winter. Caused by the release of chlorofluorocarbons (CFC) that break down the ozone molecules, the hole allows deadly ultraviolet radiation through onto the earth. Despite the outlawing of aerosols and in refrigeration, the CFC already released will last for 100 years. As the hole grows yearly, since the ozone cannot repair itself once destroyed, this may lead to the destruction of the phytoplankton on which krill feed, again endangering the Antarctic's food chain. Garou from all tribes come to the Antarctic to fight for its survival. Most commonly, Get of Fenris and Wendigo find they can best tolerate the conditions there, making them strange bedfellows indeed.

The Thing Under the Ice

The dangers to the fragile ecosystem of Antarctica would be enough to summon Garou to defend it, but there exists an even greater danger under the ice, a peril they cannot now fight, only watch.

This is the legend:

Long ago, when the land was green and pleasant (a time only remembered by the Mokolé), a terrible Wyrm creature came into it and began slaying all who lived there. None could stand against its poisoned teeth and claws, its eyes that spread madness and its black and ravenous heart. The call went out among all Garou, asking for the bravest each tribe had to offer to come to the land and battle the great evil. Champion after champion responded to the call and came, head held high and eyes alight with fervor to slay the beast and gain such glory that his name would live forever. All fell before the Wyrm's great corrupter-warrior.

While these battles took place, the evil spread its talons into everything it touched. What were once green fields became blackened twisted bogs stinking with rot. Children born in the land were blighted and warped, their limbs tangled, their minds unhinged.

After many weary years in which it seemed that Gaia's children could do nothing against so great a foe, a young Stargazer proposed a novel solution. Her travels in the Umbra had convinced her that what could not be cured must be cut out. Working from visions Gaia sent her in the stars, Carves-the-Homeland began tracing the places where Gaia's bones could be eased apart to set the spoiled green land adrift. She asked her greatest rival, Sees-the-Moon's Shadow, a mighty Theurge, to call together others to bind the evil into the land it had ruined. Then she and a hundred others began to gnaw upon the land's roots until they snapped. Fully half of them fell into the rift created when the land broke apart. The others rode with the drifting land out into the southern seas, swearing themselves to become the Sept of the Bitter Loss, there to keep watch and make certain the Wyrm spawn could not rise again.

The nights grew longer and colder as they rode the land and ice began to cover great patches of it. Even their fur could not keep them from the cold and many perished. As the trees died and the grass shriveled, the small animals also died and Carves-the-Homeland, Sees-the-Moon's Shadow and their fellows also died of starvation. As they died, each wove his or her bones into the ice to strengthen the trap confining the Wyrm creature. Finally there were none left and Gaia stopped the land on the extreme southern tip of the earth, held suspended in frigid, clear ice. Though eventually man found the exiled land once again, it is no longer green, but a purified white expanse. Garou visiting Antarctica instinctively feel that all is not right here, however. Each can feel that somewhere under the ice sleeps something terrifyingly corrupt and dangerous and each fears its waking. Still, they can take comfort, for when the storms whip into frenzy and the snow swirls high enough to cover the aurora australis with its deadly white veil, they can hear within the wind the howls of their ancient kin.